I0523677

TO BRAVE MEN

ALAN P. LANDAU

To Brave Men (2024)
©2024 Alan P Landau

 A catalogue record for this
book is available from the
National Library of Australia

The right of Alan P Landau to be identified as the moral rights author
of this work has been asserted
by him in accordance with the Copyright Amendment (Moral Rights) Act 2000.
This book is copyrighted by the author.
Apart from any use as permitted under the Copyright Act 1968, no part may be
reproduced, copied, scanned, stored in a retrieval system,
recorded, or transmitted,
by any form or by any means,
without the prior written permission of the publisher.

ISBN: 978-0-6455803-7-2 (Paperback)
ISBN: 978-0-6455803-8-9 (Ebook)
ISBN: 978-0-6455803-9-6 (AudioPlay)

Contact details for the author can be found at
www.landaubooks.com

This book is based on actual events, however, it is a work of fiction.
Names, characters, places and incidents are either a product of the author's imagination
or are used fictitiously and any resemblance to actual persons, living or dead,
business establishments, events or locations are entirely coincidental.
The views or comments expressed in this novel are not those of the Author.

Cover design : Rachel De Bruyn, Australia
Editors: Martin Robinson (Australia) and Cindy Kramer, (South Africa)
AudioPlay music composed by Martin Robinson, Australia

First published 2024

I dedicate this book to three very special friends who
played a big part in my childhood years.
My brother, Rob Landau,
and my neighbours,
Martin and Trevor Robinson.
Despite their concerted efforts, I survived.

LANDAU BOOKS PUBLICATIONS

THE LANGBOURNE SERIES :
By Alan Landau
(In sequential order.)

Langbourne

Langbourne's Rebellion

Langbourne's Empire

Langbourne's Evolution

Langbourne's Loyalty

Langbourne's Legacy

By Brenda Kate

Of Sand and Stars

E-Mail: alan@landaubooks.com
Web: www.landaubooks.com
Facebook: www.facebook.com/landaubooks
Instagram: www.instagram.com/landaubooks

"History is not just a collection of facts,
but a story waiting to be told." - Unknown

"The past cannot be changed, forgotten, or erased.
It can only be accepted." - Unknown

FOREWORD

I am not a historian, I just like to tell stories. This novel is, therefore, a work of fiction, the inspiration for which is based on a true story. I have tried to keep it as factual as possible, but I must apologise to my readers if I have been remiss or slightly inaccurate in some areas.

It is my wish that this book be experienced as an engaging novel, particularly by a younger generation who might not normally gravitate towards historical accounts, and hopefully, they will share this story with friends, thus perpetuating a significant occurrence that has almost faded from collective memory.

There are several interpretations and some strongly held views on the events depicted in this novel, so I would encourage my readers to research them further should they be inclined. Many good publications on the subject can be found at the end of this book.

Alan Landau
2024

CHAPTER ONE

Minnesota 1862

Rebecca Burnham looked beyond the shirt that she was hanging on the frayed washing line. A man was pushing his horse hard. She froze momentarily, arms still held above her head and looked towards her husband, Edwin.

Reverend Edwin Burnham had also noticed the rider approaching them and carefully lowered his bucket. Usually, when visitors arrived, they ambled along easily on their horses as the Burnham farm was not far from town. A hurried rider did not bode well.

"Ed?" Rebecca called to her husband in urgent trepidation. She pushed a stray lock of hair from her eye with the back of her hand.

Edwin looked at Rebecca, a very attractive and petite woman with long, fair hair tousled by the soft breeze. Her cotton blouse and full-length skirt billowed gently.

Edwin nodded, acknowledging her concern, then slowly walked to the rickety gate to await the rider's arrival. Edwin was a physically strong man with a very gentle nature. Ever since they moved to Dakota, his untamed beard had become a well-recognised feature in town.

The rider did not take long to arrive and pulled up to a skidding halt, a cloud of dust briefly engulfing the two men. Ordinarily, Rebecca would retreat into the homestead and push the kettle over the fire, preparing coffee for the visitor. Something told her this rider would not stay long, so she remained at the washing line.

Rebecca recognised the rider as a rancher, wearing leathers and sporting a deformed Stetson hat featuring prominent sweat stains from many days of hard outdoor labour. The rancher did not dismount but spoke to her husband from his vantage point. She could not understand the mumbled conversation, but the rider's tone was urgent and concerning. She watched Edwin nod his understanding and ask questions in return. The cowboy gesticulated to the northwest, then to the southeast, and spoke again. Edwin reached up and shook the man's hand, and then, in a cloud of dust, the cowboy bolted back the way he had come.

"What is it?" Rebecca asked as Edwin joined her at the washing line.

Edwin sighed heavily. "That was Thompson from just past the bend in the river. He brought news that the Indians are uprising."

Rebecca was immediately concerned; the urgency of the cowboy coming and going was alarming.

"Should we be worried?" she asked.

"Yes," Edwin replied softly, running his fingers through his hair. He looked up at the skies as if for divine guidance.

"What did he say?"

"The chief and his braves from the reservation attacked New Ulm on the weekend. Then some of the braves attacked the Morrison homestead on Monday."

"Oh no," Rebecca felt her legs go weak. "Was anyone hurt?"

Edwin sighed again and stared blankly out over the land.

"Ed," Rebecca pressed him for an answer, dread overcoming her.

"They killed Morrison and his family. No survivors."

"Oh no," Rebecca repeated, reaching for the dry log beside her before her legs gave way. She sat heavily upon it.

"On Wednesday, they attacked Old Man Rodger's place. They killed him, his wife, and their ten-year-old daughter. Scalped them all."

Rebecca groaned in disbelief and horror.

"We have to leave, Becca. We have to leave right now! They will be here in about two days."

"You're a man of the cloth, Ed. Surely they will leave us alone."

Edwin ushered Rebecca along the log slightly and then sat beside her. "I have a good relationship with the chief, so I would think his men would pass us by, but the Sioux seem to be riding with bloodlust. They are in a frenzy, and Thompson thinks we probably likely be just as much a target as everyone else."

"I don't believe it, Ed. I know many of the squaws in his camp, and they are very hospitable to me. Besides, we can't leave. Old Moke died last week."

Edwin sighed heavily again. "Old Moke was a lovely horse. I miss the old boy."

"We could walk to Mankato," Rebecca suggested.

Edwin shook his head in resignation. "I've thought about that. Fred is only two years old. The going would be too tough on you and the boy. Besides, the braves would outrun us in a heartbeat."

"What are we going to do?" Rebecca implored.

"Thompson suggests we move to town immediately or arm ourselves and repel any attack. That would be our best chance. In any case, it might not even come to that. As you say, we have no quarrel with the Indians."

Rebecca's maternal instinct suddenly came to the fore. "Edwin, I'm not going to risk my son at the whims of people who have turned savage. We will have to do something to ensure Fred's safety."

"What do you suggest?" Edwin asked.

"Let us leave for Mankato without delay. You can borrow a horse and cart from one of our neighbours, then come back and get Fred and me."

"I don't want to leave you and Fredrick out here on your own," Edwin objected.

Rebecca stood up. "Go now," she said. Her tone was sharp, catching Edwin by surprise, "and get a gun and bullets."

"Becca, a man of the cloth doesn't...."

"Get a gun, Edwin," Rebecca demanded. "Not to kill anyone, heaven forbid, but for protection and to ward off any attack."

Edwin acquiesced. "Alright, I'll leave now."

"Right now," Rebecca insisted and walked towards their homestead. "I'll pack you some food and water, and then you leave. Come straight back, you hear!"

Edwin wasted no time. He changed his shoes, donned his hat, and threw the leather saddlebag that Rebecca had packed with some meagre provisions over his shoulder. He tousled Fred's hair as his two-year-old son toddled past, oblivious to the turmoil around him, and then Edwin strode out the gate.

***

Rebecca took the dry washing off the line and walked back inside. Fred was beating a blackened pot with a stick, enjoying the hollow noise it made. It had been a good seven hours since Edwin had left the homestead, and Rebecca found herself constantly scanning the landscape nervously, anticipating his arrival.

The flat lands of Dakota stretched into the far distance. The tall grass that blanketed the undulations looked like a golden blanket had been cast over the earth. Thickets of tall green trees threw their long, dark shadows over the landscape.

"It will be dark soon," Rebecca told Fred, but in reality, she was speaking to the open land beckoning to her.

She opened the lid of a saucepan that had been sitting on the stove earlier in the day. The mashed vegetables had gone cold. She had been so preoccupied with the events that she had forgotten to keep the fire going.

"I suppose I should feed you now," she smiled at her son. "Sorry, dinner is cold tonight."

Fred had an insatiable appetite and seemed to enjoy vegetables, so it didn't take long to feed him. Milk served as a welcome treat after his meal, and Rebecca knew he would soon fall asleep just as darkness enveloped their smallholding. She would be left to spend the night alone, something she hadn't done in many years.

Looking out across the plains, Rebecca estimated there was about an hour of daylight left. She rekindled the fire, then changed Fred into his nightwear. Leaving him to play with a small carving of a horse she called Young Moke, Rebecca stepped outside and stood on the porch, surveying the land. Her thoughts oscillated between the Morrison and Rodger families.

She had heard stories about the Indians thriving on torture and tried to push those tales out of her head. She knew that a cowboy's greatest fear was being captured alive by an Indian. Casting one last look over the landscape, Rebecca turned to go inside and put Fred to bed.

As she turned, she thought she saw a movement in the distance. She froze and carefully turned to look in the direction that had caught her attention. There was nothing there, and she realised her nerves were playing tricks on her. But suddenly, there it was again–a speck in the distance.

"Oh no," Rebecca moaned and closed the door. Turning to the window, she searched the grassland for the speck she had seen, and then unmistakably, she saw several Indians coming towards the homestead. They were jogging with a relaxed lope in her direction.

"Oh no," Rebecca almost wailed. "What do I do? What do I do?"

Rebecca knew she must not panic, so she took a deep breath and walked inside, closing the door behind her. She knew too well that if she ran, they would track and quickly overtake her. She couldn't run far carrying a two-year-old, especially not with a dozen fit braves driven by bloodlust right behind her. She was in big trouble, and she knew it.

"Fred," she said to her son in a motherly tone. "We need to hide you."

Rebecca looked around frantically. Her eyes fell on a large woven straw basket.

"Oh please, Lord, help me," she whispered to herself.

She folded a blanket and placed it inside the basket. Gently picking Fred up, she put him in the basket and started humming a lullaby, as she did every night. Rebecca stared out the window this time, watching her attackers getting closer by the minute. She estimated that she had about fifteen minutes before they surrounded the house.

Rocking Fred in the basket, he mercifully began to close his eyes. Very gently, Rebecca carried her son in the basket out the front door and walked to the edge of a cornfield just yards from the homestead. Taking only two steps into the green corn stalks, she laid the basket softly on the ground and then, picking some cobs off the surrounding stalks, placed them in the basket on top of Fred.

"Don't cry now, my son. Don't cry, whatever you do," Rebecca pleaded.

Stepping out of the cornfield, she walked calmly back to the homestead. Before she reached the porch, she glanced carefully in the direction of the approaching braves. She couldn't see any and assumed they had spotted her and gone into hiding. It was easy to spot her, she thought. She was a white woman and dressed in white clothing against a dark house in fading sunlight.

Rebecca entered the house and closed the door as naturally as possible, immediately heading for the back window. She climbed out and sprinted towards the edge of the property, just thirty or forty yards away. Hiding behind some scrubby bushes, covered by the rugged grass, she lay panting, desperately trying to control her breathing.

Rebecca was distraught; she was at the back of her house, and her son was sleeping in a basket at the front. Suddenly, she remembered that the braves were known to yip and yelp when attacking, and she worried that the noise might wake Fred up. What if they started shooting? Fred would become a trophy if he woke up and cried. Tears started streaming down Rebecca's cheeks.

With a start, Rebecca watched as five braves ran to the back of the house. They were completely silent, which scared her even more. She couldn't hear their footfalls or the rattle of their beads; they were like ghosts. They carried tomahawks, bows, arrows, knives, and rifles. She knew that if anyone was in the house, they would be doomed.

Suddenly, a cry went up from the front of the house, and the sound of breaking glass tinkled through the cool evening air. At that exact moment, a brave, with his back to her, lit the tip of his arrow and, drawing his bow, let the burning projectile fly through the air and through a window. A rear window next to it illuminated instantly.

Then the war cry began, and the bizarre whooping filled the air, interspersed with rifle fire. Indians ran around the home in frenzied circles, their movements becoming an indiscernible blur in the low light. Rebecca began sobbing, worried that Fred would awaken to the sudden noise and his resulting death would be her fault.

There was a lull in the noise, and Rebecca's heart sank. Three braves were looking for her footprints. They had realised that no one was in the house, and they would track her. She slunk backwards into a shallow gulley, then ran for dear life. She knew she had one chance of escaping: darkness. All she had to do was stay ahead of them until night came, then she might, just might, survive until daylight.

Realising that running too hard would quickly deplete her energy, she forced herself to slow into a jog and zigzagged as much as possible. Only when it was fully dark did she dare to look back, and over the tops of the trees, she could see the orange glow of her home burning.

A sob burst from her throat. She stood still for a moment, gathering herself, then, with her back to the fire, she began walking towards Mankato.

***

When Edwin Burnham walked into Mankato, he found it eerily quiet. The ramshackle old town, with its wooden buildings and dusty streets, was deserted. He had never seen it like that and wondered where all the people were. It was mid afternoon, and he reminded himself that it was not a Sunday afternoon.

A hidden voice called out to him. "Come this way, Reverend."

Edwin looked around but saw no one. Then, at the next corner, he spotted a man waving his hat in the air.

"Over here, Reverend. This way," the man called.

Edwin quickened his pace, suddenly feeling a little uneasy.

"What's going on, Mr Green?" Edwin asked as he approached the man, recognising him as one of his congregants.

"The Indians are on the warpath. They attacked New Ulm and caused a lot of death and destruction. Our scouts say the Indians are on their way here now."

"Where is everyone?" Edwin asked, casting furtive glances over his shoulder.

"They're in the town square. Head over there now; I'll keep a lookout," Mr Green replied.

Edwin thanked the man and made his way to the familiar town square. He was shocked by what he saw when he arrived. Nearly three thousand citizens were packed into the square, milling around or seeking shelter in whatever shade they could find. Speaking to some strangers, he discovered that they were anxiously waiting for an Indian attack. The town square had been fortified to protect the residents, with wagons, crates, and barrels strategically placed and armed men positioned defensively.

The mayor, a deeply religious man, was engaged in a conversation with an armed cowboy. Edwin spotted him and approached.

"Good evening, George," Edwin said, interrupting their conversation and shaking the mayor's hand.

"Reverend, thank the Lord you've made it here. I've been worried about you," George replied.

"I heard about the Indians declaring war, so I came into town to buy a gun and ammunition."

George grimaced. "Sadly, we're short on weapons. What you see here is all we have. No one will sell or lend you a gun. Stay here; it's the safest place for you. Where's Rebecca? She can stay with Linda until this blows over."

"She's at the farm," Edwin replied nervously. "With Fred."

"What? You left them on the farm?" the mayor exclaimed incredulously.

"Yes, well, I didn't know..."

"Heavens, Edwin! The Sioux are on a rampage. Chief Little Crow has ordered his braves not to take prisoners."

Edwin looked at the mayor in horror, fear etching his face.

The cowboy interjected, "I'll gather a posse, and we'll set out at first light, George."

It was decided that six men would leave the fortification as soon as it became light enough and attempt a rescue. Normally, Edwin would have stayed with the townspeople in the square, offering words of support and encouragement, but on this night, he wanted to be alone. Distraught, he sat quietly by himself on the dusty road, wondering what his naivety had done to his family.

At first light, a posse of six hardened men departed the town to search for Rebecca and Fred. At the mayor's insistence, Edwin remained within the town's fortifications. The posse returned later that day to an extremely anxious Edwin. They had found Rebecca at a neighbour's home, six miles from their own. She was alive and unharmed. They continued to the Burnham's homestead with Rebecca, and against all odds, Fred was still sleeping in the basket of corn where Rebecca had left him.

Rebecca fell into Edwin's arms when she reunited with him and Fred, and wept with relief.

"They destroyed our home," she said, wiping tears from her eyes. "There's nothing left."

"But you survived, and so did Fred," Edwin said, overwhelmed with emotion.

The child had narrowly escaped the clutches of death. Little did Fred know this was just the beginning of his dance with fate. His tormentor would keep returning, with even more sinister and relentless pursuits.

CHAPTER TWO

Scotland 1862

Allan sat completely motionless at the dining table, transfixed by the sight of his father expertly cutting into the roast chicken with his finely sharpened carving knife. The succulent meat gleamed in the flickering candlelight, enticing both Allan and his mother, who watched with anticipation from across the table.

Robert Wilson, a robust man who laboured on the rail tracks in the frigid regions of Scotland, deftly sliced enough meat to provide each family member with a generous portion. He meticulously placed the utensils on the edge of his plate and bowed his head in gratitude for the meal.

The wait seemed agonisingly long for Allan, and he couldn't help but feel that his mother shared his eagerness to indulge in their customary Sunday afternoon roast. Finally, the formalities concluded and Robert began serving the meal to his family. As everyone politely and thoroughly devoured their food, a sense of relaxation settled over the table.

With a stern tone, Robert reminded Allan about proper table manners when he noticed his son holding his fork incorrectly. "Manners," he said firmly.

"I apologise, Father," Allan quickly responded, promptly flipping his fork over.

Nervously, Mavis Wilson interjected, "Allan, your father has something important to discuss with you."

Allan looked at his father with anticipation but remained silent.

Completing his bite of chicken, Robert cleared his throat and began. "I have received a letter from Kirkwall Grammar School up north."

"In Orkney?" Allan inquired, aware of its location as his eldest cousin had attended that school.

"Yes, exactly," Robert nodded solemnly. "They have accepted your enrolment. Since you'll be turning six this year, you need to start right away."

This was exciting news for a young boy, and Allan couldn't wait to go.

***

The journey to Kirkwall was arduous and uncomfortable, endured over two days of inclement Scottish weather. The school itself was an imposing establishment made of brown bricks, adorned with high spires and sharply pitched tiled roofs. Its outer walls boasted tall, thin windows, a feeble attempt to invite light while inadvertently allowing the heat to escape. In an unsuccessful effort to retain warmth, the windows and vents remained closed.

Robert and Mavis, accompanied by their son Allan, met the headmaster–a delightful chap–who was introduced to Allan as "Sir," as instructed by his parents. Polite handshakes were exchanged, and the headmaster proceeded to explain some important matters to Robert and Mavis. Once finished, he kindly allowed the parents to bid farewell to their young son before departing, confident in the headmaster's caretaking abilities.

As they left the headmaster's office, Allan overheard his father reassuring his mother that he would be in capable hands. The door closed with a foreboding bang, and Allan's attention was drawn to a broad black leather belt that hung from a hook on the back of the door.

"Right, Master Wilson," the headmaster grinned. "I see you noticed the belt hanging on the door."

"Aye, sir," Allan confirmed, suddenly feeling a bit intimidated by the man.

"Do you know what that is?"

"A belt, sir?"

"No, it is called a tawse. Do you know what a tawse is used for?"

"No, sir," Allan replied, growing increasingly uncomfortable without his parents' support.

"It's used to discipline your backside if you misbehave or break any school rules. You wouldn't want me to use it on you, would you?"

"No, sir," Allan said nervously.

"Good, because it hurts. It hurts a lot. Do you understand?"

"Aye, sir," Allan nodded vigorously.

"I'm pleased we have an understanding. Now, please, open the door."

As the door swung open, the headmaster cast his gaze beyond Allan's shoulder and caught sight of a passing boy.

"You, boy!" he bellowed.

Startled, Allan turned to look over his shoulder. Equally startled and timid, an older boy, thin and a few years older than Allan, came to a halt and stared at the headmaster in trepidation.

"Don't just stand there, child. Come inside," the headmaster beckoned imperiously.

The apprehensive lad quickly stepped inside the inner sanctum of control, hierarchy, and power. Allan couldn't help but notice the fear emanating from the other boy, which only heightened his own sense of dread.

"Dawson, is it?"

"Aye, sir."

"This is Master Wilson," the headmaster waved dismissively at Allan. "He is now under your charge. Take him to Mrs. Aldridge, show him where he will eat, and so forth."

"Aye, sir," Dawson said nervously.

"Right, off you go. Close the door behind you. Oh, and Dawson, since Wilson is under your charge, any tawse lashings he receives, you will receive equally. Understand?"

"Aye, sir," James Dawson agreed, stifling a sob.

"Go," the headmaster dismissed the two boys, focusing his attention back on his paperwork.

Dawson grabbed hold of Allan's sleeve and yanked him backward. Allan managed to break free and hastily grabbed his small suitcase before darting out the door. Dawson almost slammed the door shut behind them but caught himself just in time.

The two boys hurried down the crowded corridor without uttering a word. It was only when they turned a corner that Dawson finally stopped. He stared at Allan with a sense of frustration. Allan met his gaze, feeling as though he was being regarded as a repulsive creature caught between two slices of bread.

"What kind of kid are you?" Dawson threw a condescending nod in Allan's direction.

"What do you mean?"

"I'll tell you what I mean," Dawson frowned. "You better not get into any trouble, because I'll suffer the consequences alongside you. And if I have to endure the tawse because of you, there will be consequences for you too."

"I won't cause any trouble," Allan said emphatically. "Is the tawse really that painful?"

"Aye, it certainly is. I've had my fair share of the tawse, and I don't want you adding to it."

"I won't," Allan said nervously.

"Aye, you'd better not. Now, come with me."

***

The tenth day of Allan's enrolment at Kirkwall found him in the headmaster's office, bent over a chair with his pants embarrassingly pulled halfway down his legs. With buttocks tingling from a thrashing from the tawse and holding back tears, he exited the office, tucking in his shirt. Dawson stood against the wall opposite the door with a look of doom on his face.

"Sorry, Dawson," Allan said pitifully.

"I heard three," James grumbled.

"Aye, three," Allan admitted and took a moment to rub the right side of his britches, hoping to dissipate the sting.

"Dawson!" came the muffled shout from the headmaster.

James pushed himself from the wall, glaring angrily at Allan, and then entered the inner sanctum.

Allan heard three thwacks in rapid succession, and then James exited the office. Closing the door, he rubbed his posterior and looked threateningly at his charge. Allan appeared traumatised.

"Don't let that happen again," James threatened and noticed Allan's chin wobble briefly.

***

As the years passed, Allan's academic prowess was barely average, he possessed an unparalleled love for sports, particularly cricket and rugby, which had captured his heart.

Every day after his lessons, Allan would rush to a back street or an open park, craving the thrill of competition. With a borrowed bat or ball in hand, he felt a sense of purpose and determination that eclipsed his academic endeavours. Whether it was the grace of cricket or the thundering excitement of rugby, Allan displayed a strong passion for the games.

As Allan honed his skills, he formed a close-knit group of friends who shared his love for sports. Together, they would spend countless afternoons practising, competing, perfecting their techniques, and dreaming of victory. In the world of ball sports, they found solace, camaraderie, and an opportunity to forget the challenges of academia.

Another favourite Scottish activity Allan enjoyed and excelled at was tossing the caber. This involved balancing a heavy log on one end, then taking a run-up to a mark and tossing the log as far as possible. Taking after his father in stature, Allan's physical prowess developed well. He became barrel-chested with powerful arms, and his height made him stand out amongst his peers.

One Saturday afternoon, as their group laughed and shared stories near the cemetery, a rival gang from a neighbouring village was seen walking towards them. This gang was known for their nasty antics and hooligan behaviour, and their approach looked ominous.

"Allan, look," Murray tapped his friend on the shoulder and nodded in the direction of the approaching youths.

"Are they those cretins from across the river?" Allan asked although he knew the answer.

Murray nodded. "Aye, those be them. They look like they're spoiling for a fight."

"I think we should leave," a smaller boy called Andrew said nervously.

"Nay," Allan smiled. "I'm sure they will pass us by. If they want to fight, let them come to us, and let's show them how tough we Kirkwall lads are."

As the gang approached, their menacing eyes gleamed with condescension and aggression. Allan knew they were up to no good and wanted to prove a point.

Courage welled up within him, stirring his natural leadership qualities.

He rallied his friends and instructed them where to stand on his command moments before any punches were thrown.

As Allan and his friends became surrounded by a foe that outnumbered them, an older resident of the village came around the corner and, with some amusement, gauged the outcome of the conflict.

"Aye, laddies," the old man called to Allan and his friends, "I might suggest you make a run for it."

Allan turned to face the man, who was smiling broadly. "We're not gonna run, sir, but we thank you for your advice. We're gonna fight."

"Suit yourself, laddie. Suit yourself," the man laughed and continued walking around the corner and out of sight.

The moment the man disappeared, the fight erupted. Quick reflexes learned from copious sporting games and competitions, coupled with Allan's leadership and strength, ensured that his group kept the advantage–their determination to work together and protect each other paid dividends. The gang, humbled by its unexpected defeat, retreated and ran, humiliated. Allan's group chased them, hurling insults.

Word got out fast, and Kirkwall school rejoiced at the courage demonstrated by Allan and his mates, and their status in the hierarchy of their fellow pupils soared. From that day forward, Allan's quiet determination was regarded well, not only as an athlete but as a leader. It unlocked his latent potential and paved the way for a journey of growth and self-discovery.

CHAPTER THREE
Africa 1862

"Mjaan," the old man called to his son.

"I see you, Father," Mjaan beamed.

"Follow me," he said.

Mjaan obeyed immediately. He picked up his weapons and followed his father down a narrow path that meandered through the village. They walked in silence.

When all sounds from the village had quietened, the old man walked into the shade of a large tree. He found a dry log partially eaten by white ants and sat gingerly upon it.

Mpilo was a very old man for a Matabele. He had survived many conflicts against some of his own people and also against the Afrikaner Boers in the south. He had recovered from two spear wounds and a fragment of a white man's bullet that had glanced off his ribcage. His face was deeply lined with wisdom. He had lost most of his teeth, but still, when he smiled, it was contagious.

Despite Mjaan being the commander of a new Matabele impi and demanding respect, he knelt in front of his father in reverence and looked at the soil under his feet. He could tell the grey-haired old man had something important to tell him and anxiously waited for the knowledge he would impart.

"You wish to speak with me, Father?" Mjaan spoke softly, then waited for a response.

"You have returned victorious, I see."

"Yes, Father," Mjaan smiled inwardly. The rowdy jubilation exhibited by Mjaan and his men when they entered the village that morning was not missed by many.

"Are your new warriors initiated now?"

"Yes, Father," his son replied with a hidden smile. "The six new ones bloodied their spears on Mashona men for the first time. All others washed their spears with Mashona blood too. Our impi is stronger than ever now."

The grey-haired man nodded his approval. Each time a warrior washed his spear in blood, it was believed it made him stronger. Mpilo was proud of his son; his physique exuded power and strength.

Mpilo smiled broadly. "I hear you brought back many good cattle for the King."

"Yes, many. The King will be very pleased. We have also taken twenty-six young girls. They will make good women for our tribe."

"That is good," his father commended softly.

"We will feast well tonight. Will the past member of a great impi honour us with his presence?" Mjaan extended an invitation to his father, knowing it was unnecessary.

"I am an old man now, and my time to move to the spirit world grows near. I will share your jubilation. But first, there are some things you must know."

Mjaan's curiosity heightened, his senses alert to what his father had to say. "I'm listening, Father," he said and respectfully lowered his gaze once more.

"Our King Mzilikazi was a fierce warrior, a commander under King Shaka, the King of the Zulu nation. He rebelled against him one day and fled to the north, taking his impi with him. But he was beaten by the tribes there, so he turned west and, for many years, fought with the tribes there, and also the Afrikaner Boers.

This became difficult, so our King fled further north after being driven away. He crossed the Limpopo River and claimed all this land for the Matabele people."

Mjaan knew the history well but kept silent, allowing his father to repeat the story. It seemed important to the old man, and Mjaan was required by custom to allow this with due respect.

"King Mzilikazi needed to ensure our tribe, our nation, became very powerful and wanted to find a new settlement for us. We travelled north and crossed the great river until we came to this place. He then split us into two groups. Half the tribe remained here to wait for the King. These were the women, children, old men and Indunas. The others, the warriors, continued onwards, travelling deeper into the new land, looking to expand our territory and strengthen our army.

"It was a very difficult journey for the King. The country was not good. There was sickness and the Tsetse fly was terrible. The people they found were hostile. They were away for many years and suffered greatly. Finally, our King returned to us, and we were reunited."

Mjaan knew what came next in the story. This story would be told around the fire at every celebration. He politely remained kneeling on one knee, however, and listening attentively.

"The King found insolence and disorder when they returned to this village. The people here claimed they thought the King had died because he was away for so long. Therefore, many chiefs decided to crown his first-born son, Nkulumane, as the King of the Matabele. Mzilikazi was angry when he saw this, so he killed all the chiefs and all his sons so that nobody could threaten his reign, not even his children. They were thrown off the cliffs at Thabazinduna."

Mjaan looked up at his father, wondering where this was going. Usually, stories of the past were told at night, over the fires, or while drinking beer. He didn't understand why he needed a history lesson away from the village and prying ears in the middle of the day.

"I know the story," Mjaan smiled his appreciation, but he had a frown on his forehead. "Thabazinduna; the hill of chiefs. It is also thought Nkulumane went into exile across the big river in the south and was not killed because he was King Mzlikazi's favourite son."

"That is so," Mpilo said, shaking his head forlornly. "It is said that King Mzilikazi allowed Nkulumane to flee, but it is also believed he did not survive and died in King Khama's land. The story is shrouded in mystery."

The old man's eyes took on a distant look as he cast his gaze at the horizon. "Now, son, I will tell you a part of the story you do not know. King Mzilikazi had several wives. Just after we crossed the Limpopo River, and before we split in two, one of his inferior wives, Queen Fulatha Tshabalala, fell pregnant. The King was not aware of this at the time we split. She later gave birth to a son. When King Mzilikazi returned and saw that Nkulumane had been crowned King, everyone knew a great anger would come upon the King; everyone was terrified. They knew there would be a big killing.

"When Queen Tshabalala realised that if the King discovered she had a son in his absence, he would throw that child off the cliff too, so she sent him into hiding with his nurse. Not many people with high status escaped the King's wrath. Even Queen Tshabalala was thrown off the cliff."

Mjaan straightened slightly in surprise. "So the King has a son that he is unaware of?"

"Many chiefs know but do not talk about it for fear the King will throw them off the cliff. Even you must not speak of this, or else you will find yourself talking with the bones of many chiefs at the bottom of Thabazinduna."

Mjaan nervously wiped the sweat off his brow with the palm of his hand. "I will not speak of it."

A smile crossed the old man's face. "There is more to this story," he said, then became serious again. "One night, not so long ago, I was awoken by a noise outside my hut. One of our spirit mediums was drunk, maybe with beer, or maybe with his herbs, I do not know. He had fallen by my door, so I went to help him stand again. He told me something that maybe he should not have."

"What did he say, Father?" Mjaan was suddenly skittish. Anything to do with the spirits made him nervous.

"He said when King Mzilikazi is taken to the spirit world, there will be much infighting because nobody will be able to decide who will be the next King. The village will be divided in their decision between Nkulumane, if he lives, and Queen Tshabalala's son. Matabele blood will be shed in the fight to decide."

"Do you know who this son is, Father?"

"Yes, he is the one they call Lobengula."

"Ghaw," Mjaan said in surprise. "I know of him. He is not a child."

"No, he is not. He has had 27 summers. You were born eleven summers before him. After his nurse had died, Lobengula was taken in by another family. When he reached his adult year, he did his duty in a powerful impi, as is the custom for all young men. He is a good warrior."

Mjaan knew Lobengula to be very smart and held him in high regard. He was tall, strong, handsome, and level-headed. When men were debating around the fire, Lobengula had a calculating mind and was an excellent orator. He could debate complex issues and was also excellent at mediating when villagers complained. His ability to resolve disputes often prevented unnecessary audiences with the King, which would invariably result in one of the parties being killed for their trouble.

The old man continued. "There was one more thing the spirit medium said. He told me that the commander of a very powerful impi would lead the fighting that would decide who the King would be. It is this impi that will win to ensure the correct King is crowned. But it will not be the Royal Guard. This new impi will destroy the Royal Guard."

"Ghaw," Mjaan exclaimed. "That means Mbiko, the commander of the Zwangendaba impi, will be defeated. How is that possible?"

"I only tell you what the spirit medium told me. But, what I say now is very important, my son. Listen to me well."

"I listen, Father."

"You must know this because the next King of the Matabele will be either Nkulumane or Lobengula. The white people in the south are starting to look towards Matabeleland now. They want our country, and there will be fighting. If Nkulumane is elected King once more, there will quickly be a bloody war against the white man, but if Lobengula is King, he might treat the white man with diplomacy. But, maybe even the best diplomacy won't work against the white man."

Mjaan sighed. "Father, you have told me much today, some of which is disturbing."

The old man stood up carefully; his old bones creaked with age. "We will never speak of this again, my son. Now come, we must celebrate your victory."

As they walked back to the village, Mjaan noticed that his father's pace had slowed considerably since the last time they had gone for a walk together. He slowed his steps to keep in time with Mpilo.

Mjaan enjoyed spending time alone with his father. "Father, please tell me again about your last battle with King Mzilikazi."

"Ahh…" Mpilo sighed, "it was a good battle. But I have told you about it many times before."

"You have," Mjaan nodded with a smile. "But I always like listening to the victories of my father."

"Our King was a ferocious warrior. He made us train and exercise all the time. There was never a time when we were not strengthening our bodies. We were powerful."

"How did you strengthen your body?" Mjaan asked curiously.

"In the same way you and your impi practice fighting today–but harder. I fear the new impis are not as strong as we were. When King Mzilikazi was younger, he would watch us all the time, and he was a tough master. His Indunas were even harder. We fought some tough battles for him."

Mjaan nodded gravely. "I know of these battles. They are often told around the fire."

Mpilo's eyes clouded over as he recalled some of the exciting adventures of his youth. "My son, listen to the elders carefully, and remember their stories. There are not many of us left now. We are old, and the hair on our heads is white with time. These stories must be told to youngsters often so that we remember and never forget."

Mjaan smiled pleasingly. "I will do that father, and I will make sure my impi is the strongest in the land."

CHAPTER FOUR

Minnesota 1868

"Where is that boy?" Rebecca Burnham grumbled as she stirred a watery stew over the cooking fire.

Edwin stood at the cabin door, arms folded, looking out at the vast plain that stretched out for miles around. Winter was setting in, and, although there was no snow on the ground, the morning had been greeted with a blanket of fine frost, which had given way to brown, dry grass only hours after the sun touched it. The daily changes to the landscape always fascinated him. Now the late afternoon shadows from the patches of woodland were growing long.

"Here he comes," Edwin said calmly.

Rebecca walked up to the door, wiping her hands on her apron. She watched her son, loping at an easy pace, ascend a ridge.

"I told that boy to be home well before dusk. I worry about him. It's turning cold now," she stated curtly.

Edwin put his arm around his wife's shoulders and pulled her close. "He'll be fine, don't worry about him."

"After what Chief Little Crow did to our home when he was a baby, I don't trust the Sioux one bit."

Edwin smiled. "That was a long time ago. Hostilities are over, and we are all getting along fine now. If I were concerned, I would do something about it. The Sioux seem to have taken Fred in as their own. They enjoy his company, and their kids have a lot of fun with him, too. Besides, he needs friends his age."

"Huh," Rebecca almost grunted. "The boy needs an education. He needs to go to a proper school."

Edwin relaxed his hold on Rebecca and stepped onto the veranda. He took a seat in a rickety wooden chair and gave a deep sigh. "We've been through this before, Rebecca. The nearest school is too far to travel to each day. Besides, he's getting a great education from the Sioux, and it's the kind of education he needs out here."

Rebecca stood her ground. "He'll be eight next year, and if he moves to one of the cities when he grows up, he'll need a proper education. I don't want him ending up a cow hand."

"So what if he does? It's an honest job." Edwin smiled at Rebecca, then looked into the distance and pointed to his son, who was drawing closer. "Look at Fred; he even runs like a Sioux Indian."

"How do Indians run?" Rebecca said sarcastically.

"Well, look. He's loping along at ease; his head and shoulders are not bobbing like most of us do. He's so relaxed."

Rebecca shivered and returned to the pot on the fire, dismissing what Edwin had just said with a grunt.

Fred arrived at the homestead and greeted Edwin. "Hello, Father," he said joyfully. He was hardly out of breath.

"Where did you learn to run like that?" Edwin asked, somewhat bemused.

"Like what?" Fred asked.

"Like a Sioux Indian."

"Oh, that," Fred smiled. "My friend, Tashunka, was being trained by his father, so he told me to learn too. If you run fast, you get tired fast. This way, if you go slower and use only the muscles you need, you can run for a very long time."

"Is that a fact?" Edwin scratched his chin and smiled.

"Tashunka's father told us that he ran down a cowboy who was on a horse. All Indians can do that. He said the cowboy shot someone in the village one day and took off on his horse at a gallop, so Tashunka's father picked up his tomahawk and started running after him. The cowboy pushed the horse too hard, so he had to stop and let the horse walk and drink occasionally. But Tashunka's father kept running steadily and didn't stop; he just kept following his tracks. It took him two days to catch the cowboy. When he caught him, he scalped him."

"Oh, please!" Rebecca shouted from the kitchen. "Enough of this violent talk. Edwin!"

"Yes, dear," Edwin stood up. "Fred, we don't discuss killing and stuff like that in this house; you know the rules."

"Yes, but Father, you asked me."

"It upsets your mother. No more of those stories, you understand?"

"Alright, Father," Fred concurred, dejected.

"You see," Rebecca continued, "he needs a proper education. Who knows what else those Sioux are teaching him."

When they had sat down to eat, and after Edwin concluded a lengthy and heartfelt thanks to the Lord for the meal that He had provided, Rebecca probed Fred on what else the Sioux had taught him.

Surprisingly, what Fred revealed held his parents in awe. He was learning how to track various animals, horses and people. He could identify an animal by its footprint and determine its size and age, and sometimes if it was a male or female. He learned how to find water in a desert and determine what plants he could eat, what he could use as a poison, and what could be used for healing.

One of the core lessons the Sioux taught their youngsters was how to train their eyes to see at night. This was an important lesson, which they practised regularly on moonless nights.

Fred's favourite lesson was camouflage and backtracking–hiding his tracks as if he were being hunted or pursued. These lessons, Fred informed his parents, he regarded as a game, not a lesson, and they would play these games every day.

Fred had a real affinity for horses and spent a great deal of time with the horses of the Sioux village. The Sioux had noticed his strong connection with the animals and the horses' acceptance of him, so they encouraged Fred to ride and practice equestrian skills regularly. Fred proudly claimed that he could almost talk to the horses, and surprisingly, they could talk to him. He could read signs from a horse by feeling a twitch in a muscle in its neck or how an ear twisted back, the flick of a tail or the toss of a head.

"So, do they let you ride their horses every day?" Rebecca asked.

"Yes, most days," Fred replied, somewhat surprised at the question.

"Bareback?"

"Mostly, why?"

"Well, I'll be," Rebecca said in awe.

"You see, the boy is getting an education," Edwin smiled contentedly, "and probably the best education a boy can get in these parts."

Fred told his parents how he had learnt to snare smaller animals, how to light a fire, gut, skin and then cook his catch. Because his father was a man of God and was against guns, he felt it best to avoid telling him he was good with a bow and arrow, and a spear. His favourite tool, which he also failed to mention, was a hunting knife.

Tashunka's father, known as Dakota, had given him a beautiful knife as a prize the previous year. Fred had managed to track Dakota down ahead of all the other young braves during a tracking lesson. Dakota had used his best skills to run and hide from the boys, but still Fred had found him with relative ease. What gave Dakota's position away was a lesson Fred had been taught earlier, and that was to watch for birds and their behaviour. He had noticed three birds flying fast in a westerly direction despite Dakota's trail going south. All he did was follow where the birds appeared to come from before he picked up Dakota's trail again.

Fred never told Dakota or Tashunka how he did it–it was his secret. The knife was also kept a secret from his parents. Each day, as he ran off to play with the children of the Sioux village, he collected his knife from a hollow in a tree, and every evening when he ran home, he would hide it there again.

Being young and fit, running was never a bother for Fred. It was a six-mile run to the village from his home, and sometimes, he would arrive just in time to join an informal lesson that involved a lot of running. Fred was convinced that sometimes the Sioux waited for him to arrive before they immediately began their running lesson. Fred never saw this as being unfair, and he never let on that he was tired. Then, of course, he would have to run home in the late afternoon to prevent a scolding from his mother. In time, he developed the ability to run great distances without any apparent effort.

"Mother, Father," Fred drew his parent's attention as soon as he had finished his meal, "tomorrow night is a celebration at the camp. The chief will be telling the children stories and traditions around the fire afterwards. Please, may I spend the night there?"

Rebecca looked at Edwin. "Oh, I don't know...."

"It will do him good to learn a bit more about the Sioux," Edwin interrupted his wife.

Rebecca looked at Fred uncertainly. "Have you heard any of these stories before?"

"Tashunka has told me some, but I have never heard the chief tell any."

"What story did Tashunka tell you?" Rebecca asked suspiciously.

"It was about seven grandfathers; each one had a special power that the tribe needed to understand. They were truth, humility, bravery, honesty, wisdom, love and…. and…. respect," Fred said, smiling as he counted off the attributes on his fingers.

Rebecca looked at Edwin sideways. "Do you think Chief Little Crow knew that story?"

Edwin cleared his throat and wiped his mouth on his sleeve. "I think Fred could spend the night out."

Rebecca frowned. "Alright, but I want you back here for breakfast the next day."

"Thanks, Mother, thanks, Father," Fred enthused.

"Before you go tomorrow," Edwin said, "I finished making that door for the new barn today. Please help me hold it in place while I secure it to the frame."

"Sure, Father," Fred smiled. "Will the barn be ready soon?"

He was excited because once the new barn was ready, they would buy sheep, and perhaps a cow.

"Maybe within a week," Edwin winked.

***

The following morning brought with it the start of winter. The frost was heavy on the ground, and some smaller puddles had iced up. After a hot breakfast, which included some of the previous evening's leftover stew, Edwin and Fred dressed warmly and walked outside.

The heavy wooden door that Edwin had built was carefully put in place, and, while Fred held it steady, Edwin secured it to the frame. When the job was done to Edwin's satisfaction, father and son walked back to the homestead. Rebecca was collecting eggs from the chicken coop.

"Done already?" Rebecca smiled at the two men in her life. They were an odd contrast, she thought. Edwin was tall and slender with an unkempt beard, while Fred was short with a more rounded face. Short though Fred was, he had a good physique, even for his age, and on the rare occasion that he gave her a hug, Rebecca knew he had a strength far beyond his years. It was the ice-cold blue eyes that made him striking.

"Yes," Edwin smiled back. "A lot easier when you have good help."

"May I go now?" Fred asked eagerly.

"Of course," Rebecca put an arm around Fred's shoulders and steered him to the house. "I packed a haversack for you with an extra blanket. You'll need it tonight."

"The teepees are warm inside, Mother. You need not worry," Fred calmed her protective maternal instincts.

Rebecca looked over her shoulder and suddenly stopped. "Edwin, what are you doing?" she exclaimed.

Edwin was bent over, trying to lift a log that looked a little too heavy for him.

"I need to move this log to the barn. It's not heavy," he grunted.

"Wait," she urged her husband, "Let's get Young Moke and drag it over to the barn. You'll break your back like that."

"The horse is lame. She did something to her leg yesterday. I'll do it; it's not that heavy," Edwin moaned as he lifted the cumbersome log and steadied it across his chest in the crook of his arms. He straightened up and turned slowly. "I'm fine," he repeated.

"Silly man," Rebecca muttered and turned to walk inside with Fred.

As Edwin neared the new barn, he stepped on a patch of mud just in front of the doorway. The water in the mud had frozen to ice overnight, and, suddenly, Edwin's right foot slipped from under him. He went down with a sickening thud.

Rebecca and Fred turned at the sudden sound and saw Edwin lying on his back with the log across his chest. His head was flung back as he tried to scream, but no sound issued from his throat. It was a frightening sight.

Rebecca shrieked and ran to Edwin's aid. Fred got there a split second before her and lifted one end of the log off his father's chest. Rebecca was suddenly at his side, and together, in one fluid motion, they lifted the offending log off her husband.

Edwin wheezed and clutched gingerly at his chest. His eyes were closed, and he coughed once, softly, and winced in extreme pain.

"Father," Fred implored, his face etched in concern. "Are you alright?"

"It's alright," Rebecca fussed. "We're here, we're right here."

Kneeling on the ground on either side of Edwin, Fred and Rebecca felt the cold soaking through their warm clothing to their knees. They quickly realised that the man should not be lying on the ice-cold ground.

"Take it easy," Rebecca crooned. "Catch your breath; then we need to get you inside. Do you think you can walk?"

Edwin coughed softly once more, then nodded gently, his eyelids clenched tight in pain. A smudge of blood appeared on his lips.

Fred looked at his mother for guidance and reassurance. When she looked up at him, his jaw dropped. A look of horror gripped Fred's face.

Rebecca cocked her head at Fred. "What's the matter?" she asked gently.

"Your face, you have blood splattered all over it," Fred whispered hoarsely.

Rebecca rubbed her face with her hand, then looked at her palm. Fred was right; her hand was smeared with bright red blood. They both looked down at Edwin, and traces of blood were visible at the corners of his mouth.

"We've got to get you inside," Rebecca told her husband, "and quickly. Fred, help me."

Fred and Rebecca stood up. Rebecca supported Edwin under his arms, carefully raising him to his feet, and Fred did his best to steady his mother. Slowly, the three of them walked back into the homestead. Despite Edwin objecting that he would be fine, Rebecca took his jacket off and laid him on a bed, quickly covering him in blankets to warm him.

Fred stoked the fire and put the kettle on it. He didn't really know how to help his parents, but he felt he had to do something.

Rebecca called Fred over. "Saddle up the horse and ride into town. Tell Doc Williams to get here as fast as he can."

"No," Edwin wheezed and waved a dismissive hand at her. "I'll be alright shortly. I just need to rest."

"You need a doctor, Edwin. You have broken some ribs and punctured your lungs. Fred...."

Edwin coughed again and gripped his chest. This time, there was no mistaking a spray of blood.

"The horse is lame," Edwin wheezed through a groan. "Can't be ridden."

Fred tapped his mother on her shoulder. "I'll run into town. I'll bring the doctor back."

Rebecca looked at her son in consternation. She didn't feel that she could expect her seven-year-old son to run twenty-five miles into Mankato, yet they desperately needed a doctor. Fred didn't wait for any further instruction or objection; he simply turned on his heels and ran out the door.

Turning down the track that would eventually take him to Mankato, Fred forced himself to remember the Sioux training that Dakota had drummed into him. He curbed his pace, controlled his breathing, and settled into a rhythm. Looking toward the bend in the road ahead he put his mind to reaching it; once there, he aimed for the next bend.

So Fred went, aiming for the next landmark, controlling his breathing, and loping at a steady, gentle pace. He tried hard to put the image of his father lying under a log out of his mind. Each time that image flashed through his mind he knew he would lose his rhythm, so he forced himself to concentrate on his pace.

When Mankato came into view, Fred was surprised at how easy the run had been. He still had energy and had not slowed once. As he entered the town, he called to the first pedestrian he encountered.

"Where can I find Doc Williams?" he shouted without pausing. "Emergency," he added.

The pedestrian pointed to the saloon across the street. "In there," he called back.

Fred sprinted to the bar and pushed the doors open. The attention of the customers was immediately drawn to the door, and a sudden silence filled the room.

"I'm looking for Doc Williams," Fred shouted. "My father is hurt."

An elderly man stood. "You're Reverend Burnham's son, aren't you?"

"Yes, Sir. Father's had an accident this morning, at the farm. Crushed his ribs. We need help, please."

"Come with me, son," the doctor said kindly. "Let's take my buggy, and you can tell me what happened. Mr Brown," he called to the bartender, "would you mind stabling Master Burnham's horse until we get back?"

"It's alright," Fred interjected, "I don't have a horse, Sir. I ran here."

The silence in the saloon was broken by a low murmur from the patrons.

"It happened this morning, at the Reverend's home?" the doctor asked, consulting his fob watch.

"Yes, Sir. Please hurry."

Doc Williams cast a look at some of the patrons, then shrugged. "Alright, let's go."

***

Edwin recovered, but not fully. He was bedridden for three weeks, and when he finally attempted to do some physical work, he was forced to return to bed. The cold winter air slowed his recovery.

After the accident, without the support of Edwin's strength, the family could no longer afford to remain on the farm. The buggy was sold, then the horse, and ultimately the property. With a heavy heart, Fred said farewell to his adopted Sioux family, and the Burnhams moved to Mankato.

Edwin got a job at a general store to supplement a stipend he got from the church, but he struggled to do a full day's work. The community was kindly. As Edwin was a loved pastor, they turned a blind eye to the restrictions imposed on him by his handicap, which resulted in him being able to do less than previously with regard to his clerical responsibilities, but it was not ideal, and Edwin was also often struck by medical complications.

Rebecca tried to get Fred into a school, but he was not suited to formal learning. Edwin's friend offered Fred some part-time work at his stables. Fred enjoyed looking after horses but his pay dwindled to nothing very soon after starting. It didn't worry Fred, he just loved being around horses. Hard times slowly but surely fell upon the Burnham family, and, just as surely, Edwin's health deteriorated.

It had been a year since Edwin's accident. Winter had returned, and Edwin was confined to his bed with pneumonia. Doc Williams closed his leather medical bag, bade Edwin farewell, and allowed Rebecca to walk him to the door. Fred followed them out. He was feeling depressed. His father was poorly and thin, they were broke, and food was not easily available. Fred's part-time job at the stables had come to an abrupt end with the arrival of winter, and sitting around their small room on the church grounds with an incapacitated father tested his patience.

"Thanks for coming, Doctor," Rebecca said forlornly.

Doc Williams turned to face Rebecca. "Mrs Burnham, may I make a suggestion?"

Rebecca looked up at him expectantly and nodded.

"Winter in Minnesota can be very harsh, and this cold weather is not doing your husband any good. His lungs have been badly weakened. If he is not careful, he may die from complications. I strongly suggest you move to a warmer climate."

"Where do you suggest?" Rebecca asked apprehensively.

"California would be my suggestion," the doctor said. "Not only is the weather better suited for Mr Burnham's condition, but the medical help there is better than anything I can give in Minnesota. It would be the best thing for him overall."

"Thank you, Doctor," Rebecca said woefully. "I'll talk to Edwin this afternoon."

"Good Day, Mrs Burnham," Doc Williams doffed his hat, then left.

Rebecca closed the door behind him and turned to Fred. He was looking at her with expectant eyes."

"California?" Rebecca mused.

"Your good friend lives in California, doesn't she?" Fred asked, but it wasn't really a question.

CHAPTER FIVE
Africa 1868

Mjaan remained crouched, motionless as a granite rock. He could almost have been mistaken for one. A rivulet of sweat ran down his brow and into his right eye. It stung a little, but he didn't flinch. He'd been trained not to make any sudden moves at a time like this. His second-in-command stood, unmoving, to his left and slightly behind, watching his leader peripherally.

With his spear in his right hand and shield in his left, Mjaan slowly began to stand until he could see just above the top of the grass which, like him, was barely moving in the hot, still air. He froze again, perfectly still and silent, like a stalking leopard.

About thirty yards ahead was a Mashona village. Mjaan counted seven huts in a semi-circle, one in the process of being built. An old man sat on a large stone, smoking a rolled cigarette. Two women walked past the cleared area's centre, clay pots on their heads. They were chatting, one giggling. Another two young women were pounding dried maize in a wooden mortar, taking turns to smash the kernels, one after the other. It was the sound of the pounding that had alerted Mjaan's spies to the village's whereabouts.

Mjaan slowly sank back to his haunches and looked at his second-in-command. Ngwenya was a lithe man in his mid-twenties, a fearless warrior who deserved his rank. Mjaan nodded, confirming the attack would go ahead. With a nod in response from Ngwenya, Mjaan understood that the other warriors were in place and ready. The village was doomed.

Allowing power to surge through his body, Mjaan quietly got to his feet and stood to his full height, his muscles almost quivering in energised anticipation of the massacre that was about to unfold. He raised both arms, brandished his stabbing spear and shield, and drew a deep breath.

"Ghee!" Mjaan bellowed loudly, allowing his call to arms to fade as all air was expelled.

His cry was answered immediately by over a thousand warriors, who jumped to their feet in reply.

"Ghee!" The terrifying war cry resounded in unison.

The villagers froze, fear and confusion holding them immobile. When the two women saw Mjaan they gave blood-curdling screams. The pots being carried on the women's heads crashed to the ground, and, as the women turned to run, they were briefly shielded by a magnificent spray of water that glistened in the bright sunlight.

Men, women, children, and grandparents came running out of the huts, only to find a hoard of merciless, bloodthirsty Matabele warriors descending upon them. As the shower of sparkling water dropped back to the dry earth, a new deep red colour replaced the clear liquid; Mashona blood.

The attack didn't last long. It was over almost as soon as it had started. Lying on the stained earth in the semi-circle were fourteen mutilated bodies. All the men of the village were dead, including the old man, his cigarette sympathetically smouldering to its death along with him. All the children had been killed beside their grandmothers. Five young women under the age of sixteen were spared. They were the Matabeles' prisoners, their prize, and the King would be well pleased with these girls. They would make good slaves for the villagers of Gibixhegu.

Mjaan pointed to his second-in-command, then moved his spear in an arc before him. With a quick command, ten warriors bolted into the fields and bushland beyond the village, searching for people who may have been outside the village confines when the attack started. They returned an hour later with two more young girls and a report that one middle-aged man was dead. Thirty cattle were added to their bounty.

The attack was complete, and there would be a celebration that night. Mjaan smiled: it was too easy—just as it always was when fighting the Mashona.

* * *

Tension filled the air as a young warrior approached Mjaan and Ngwenya. He carried a clay pot containing boiled goat meat and a thickened maize paste, the spoils of their latest raid.

Mjaan and Ngwenya accepted the offering with a grunt of thanks. Mjaan chewed a mouthful of the food, his brow furrowed in thought. Ngwenya knew better than to interrupt his superior when he was in this mood.

After a moment, Mjaan rolled some of the thick maize porridge in one hand and dipped it in the watery gravy. "Ngwenya," he said softly, "something is troubling me, but I am not sure what it is."

Ngwenya stopped eating, anticipating that he would have to answer his commander shortly.

Mjaan had a distant look in his eyes. "Our attacks on these Mashona cowards are too easy."

Ngwenya smiled. "That is because we are powerful, and they are weak. Their flesh is too soft for Matabele spears; they are very easy to kill."

"I think this is what is worrying me, Ngwenya." Mjaan paused momentarily, then continued dipping a small ball of maize in the gravy. With one finger, he scooped a chunk of meat into the porridge and put the contents in his mouth.

"I am curious why an easy kill should concern you," Ngwenya spoke respectfully.

"Mmm...." Mjaan waved a warning finger in the air as he chewed. Ngwenya held his silence.

Mjaan swallowed noisily. "We have raided three villages since we left Gibixhegu, and each has been very successful. All our warriors have blooded their spears well, and we have many young women and cattle to take to the King."

"That is so," Ngwenya agreed and commenced eating again.

"How many of our fighting men have been hurt in battle?"

Ngwenya spoke through a mouthful of food. "None. We don't have an injury among us. Not even a blister from all the distance we have marched."

Mjaan looked at their temporary camp, where all his warriors relaxed and enjoyed their meal. Off to the right, the young women cowered under the shade of a tree.

"That is what worries me," Mjaan had a puzzled look on his face. "It is too easy. Our men are not getting proper practice in fighting a battle. These Mashona are too weak, and they are cowards. They can't run away fast enough. We are becoming weak."

"Maybe, my Induna, it is because we are just too strong and powerful. We are Matabele. To speak our name makes the strongest Mashona shake."

"No," Mjaan objected, then put some more food in his mouth. "My father would tell me of his battles. They were hard-fought. They were tough, very tough. Our men are not being tested hard enough. If we were attacking a village belonging to King Shaka, to the south, it would be very different. We would be as soft as the Mashonas if we were to fight King Shaka."

Ngwenya knew about the reputation of the Zulu tribes south of the big river. In earlier days, his King, Mzilikazi, was driven north by King Shaka's forces and then again by the white Boer settlers. Mzilikazi had crossed to the north of the Limpopo River and settled his people there.

They allowed the Mashona people to live as slaves in the land he took, and King Mzilikazi demanded tribute from them in cattle and maize. They collected this tribute, or tax, through raids on the villages. The Matabele maintained their superiority by killing men and older boys of fighting age. Young boys could be brought back and blended into their own armies to strengthen their impis, and, of course, young women were very useful for contributing to the growth and strength of Gibixhegu.

"What are you suggesting?" Ngwenya asked curiously.

"I want to attack one more village before we return to the King. This time, I want to make it more difficult for our men; I want them to face a stronger fight."

"How can we do this?" Ngwenya was intrigued. "How can we make the Mashona stronger against us? Surely we do not want the Mashona to be stronger than us?"

Mjaan smiled mischievously. "No, but let us send some runners ahead to warn the next village we are coming. Let them prepare and be ready for us. Let them sharpen their spears."

Ngwenya beamed. "This is a very good idea, Induna."

"But more," Mjaan pointed a finger in the air as another idea crossed his mind. "Let us only send half our impi to fight this time. Send the lowest rank only, and make sure the Mashona men outnumber them."

Ngwenya grinned. "I will arrange that, Induna."

***

Two days later, Mjaan's spies found a large village, suitable for their latest battle plan to put the junior warriors to a powerful test. There were over thirty huts, and the scouts had observed many strong men and an equal number of young girls. From the tracks on the ground, they had noticed numerous fat cows, just ready for the taking.

Mjaan paced back and forth like a caged leopard. He regretted the idea of sending in a handful of junior warriors to see how they coped when the odds were tilted against them. This regret was because he could not participate in the attack. At forty-three years old, Mjaan believed he was at his peak and unconquerable, and now it irked him that he could not blood his stabbing spear on a miserable Mashona man.

But, he had to console himself; it was his idea to strengthen his impi with tougher challenges, although he was annoyed his plan had excluded him from the action. Ngwenya was there, but only to watch and report back. The Mashona had been warned that they were coming and to prepare. He knew they would be sharpening their spears, but strangely, Mjaan hoped his junior warriors would fail.

If that were to happen, Ngwenya would send a runner to Mjaan with a message, and the remainder of the impi would descend on the village with their full force and totally obliterate it. Of course, punishment and ridicule would follow, but that was the consequence of failure.

The settlement was only half a mile away, so Mjaan was sure he would hear the blood-curdling screams heralding the commencement of the offensive. As yet, all was quiet. He paced and paced, and the men standing behind him waited anxiously. They wanted blood just as much as Mjaan.

Then something strange happened. Mjaan heard a low rumble coming from his men. He looked to discover what they were mumbling about. Ngwenya and a handful of warriors were trudging back through the bush towards him. They looked dejected.

"What is the problem?" Mjaan asked, confused.

Ngwenya kneeled at Mjaan's feet. "My Induna, the village is deserted. The Mashona cowards have run away. They are worse than dogs."

Mjaan looked at Ngwenya in disbelief. "What? They ran away? Even after we gave them notice to prepare for us?"

"Yes, Induna. They have run into the hills and are hiding."

Mjaan fumed in anger. "They cannot do that to the Matabele. We must find them and kill them. All of them!"

Mjaan looked at the men of the impi, who were watching him expectantly, bloodlust in their eyes. He lifted both hands to the sky, then, theatrically, brought his spear downward to point in the direction of the village.

"Ghee!" his deep voice carried far.

His cry was immediately taken up by his impi, charging through the bush, past the village, and into the hills beyond. They were thirsty for blood. They had a commander who was angry, and he had let them do as they pleased. It was open season, and the men would make the most of it.

When the sun set that evening, Mjaan and his warriors were furious with the Mashona people. They had not found a single member of the village, and, adding to the disrespect, they didn't find any of their cattle either. They did stumble upon a big hoard of grain, however, and some fermented beer which they immediately appropriated.

Mjaan did not want to return to Gibixhegu after a failed raid, so he ordered that they remain one more day and vent their anger on another village before returning to the capital in the south. Scouts were sent out before sunrise. By mid-morning a village to the east had been located.

It was a sad day for those villagers. The Matabele were ruthless and exacted a brutal revenge. Later that evening, with anger and humiliation vented, Mjaan commanded his impi to return to Gibixhegu at first light.

***

When Mjaan and his impi entered the royal village he handed his bounty over to the Royal Guard. Their task was to select the finest cattle and distribute them among the various impis. Among the herd, there was only one black cow, highly sought after for making shields for the Royal impi.

After dismissing his own impi, Mjaan made his way to his hut. As he approached he noticed his wives sitting outside, wailing pitifully. His heart sank; he knew what this meant. Bracing himself, he waited for his senior wife to approach him and deliver the news that his father had passed away and was now walking with the spirits.

"When did he depart?" Mjaan asked, managing to keep his emotions in check. He had expected this to happen soon and had mentally prepared himself. No matter how much preparation one makes, however, the news of a loved one's passing is always difficult to accept.

"He left during the night, my husband," she said, her gaze fixed sadly on the ground. "You have returned just in time. According to tradition, your father is to be buried today. The grave has already been prepared."

Mjaan's anger surged immediately. If it hadn't been for the debacle with the cowardly Mashona at the second-to-last village, he would have made it home a day earlier and could have been at his father's side during his final moments. His anger grew to unsurmountable heights; he placed the blame for this woe squarely on the Mashona.

***

After his father's funeral, Mjaan took the first watch over the grave to ensure witches did not interfere with the deceased, in accordance with Matabele traditions and beliefs. Guarding the grave was expected to last several days. Once the inyanga, the traditional healer, declared the burial site safe, Mjaan wasted no time in rallying his impi together for a massive raid on the Mashona to the north.

Incensed, Mjaan pushed his men at a fast pace until they crossed the Bembezi River. Once across he allowed his men to rest for only one day to gather their strength. He whipped his subordinates into a frenzy as he paced impatiently, inspecting the ranks and checking the blades of their killing tools.

The raid commenced in a brutal and bloody manner. Each day, Mjaan's impis swept northwards, killing every man, woman, and child in their path, leaving a horrific trail of destruction. After the fourth day of slaughter the warriors made camp for the night at the base of a granite outcrop. Despite their normal enjoyment of a battle, talk around the cooking fires turned to solemn whispers as they questioned their leader's excessive lust for blood.

Mjaan sensed a commotion coming from the men to the south of the camp and looked curiously at Ngwenya. "What can that be?" Mjaan asked.

Ngwenya, looking weary, stood and peered towards where the excited chatter was coming from. "I see some men bringing a messenger to us."

Mjaan patiently awaited, curious as to why a message was being sent to him at such a time. It didn't take long before a small group of his loyal soldiers escorted a young, vigorous man to him. On seeing Mjaan, the man dropped to his knees and then lay prostrate face-first on the ground.

"Come," Mjaan demanded.

The messenger immediately crawled forward on his hands and knees and stopped at Mjaan's feet. "Oh, Induna," he almost wailed, quivering in fear. "I bring bad news."

"What is your message?" Mjaan asked, feeling a hollow pit in his stomach.

"Our mighty and powerful King Mzilikazi has passed to be with the spirits."

An uncomfortable silence descended upon the camp.

"King Mzilikazi is dead?" Mjaan stood slowly, disbelief evident in his expression. "When?"

"Two days after you left, oh Induna."

An uncomfortable silence cloaked the camp. Mjaan turned away from the messenger and walked into the tall grass, where he stopped in deep thought. The tension in the camp was so taut that not even a bird seemed to chirp in the treetops.

The conversation he had had with his late father six summers ago tugged at his memory. He tried to recall what his father had told him; it had something to do with the commander of the Zwangendaba impi. Mjaan was confused.

He returned to the quivering messenger. "Stand!" Mjaan ordered. "The commander of the Zwangendaba impi? Does he live?"

"Yes, my Commander. He lives. He is protecting the King's grave as we speak."

"How did our King die?"

"Sickness, my Commander," the petrified messenger quaked.

"Sickness?" Mjaan said under his breath, then looked the runner in the eye with a threatening scowl. "The King was well when I left. This is sudden. Was it a bad spirit?"

The question scared the man terribly, nearly causing his legs to collapse under him. He did not want to invoke any anger from the spirit world.

"The inyanga said sickness, my Commander."

"A bad spirit?" Mjaan looked at Ngwenya angrily.

The messenger tumbled at Mjaan's feet; it was too much for him. Not only was he in fear of Mjaan and the burden of bearing the most terrible news along with the invocation of the spiritual world, but he was also physically exhausted.

Mjaan looked down at the man, then back at Ngwenya. "We will return at first light, and we will go fast. Inform your men."

***

Mjaan and his impi entered the Royal Village at a steady trot while a mournful baritone chant resonated from his warriors. People moved aside, either out of respect or fear. One of King Mzilikazi's senior advisors stood firm in the road, signalling Mjaan to halt.

The impi stopped as one, the warriors barely panting. Mjaan walked purposefully up to the advisor, stopping just feet from him. It was customary for an advisor to update the commander on any important news during his absence.

"The news of the King's death has reached my ears," Mjaan spoke first.

"You have heard correctly," the advisor replied softly.

"Our King was well when I left. What caused his death?"

The advisor looked uncomfortable, glancing left and right. "It is unknown. He wasn't in the best health."

"But not unwell enough to die."

The advisor shrugged, opting to remain silent.

Now Mjaan grew nervous. "Where is the spiritual leader, Busangwane?"

"He has been in the Matobo Hills for several days but returned upon hearing the news, just like you did."

Mjaan shuffled uncomfortably. "If the King wasn't well as you claim, who was treating him?"

The advisor wiped his forehead with the back of his hand, beads of nervous sweat appearing on his brow. Mjaan noticed this.

"The traditional healer, the inyanga, was treating the King. The King passed away a few days ago at his capital, but the Council of Chiefs decided to withhold the news. They have only announced his death now."

Mjaan grunted, looking down at his feet in contemplation. When he looked up, his eyes burned with anger.

"What are you telling me, Advisor?"

The man trembled slightly before answering. "I am merely relaying what has transpired with our King. He rests in the Royal Dwelling, protected by his twelve Queens and the Zwangendaba impi. I am also here to inform you that there will be a Council of Chiefs tonight. All commanders are required to attend as the chiefs need to discuss the succession of the next King."

Mjaan raised an eyebrow. "And who do they propose as the next King?"

"They are considering sending emissaries to see if Nkulumane is still alive."

"Nkulumane? The one who was King for a brief period and caused resentment towards King Mzilikazi?"

"That is the one," the advisor sighed. "Lobengula Kumalo is another contender for the throne."

"Is it possible that the sangoma cast a spell on the King?"

The advisor shuddered but remained silent. The fear in his wandering eyes spoke volumes.

Mjaan pondered the ground at his feet, then locked eyes with the advisor. "Is it not true that the inyanga bestows magic upon the Zwangendaba impi, the protectors of the King?"

"That is true," the man replied. "Just as it is true that he grants magic to all impis, including yours."

"And is it not true that the commander of the Zwangendaba impi is the nephew of the inyanga?"

"That is also true," the advisor confirmed.

Suddenly, Mjaan straightened. Ignoring the advisor, he turned to face his waiting impi and summoned Ngwenya with a sharp nod of his head. Ngwenya responded promptly .

"Ngwenya," Mjaan said softly. "We will march quietly to the royal dwelling of our King and pay our respects. Inform the men to show reverence to Busangwane, who is at the grave. Let us proceed."

Mjaan's impi marched solemnly past thousands of wailing, mourning villagers. The large round structure of the royal dwelling greeted them through the sea of people surrounding it. When Mjaan and his warriors got close they stopped and took in the sight before them. Mjaan dropped to one knee, holding his spear with the point in the dirt, and his men followed suit.

After a respectful moment, Mjaan slowly stood and turned to walk away, but not before fixing the Zwangendaba commander, Mbiko, with a disdainful stare. Mbiko scowled back at Mjaan, almost daring him to a challenge battle.

***

After the funeral, and following an appropriate mourning period, all the important figures of the Royal Village were summoned for a special meeting. The meeting brought together the Indunas–including the royal advisors–the spiritual leaders, and the head priest Busangwane. These men gathered together from every corner of Matabeleland. The Indunas of each impi stood to one side of the gathering, eager to hear the outcome of the special meeting and discover who would be the new ultimate leader and King that they would serve.

Mjaan felt a great sense of anxiety as he looked around the gathering. There was an ominous feeling in the air, and he couldn't shake the belief that many spirits, including the spirit of his late father, were watching closely. An involuntary shiver ran through him as he searched for the Zwangendaba commander. He spotted him standing proudly and confidently at the front of the group of Indunas.

Busangwane called the meeting to order by invoking the spirits to guide them and ensure their proceedings were conducted correctly. The invocation of the spirits took nearly two hours. Finally, the chief of the Royal Village rose and slowly made his way to the centre of the gathering.

He recounted how King Mzilikazi had returned after a long absence only to find Nkulumane installed as King, resulting in the Great Anger that befell the Matabele nation. The chief narrated the tale of how King Mzilikazi had overthrown Nkulumane and had thrown many of his followers off the cliffs of Thabazinduna, leaving no clear heir to this day.

Stepping closer to the fire that burned in the centre of the dusty circle, the Royal Chief gestured to those around him. "There are many here," he declared with authority, "who believe that Nkulumane was not thrown off Thabazinduna. It is believed that he was allowed to escape the Great Anger and fled south, across the big river."

The Royal Chief paused, allowing the weight of his words to sink in. "Now, we must make a decision. Shall we send emissaries to find Nkulumane, or shall we offer the crown to King Mzilikazi's second-born son, Prince Lobengula, who is present with us today?"

An audible murmur erupted among the attendees. Mjaan's gaze shifted between Lobengula and Induna Mbiko. Prince Lobengula sat quietly beside Busangwane, observing with great interest. Mjaan recollected his conversation with his father many years ago under the cool shade of a tree. He knew something significant would be decided today, but he was uncertain as to which way the council would lean.

"What was it that my father was trying to tell me?" Mjaan pondered. *"Nkulumane was inclined toward war, while Lobengula favoured diplomacy. No, it was something else."*

The rumble of debate grew to a low roar until, suddenly, Prince Lobengula stood. The uncontrolled chatter abruptly stopped as all eyes turned towards him.

Radiating regality, Lobengula approached the fire's edge and locked eyes with the Royal Chief. His baritone resonated with surprising power throughout the assembly. "Before we decide to send emissaries to find my older brother," Lobengula declared, "let us first ascertain how many people wish to search for him or install me. If most of our chiefs wish to search, so be it. If the majority prefer me to be honoured as their King, then let that be."

The Royal Chief nodded emphatically, making it clear to all that he fully supported Lobengula's proposal. "Prince Lobengula's suggestion is well-received. Let us decide. Those who wish to search for Prince Nkulumane, please stand on this side of the fire," he gestured to his right. "Those who wish to install Prince Lobengula as our King, please stand behind him on that side of the fire."

As the attendees began shuffling to take their chosen positions, Mjaan carefully observed the unfolding scene. Initially, he believed this choice only concerned the chiefs and decided not to move. When he noticed Mbiko and some of the other Indunas leaving their assigned positions and walking towards the central fire, he realised he had to make a decision.

It was in that moment that Mjaan saw Induna Mbiko, commander of the Zwangendaba impi and protector of the King, position himself to the right of the Royal Chief, and his father's words suddenly resurfaced in his mind.

'The spirit medium told me that the commander of a powerful impi would lead the battle to determine the rightful King. This impi would emerge victorious, ensuring the correct coronation. However, it will not be the Royal Guard that prevails. This new impi will destroy the Royal Guard.'

A cold sweat broke out on Mjaan's forehead. It became clear that he must align himself with Lobengula, as the Zwangendaba impi would be defeated. Without a moment's hesitation, he chose Prince Lobengula and moved to the left of the fire. He found himself standing just to the left of Lobengula's shoulder.

The Royal Chief positioned himself in the centre, carefully maintaining his neutrality, and surveyed the assembled individuals. The split in support was nearly equal. He turned his attention to Prince Lobengula.

"The division is evenly split. What is your decision now, Prince Lobengula?"

"Let us dispatch emissaries to seek out my brother and determine if he is still alive. If he is, he must be brought back urgently and crowned King."

"That is a wise decision," the Royal Chief concurred. "Therefore, this Council of Chiefs is now adjourned."

As the meeting concluded and the attendees dispersed, Lobengula tightly grasped Mjaan's wrist. The strength of his grip caught Mjaan off guard.

"Who are you?" Lobengula whispered.

"I am Induna Mjaan of the iNgubo impi, my Prince," Mjaan replied.

Lobengula's expression took on a sinister tone. "Did you see the faces of those on the other side of the fire?"

"Yes, my Prince. My eyes have seen them."

"Do not forget those faces. They are now my enemies."

"I will not forget," Mjaan nodded solemnly.

Lobengula released his grip on Mjaan's wrist. "Observe them all again and do not forget who they are."

Mjaan and Lobengula stood silently, watching the crowd disperse. Mjaan was certain he would remember all who stood opposite, but to be sure, he tried hard to commit the prince's enemies to memory.

Looking at the Royal Chief, Mjaan was not convinced if he would be regarded as an enemy or not. Probably not, he thought, but it didn't escape his notice that the man was looking a little nervous, his eyes darting across to Lobengula furtively. Then again, Mjaan understood that everyone at the gathering was at a heightened state of anxiety.

Whichever way a decision went, knew that many people would die once a new King was crowned.

The crowd had thinned to just a few people before Lobengula turned to face Mjaan.

"I have been observing you and your impi returning from battle. You and your warriors are powerful and victorious. If I become King, I will appoint your impi as my Royal Guard."

Mjaan hid a smile, his gaze dropping to the ground. "I will serve you with honour," he declared sincerely.

His father's words echoed in his mind, confirming that he would lead the most powerful impi in Matabeleland. It was he who would emerge triumphant against Induna Mbiko and the Zwangendaba impi.

CHAPTER SIX
Scotland 1868

"Come on, Wilson!" someone shouted from the stands.

Allan smiled quietly to himself as he walked back to the crease. It was fitting, he thought, that as the captain of the Kirkwall Grammar School Cricket Team, he would be left to face the last ball of the match. It was also the last ball of the season. The team needed a boundary–four runs would give them the win he so desperately wanted. Anything else, and his team would walk off the field, disheartened.

Allan had filled out during his years at Kirkwall. He was the toughest lad of all the boys. He stood proud, barrel-chested, and oozing confidence. Although respected and liked by all the pupils at the school, academically he was wanting. It made his classroom life at Kirkwall miserable, but he was in his element once on the sports field, amongst fellow boys of his year.

Allan's natural leadership qualities had earned him the captaincy of the school's senior cricket team and good standing on the rugby team as well. With only one month left of his final school term, Allan was determined to end his miserable time under the everyday threat of the headmaster's tawse and leave victorious. His team and the school depended on this final ball of the match.

Turning to face the bowler, a lanky boy his own age with a sinister smile, Allan planted his feet firmly on the ground and hit the earth between his feet several times with his grubby willow cricket bat to align himself with the bowler, bat, and wickets. The solid, hollow sound suggested an air of confidence.

Allan stared down the bowler, then replaced the stare with a concentrated frown. The bowler's arm arched high before he released the ball at a blistering pace. Allan watched its trajectory and almost smiled in that split second the ball took to reach him. It was a perfect length, meaning he would need to step forward slightly, allowing him to put his entire body weight into the swing.

The ball hit the sweet spot of the bat with a satisfying whack that reverberated across the field. Allan knew at that moment the score would not be the hoped-for four, but a match-winning six. The ball was still rising when Allan raised his arms in a victorious salute to the cheering of his peers from the sidelines.

Later that day, as players, teachers and guests drank strong sweet tea and nibbled cheap, stale biscuits under a faded canvas sheet strung between some trees, Allan felt a light tap on his shoulder. He turned to see a former pupil grinning at him.

"James Dawson," Allan exclaimed in delight and shook James' hand.

Allan noticed that James was still as gaunt as he had been the day they met, and the day he left Kirkwall some years prior. His nose seemed a little longer and sharper than Allan remembered, and he thought a strong wind might blow James over if he were not careful.

"Congratulations," James smiled. "Seems you are a little better at sports than you were at mathematics and English."

"Indeed," Allan chuckled. "Unfortunately, that side of it hasn't improved much. I still get the business end of the tawse because of it."

James chuckled. "I'm pleased you're not sharing it with me anymore."

"Yes, I'm sorry you had to deal with that because of me," Allan apologised.

"Think nothing of it," James shrugged, a genuine smile lighting up his face. "That's the way things are in life, I suppose."

Allan shook his head. "What I find unfair is that they beat the girls with the tawse as well as the boys. That shouldn't be allowed to happen."

"I agree," James nodded.

"What are you doing with yourself these days?" Allan changed the subject.

"I live in Fochabers now. I have a job at a general dealer's store. I'm just up for the weekend to visit my parents and noticed that the annual cricket match was on against our old-time rival school, so I thought I'd waste a few minutes here. When I learned you were the team's captain, I stayed a bit longer."

"Fochabers," Allan mulled. "I'll be there next year. My parents want me to improve on my poor academic abilities."

"Ahh…." James smiled, "Milne's Institute."

"Quite," Allan nodded.

"Well, I must be off," James said. "Well played, and good day to you."

"Hold on one moment, please, if you would?" Allan requested as he put his teacup down. "I have something I would like to give you before you go."

"Give me?" James said, bemused. "What?"

"It's in my trunk, at the school. Let me walk you out, and we can fetch it."

James shrugged and followed Allan out of the pavilion. The walk to the school premises was short, and it took Allan only a moment to unlock his trunk and retrieve a parcel wrapped in old newspaper and tied up with a length of jute twine.

"For you," he said, smiling broadly, "with my thanks for all you did for me. Not to be opened until you are back in Fochabers."

"What is it?" James asked curiously as he weighed the gift in his hands.

"It's a secret. Something to remind you of me. Safe travels, and perhaps we will cross paths in Fochabers one day."

"Perhaps," James said. "Thanks for the gift."

When James arrived in Fochabers, he remembered the gift Allan had given him. Unwrapping the newspapers, he laughed at what he found– the infamous black leather belt that was used as a tawse which hung on the back of the headmaster's door. He found out later that Allan and his small group of friends had been involved in the theft, in protest of the inclusion of girls in the beatings. Although the thief had never been identified, the reason the tawse had been stolen was known, and the policy of beating girls with it came to an end.

CHAPTER SEVEN

Africa 1869

It had been two years since emissaries had been sent to find Prince Nkulumane, who was believed to be in the country to the south of the big river. A strong lead had sent them as far as Basuto territory, but that had led nowhere. The emissaries returned and reported that Nkulumane was dead, even though they weren't absolutely sure. Based on that, the Council of Chiefs offered the crown to Lobengula. There was still opposition to this, especially from Induna Mbiko of the Zwangendaba impi. Frustrated, Lobengula addressed the Council and demanded that a decision be made.

A meeting of the Council of Chiefs was called, and, as was the custom, a fire was made in the centre of the circle, around which all the delegates congregated. After the formalities were completed and Busangwane had summoned the appropriate spirits, the Royal Chief called the meeting to order.

Lobengula rose and walked to the edge of the fire. "There is too much indecision and opposition to the appointment of a King. I propose that we allow a weapon of war to decide the matter."

The rumble of mumbling that swept the meeting indicated that the chiefs were interested in this idea.

"The biggest opposition to me, Prince Lobengula, is Induna Mbiko of the Zwangendaba impi and those chiefs that take his side. We all know who they are." Lobengula paused. "I propose a battle between the Zwangendaba impi and the iNgubo impi tomorrow at sunrise."

Adrenaline surged through Mjaan's veins. Tomorrow he was going to lead his men into battle against his own people, and not only that, against warriors who were highly trained and ready to kill. He looked at Mbiko, who returned his gaze with a cunning smile.

The chatter from the attendees was cut short as Lobengula raised his arms to silence them.

"Weapons will be assegais and shields. The battle will be decided when only one impi remains standing and the other fights no more. I choose the iNgubo impi. If my impi wins, then I accept the crown. If my impi loses, I will stand back and leave the chiefs and Zwangendaba to find a suitable King."

Mjaan fixed his gaze on Lobengula, forcing himself not to look at Mbiko. The drive to stare the Induna down was strong, but he comforted himself knowing the time would come in the morning.

"I have spoken," Lobengula said authoritatively, then walked back to the seat allocated to him and sat down.

The Royal Chief walked to the fire and looked at all the attendees. "Do you all agree with what has been proposed?"

A resounding cheer of approval went up.

"Are there any objectors?"

The crowd barely moved. There was an uncomfortable silence: nobody dared contradict the cheer that had gone up only moments prior.

"Then it is decided. The two impis will meet at the river before sunrise. When the sun greets us, let the battle begin."

As the meeting broke up, Lobengula signalled Mjaan to come to him. He obeyed immediately and dropped to one knee.

Lobengula smiled. "Now you know why I have made you train very hard."

"I understand," Mjaan said without looking at Lobengula. "We are ready. I want to thrust my spear into Mbiko's throat tomorrow."

Lobengula assumed a sinister grin. "We must not spare anyone. We must win tomorrow."

"We will win, my Prince. I know because my father told me so before he died."

"Is that so?" Lobengula smiled, but there was a frown between his eyes. "Your father was telling the truth, and we will win tomorrow. This is good to hear. Now go tell your men to rest, for tomorrow will be a hard day."

.

* * *

As the eastern horizon began to show signs of changing colour, a deathly quiet hung over the plain on the north bank of the small river. An unusual silence hung ominously in the air as over two thousand warriors stood at the ready, poised to attack those of their own clan. Tensions ran high as the warriors eagerly awaited the arrival of the sun so that they could unleash their repressed fury upon each other.

Mjaan turned his gaze away from the skyline and faced his men. He was pleased with what he saw. Standing proudly, Mjaan was dressed only in a loincloth made of leopard tails, firmly holding his black and white shield in his left hand and his iklwa–his short stabbing spear–in his right, the glinting blade menacingly reflecting the fading moonlight.

Over the past year, Mjaan had relentlessly drilled his impi, sending them into battles against the Mashona whenever possible. He devised war games and physical exercises that could be classed akin to torture, all in an effort to toughen bodies and sharpen reflexes. Inflexible discipline left no room for tolerance of any kind.

The iNgubo impi trained in secret, away from Mbiko and his men. Mjaan was confident that his warriors were the best in the Kingdom and that they were prepared for this battle. They were not just ready, they thirsted for blood. They *needed* blood.

The previous evening Mjaan had spoken gravely to his men, explaining what was at stake and the reasoning behind their intense training. The time had come to demonstrate their loyalty, dedication, and unwavering commitment to their ancestors, their nation, and their future King.

In accordance with Matabele tradition, it was customary to remain on the battlefield after a battle and mutilate the bodies of those killed. It was believed that opening up the bodies would release the spirits trapped within, and that failure to do so would result in the dead person's spirit haunting the warrior who killed them. This battle would brook no exception.

As tensions heightened with the imminence of the rising of the sun, Mjaan felt a presence beside him. In his peripheral vision, he could tell it was a warrior, a large and imposing figure, also almost naked and armed with a shield and spear. This confused Mjaan, as only Ngwenya would approach him at such a time, yet it was not Ngwenya. He turned to see who it was and immediately fell to his knees.

"My Prince," Mjaan whispered.

"Stand," Lobengula commanded in a low voice. "Are you ready?"

"Yes, my Prince. Why are you here?" Mjaan asked, surprised.

"I will fight alongside you," Lobengula declared, a mischievous grin appearing on his face.

"It is not necessary, my Prince," Mjaan objected. "We will win for you. The spirits have assured us."

"I will fight because the spirits have foretold our victory," Lobengula explained. "Besides, I have a score to settle with Mbiko. Tell me, Induna, what is your strategy now?"

Mjaan surveyed his warriors and answered, "We will wait for Mbiko's charge. Once he begins, we will observe his strategy and adapt ours accordingly."

Lobengula nodded in understanding. "You are a strategist, indeed."

Mjaan expressed his gratitude. "If Mbiko charges straight at us, we will form the Horns of the Buffalo and flank him on both sides."

"I fear he is too cunning for that. He will likely form the Horns of the Buffalo first, putting you at a disadvantage," Lobengula warned.

"Yes, that is a possibility," Mjaan acknowledged. "If he does, we will tightly group together and counter his flanking manoeuvre."

Lobengula nodded but with some doubt. "You may still find yourselves in trouble."

Mjaan grinned confidently. "What you see behind me, my Prince, is only half my impi. The other half is lying in wait on the flanks. They moved into position last night."

Lobengula couldn't help but suppress a laugh. "Very clever, Induna."

"If Mbiko charges straight ahead, my flanks will sweep behind his lines and attack from the rear. If he forms the Horns of the Buffalo we will draw them in and hold them until my flanks strike from the rear and sides."

Lobengula nodded approvingly, then pointed to the skyline. "The time is upon us. Let us fight."

Every soldier on the battlefield turned their attention to the horizon, awaiting the moment of battle. The sun hovered just below the horizon. A tense shuffling sound reverberated through the ground as warriors on both sides prepared for imminent combat.

A sliver of sun emerged above the horizon, brilliant even at that early hour. All heads turned to face their enemies, and both Indunas raised their spears to the heavens.

"Ghee..." Mjaan bellowed, and his men echoed his call.

"Ghee..." came the response from the far side of the field.

Mjaan momentarily charged forward, then suddenly halted, prompting his impi to do the same. This provided enough time for Mbiko's impi to react, and they charged.

Mbiko's strategy was exactly as Mjaan had anticipated; they swiftly formed the traditional Horns of the Buffalo. The fastest runners positioned themselves on the outer edges of the 'horns', preparing to encircle their enemies. The centre charge followed slightly behind, giving the outer runners time to complete their formation.

Mjaan urgently commanded his men to square up and fortify all sides, including the rear. Mbiko's men were upon them and the expected slashing and stabbing ensued. At first, the thudding sound of iklwa striking hardened hide shields dominated the battlefield, but the screams of men, either rallying their courage or succumbing to death, began to drown out the thuds.

Mjaan deflected a parry from a young warrior and swiftly countered with a piercing strike to his opponent's throat. The man fell instantly, revealing another bloodthirsty warrior behind him. Capitalising on the opportunity he struck with his iklwa, finding the attacker's throat. Another enemy was out of the battle.

Suddenly the battle cries shifted in tone—Mjaan's flanks had arrived and were inflicting substantial damage on Mbiko's rear and sides. The plan was succeeding.

Amidst the chaos Mjaan found himself face-to-face with Mbiko whose spear was raised, poised to strike. Mjaan raised his shield and ducked under it, his eyes fixed on Mbiko's abdomen. His spear was readied for the killing blow, but, at the last moment Mjaan made a critical decision. He would not be the one to end Mbiko's life; that honour belonged to the King, to Lobengula. With grim intent he aimed his spear at Mbiko's groin, driving the blade in deep. A scream of pain escaped Mbiko's lips.

Retracting his spear, Mjaan watched as Mbiko dropped to his knees, his eyes pleading, aware of his imminent demise. Mjaan stood tall and kicked the Zwangendaba commander backwards, confident that he would remain motionless until the battle's end. He then turned his attention to the next warrior.

To Mjaan's dismay, he only managed to slay two more men before the battle, seemingly lasting mere minutes, ended. Faithful to their strict training, the iNgubo impi refrained from cheering and quickly reformed their ranks, awaiting their Induna's next command. Lobengula stood out on the battlefield, covered in blood, making his way towards Mjaan with a determined stride.

"You have emerged victorious," Lobengula adulated.

"I have spared Mbiko for you, my King," Mjaan addressed Lobengula as the rightful heir to the throne.

"Take me to him," Lobengula snarled.

When they found Mbiko, he was still alive but bleeding profusely. Lobengula placed the tip of his iklwa against the helpless man's throat, staring at him briefly. Silently he thrust the iklwa into the Induna's soft flesh.

Mjaan nodded in approval. "I shall leave you to release his spirit, my King. I must address my men now as they must do the same for those they have slain."

"Very well," Lobengula grunted. "If any members of the Zwangendaba impi survived, their spirits must follow their fallen commander."

"It shall be done, my King," Mjaan grinned.

Later that evening, the Council of Chiefs declared Lobengula's conduct on the battlefield admirable and deemed the dispute resolved without further arbitration.

"We extend to you the position of King," the Royal Chief spoke on behalf of all the dignitaries.

"I accept," Lobengula smiled as he stood beside the flickering flames of the fire.

***

On a cool September morning in 1869, the Matabele nation crowned King Lobengula as the second King of the Matabele. A massive celebration took place, and many cattle were slaughtered to prepare for the feast that followed. Shortly afterwards, anyone believed to have opposed Lobengula's ascension to the throne was brutally put to death. This included Mbiko's entire village, as well as his dogs and goats.

CHAPTER EIGHT

California 1871

After an exhilarating journey on a paddle steamer down the west coast of America, followed by an uncomfortable stagecoach ride, the Burnhams finally arrived in Los Angeles in the first few days of the new year. Despite their exhaustion, they held onto their hope for a prosperous and exciting new life.

Life in Dakota had been harsh for the Burnhams. When Fred was almost three years old, they had welcomed a second son, but the child had tragically passed away three years later. Two years after that, they were blessed with a daughter, but she only survived eight months. This journey to California was particularly challenging for Rebecca, as she was noticeably pregnant.

In 1871, Los Angeles buzzed with energy. This was especially exciting for young Fred, by then a robust young boy, and he eagerly immersed himself in his vibrant new community. He marvelled at the diverse mix of people he encountered, including Mexicans, Indians and Chinese, each representing different cultures and races. The sheer number of individuals in Los Angeles astounded him; he had never witnessed such a bustling crowd.

What captivated him even more were the vivid colours that surrounded him at every turn, from the vibrant paint on buildings to the eye-catching signs in shop windows, even the clothing of the Mexican men and women. The sombreros, unique to the Mexicans, never ceased to impress him. Women wore makeup that added a touch of mystery and allure. Every aspect of this new world ignited his curiosity, turning his experience into a delightful sensory adventure.

Fred's outgoing nature and captivating smile appealed to the eclectic residents of his new home city, and he made friends easily. He found the older men particularly interesting and was especially intrigued by their tales of adventure and near-death experiences. One scarred old man with deep wrinkles had worked in the fishing industry. He told stories of exotic tropical islands and treacherous encounters with massive whales using nothing more than hand-thrown harpoons. This inspired Fred one evening to declare that he would become an experienced sailor, exploring the seas and distant lands.

Another larger-than-life character had Fred enthralled with his adventures in China, where he had trained with Shaolin Monks and learned secret fighting techniques. Then, other stories of the Samurai swordsmen in Japan convinced Fred that he would prefer a trip to Japan rather than pursuing a career as a fisherman. He wanted to learn their fighting style and acquire a sword capable of slicing bullets in half while in flight. All too soon, though, this ambition was replaced by a desire to discover hidden tombs in the pyramids of Egypt.

Rebecca and Edwin would often shake their heads in bemusement at the dinner table and smilingly wonder what Fred's next fascination would be. Little did they know that before long, an incident would forever change the course of Fred's life.

Edwin cleared his throat and pushed his empty dinner plate away. "Fred," he began, "tomorrow morning, I would like you to accompany me on a mission."

"What kind of mission?" Fred's curiosity was piqued.

"I believe you will find it enjoyable. Many people in this town are angry because of..."

"There are no angry people here, only happy and friendly people," Fred interrupted. "I like them all."

Edwin raised his hand to quieten his son. "In this area, yes, but in rural California, there are some very unhappy people. You only see the friendly ones, Fred. I want you to see the ones who are not happy," Edwin explained with a smile. He wanted Fred to drive the buckboard because his chest pain made controlling horses or mules difficult. "You see, as more and more people come to California, conflicts arise over water rights, grazing territories, and ranch boundaries. People have become so angry that they are resorting to violence over trivial matters."

"They are?" Fred asked, surprised.

"Yes, and the laws here are not being respected. They don't call this 'The Wild West' for nothing. Tomorrow, I am going south to negotiate with some Mexican ranchers on behalf of American ranchers. The church has asked me to speak to the Mexicans because I am a neutral party."

"What does neutral mean, Father?" Fred asked, thinking it had something to do with a church greeting.

"It means I don't take sides. I am neither a friend of the Americans nor the Mexicans, just a holy man. I know what the Americans want, so now it's time to see what the Mexicans want and if we can come to an agreement."

"That sounds good. What time do we leave?" Fred asked eagerly, his attention grabbed by the unusual opportunity.

"We will leave after breakfast," Edwin replied with a smile. He was pleased that Fred would be joining him because, in his mind, having his young son with him would help dispel any suspicions the Mexicans might have about his motives in the negotiations.

"I'll be ready," Fred promised, seeking to be excused from the table before disappearing on his own mission.

"He's an excitable child," Edwin muttered to himself, but he couldn't hide his grin.

Rebecca placed a soothing hand on her husband's arm. "He's young and adventurous. I'm sure you were just like him once."

Edwin stifled a laugh, clutching his chest.

"You need to see a doctor, Edwin," Rebecca said sternly. "It's getting worse."

"I'll be fine," Edwin reassured her. "I'll see the doctor once we return tomorrow afternoon if it will ease your worries."

***

Before breakfast was served, Fred had the mule harnessed to the buggy and was ready to go. Rebecca insisted that the two eat something before they departed. As the morning sun was beginning to generate its uncomfortable heat Edwin and Fred left town, heading south at a leisurely pace.

It took only two hours to reach the homestead where the meeting was scheduled to take place. Edwin and Fred were received coolly by half a dozen Mexicans from the surrounding properties. After some forced smiles and cordial conversation, sentiments warmed, and the ranchers settled down to listen to Edwin.

They weren't exactly enthusiastic about the terms the American ranchers proposed. They disagreed with more points than Edwin had hoped for, but they agreed it was a starting point and would entertain further discussions at a later date.

As Edwin struggled to board the buckboard a kindly Mexican helped him up. Feeling concerned for him, the Mexicans decided to escort him halfway back to town, giving them a chance to talk further.

Fred listened idly as he steered the mule homeward. The talks had been only vaguely interesting to him. The group had not quite reached the halfway mark when Fred noticed a man on a horse waiting in the middle of the road.

"Who's that, Father?" Fred interrupted the conversation without taking his eyes off the man.

Edwin squinted at the lone figure in the distance. "I think it's Mr Johnson. What's he doing here?"

The Mexicans suddenly began speaking quickly in Spanish, causing Fred to look at them in confusion. He hadn't seen them this excited during the negotiations, and Mr Johnson seemed to be the cause of their agitation.

"What is he doing here?" the leader of the Mexicans demanded.

"I don't know why he is here," Edwin replied, perplexed. "Let me go ahead and ask him."

"What's the matter?" Fred asked, starting to feel alarmed.

Edwin ignored the question. "Fred, move on up; let's see what he wants."

The lead Mexican rancher, a large man with an unruly moustache, suddenly pulled his revolver from its holster, creating a chain reaction with his compatriots, who also drew their weapons.

"Mr Johnson is the instigator of all this trouble," the Mexican almost growled, "and you bring him here?"

"No," Edwin protested. "I told him not to come. Wait, wait. I'll speak to him. Fred, move it!"

"You are not neutral," the rancher accused. "You are on their side."

Fred flicked the reins and gave a sharp cry, and the mule lurched forward. Behind him, he heard a metallic click. Swivelling around to see what it was, Fred saw six rough-looking ranchers pointing their guns at him and his father.

"Go!" Fred shouted and again flicked the reins sharply. The mule immediately responded and broke into a trot. The moment that happened, a shot rang out, and Fred was sure several bullets whizzed around his head. It felt like forever, but finally, they left the ranchers in their dust and escaped to safety with Mr Johnson.

Johnson pulled up and waited for the Burnhams to catch up with him. Once they did, Edwin could hardly contain himself.

"In the name of the heavenly Father, what do you think you are doing coming onto their land?"

"Reverend," the apologetic American said, "I was so anxious to find out what had happened with the negotiations that I thought I would meet you along the track."

"Are you alright, Fred?" Edwin suddenly looked at his son.

"That was amazing," Fred beamed, adrenalin still pumping. "I'm fine, Father. How about you?"

"I'm fine," Edwin grunted, then turned to Mr Johnson, anger burning in his eyes. "You could have gotten us killed, you fool!"

"I didn't expect them to accompany you on your return."

"No, of course you didn't," Edwin managed, before grasping his chest in agony.

Fred stood and looked back at the settling dust. "Did you see all those bullets? That was so exciting. We dodged them all."

"They wouldn't miss from that distance. I think they were just warning shots," Johnson tried to downplay the seriousness of the incident.

"Sit down, Fred; let's go," Edwin said, then glared at Johnson. "I'm done with you lot."

Fred flicked the reins, and the buggy jerked noisily past the American.

"Reverend, wait a minute," Johnson pleaded. "Were the talks promising?"

"Thanks to you," Edwin sneered, "not anymore."

As they rumbled homeward, Edwin struggled with his breathing while Fred found his near-death experience exhilarating.

In that instant, Fred knew he had found his direction in life.

CHAPTER NINE
Scotland 1871

James Dawson stared at the numbers on his clipboard, his brow furrowed in confusion. The numbers just didn't make sense. He sighed, realising he would have to trudge back to the dreary storeroom and do another round of counting.

Annoyed, he spun around and accidentally bumped into a young lady standing behind him. She gasped, and the tin tea caddy she was holding slipped from her hand, crashing to the floor with a loud clatter.

"I do beg your pardon," James apologised profusely, quickly scooping the container up off the floor.

"It is quite all right, sir," she smiled. "No harm done."

James couldn't take his eyes off her smile. It was captivating. "I'm afraid I was lost in thought and didn't notice you behind me," James continued to apologise.

"As I said," she reassured James, "no harm done."

"May I find you another one of these, unblemished?"

"No, I didn't want it anyway, I was just looking," she said, putting the tin back on the shelf.

"I must apologise once again," James said in embarrassment as he turned to walk away. "Good day to you, ma'am."

"I say, did you go to Kirkwall Grammar?" she asked.

James smiled. "Yes, I did."

"I thought I recognised you."

"Forgive me," James said shyly, "I can't remember you. I dare tell you that I did not enjoy my time there."

"May Thomson is my name. And you are?"

"Dawson. James Dawson," he smiled for the first time.

"Nice to meet you, James," May said, and her beautiful smile reappeared. "Well, I must be going, but I now know that you work at Fochabers General and Fabrics, so we may... bump into each other again one day."

James smiled at her humour. "I'd like that."

"Good day to you, James," May said and turned to walk out of the store.

She was halfway down the aisle when she suddenly turned and looked back. James was staring after her and jerked in surprise; he had been caught.

May smiled. "By the way, I didn't enjoy my time at Kirkwall either. That headmaster knew how to wield that tawse, until someone stole it," she remarked before she turned and walked away, leaving James feeling like jelly.

"I'll marry that girl someday. I know I will," he said quietly to himself.

***

Allan's time at Milne's Institute in Fochabers was a significant departure from Kirkwall Grammar. The instructors were highly skilled, and the students were treated with a reasonable level of respect, which greatly relieved Allan. The freedom to learn and participate in various activities without strict discipline or punishment allowed Allan to truly thrive.

After settling into his new environment and forming new friendships, Allan discovered that the teachers were readily approachable, greatly improving his academic achievements. This, in turn, made his parents extremely proud of him. Furthermore, Allan still excelled in sports, and the physical exercise further enhanced his already remarkable physique. He also actively participated in community projects and joined numerous clubs and societies.

With a well-stocked and welcoming library readily available to him, Allan developed a newfound love for literature. He expanded his knowledge of the world and uncovered intriguing stories and educational treasures hidden within the pages of old books. Education suddenly became a source of joy for Allan.

CHAPTER TEN

California 1874

Dr Simpson emerged from Edwin's bedroom and looked at Rebecca solemnly. She sat anxiously, her hands clasped tightly in her lap.

"Mrs Burnham, I'm afraid the prognosis is not good," Dr Simpson said.

Rebecca sighed in resignation and stared at the floor.

"The tuberculosis is well advanced. We can only hope and pray now," the doctor quietly informed her.

Later that night, Edwin took his last raspy breath, and Rebecca broke the news to Fred at the breakfast table the next morning. Howard, his younger brother, now just three years old was too young to understand what had happened.

The funeral took place three days later, by which time Rebecca had assessed her precarious situation. Penniless, unemployed, and facing an impending eviction from the church-subsidised housing, she was far from comfortable. On top of that, she had to care for a young boy and a toddler.

After the funeral, Rebecca sat Fred down at the kitchen table and poured him a cup of hot tea. "Frederick," she began, using his full name to indicate the seriousness of the conversation, "we have no money. In fact, we have nothing, and I can't rely on the congregation's support for much longer. Therefore, I have written to my brothers in Iowa asking if they will take care of us there."

"Iowa?" Fred asked, incredulous.

"It's our only option," Rebecca replied.

"Mother, I don't want to go to Iowa. I want to stay here. I have friends now, and I can find work. I can take care of us."

Rebecca smiled sweetly. "I know, Fred, and I appreciate your willingness to support us, but you're just a young teen and won't be paid enough to support a family."

"I will too!" Fred objected.

Rebecca shrugged. "Even so, you would need a man's job to support the three of us. No, I'll take you and Howard to Iowa as soon as my brothers agree, as I know they will."

***

Two weeks later Rebecca received a reply from her brothers in Iowa. It was a very compassionate letter, offering to take the family in and support them on one of their properties. There was one caveat, however; they wouldn't pay for the fare to get them from California all the way to Iowa.

Desperate to leave as soon as possible Rebecca contacted a good friend and borrowed the fare to make the trip. She knew it would take a long time to repay, but she resigned herself to the fact and decided to cross that bridge when she got to it. She simply had to leave California soon.

Fred was adamant that he did not want to go to Iowa and so, after much persuasion, he convinced his mother to agree to leave him behind if he could find a decent job. On Fred's finding employment at Western Union Telegraph as a mounted rider, delivering telegrams on horseback to outlying settlements, Fred's mother held to their agreement. Rebecca purchased just two tickets with the borrowed money and boarded the stagecoach for the two-thousand-mile journey to Iowa.

***

Freedom at last! With no father to constrain him to the ways of the church and his mother's blessings to encourage him, the world suddenly became Fred's oyster. That he might be lonely never entered his thoughts. The idea of riding through the wide-open land of California on his own gripped his imagination, and he fully embraced his future.

Fred was skilled with horses, having learned much from the Sioux Indians during his early childhood, and he possessed a strength and stamina that exceeded his years. He earned a good wage and found that he could earn even more by working extra hours. It didn't take long for him to realise he had far more stamina than his co-workers.

Fred was given a team of four horses which he rode in rotation to prevent them from tiring too quickly. He often outperformed the senior riders in the company, sometimes doubling or tripling their productivity. He loved being outdoors. He had found his dream job right from the start, and in just one year, he had repaid his mother's debt in full.

One day, when the sun was high, he rode into a small outpost, dropped off a satchel, and immediately walked out to mount his horse. Sitting on the sidewalk outside the general store, a grizzled older man called out to Fred.

"Hey, young man, come here a minute."

Curious, Fred led his horse over to the man. "Yes, Sir?"

"I've been watching you for the past month or so. Don't you ever stop and rest? It's hot as blazes out there."

"No, Sir," Fred smiled. "I rest on the backs of my horses. I eat, drink, and sometimes even sleep while riding."

The man laughed heartily. "To be young again! Tell me, son, can you use a rifle?"

"Yes," Fred said cautiously. "My father taught me when we lived in Minnesota. He was worried about Indian attacks."

"Good for him," the man said, magically producing a small bottle of whiskey from his pocket and taking a swig. He offered the bottle to Fred. "Want some?"

"No thanks," Fred frowned.

"Do you know how to hunt?"

"Yes, I know how to hunt," Fred confirmed. He knew how to hunt, trap, track, and skin wildlife, thanks to his years with his Sioux friends. He was proficient at it.

"There's a job for a fellow like you down by the silver mines further east. I think you'd enjoy it. The pay's good, too."

"Yes?" Fred said, shuffling in his saddle. "Doing what?"

"Hunting."

"Hunting?"

"Yeah. There are a lot of people working in those silver mines, and they all need to eat. I have a friend named Remi. He owns the transport wagons that ship the silver into town. It's a big operation, and he's got many guys that also need to eat. Go find Remi, and he'll give you a job hunting fresh meat."

"I've seen those wagons. Yeah, alright, I'll look out for him. Thanks."

Two weeks later, Fred started work as a hunter for Remi's transport company. He would spend several days at a time in the wild, tracking and hunting animals. Always on his own, he began to understand the land and reading the tracks and signs left by animals and humans became second nature to him. By reading footprints left in the desert sand, he could associate boot prints with their owners and, at times, even age the men who left the footprints.

Driven by his love for the wild and the lure of easy money, Fred became a highly efficient hunter. He would often return with four times the amount of meat as the other hunters. This caused some jealousy from the other hunters, but it didn't bother Fred.

Fellow hunters weren't Fred's only competition: Mexican bandits were also in the desert. Once, when his horse was stolen while he was on foot to shoot some game, Fred gave chase on foot and almost caught up with the thief, planning to get his horse back by force if necessary. Luckily, he stumbled upon some Mexicans who informed him they had just seen the man he was after riding his horse. They recognised him as a notorious bandit, known to kill anyone who challenged him without hesitation. Understanding that discretion is often the better part of valour, Fred reluctantly accepted the loss of his horse and trudged back to his base, angry and dejected.

While with the transport company, Fred encountered many interesting people who always found his companionship worth their time. Two men in particular took an extraordinary amount of time to teach him their hard-won skills. They shared their knowledge about scouting, reading the signs of the land, and understanding Indian and Mexican cultures. Fred felt these life lessons were important, so he listened carefully and constantly questioned his tutors.

Just as he turned fourteen, Fred received a letter from his uncle in Iowa, who kept him up to date on all the news about his mother and brother. A friend, the local newspaper editor, delivered the letter. It noted that, as Fred's formal education was lacking both secularly and in the Christian faith, he was now expected to return to Iowa and enrol at the school with his cousins. The letter was worded in such a way that Fred felt he had no choice but to comply. With great reluctance, he resigned, bade farewell to his friends and colleagues, and bought a ticket for the north.

CHAPTER ELEVEN

Africa 1874

It had been a splendid four years since King Lobengula ascended the throne, and his loyal subjects lived in harmonious contentment under his rule. Mjaan, the valiant protector of the King, carried out his duties with unwavering loyalty, commanding respect and fear from other impis. As Lobengula's tally of wives approached a remarkable one hundred, anticipation grew for the upcoming spring dance, where twenty-one young girls would eagerly vie for the coveted position of being the King's bride. Often, the King would choose several.

"Mjaan!" came an exasperated grumble from the slightly open door of the King's kraal.

With utmost respect, Mjaan entered the kraal and crawled across the dusty floor, humbling himself and pressing his face against the ground.

"I see you, mighty King," Mjaan uttered reverently.

"Stand," commanded Lobengula.

Mjaan complied without hesitation.

The King gingerly extended his aching leg. "My foot is plagued with pain, and it worsens hourly. Fetch the healer for me, swiftly."

Mjaan quickly exited the dimly lit room and summoned Ngwenya to seek the healer's assistance. Ngwenya, in turn, dispatched five other warriors. Within moments, the esteemed healer, sometimes called the witch doctor, entered the King's abode. With due permission, he attended to the King's ailment.

The instant he laid a hand on the slightly swollen ankle, Lobengula shouted in pain.

"Take care, you fool!" he admonished. "The pain is unbearable."

The healer examined the royal foot without making contact, suddenly realising the source of the problem.

"My King," he spoke cautiously, keeping a distance. "I know what is causing your suffering. I have *muthi* that will fix this problem."

"What afflicts me?" Lobengula demanded. "My foot was perfectly fine yesterday."

"Someone has cast a spell upon you. You have fallen victim to an evil spirit."

"No," Lobengula exclaimed, astonishment etched across his face. "Who would dare do this to me, the King?"

"We must conduct a 'smelling out' to identify the culprit or culprits."

"A 'smelling out,'" Lobengula nodded thoughtfully. "Indeed, we must proceed with that. Mjaan, gather all the Indunas present in the village and bring them to the goat pens. Bring the villagers, too. We shall reveal the perpetrators with a 'smelling out'."

When the high priest, Busangwane, arrived, Lobengula turned his attention to him. "Someone has unleashed an evil spirit upon me, and it has invaded my foot. Observe! Look at my foot!" he demanded with such anger that spittle escaped his mouth. Busangwane was horrified that someone would do such a thing to the King.

"I agree with the healer. A 'smelling out' must be done," Busangwane scowled.

Lobengula exited his kraal with the help of Mjaan and Ngwenya and sat uncomfortably on his throne to watch the proceedings. Busangwane turned his gaze to the assembled villagers and Indunas, a sinister look in his eyes.

Approaching the first man, he sniffed his neck and shook his head. He repeated the process with the next individuals, shaking his head in disapproval. Only upon reaching the eighth person, a brawny Induna, he dramatically halted after sensing an unfamiliar scent. Returning to him for certainty, he then turned to Lobengula.

"It is him!" he exclaimed in a high-pitched falsetto. "He is the one who cast the spell upon you."

The Induna's eyes bulged with fear, and though he attempted to protest, no words escaped his lips.

Mjaan stepped forward and forcefully escorted the hapless man to the pen's edge. Lobengula stared at him, profound disappointment in his eyes. He had trusted his Induna and had high aspirations for him. The Induna fell silent, knowing that any utterance would be in vain. Mjaan glanced at Lobengula, who nodded in approval.

Instantly, Mjaan raised his impeccably crafted knobkerrie into the air. A masterpiece of mahogany wood, its straight and gleaming shaft bespoke supreme efficiency and purpose. The polished wooden knob on the end, once formed from a knot in the wood, shone with equal brilliance. Mjaan brought the knob crashing down upon the Induna's head in one fluid movement. The resounding crack echoed throughout the royal village, and the Induna crumpled where he stood.

A scream erupted from Busangwane, capturing the attention of all present. He was busy sniffing another man's neck.

"This one, too! He is wicked! He rides on the backs of jackals under the cloak of night, poisoning innocent souls."

Mjaan strode towards the trembling man and hauled him beside the lifeless Induna. Turning him to face Lobengula, and without waiting for the King's approval, Mjaan delivered a strong blow to the back of the man's head. Like the man before him, he was dead before he hit the ground.

The next time Busangwane screamed his nerve-shattering cry, a thin warrior standing in the middle of the assembled people couldn't take the strain and bolted. Knocking over three of his comrades, he ran for the opening of the pens. He was slight on his feet, driven by adrenaline and fear–fear of the evil spirit that smelt him out, and fear of what was about to happen to him.

Mjaan calmly let the man run, but, carefully raised his spear, drew his arm back and threw the projectile at the fleeing warrior. His aim was perfect, and the spear found its mark between the warrior's shoulders. Mjaan's prowess as the King's bodyguard would be talked about for years to come.

The sombre scene unfolded as Busangwane continued sniffing necks, smelling breath, and prodding eyes and nostrils. By the night's end, thirty-six individuals lay dead at Mjaan's feet.

It would take a full week for the King's foot to heal from the evil spell that had befallen him.

CHAPTER TWELVE

Scotland 1874

Allan left the Milne's Institute gates for the final time and met his parents on the pavement. He shook hands with his father and gave his mother an embracing hug.

"Well, there we have it, I dare say," Allan smiled broadly.

"Very proud of you, son," Robert said. "Very proud of you indeed."

"Top of the class," Mavis gushed.

"I enjoyed the Institute, but I'm glad to move on with my life now," Allan smiled coyly, humbly accepting the appreciation.

"Speaking of which," Robert put his arm around Allan's shoulders and led him away from the gates, "I spoke to my friend, Albright, at Fochaber's Bank–the one I was telling you about–and he has set you up with an interview tomorrow morning."

Allan wasn't too pleased to hear this, but he hid his feelings behind a smile. "Well, I was hoping to take a couple of days off to celebrate and perhaps go down to the coast for a few days."

"Nonsense, my boy. I say, 'strike while the iron is hot,'" Robert chuckled at his use of the old adage. "There'll be plenty of time for celebrations later."

"Alright," Allan sighed. "What time tomorrow?"

***

"Good morning, Mr Albright," Allan smiled as he entered the manager's office at Fochaber's Bank the next morning, hoping he hadn't knocked on the door too heavily.

"Ahh," Albright stood up from behind his desk and extended a welcoming hand, "Mr Wilson. Welcome to Fochaber's Bank. We have been expecting you. Your father, a good friend of mine as you know, has spoken very highly of you. Furthermore, your achievements at Milne's Institute speak volumes." The bank manager gestured to a chair. "Take a seat, would you?"

"Thank you," Allan gratefully accepted the offer and sat down as he was bade.

Mr Albright shuffled through some paperwork before him, then pointed at a line of text.

"First place in tossing the caber last year?" Albright grinned and raised a questioning eyebrow.

Allan laughed in embarrassment. "That won't have much bearing on my career here as a banker."

"True," Albright agreed with a chuckle. "But it does tell me that you enjoy physical pastimes. Do you play tennis?"

"No, sir." Allan shifted uncomfortably. "Cricket is more my sporting passion."

"Hmm…" Albright frowned. "Can't hold that against you, I suppose," he commented with a grin.

The interview went well, and Allan got the job. From the start, he had had a strong feeling that he would secure the position. He suspected the manager had been specifically instructed to hire him—no matter what.

As the interview drew to an end Allan realised that, without his demanding father by his side, he might have some flexibility in negotiating the start date. So, when he was informed that he would be able to start the next day, he quickly mentioned a family commitment in Aberdeen and proposed starting one week later. Thankfully, his request was accepted without any questions. Later that evening, at dinner, he happily informed his parents that he would be able to start working in a week's time.

"So, considering this," Allan smiled sweetly at his mother, "I think I might take the opportunity to visit Cousin William in Aberdeen." He glanced at his father, and added, "That is, if you don't mind."

Mavis looked at Robert, her face beaming. "That would be a wonderful idea, don't you agree, Robert?"

"Yes, absolutely," Robert forced a smile in agreement.

One week later, as agreed, Allan presented himself at Mr Albright's office once more.

"Reporting for duty, sir," Allan confirmed, feeling a little more relaxed.

After a short conversation, Albright stood up, as did Allan.

"Follow me," Albright commanded as he exited the office. "Your training with us begins today, so we had better get on with it. Come with me. Mr Smithers has been assigned as your immediate supervisor."

***

It had been six months since Allan joined the bank as a trainee, during which time he had been stationed at a desk opposite Mr Smithers, meticulously checking ledger entries. Sporting a dark, manicured moustache, Allan's handsome features and good physique made him appear five or six years older than his actual age.

Briefly glancing at Smithers, Allan subtly shook his head before returning to the heavy ledger before him. Smithers seemed insignificant, with thin, sparse hair and a constantly dripping nose that caused him to sniffle. He appeared older than his early 50s and wore the same unremarkable suit daily, scrutinising his work through a thin-rimmed monocle.

Allan believed Smithers' habit of scrunching one eye caused his incessant sniffles. Initially, it was unbearable, but with time, Allan learned to accept and then eventually ignore the man. He couldn't, however, ignore the lack of learning opportunities—each day consisted of checking and verifying ledger numbers. Smithers rarely uttered a word, and Allan felt his life was slipping away. Nonetheless, he worked diligently, hoping his industriousness and patience would eventually yield results. He envisioned a future where he would have an office like Mr Albright's, welcoming new apprentices and ensuring they learned every aspect of the banking world within their first six months. As a manager, he would regularly check on his trainees and monitor their progress.

It occurred to Allan that Mr Albright hadn't spoken to him at all since he had begun working at the bank. He found it odd that, despite Albright's friendship with his father, there had been no effort to engage with him. Perhaps, Allan thought, Albright was intentionally avoiding him. Whatever the reason, it was unsettling.

Glancing at his pocket watch, Allan cleared his throat. "Mr Smithers," he said, "I believe it's my lunch hour. I'll be back by two o'clock as usual."

Smithers didn't look up but nodded his approval.

Careful not to scrape his chair against the wooden floor–an action that, he had been informed, irritated Smithers — Allan silently left the room.

"I hope I never end up like him," Allan muttered as he stepped onto the pavement and turned sharply right, accidentally bumping into a young woman who let out a small yelp.

"I apologise," Allan quickly said, holding the woman's shoulders to ensure she didn't fall.

She recovered swiftly. "Please don't worry. I am all right."

"I'm truly sorry," Allan said, blushing profusely and releasing his hold on her. "I should have been more aware of my surroundings."

To his surprise, he recognised her. She was lovely, with dark hair and a captivating smile. His heart skipped a beat.

"No need to worry at all," she smiled, lightly straightening her skirt.

At that moment, a tall, thin man approached and stood beside them.

"Are you all right, May?" the man asked with concern.

"Hello, James. Yes, I'm perfectly fine, thank you," May replied, her smile drawing Allan's attention again.

Allan averted his gaze from her and looked at the newcomer. "James Dawson?" he exclaimed in surprise.

James appeared taken aback. "Wilson? What are you doing here? I thought you were at Milne's Institute."

"I work here now, at Fochaber's Bank," Allan explained, pointing over his shoulder with his thumb.

"You two know each other?" May inquired.

"We attended Kirkwall together," James replied dryly.

"We did," Allan smiled. "It feels like a lifetime ago."

"Come on, May, we're going to be late," James interjected irritably. "Good day, Wilson."

James whisked May away down the pavement in one smooth, jealous motion. Allan watched the couple as they walked away, his smile widening. May glanced over her shoulder briefly, locking eyes with Allan, and his heart fluttered.

Allan smiled broadly. "I am going to marry her someday."

Sitting in the tea house, James Dawson stared into his half-finished cup of tea. The intricately decorated porcelain cup did not hold James' attention, though. Not truly seeing it, he was also absent-mindedly unaware of the chatty conversation May was trying to engage him in. His right hand rested in his coat pocket, gently turning a ring box between his fingers. Carefully, he allowed the box to drop to the base of his pocket and then reached for a folded envelope that lay beside it. He felt the texture of the paper between his thumb and forefinger before reaching for the ring box again, carefully tracing the corners and the slightly raised brass hinge. He found himself in a dilemma, only to have his thoughts abruptly interrupted.

"James? James? Are you alright?" May inquired with concern.

"I apologise, my dearest May," James blushed in embarrassment. "I'm afraid I was lost in thought."

"It certainly seems that way," May forced a smile. "Would you care to share those thoughts with me?"

James sighed, contemplating his words. Finally, he let out another sigh. "A troubling dilemma has recently come my way."

"Tell me more," May said, a crease of concern appearing on her forehead.

James paused, deep in thought. Finally, he sighed once again, and answered her query, "I received a letter from my brother yesterday."

"Your brother in Africa? The store owner?" May asked, seeking clarification.

"Yes, indeed, in Bechuanaland. It seems he is doing exceptionally well and has asked me to join him as he now is in need of assistance."

"Well," May leaned back in relief, "I don't see that as troubling. On the contrary, it sounds like good news to me."

"My dear May, the thought of leaving you is what is troubling me," James confessed.

His dilemma was more involved than that. He desperately wanted to marry May and was on the verge of proposing to her. He knew, however, that working where he was currently employed did not make him an appealing marriage prospect, particularly considering his salary. Nevertheless, he had decided to take the risk and propose that afternoon, hoping for a positive response. But then the letter arrived, shifting the dynamics of everything in his life. Should he take the opportunity to earn his fortune alongside his brother, possibly even owning a business, before marrying the love of his life? Or would he risk losing May to another suitor while he was away? If she accepted his proposal, would she give up her lifestyle in Scotland to venture to the wild, untamed continent of Africa?

Oh, the questions that plagued him that day. He placed his hand back in his coat pocket and lightly touched the ring box.

May smiled sweetly. "I'll miss you too, James, but I believe your family comes first."

James released his grip on the ring box and touched the envelope, then returned to the ring box. He was torn, unable to make a firm decision. He suddenly realised that he didn't possess the courage to make up his mind.

"Do you think I should go?" James entrusted his fate to May.

"I believe so," May stated firmly, "although I will miss you terribly. When would you leave?"

James' fingers slipped off the ring box, swiftly retrieving the envelope from his pocket. His fate had been decided in that split second. He flattened the envelope on the table with his palms.

"I need to get to Southampton to catch the steamer. My brother asked that I get to him as quickly as is practical."

May leaned forward, tenderly holding his hands. "You must go, James. I truly believe this is important, and you could establish a successful life there. Rumours suggest that people in the southern part of Africa become very wealthy very rapidly."

James smiled. May was right. He decided that he would amass his fortune in Africa and return for her as soon as he could. With newfound prosperity, the odds of her accepting his proposal would be much more certain.

"That settles it," James confirmed confidently. "I will go to Africa."

CHAPTER THIRTEEN
California 1875 - 1885

Fred had completed a few years of school in Iowa and, although he detested it, he had tried to stay the course. Two things kept his sanity intact: his friend John London, and the shenanigans the two of them got up to. John shared Fred's interests in bushcraft, tracking and the outdoors. Also, like Fred, he was a skilled equestrian.

Staunch Christian relatives surrounded Fred, and the town itself was extremely religious. No excitement was to be found in the confines of the church's jurisdiction. The ultra-religious town council had even banned weekend sports and festivities. An air of despair hung over all the youngsters in town.

Boredom frustrated Fred, so he formed a tight gang of school friends of which he naturally became the leader. They engaged in pranks, particularly targeting the town elders and the head of their church, which became a source of great excitement and laughter for them. These shenanigans provided the missing entertainment and distractions they needed to ease the boredom that plagued them. The pranks ranged from jamming household doors shut to relocating signposts at the wrong street corners and releasing stray cattle to roam through residents' carefully manicured gardens at night. Residents in the school neighbourhood were exasperated by the practical jokes that swept through the community. Although Fred and John and their gang were the suspected culprits, they were never caught.

These annoying, but ultimately harmless pranks came to a decisive end when Fred discovered how to make gunpowder, a high explosive used in mines. He devised a plan to blow up a tree that stood proudly in the centre of the priest's front garden. Fred underestimated the power of the gunpowder, and the explosion blew the targeted tree into splinters. Furthermore, every tree within a fifty-yard radius lost its leaves. The rectory also had its windows shattered. The mischievous gang made a pact to keep the event a secret, but one member could not handle the guilt and ultimately betrayed them, leading to the elders punishing everyone involved. The gang disbanded, and misery descended on the youngsters.

One morning soon after Fred received a reprimand from his headmaster for failing yet another test. He was returning to his classroom when he heard a girl's voice reading aloud from a book. Intrigued, Fred followed the sound to an open classroom door on his right. A pretty girl, close to him in age, was sitting on a wooden chair facing the class and reading an adventure novel. Fred stood silently listening to the story, captivated by not only her melodious voice, but also the story he was hearing. The account was about Africa, and it spoke to his adventurous spirit. Ignoring that he was due to return to his class, Fred listened until the bell rang and the class adjourned.

Over the next few days, Fred's emotions were all over the place. He found he had a growing desire to explore Africa's wilderness, from rivers and forests to deserts and wild animals. This desire for exploration constantly played on his mind, causing his attention to wander during lessons. Over time, he found himself troubled by falling grades and unremitting reprimands from his teachers.

One morning, Fred unexpectedly chanced upon the girl who had unknowingly re-ignited his adventurous side.

"Hi," Fred greeted her, catching her by surprise.

"Hello," she replied with a captivating smile. "I saw you listening to me read last Tuesday."

"Yes," Fred blushed. "I hope you didn't mind?"

"No, not at all. It's a good story, isn't it?"

"Yes," Fred nodded. "It has made me want to go to Africa when I leave school."

She laughed. "Me too. It sounds like an exciting place."

"I'd like to hear more of the story. May I come by your class again?"

The girl shook her head whilst smiling warmly. "I won't be reading any more of the story; we all take turns in class. A copy of the book is in the school library, though. It's called "Adventures in the Great Forest Regions of Equatorial Africa". Why not read it yourself?"

"Oh..." Fred felt embarrassed. "I don't like reading much. It was just so nice listening to you read."

She smiled appreciatively. "Your name is Fred, isn't it?"

"Yes," Fred beamed. "Fred Burnham. And yours?"

"Blanche Blick."

"Well, Blanche, I really enjoyed your reading. You have a nice voice and read well."

"Why, thank you, Fred," Blanche said, blushing. "It was good to meet you, but I have a class to get to."

"Good to meet you too," Fred beamed, hope of another meeting lifting his spirits.

***

Three days before the end of the school break and the start of the new school year, Fred and John sat in the loft of a nearby barn. They were in low spirits, dreading another year of intolerable lessons and strict teachers.

John tried to lift the mood. "It's my birthday next week, and my Ma has arranged that we go on a picnic. You're invited."

Fred did not immediately reply, and John looked at him curiously.

"I have something to tell you," Fred smiled conspiratorially. "I've decided I'm not going back to school. I'm going to run away tomorrow."

John was surprised. "What do you mean?"

"I can't take it anymore. I've had enough. I'm leaving. I'm going back to California."

"You can't do that," John insisted. "Your uncle will..."

Fred raised a hand to silence him. "I can't do this anymore. Before I came here, I had two jobs. They were exciting and wonderful. Now they want to lock me in a classroom with teachers who can't teach me anything useful."

John remained silent. Fully understanding Fred's feelings, he still felt a sense of sadness at hearing of Fred's plans. Silence stretched between them.

Finally, John sighed. "So, what's your plan, Fred?"

Fred flicked away a piece of straw he had been chewing on. "I'm leaving tomorrow night. I have to prepare a few things first."

Another uncomfortable silence settled between them. The idea of breaking up such a close-knit pair of friends was almost unthinkable, like losing a family member. Fred recognised this but couldn't face another year trapped in school, especially after having previously tasted freedom and adulthood.

"How do you plan to do it?" John asked. "They'll track you down and bring you back."

Fred grinned. "They won't be able to find me until it's too late. They wouldn't even know where to start. The Sioux taught me well; I'm really good at this."

"Are you going on foot, wearing moccasins?" John suggested.

"Nope," Fred smiled broadly. "I'm going to kayak down the river for the first fifty miles or so. No footprints."

"Where will you get a kayak?" John asked, his curiosity piqued.

"There's an abandoned kayak in the reeds, just outside the doctor's place."

"I know the one," John nodded slowly. "It's in bad shape. It won't float."

"I have been secretly patching it up. It'll handle the rapids well enough now."

Fred quietly slipped out of his room the following night and pushed the repaired kayak into the gently flowing river. As he set off, his thoughts turned to wild adventures in Africa. Excitement coursed through him, but a hint of unease tugged at his heart. He knew he wasn't just running away from school but also from his mother and what she thought was best for him.

***

Fred's escape went according to plan as he paddled past villages under the cover of darkness. During the day, he slept in the kayak, hidden among the reeds. When he found a settlement about fifty miles downriver, he abandoned the vessel and continued his journey on foot toward Kansas.

Along the way, Fred managed to find jobs, mostly as a cattle herder, which allowed him to save enough money to buy an old horse. Despite facing harsh and icy weather that nearly took his life on one occasion, he persevered through these challenges and continued to make his way towards Texas.

Unfortunately, one day his horse was stolen, leaving him penniless, hungry, and cold. Undeterred, Fred pressed on. His journey led him to the vast expanse of the Tonto Basin, a land about sixty miles northeast of Phoenix, Arizona. His emaciated frame bore witness to the hardships he had endured, and his worn-out clothes told a story of resilience. In desperate need of sustenance, he stumbled upon a small farmstead nestled in the sprawling landscape. Fred approached the abode, and the family living there showed kindness and compassion, welcoming him with open arms. They not only provided him with nourishment and clothing but also offered valuable gifts of employment, friendship, and love.

Fate had a cruel twist in store for Fred in this newfound sanctuary. A bitter feud erupted between three families in the Tonto Basin, revolving around grazing rights and territorial boundaries. Unexpectedly, the benevolent family that had taken Fred in became entangled in this escalating dispute. Days turned into weeks, weeks became months, and the animosity raged uncontrollably. In a tragic turn of events, a life was senselessly taken, igniting a chain reaction of deadly, vengeful attacks. Fred's adoptive father became enraged and shot a sheriff. Fred was wrongfully accused of the murder, resulting in a bounty being placed on his head. He had no choice but to flee.

During his subsequent travels, Fred befriended a young man in Phoenix, whom he believed had the right attitude to life, but he soon found out that that was not the case. His new friend had a plan to make easy money through horse and cattle theft and sought an accomplice. He approached Fred with a very compelling proposition. Given Fred's desperate situation and his status as a wanted man, Fred was mightily tempted and briefly considered joining in with his friend's criminal ambitions. Despite the heavy pressure from this young man, though, Fred asked for one day to consider it. He rode out into the desert for the night to think it over without any distractions.

A friend of Fred's uncle lived in Phoenix, whom Fred avoided but occasionally bumped into. On returning to town, Fred saw this man by chance, who had a letter from his uncle for him that had arrived about a month prior. The letter reminded Fred of his honourable family lineage and affirmed that he was not a villain. Fred felt as though this letter served as a divine sign, leading him to decline the wayward offer from his friend immediately. Later, Fred discovered that his friend had met a tragic end during his nefarious pursuits. This incident shook Fred to his core once again and reinforced his desire for a fresh start.

Realising that his physical features, such as his short stature and cleft chin, made it impossible to hide his identity, Fred determined that he needed to start anew. Unfortunately, there was still a price on his head by a rival faction in the Tonto Basin. He decided his only option was to ride off and find a town where nobody had heard of him.

***

Fred found himself in a town called Tombstone and quickly found work doing manual labour. He now found the time to think deeply about the life he had been living and realised he had become entangled with the wrong people. He yearned for a fresh start. He didn't earn much in Tombstone, but it was enough to keep himself fed and housed, and, most importantly, anonymous. Not having friends, Fred would find himself eavesdropping on conversations between older folks, hoping to find opportunities for personal growth and, hopefully, to gain the freedom of movement that he so deeply desired.

One day, Fred came across an old-timer named Holmes, who had been a scout at one time. Holmes was an expert in tracking and possessed exceptional skills in woodcraft, ropes, knife-work, axe-work, making shelters, shooting, butchering, sewing, curing food, and cooking. Despite Holmes' being frequently inebriated with whiskey, Fred listened carefully to him and was soon captivated by Holmes' stories of earlier days.

Holmes was a cantankerous man with minimal manners and a foul mouth, but that didn't concern Fred. What truly caught his attention were Holmes' stories about tracking Indians and bandits. Other boys Fred's age would join in, listening to these intriguing tales, but they eventually grew weary of Holmes' insults and belittling. Not Fred, however, he continued listening and learning, spending more and more time with Holmes. When Holmes realised Fred's genuine interest, his attitude towards him changed, and he took Fred under his wing.

"I'm getting old, kid," Holmes slurred one afternoon, "and I have nobody to pass on all my years of knowledge to. If you want to learn, I'll teach you. Do you want to learn about scouting and woodcraft?"

"Yes, Sir!" Fred nodded eagerly.

"Well then, get your saddle and horse, and meet me here tomorrow morning. We're going into the desert and won't return for a fortnight."

Fred underwent intense training from that day forward. Holmes was a tough but effective teacher who demanded perfection. Knotting ropes had to be precise, neither too tight nor too loose. The condition of the rope mattered too, as a frayed one could harm horses when used for hobbling. Tracking lessons were rigorous, followed by lessons on weather, plants, birds, and reptiles.

Apaches were a frequent topic of discussion. Holmes' discussions about their extraordinary scouting skills fascinated Fred, but what truly made them dangerous were their cunning and brutal methods of torture and murder.

"Never, ever, let an Apache catch you alive," Holmes warned.

Holmes noticed that the Sioux had already honed Fred's senses. He was better than most Westerners in that area, but he wanted more improvement. Developing Fred's senses was a crucial aspect of his becoming an excellent scout. Smell, sight, touch, taste, and hearing were all essential, and so was intuition.

During Fred's training with Holmes, his peripheral vision improved immensely. Training his eyesight to see in the dark was of paramount importance. He came to almost unconsciously monitor the flight patterns of various birds and to better understand weather patterns. Holmes also emphasised the importance of a person's sense of smell. The scents of plants, animals, and humans all told stories that could be read if one knew how to interpret them. Fred believed Holmes when he said that his sense of smell would save his life many times over, and Holmes set numerous lessons in that area.

Fred became adept at surviving in the desert with scant provisions. Holmes would frequently send him into the desert for a week to ten days at a time with minimal food and water, not only to learn how to survive but also to learn how to live in isolation for extended periods. Fred learned that reading the night sky was just as crucial as understanding the shadows of the cactus trees.

One essential lesson Fred found that he still needed to learn was how to shoot with accuracy, and he realised that this was a lesson he needed to teach himself. Using a portion of his savings, Fred purchased a Remington .44-40 revolver and invested in a thousand rounds of ammunition. Practising in the isolation of the desert, he shot at a small metal drum daily. He fired from various positions and angles, perfecting his aim while standing, sitting on horseback, trotting, cantering, and even galloping. He also practised these techniques with his left hand.

Around this time, conflicts with the Apaches intensified, and, for a period of time, Fred offered his services as a scout to the United States Army, spending days searching for and evading the Apaches. He was hot on the trail of Geronimo when the Apache leader finally surrendered, bringing an end to the killings. Fred closely followed these developments through newspaper reports but became disheartened by how the Apaches were treated. Despite the horrors of the war with the Apaches, Fred couldn't help but admire their scouting and hunting techniques, raiding strategies, connection with the wilderness, and their freedom to roam wherever they pleased.

***

Fred then became a deputy sheriff, tasked with recovering tax debts for the government. Using his scouting and tracker skills, he would locate offenders across the vast open areas of the Arizona and New Mexico deserts, reporting their whereabouts to the Sheriff.

During his travels, Fred encountered numerous prospectors. While most were broke, some had discovered highly productive gold and silver claims. The tantalising tales of where to find gold, and the subtle clues hidden within the vegetation, rivers, and soil colours, sparked Fred's dreams of striking it rich with ease.

Eventually, Fred left his job as a deputy and joined forces with acquaintances to pursue prospecting. He invested his hard-earned savings in provisions for his expeditions. He would spend weeks in the desert, tirelessly digging, chipping, and panning for the elusive minerals. Unfortunately, despite his efforts, little of substantial value was found. The money earned from occasional small finds was poured back into prospecting, but a favourable balance between income and costs was proving to be elusive.

Broke and disheartened, Fred found time to reflect. His thoughts turned to Blanche in Iowa, the woman who still occupied his troubled heart. One morning he made a decision. Fred bade farewell to his fellow prospectors, mounted his horse, and set off with the intention of finding Blanche.

***

Rebecca was surprised, angry, and at the same time happy to see Fred–not only because of his unexpected arrival but also due to his physical appearance. The lad seemed incredibly thin, and his clothes were well beyond their prime, desperately in need of repair or, more fittingly, disposal. Rebecca's family promptly bought him a few clothes and then took him to the backyard for a much-needed haircut and shave. The next day, Fred paid a visit to his old friend, John London. Rebecca directed him towards a saddlery at the end of the main street, where he would likely find him.

"Still working with horses," Fred remarked from the doorway.

John spun around in surprise. "Well, I never! The boy has returned."

"Yeah, I arrived yesterday. How have you been, John?" Fred approached and warmly shook his hand.

"I have a job," John replied. "Nothing too exciting—certainly nothing like what you've been up to, judging by your appearance."

Fred laughed. "You should have seen me when I got back. Ma burned my clothes in the backyard."

"I heard you've been fighting Indians and bandits," John said.

Fred shrugged. "I've had some close calls. I've been prospecting too."

John leaned back on a bench and wiped his hands on an apron. "Are you rich?"

Fred laughed again. "No, as broke as can be. I caught the gold fever but found nothing."

"So, what are you going to do now?"

"Can't say for sure. Maybe go back to scouting for the government. The pay is decent."

"If you do, I'll come with you. I may not be as skilled a scout as you, but you taught me well."

"Yeah," Fred said with a broad smile. "I'd like that. Now, tell me, John, what's the news on Blanche Blick?"

John grinned wryly. "She's moved about two hundred and fifty miles away to Prescott, with her family. She's working as a teacher now."

Fred hesitated before asking his next question. "Is she married?"

"Last I heard, no. But it's not for lack of suitors. I know of two men who have proposed to her, and she turned them down outright."

"Why?" Fred asked curiously.

"Beats me. I think she's waiting for Mr Right."

Fred shrugged. "I'm willing to take my chances with her if she's still unmarried."

"You?" John laughed. "Good luck, my friend."

"I've always had my heart set on her," Fred admitted shyly.

***

Fred stood outside the school gates, patiently waiting for the rush of kids to pass. Soon, Blanche emerged from the building. Upon seeing Fred, she stopped in her tracks, causing his heart to flutter uncontrollably.

"Hello, Blanche," Fred greeted her with a shy smile. "Do you remember me?"

Blanche responded with a sweet smile. "How could I ever forget you, Frederick Burnham?"

Fred's smile widened. "I never forgot about you."

Blanche's captivating smile remained. "You've always been on my mind too," she said lightly.

Fred cleared his throat. "Would you please walk with me?" he asked.

They walked slowly along the pavement.

"Blanche," Fred decided to get straight to the point, too nervous to beat around the bush. "Please forgive me for being forward, but my heart has always been yours, since the first time we met. I have returned to ask your father for your hand in marriage. Before I ask him, I need to know if you will have me as your husband?"

Blanche stopped and faced him, her smile widening. "I knew you would come back. Of course, I will marry you. But, it all depends on my father."

Fred beamed with joy. "My heart has ached for you since the day I left. We must not waste any more time. Where can I find him?"

Blanche giggled. "You haven't changed. You want to do everything now, now, now. Tomorrow you can speak to him. I'll inform him tonight at dinner that you wish to see him. My father does *not* appreciate surprises."

For the rest of the day the couple strolled through the parks. Fred recounted his adventures, close calls, and past mistakes. He made sure to emphasise his reformation and his realisation that associating with some of those whom he had met along the way was terribly wrong.

The following evening, Fred met the Blick family. The meeting started awkwardly, but Mr Blick strategically arranged for Fred to have a private conversation with him.

"Fred," Mr Blick spoke sternly. "Before I grant my permission for you to marry my Blanche, there is something you must understand."

"Yes, sir?" Fred waited nervously.

"Your reputation in Iowa is less than savoury. You were the one who blew up that tree in..."

"Yes, it was me, sir. I know it was wrong. I was young and wild then."

"And you're still young and wild," Mr Blick snorted. "Tell me, how much money do you have? Can you support my daughter and the family you may have?"

"Not at the moment, sir," Fred admitted sadly. "I lost everything while prospecting for gold. But I know I will succeed. It's just around the corner. Besides, I can always seek employment as a scout with the American government."

"Finding gold is always just around the corner," Mr Blick said sarcastically. "Here's the deal, Mr Burnham. I will give you my blessing to marry Blanche under one condition. Just one."

"And that is?" Fred asked eagerly.

"That you earn enough money to support my daughter. Only then will you have my blessing to marry her."

Fred took a moment to digest this. "Alright, sir. I accept that. Thank you."

Later, Fred explained the agreement to Blanche and informed her that he would be heading back to Arizona the following day to seek his fortune. Blanche's emotions were torn. She wanted Fred to stay, but she also wanted to marry him. She doubted Fred would find his fortune in gold prospecting, but she had no choice but to let him try. She knew that she would be marrying the man she had always loved, but the emotional toll of having to wait alone once again weighed heavily on her.

***

Fred spent nearly a year in Arizona with new partners, prospecting in arid areas where even desert horses struggled to endure. As a result, they walked everywhere and had to carry survival supplies as well as their tools, along with enough water to separate the dirt from the flecks of gold.

One day, Fred's luck changed. He and his group found gold nuggets as big as quails' eggs and a vein in a ridge of quartz that showed great potential. Fred and his partners cashed in the gold they found and then sold the claim for a massive profit. Suddenly, unexpectedly, Fred was a millionaire. Before returning to marry Blanche, he travelled to Pasadena and bought a citrus estate. He knew nothing about farming citrus, but owning land was prestigious, and he knew Mr Blick could not reject a wealthy man who owned property. Fred then returned to Iowa to claim his bride.

Fred and Blanche were married in Iowa. Afterwards, they returned to Pasadena to their citrus estate. Within a year, Fred had arranged for his mother and Blanche's entire family to move onto the estate with them. It didn't take long for Blanche to become pregnant, and Fred was a happy and proud man. Growing citrus, however, was a painstakingly slow process, and it drove Fred crazy. Accustomed to a life of excitement, danger, and unpredictability, he became increasingly restless. Before Roderick was born, Fred had journeyed back to Arizona again to prospect for gold and silver.

For the next seven years, Fred kept moving, exploring other commercial ventures, and crisscrossing the American continent on the new rail network. He returned home to his wife and family, but the citrus business was not making any money and was, in fact, running at a steep loss. His prospecting efforts were dragging him down, and his investments were almost worthless due to the economy dropping steadily.

One evening after dinner, Blanche brought Fred his customary cup of tea on the wide veranda of their home. Fred thanked her and slowly drank the beverage.

"This country is too modern for me now." Fred moaned. "I don't like it."

"What do you mean, my darling?" Blanche asked.

"Well, the rail network, for one. You can travel to places in a day that used to take weeks. Law and order are under control; it's not the Wild West it used to be. I'm restless. I need adventure, excitement."

"Have you any ideas?" Blanche asked curiously, wondering where this conversation was going.

"There's gold to be found in Panama. It's a new and exciting country. The government was building a canal to link the Pacific and the Atlantic Oceans, but they had to stop because of tropical disease. Imagine the opportunities for us."

"Well," Blanche sounded pensive, "I'm happy to follow you."

"You would?" Fred smiled. "Truly?"

"Yes," Blanche smiled back. "You're not the only one bored on this citrus farm."

Fred was elated. "This will be a new chapter in our lives. We will move to Panama, the new frontier. Let me put my mind to this, Blanche," Fred grinned. "This excites me."

"I know," Blanche winked. "Now come to bed; it's late."

As they walked inside, Fred picked up a newspaper from the sideboard. He had noticed a headline.

"Blanche," Fred tapped his finger on the headline, "have you heard of this man, Cecil John Rhodes?"

"Yes," she replied. "He's in almost every newspaper at least once a week these days. All my friends talk about him. He's in Africa, isn't he?"

"Yes," Fred pondered. "I've been reading about him too, and some of my business partners constantly talk about him. He wants to build a railway line from Cape Town, at the southern tip of Africa, right up to Cairo in Egypt."

"I know," Blanche agreed. "I read about that."

"They think he is the richest man in the world; he owns diamond mines and has a vision to take over most of Africa for Britain."

"Africa," Blanche almost whispered.

Fred embraced Blanche lovingly. "Remember when we first saw each other? You were reading a book about an adventure in Africa."

"I remember it well."

"My heart has been restless from then on. I fell in love with you, watching you read so peacefully; the sound of your voice, your beauty, and the story stirred my inner desire to explore Africa. It was a life-altering day for me."

"I fell in love with you too, Fred," Blanche sighed. "I knew you would return, and I was right."

"Africa," Fred mused. "A new frontier. I've always wanted to go to Africa. I know a man like Rhodes could use my scouting skills there."

"Africa," Blanche said dreamily. "I'll follow you to Africa, my darling, if that's what you want to do."

Fred smiled mischievously. "Africa, not Panama."

CHAPTER FOURTEEN

Africa 1875 - 1885

Mjaan ducked his head at the low head-jamb and entered his hut. His wife could see that he had had a tough day.

"Come and sit," Thandiwe pulled out a stool that was against the side wall and placed it in his favourite place. "I will fetch you a gourd of beer."

"Thank you," Mjaan said as he sat. He was over fifty years old but looked much younger than his years.

"I can see you are going on a raid soon," Thandiwe said as she took a dried calabash shell from a makeshift box. "I can tell from your face you are thinking of war."

Mjaan smiled at her perceptiveness. "Not war. The fruits are nearing harvest, and the moon draws full."

"Ahh...," she said knowingly. "The iShumba dance is near."

Thandiwe dipped the open end of the calabash into a clay pot filled with fermented millet beer and passed the gourd to her husband. He took several long pulls of the rancid concoction, then handed back the empty container with a sigh of satisfaction.

"It will be a big celebration this time," Mjaan smiled contentedly. "We have many new warriors who want to wash their spears with blood. They constantly beset me for their opportunity to become men."

"I can understand why they are anxious for the dance. Do you know which way the King will throw his spear?"

Mjaan grunted. "We can never tell which way the spear will fly until the King throws it."

Savouring his second gourd of home-made beer, Mjaan reflected on the up-coming dance. The iShumba dance happened only once a year at the harvest full moon. Many cattle were slaughtered, and a great deal of beer was consumed. The dance and feasting lasted three days, and on the final day, at the end of the celebrations, the King would walk out of his Royal Compound with his spear and survey the land about him. Thousands of warriors would then gather around the King, their anticipation of coming warfare intensified.

Once the King was satisfied that everyone had gathered, he would raise his arm and throw the royal spear in the direction of his choice. The King was meant to choose a random direction, but his spear was more often than not thrown northwards, in the direction of the Mashona people. The new warriors would then erupt into cheers of excitement, and take off in the direction that the spear had been thrown.

The newly-appointed warriors would run for days in the indicated direction, and anyone in their path would be brutally slain. If they came across a village, the entire village would be slaughtered. That is how it had been done throughout Mzilikazi's and then Lobengula's reign.

"Is that why you are troubled?" Thandiwe asked quietly when she discerned that his thoughts were completed.

Mjaan looked up at her. "No, the dance does not concern me. What troubles me is that the settlers in the south are creeping northwards and want to enter our country to speak to the King. We know not why, and the King is concerned. I am not sure how to advise him.

"There is another problem. The Portuguese in the east are also pushing towards us. They are becoming a problem too. If it was up to me I would send many impis to kill them all and be done with this problem.

"How do the other advisors speak?"

"Ghaw!" Mjaan exclaimed. "I think they are all stupid. They talk around and around and give no good advice. If I find it frustrating, can you imagine what the King thinks? Now, the King has to deal with the British, the Portuguese and even his own advisors and Indunas. The King is a troubled man and is often inflicted with pain."

"What will you do, my husband?" Thandiwe asked respectfully.

"I will speak to the King early tomorrow and ask if I can take some of my impi south and spy on these people. Maybe I can find out what they want."

"That is good, my husband," Thandiwe nodded gravely. "Will you wait until after the iShumba dance?"

"I will wait," Mjaan smiled broadly. "I want to be at the dance. I want to witness the throwing of the spear so that I can take my men on the raid. As our elders say, 'Never let a man's blood dry on your spear. Keep it wet with the blood of your enemy.' When the raid has ended we will go south to observe the white men's actions."

His mind made up, Mjaan handed the empty gourd back to Thandiwe and left his hut in order to check on his new recruits.

CHAPTER FIFTEEN

Scotland 1875 - 1885

It was about lunchtime when May Thompson approached Fochaber Bank. The day was hot, so she held a dainty parasol over her head to keep off the sun, making her look even more appealing to passing men who tipped their hats in gentlemanly fashion as they walked past her.

It had been two weeks since she had re-encountered the strapping young Allan Wilson. James Dawson had left for Africa, and she smiled inwardly, thankful that she had finally escaped his attentions. She had begun to worry that he might propose to her, so she was relieved when he told her he was leaving for faraway lands. *'Rejection is always awkward,'* she thought to herself as she strolled along the sidewalk.

Allan walked out of the bank's main door promptly at one o'clock. It was his lunchtime, and the bank was strictly punctual. As he stepped on the pavement, his eye caught May. His attention was instantly captured by her beauty and how she carried herself under her parasol.

"Miss Thompson," Allan smiled broadly as she drew near. "Fancy seeing you here."

"Mr Wilson!" she smiled sweetly, "I hoped we might bump into each other again, but not quite so...."

"Dramatically?" Allan suggested.

"Quite," she cocked her head shyly.

"How is my friend Mr Dawson?" Allan asked as they walked towards the nearby park.

"He has left for Bechuanaland, a country somewhere in Africa. His brother needed him there."

"I see," Allan smiled. He had assumed May and James were romantically involved. This bit of news pleased him immensely.

"It's my lunch hour," Allan suggested. "Would you have time to take a walk in the park? It is a beautiful day, after all."

"That would be lovely," May agreed.

The lunch hour allocated to Allan by the bank flashed by too quickly for him. Both he and May found similarities in their humour and had a most enjoyable time together, so much so that Allan asked May if she would join him for lunch the following week, at the same time. To Allan's delight, she readily accepted. He returned to the bank with a distinct spring in his step. Not even Smithers' sniffing could sully his mood that afternoon.

***

Allan began courting May, and, after only two months, he got down on one knee and proposed. She accepted immediately, much to the delight of family and friends on both sides.

Despite Allan's best-laid plans and aspirations, his future at Fochaber Bank began to falter. Smithers' persistent sniffing was driving him insane. The repetitive checking of ledgers in the damp and gloomy room, alongside Smithers, filled him with a sense of desolation and decay. Not even the lovely May Thompson could elicit a smile from the typically happy, amiable young man.

It soon became evident to Allan that he could not advance up the corporate ladder readily, so he began exploring other career options. Allan was fully aware that his father would strongly oppose any decision for a change in career that he might make.

One afternoon during his lunch break, he came upon an advertisement in the local newspaper. The British Permanent Colonial Forces of the Cape Colony in Africa were recruiting members for the Frontier Armed and Mounted Police Force in Basutoland.

This resonated deeply with him. He had heard favourable reports of the colonial forces in Africa, and even his former mentor, James Dawson, had ventured to Bechuanaland as a trader. With his mind made up, Allan returned to the bank and tendered his resignation. That evening he faced the daunting task of informing his future bride that their wedding would have to be postponed until he established himself in Africa.

He harboured hopes that his fiancée might join him in Africa after they were married, but May was not happy about leaving Scotland. She did agree, though, to await his return.

Sharing the news with his parents proved even more challenging than telling his bride-to-be. Robert was furious, and Mavis was overcome with tears, going through three handkerchiefs during the conversation. It was a dreadful evening, but Allan stood his ground, and, ten days later, he had enlisted and embarked on his adventure to the southernmost tip of Africa.

***

Basutoland was not what Trooper Wilson had expected. Indeed, there was plenty of sunshine and fresh air, but that was about where the positives ended. The food was bland, water was scarce, and the countryside appeared brown, dry, and brittle. A devastating drought had plagued the region for the past two years, worsening conditions and fraying the tempers of the population. The Basuto people were overtly hostile, making everyone jittery. Furthermore, the horse assigned to Allan proved uncooperative, which didn't help his mood.

After two months of settling in, Allan had accepted his circumstances and wholeheartedly embraced any opportunity that came his way. With his calm temperament and robust build, he found himself enjoying a pleasant camaraderie with his fellow soldiers. When they weren't engaged in rigorous training, there was often laughter, with Allan usually at the centre of proceedings. His equestrian skills improved, and he became an excellent marksman both on and off horseback.

The on-going drought, the most severe in living memory, heightened the population's tensions to the point of snapping like an over-taut piano wire. Tribal conflicts erupted when members of the Gcaleka tribe attacked the Fengu tribe at a gathering, escalating into a full-blown war. British Colony's Frontier Armed and Mounted Police were established as a paramilitary force to secure the borders, protect British interests, and maintain control over the local population. They were predominantly responsible for keeping the peace, preventing crime, suppressing potential rebellions, and dealing with conflicts arising between different factions.

Unexpectedly Allan's unit found themselves thrust into the midst of battle. The conflict was brutal and raged on for nearly two years. By the time hostilities ceased, Allan, now a seasoned soldier, received the South Africa Medal.

The Morosi Campaign commenced a year later, presenting yet another arduous conflict between the British and Chief Morosi in Basutoland. This time, it was more of a tactical war, and Allan's experience gained from the previous engagement served him well. It was a gruelling and bloody struggle, but Allan's ability to command and strategise earned him much praise despite his low rank. Once the war concluded, he was awarded a clasp for his South Africa Medal.

Upon the war's conclusion, it was decided that the Frontier Armed and Mounted Police Force was no longer necessary, and so it was subsequently disbanded. A new force, the Cape Mounted Rifles, was established, and Allan willingly transferred to that. Due to his proven courage and natural leadership abilities, especially under fire, Allan was promoted to the rank of Sergeant.

Peace was short-lived, as war once again ravaged the land. This time, it was the First Anglo-Boer War, and Allan found himself on the losing side as the Boers emerged victorious. Nonetheless, Allan's military prowess was acknowledged, and he was awarded another clasp for his South Africa Medal.

Allan's life was hurtling along in an unexpected direction. From a career in banking, he now found himself to be a seasoned soldier with a wealth of combat experience. It astonished him that he had already fought in three wars despite being only 23 years old.

In one respect, he yearned to return home and marry May. Their relationship was strengthened by the copious and open correspondence they maintained, but long-distance relationships were difficult. Allan had tried hard to persuade May to come to Africa and join him in marriage, but she held steadfast to her refusal to leave Scottish soil. This troubled and upset Allan, but he resolved to find a way to persuade the love of his life to reconsider. In the meantime, all he could do was continue striving for promotions until such time that he earned a respectable wage, and hope that, in time, May might change her mind.

CHAPTER SIXTEEN

Africa 1875

In time, Allan's contract with the Cape Mounted Rifles came to an end, and he decided it was time to take his life in a new direction. The idea of making his fortune as a trader had begun to appeal to him, so, with this thought nagging at him, he accepted his discharge and left the military.

With a renewed enthusiasm for adventure and opportunities, Allan outfitted himself with a wagon, six oxen, and a horse. Rigorous training along with strict military discipline and traditions no longer bound him. He loved the wildlife and the picturesque landscape. Life in remote areas suited him, and his occasional encounters with explorers, traders, missionaries, and their extraordinary tales of adventure captivated him. Prospectors, in particular, intrigued him with their stories of discoveries of immense wealth and treasures, a rarer occurrence than the ubiquitous stories of hardship and misfortune.

Soon though, the challenges and hardships faced by Allan began to affect him directly. Trading was proving difficult as his kind and compassionate nature hindered his ability to negotiate ruthlessly. He found it difficult to hard-sell his products and often resorted to offering significant discounts just to make a sale. Unfortunately, these practices were impacting on his profitability in a significant way. May frequently crossed Allan's mind, but since he was not much better off financially than he had been when he arrived in Africa, he resolved to give his new venture a fair chance before considering a return to Scotland. Despite the distance, Allan's relationship with May remained strong through their extensive correspondence. He would write lengthy letters about his adventures at least once a week. In return, May would respond with equal frequency, but Allan would only receive her letters every couple of months when he passed through a small settlement town called Mafeking.

Allan bought most of his goods from a large trading establishment in Mafeking called Weil and Co., owned and operated by a man named Julius Weil. Weil was the largest trader in the region, with branches all over the southern part of the continent. Weil and Co. acted as a post office too. It was here that Allan received his mail from May, the main reason Allan enjoyed his return visits to Mafeking. After restocking his wares, he handed over a lengthy letter to May, explaining his whereabouts and endeavours and reaffirming his love and commitment to her. While at the counter, Allan was approached by a man with a friendly smile.

"Good day, Sir," the man said warmly. "Forgive me, but I couldn't help but notice your accent. You must be Scottish."

Allan beamed. "Indeed, and you must be a fellow Scot, judging by your accent."

"Yes, born in Stranraer, Wigtownshire, but mostly lived in England," the short man smiled.

"Glenurquhart," Allan said, "in the Highlands. The name's Wilson, Allan Wilson," he continued, extending his arm in friendship. "Pleased to make your acquaintance."

"Jameson, Leander Starr Jameson," the man returned the greeting with a firm grip. "If you are not occupied, perhaps you could join me in the hotel bar for a drink and exchange some stories? I'm keen to discover more about this country and the people around here."

"I'd be delighted," Allan agreed. "I don't partake in alcoholic beverages, but I'd welcome a lemonade."

"Then you are in good company," Jameson laughed.

The two men were complete opposites in every way. Allan was robust, tall, and barrel-chested, with broad shoulders and a slim waist. With his mop of dark hair and prominent moustache, he turned heads wherever he went. On the other hand, Jameson barely reached Allan's shoulder in height. He had a slight stature, a receding hairline, and a soft-spoken manner. From their initial handshake, Allan deduced that Jameson likely held a desk job–an administrator, perhaps. Allan found him an excellent conversationalist, and he quickly warmed to his fellow countryman.

Upon their arrival at the hotel across the street, Jameson purchased two lemonades and found an empty table. Allan took two large gulps to quench his thirst and then turned to Jameson to satisfy his curiosity.

"What brings you so deep into the African continent?" Allan inquired.

"I could ask you the same question, Mr Wilson," Jameson chuckled. "I was a medical doctor in London for many years. Unfortunately, my health declined due to overwork, so I came to Africa. I've been practising at a more leisurely pace in Kimberley, just south of Mafeking."

"I know Kimberley," Allan smiled, making a mental note to address Jameson as Doctor from now on.

"And what about you? How do you fit into this... this arena?" Jameson smiled, gesturing at their surroundings.

Allan took a small sip of his lemonade, then carefully placed his glass on the table. "It's quite a long story, Dr Jameson. I used to work at a bank in Scotland and grew tired of it, I suppose. I saw an advertisement in the newspaper to come out and join the Frontier Armed and Mounted Police."

"Did you participate in the Gaika-Galeka campaign?" Leander frowned.

"Yes, unfortunately, and the Morosi Campaign. I didn't expect to become a soldier in a police force. I honestly thought I was signing up for a police career, never thinking there was a military wing to the force. I took my discharge when my contract was completed and became a trader."

"What rank did you achieve when you were in the military?" Jameson inquired.

Allan found the questions about his service surprising. "Sergeant," he replied.

"Did you receive any recognition for your service?" Dr Jameson asked.

This time, Allan raised a curious eyebrow. "Yes, I received the South Africa Medal, if that's what you mean. With three clasps," he added.

"Very good," Jameson smiled appreciatively.

Trying to change the subject, Allan said, "What brings you to Mafeking? There isn't much here."

"I'm making my way northward on a mission of discovery for a good friend. Have you heard of Cecil John Rhodes?"

"Of course. Who hasn't? He's a Member of Parliament in the Cape Colony," Allan grinned, "a business entrepreneur and diamond magnate."

"Exactly," Jameson nodded. "He has grand designs for the northern territories and has asked me, as his good friend, to scout around."

"I wouldn't dare cross the Limpopo River if I were you. That's Matabele country, and they have a rather unforgiving King, I'm told."

"Indeed," Dr Jameson scowled. "I have been warned, but I believe their King is approachable. One of my patients in Kimberley, a trader, has been there several times, and he seems to think it is alright."

"Well, I've had my share of violence, so I'm quite content to remain on this side of the river," Allan affirmed.

Jameson continued, "My patient has seen the King's royal village. I will meet him here in Mafeking in three days, and he will escort me to the King's village. Apparently, it's quite a process to see King Lobengula."

"So I've heard," Allan shook his head, more amused than interested. "They say he is very arrogant. He can keep you waiting on the outskirts of his village for up to a month before he'll entertain your presence. And when you finally get the invitation, you have to crawl and grovel in the dust at his feet until he permits you to sit up."

"I'm prepared to do that as long as I can see him and get a sense of who he is," Jameson replied.

"You're going through all this for your friend, Mr Rhodes?" Allan inquired.

"I'd do more for him if he asked," Dr Jameson affirmed.

Allan noticed a glimmer in the doctor's eyes when he spoke of his politician friend—a hint of hero-worship, perhaps.

Jameson continued. "We've enlisted the help of a British missionary, Reverend John Moffat. He is the son of the famous missionary Reverend Robert Moffat. King Lobengula trusts Reverend Moffat, who will serve as my translator."

Allan narrowed his eyes. The doctor's meeting with the King seemed too well-planned, as if it had a specific purpose–more than just an introductory meeting.

"Well," Allan said cautiously, "it looks like you have everything under control."

"I certainly hope so," Jameson confirmed. "By the way, my patient, or guide in this case, is a fellow Scot. I think you might know him–Mr James Dawson."

Allan nearly coughed up his drink. "Yes, I know Mr Dawson. He was my senior at school. He actually introduced me to the lady I am engaged to."

"You are engaged to be married? How unfortunate," Jameson mumbled. "It must be challenging to maintain a romantic relationship, considering the great distance between you," he added drily.

Allan had expected a more congratulatory response. "Yes," he said cautiously. "Without suitable means of communication either, I'm not sure if our arrangement still exists."

Jameson leaned back casually, giving Allan a discerning look. "Have you ever considered trying your hand at gold prospecting?"

"It has crossed my mind," Allan smiled, "but from what I gather, not many people have found gold here. If you want to find gold, you need to go to the Witwatersrand."

"I've heard there is a lot of gold to be found in Matabeleland," Jameson said, with a knowing smile.

"No, Dr Jameson," Allan laughed aloud. "You won't find me crossing that river. I do not trust the political situation there. I have heard stories about King Lobengula, and none are good."

***

Dr Jameson awoke and gazed at the dirty canvas just inches from his nose. His tent was basic, providing no room to stand. Something had roused him from his afternoon nap, but he felt so drowsy and disoriented that he couldn't quite determine what it was.

The sound came again–a tapping of two sticks together. It served as the customary way of knocking, since the tents lacked doors.

"Yes?" Jameson managed to utter groggily.

"Moffat here, Dr Jameson. The King is ready to see you now," a voice called out.

Jameson quickly crawled out of his tent and straightened his dishevelled clothes. "About time, don't you think?" he grumbled.

"You are fortunate to have only waited two weeks, Doctor," the missionary replied, suppressing a chuckle, "however, we mustn't keep him waiting any longer. We must proceed immediately. He is in a foul mood."

This news troubled Jameson. Nevertheless, he and Moffat hurried to the royal enclosure and entered. King Lobengula sat outside his kraal, a sizeable circular structure made of wood, plastered with mud and topped with a thatched roof. Jameson and Moffat saluted him, using the King's family name to show respect, and then took a seat beside three other disgruntled white men.

Once the King had finished listening to the woeful tale of one of his troubled villagers, he nodded at Moffat. Mjaan, who stood by his side, summoned the missionary. To Jameson's fascination, Moffat got down on his hands and knees and crawled toward the King.

Lobengula spoke in his native language. "Sit with me."

Moffat stood, bent at the hips, and accepted the offered seat, being careful not to stand taller than the seated monarch. "I see you, King Lobengula. I trust God has blessed you with good health since we last met."

Lobengula snorted. "An evil spirit has once again afflicted my foot. Someone in my kraal has cursed me with another evil spirit. This is not a problem your God can fix. My healers will find the culprit. There will be a 'smelling out' tonight."

Moffat's heart sank. He knew what that meant–many innocent people would die, needlessly and violently.

"Who do you bring to see me this time, Moffat? I am not pleased to see anyone today, as I am in pain," Lobengula grumbled.

Moffat looked across at Jameson, who sat on the ground, motionless, in the sun. "He is an important man from Britain. He conveys greetings from his white Queen."

Lobengula pondered this for a moment and grunted. "Very well, bring him to me."

Moffat signalled to Jameson, who, as instructed, crawled on his hands and knees toward the King. He remained in that position until Moffat interpreted an instruction for him to sit on the ground but not to stand.

Moffat spoke softly to Jameson. "The King is not in the mood to entertain visitors. Say what you need to, and I will do what I can."

Jameson humbly spoke to Lobengula's feet. "I bring greetings to the great King of the Matabele from my great Queen of the north. I also bring greetings from my Induna, Cecil Rhodes, who is honoured that you have allowed a humble man like myself to convey his wishes to you."

Moffat translated Jameson's words to Lobengula, who simply grunted in response.

After a moment, Lobengula continued. "Tell this white man to convey my greetings back to his white Queen."

Moffat looked at Jameson. "He says to take his greetings back to Queen Victoria."

Jameson maintained his gaze on Lobengula's feet. "Ask him if his right foot is in pain."

"Pardon?" Moffat said, surprised.

"It appears swollen. Inquire about it," Jameson insisted.

Moffat turned to Lobengula. "This white man asks if your foot is causing you pain?"

"Who is this man?" Lobengula exclaimed. "Is he a witch doctor?"

This prompted Mjaan and Ngwenya, both standing at their King's side, to raise their spears menacingly.

"No," Moffat quickly responded. "No, he is a medical man from the white man's country in the north. He claims that he can see you are in pain."

Lobengula raised his hand, signalling Mjann to lower his spear. "What else does he say?"

"He says that one foot is larger than the other."

"That is true," Lobengula admitted. "That is evident. What else can he deduce that he cannot see?"

"The King wants to know what other observations you have made about his condition," Moffat relayed to Jameson.

Jameson shuffled uncomfortably. "I would like to touch his foot and ascertain if it feels hot."

"You will not be permitted to touch the King, I can assure you of that," Moffat replied.

"Ask him if his foot feels warm," Jameson requested.

Moffat asked Lobengula, and this question elicited an exclamation from the King.

"I suspected as much," Jameson said. "I believe I know what ails him. Tell him I can remedy it. I possess medication for this ailment."

Moffat cautiously addressed the King. "He believes he understands what afflicts you. He possesses a medicine from the white man that can fix your foot."

Lobengula chuckled. "White man's medicine holds no power for black men."

Moffat looked down at Jameson. "You won't be able to persuade him to take any of your medication."

"Tell him he suffers from an ailment reserved for Kings. I am convinced it is the ailment of Kings."

"Gout?" Moffat questioned.

"It certainly seems so. Inquire if he experiences pain when moving his foot in any direction. If it causes extreme discomfort, it is likely gout," Jameson explained.

Moffat relayed this information to Lobengula, who refrained from moving his foot due to the pain.

Jameson smiled inwardly. "I have laudanum in my bag. It is morphine based and it will alleviate the pain within minutes. Inform him that if he permits me to administer a small dose of the medication, and it fails to provide relief, I will leave and never return."

After some deliberation between the missionary and the King, Jameson hastily returned to his tent to retrieve his medical bag. Re-entering the compound, along with his black bag, nearly incited Mjaan and Ngwenya to attack. Lobengula intervened and allowed Jameson to approach.

The morphine was in liquid form, stored in a brown bottle. Jameson poured a small dose into a stainless steel container that was slightly larger than a thimble and handed it to Moffat, who then passed it to the King. Lobengula inspected it momentarily before handing it to Mjaan for examination.

"Taste it," he ordered Mjaan.

Mjaan dipped his finger into the clear liquid and placed a drop on his tongue. His face twisted in disgust.

"A putrifying dead hyena tastes better than this, my King," Mjaan stated.

"Give it to me," Lobengula demanded, then handed it to Moffat. "Now you taste it."

Moffat followed suit and tasted the opiate. "Your Induna is correct. It doesn't taste pleasant."

"We shall wait," Lobengula declared. "Let us see which one of you this poison will kill first."

"What's happening?" Jameson whispered.

"He is waiting to see if this poison will kill one of us," Moffat replied.

"Give it to me," Jameson requested Moffat. He took the thimble from Moffat and held it in front of him, displaying it to the King. He then brought it to his lips and consumed the entire contents in one gulp. A chorus of exclamations erupted from the court. Jameson refilled the thimble and passed it to Moffat.

"Inform the King that this is not poison. I have proven this myself."

Lobengula laughed heartily, took the thimble from Moffat, and then drank the liquid. "You've brought a peculiar man to me, Moffat. You must return tonight with him. I want him to witness a 'smelling out'. He must see how we handle evil spirits according to our customs."

Moffat shuddered. This was the last thing he wanted to observe. He had witnessed a 'smelling out' before, and it had left him feeling repulsed and disturbed for weeks.

"Yes, King," he reluctantly responded.

"You may leave me now," Lobengula dismissed the two white men.

On their hands and knees, they crawled out of the royal enclosure. But before they could exit, Mjaan, who brandished his spear, obstructed their path. He grunted something, and Moffat turned to Jameson.

"The King wishes to speak with us once more."

"I thought as much. Morphine is an incredibly powerful drug," the doctor said with a broad smile. "I hope this doesn't take long–I'm going to need to have a sleep shortly."

Jameson knew that he had the King under his influence from that day forward.

***

A seed had been planted in Allan's head–a nagging seed that had nestled in his mind ever since his conversation with Dr Jameson. Maybe, he thought, there was some merit in becoming a gold prospector and taking his chances. His bank account balance was still embarrassing. He knew he had to make a change in order to improve his current financial situation.

After lengthy conversations with prospectors he had crossed paths with during his lonely treks between settlements, and reading whatever literature he could find on the subject, Allan decided to take the plunge and close his business down. Cashing in his wagon, oxen and stock-in-trade, he purchased a scotch cart, two mules and some prospecting equipment.

For four gruelling years, Allan put his back into searching for his fortune. Starting in the Witwatersrand, he made his way to Basutoland.

Unfortunately, it didn't work out. While there were occasional small finds that allowed him to continue his pursuit, overall his financial situation steadily declined.

One day, while registering a potential claim at a Basuto police station, Allan stumbled upon an opportunity to change direction once again. The head of the police force was looking for recruits, and after a quick interview with the Chief Inspector, Allan landed a job and a commission. He was delighted with the idea that he was finally doing police work–his original intention when he left Scotland. His secure employment with the force was, however, short-lived. A chance encounter with the head of the Bechuanaland Exploration Company presented another opportunity, leading him to become their Chief Inspector of Mines. Before long, Allan was offered a promotion to represent the company in a town called Fort Victoria, in Mashonaland.

"No," Allan refused. "Neither Mashonaland nor Matabeleland interest me at all."

"Why not?" Mr Kendall, the district manager, sounded hurt.

"That's part of King Lobengula's country. I've heard stories about him."

"Nonsense, Mr Wilson," Kendall dismissed Allan's fears with a wave. "It's all under control now. Five years ago, Rhodes signed an agreement with the King. Rhodes practically owns the country now."

"I've heard of this agreement, the Rudd Concession was it not? Isn't it in dispute?" Allan asked.

"Not anymore. That dispute was resolved, and now the BSAC has a Royal Charter over the country. King Lobengula has agreed not to harm any white people in his country. It's as safe as houses, Mr Wilson. I know, I was there last month."

Allan was deeply torn. All his instincts told him not to accept the job, but the promotion and salary were too hard to refuse. "Alright, Mr Kendall," Allan sighed. "I'll take the position."

***

Allan found himself quite enjoying his time in Fort Victoria, quickly realising that his initial misgivings were unfounded. The community was vibrant, and he made friends easily. Contrary to their warlike neighbours, the Matabele, the local native Mashona people were friendly and peace-loving. Lobengula's Matabele people still regarded the Mashona as their vassals and slaves, but the Mashona were more relaxed, enjoying having the white population as protectors from Matabele raids.

One day, as Allan prepared to enjoy a meal in the hotel dining room, he was taken aback when he spotted a familiar face enter the room.

"Dr Jameson," Allan greeted with a smile. "What a coincidence to see you here."

"Mr Wilson," the doctor replied, extending his arm for a handshake.

Allan was impressed that Dr Jameson remembered his name. "Please, join me," he offered, gesturing to an empty seat.

Dr Jameson took the proffered seat and promptly ordered the same meal as Allan. After a brief pause, he began to speak. "I now work for Cecil John Rhodes. I serve as his Chief Administrator for Mashonaland."

"I heard. Congratulations," Allan responded sincerely.

Dr Jameson regarded Allan curiously. "I thought you had no interest in entering Lobengula's territory."

"My employers managed to convince me otherwise," Allan smiled sheepishly.

"That's precisely why I'm here," Dr Jameson nodded. "I've been searching for you."

"Me?" Allan was surprised to hear this.

"I heard you were in Fort Victoria, and I wanted to offer you a position with me."

Curious, Allan raised an eyebrow. "Go on."

"We are in the process of building a military force as a precautionary measure, in the event of any trouble with the Matabele." Dr Jameson explained. "Although we don't anticipate any issues, it's necessary to have a force to protect the settlers. Given your military background, we believe you possess the necessary leadership qualities we're seeking."

"Well, if everything is as secure as you claim...." Allan hedged cautiously.

Dr Jameson interjected, "We already have a small volunteer force based here called the Victoria Volunteers. The current officer in command, Captain Lendy, is needed elsewhere. We would like you to assume his position as Captain."

"Captain?"

"Yes, and naturally, the position comes with the appropriate pay and benefits," Dr Jameson confirmed. "It is said that you have an exceptional ability to command and lead men, and that is precisely the leadership style we are seeking."

"Who mentioned that about me?" Allan asked, somewhat perplexed.

"Major Forbes," Dr Jameson replied confidently. "You may not have heard of him, but you will. He is based in Fort Salisbury with me. I have discussed this with Mr Rhodes too, and he confirms that we need someone like you for this important task. May I rely on you to accept this position, Mr Wilson?"

Allan couldn't help but feel the weight of Dr Jameson's persuasive manner. "I'll need to discuss this with my employer," he said cautiously.

Dr Jameson smiled reassuringly. "Of course, but I have already spoken to your employer; he is a good friend of mine. I've smoothed the way for you in that regard."

Shaking his head, Allan realised that Dr Jameson was not one to be taken lightly. "Very well then, when do I start?"

"Tomorrow morning. Meet me at the magistrate's office, and we'll get you officially enlisted. Now, let's enjoy this meal, Captain Wilson."

PART TWO

AFRICA 1893

CHAPTER SEVENTEEN

January 1893

On the first day of 1893, the Burnhams embarked on their long journey to Africa. They headed north to Vancouver, then traversed the entire width of Canada, eventually ending up in New York, back in America. From there, they boarded a steamer to Liverpool in England. They took an excursion to Paris before continuing their journey down the west coast of Africa, finally reaching Durban on the east coast of the massive continent. They disembarked in the middle of April 1893, the entire journey having taken four and a half months.

"Father, do we sail to Matabeleland?" six-year-old Roderick asked Fred.

"Oh no," Fred replied with a chuckle. "From here, we go by wagon. There is no sea from now on, just a lot of land and wilderness."

Blanche laughed. "I don't even think there is a road to Matabeleland!"

"Isn't this town amazing?" Fred marvelled at the streets and the large department stores of Durban.

"I didn't expect to find all this here," Blanche agreed. "The prices are even comparable to California. And the people are so friendly."

Once they had taken a few days to orient themselves, Fred set out to purchase a wagon and provisions for their journey north. He wanted an American buckboard pulled by burros (or, as he learned they called them in Africa, mules or donkeys). The purchase of a buckboard, however, proved impossible. He was told in no uncertain terms that he would require a larger, bulky wagon, drawn by a team of sixteen oxen, in order to survive the journey through the rugged bush. After all, this *was* Africa. Fred just could not understand why he had to pay such exorbitant prices for a large team of oxen and employ several men to drive them. He was convinced he only needed a buckboard and six mules to carry just the three of them and their provisions. Despite his constant objections, he found that he always hit a brick wall.

Luck chanced upon him a few days later when a trader told him that he had the metal frame, wheels, and axles for a buckboard he had once imported but had not been able to sell. American buckboards had no springs, which made them undesirable in Africa. The trader was delighted to get rid of the materials for a small fee. To his immense satisfaction, Fred immediately purchased timber to build a buckboard to his specifications.

Trying to purchase six donkeys to pull the contraption was the next obstacle Fred faced. Not only were the donkeys difficult to obtain, but those he finally sourced were not accustomed to being harnessed. Fred's animal husbandry skills were put to the test as he set about training them. Harnesses were unavailable, but with Fred's direction and Blanche's sewing skills, they made reins and harnesses out of cowhide. Once Fred believed they were fully prepared for the journey they left Durban, excited to set off on the next step in their adventure. Their buckboard and donkeys caused much amusement and laughter as they left the town limits, little aware of the arduousness of the four-month journey that lay ahead of them.

One month later, the Burnhams arrived in Johannesburg, the bustling city of gold, where they were again greeted with laughter. Fred wasn't concerned, however, he knew he had travelled much faster than the ox-drawn wagons, and, more importantly, his donkeys didn't need as much feed or care as the great beasts.

When Fred learned they would begin travelling through dangerous lion-infested regions from Johannesburg onwards, he joined a team of Boers headed north to Fort Salisbury via Fort Victoria in Mashonaland. He thought it prudent to travel in company for this leg of the journey. The trek was frustratingly slow, and Fred insisted that six-year-old Roderick remain in the buckboard at all times, fearing an attack from wild predators, or even, perhaps, aggressive Zulu tribesmen.

Fred learned much from the Boers. They were excellent marksmen, could shoot animals on foot or from the saddle at long range, and knew their oxen like their own children. Discipline in the trek was organised and strict. The Boers would wake at two o'clock in the morning, and within half an hour, coffee would be made, the oxen harnessed, and the convoy underway, before the heat of the day hit. The group would halt at sunrise, and prepare to eat and then rest during the hottest part of the day. Just before sunset, they would harness the oxen again and only stop at about nine o'clock at night. This schedule was strictly followed every day. The Boers had a steadfast rule that oxen must never be yoked with the African sun on their backs. To work the oxen in the heat of the day would sap their energy rapidly, and, very soon, they would be incapable of hauling heavy loads. It would be perilous to allow this.

One afternoon, as the Burnhams stood on the sandy bank of a river watching a struggling team of oxen prepare to cross, Blanche put her arm lovingly around Fred's waist.

"Isn't this country marvellous?" she said softly, admiring the beauty around her.

Fred reciprocated and put his arm around her, too. "A new frontier," he agreed. "This country is better than anything I ever expected. Imagine the opportunities. I am sure gold must be deposited in these riverbanks."

Blanche watched the lumbering Boer contingent unload a wagon to adjust its weight before entering the water. "Maybe you should go back over and give them a hand."

"No," Fred smiled. "They know what they are doing and are used to doing it their way. Besides, I'm not leaving you and Roderick alone on this side of the river."

"I'll be alright," Blanche squeezed Fred lovingly.

"I know," Fred smiled, "but I won't chance anything. I saw lion footprints just over there."

Blanche looked over her shoulder. "Where? You are joking, aren't you?"

Fred laughed. "No, I can read the ground like you can read a book. Come, I'll show you what a lion's footprint looks like if you want."

Blanche smiled. She knew Fred had exceptional tracking abilities, thanks to his early life with the Sioux and Apache Indians. She was not surprised that he had honed his skills on their journey.

"Go on, show me," she laughed. "Let's show Roderick, too; he needs to learn."

***

King Lobengula sat on his royal wagon, a vehicle gifted to him by a trader seeking concessions. He favoured this mode of transport, especially because he could sleep in it. On this particular day, his gout was troubling him, making it difficult to move, but he could hold court without leaving the wagon, looking down on his Indunas with condescension.

The day had been hot and tedious, and his Indunas had been troubling him more than the pain in his foot. Their main complaint was that he had signed an agreement with the settlers that gave away their Kingdom. Despite his assurances that he had not, he felt as though he was fighting an uphill battle against them.

Five years prior, in 1888, Lobengula had signed the Rudd Concession, granting the British South Africa Company (BSAC) the rights to mine for gold, farm, and settle in the land of the Mashona people to the north, a land that Lobengula ruled over. Rhodes presented the Rudd Concession to Queen Victoria, who granted his BSAC a Royal Charter, allowing Rhodes to establish colonial settlements in Mashonaland. The Charter also enabled Rhodes to set up a judicial system, a police force, and an administrative system. Rhodes wasted no time and sent a group of pioneers to settle the country in 1890, enticing them with promises of land and mining concessions.

After signing the Rudd Concession, Lobengula had been persuaded by Rhodes' enemies that he had been deceived. He desperately tried to have the document nullified, even going to the extreme of sending two of his emissaries to England to meet the Queen. These attempts were thwarted, and Lobengula began believing he had been played for a fool.

"My King," one of the elderly Indunas spoke gravely, "these white people are now everywhere, digging holes and building houses. Their numbers are growing by the day."

"I allowed them to do so," Lobengula responded with anger. "They are not in Matabeleland but are staying north of the Shangani River. Have they not honoured their agreement?"

There was a discontented murmuring, and the Induna pressed the point further. "Perhaps for now, but the whites are settled in the south, and now the north, and the Portuguese have been in the east for a long time. The whites will come, oh King. We cannot trust them."

Lobengula winced in pain as he moved his leg. "They claimed to come in peace, and so far, they have. They have not harmed any Matabele."

"That may be true," another Induna joined the discussion, "but they have forbidden our warriors from engaging in battle with the Mashona to maintain our traditions and culture."

"What would you have me do?" Lobengula asked, growing increasingly exasperated with the conversation.

"My King," a young Induna named Umgandan spoke, "does this agreement with the white man prevent us from continuing our ancient traditions?"

"No, it does not," Lobengula replied abruptly, attempting to swat away a fly. "Our traditions are not affected."

"Then, my King, allow us to embark on a raid to the north, where we can engage the Mashona, wash our spears with blood, and bring back cattle and women as is our tradition."

Lobengula considered the proposal. In pain, frustrated, and increasingly annoyed with his Indunas, who were supposed to support him, he concluded that Umgandan's suggestion would not violate his agreement with the white Queen in the faraway land. Perhaps, he thought, his Indunas would leave him alone if he allowed them to vent their frustrations.

"Very well, Umgandan. I will permit it. You and your impi may venture as far as the place the white man calls Fort Victoria. But I have two conditions. Firstly, you must not harm any white person, not even a little bit. If you shed the blood of a white man or woman, I will kill you and your entire impi upon your return."

"Secondly, you must take Induna Manyow," he said, pointing to an old man with white hair and a scratchy beard to match. "He will be my eyes and ears. If he does not come back with you unharmed, I will kill you and your entire impi upon your return. Now go, for the King has spoken."

***

Allan strolled down the dusty main street of Fort Victoria, his spirits soaring. He had had a restless night and had come to a decision that he had been putting off for a long time.

After sixteen years in Africa, three wars, several jobs, many hardships and some failures, he missed his family and friends in Scotland. Granted, he had a number of good and loyal friends in Africa, and he did cherish a brief romance once, but he had to consider the future. There was a lot to think about, but his decision was made, and he felt good about it.

Turning a corner, Allan thought he would call on his friend, William Judd, and tell him of his plans. Judd owned a thriving transport business in Fort Victoria, and he always enjoyed his company.

"Good morning," Allan cheerfully greeted his friend. "How are things going on this delightful day?"

"Good morning to you, too," Judd returned the salutation with a broad smile.

Judd was a short man with a round face adorned by a full, dark beard that extended from his face, seamlessly blending with the thick hair on his chest. Despite his diminutive stature, Judd possessed remarkable strength concealed beneath his loose cotton shirt.

"Is business booming as usual?" Allan inquired.

"Can't complain," Judd replied with a coy smile. "And how's our intrepid soldier and protector doing?"

"Same as usual," Allan chuckled. "The usual boring military happenings. I've been contemplating leaving and returning to Scotland. I made my decision last night."

Judd's brow furrowed. "I didn't expect to hear that from you, my friend. Aren't you enjoying yourself here?"

"Well, I have been," Allan admitted, "but the future of this country is uncertain, and I have family back home."

Just then, Judd raised his hand to silence Allan, his head cocked to the side. "Do you hear that?"

Allan listened intently. "Shouting?"

"Sounds like someone in distress. Screaming, more like it."

"Let's go and see what's happening," Allan promptly suggested, turning to leave. Judd followed, matching his pace.

As they stepped onto the street, a blood-curdling scream pierced the air from their right. About twenty heavily armed Matabele warriors, adorned with spears and shields, swiftly came into view from behind a thatched dwelling. Sporting armbands with ostrich feathers, with more feathered bands on their calves and foreheads signalling their war dress, they trotted past Allan and Judd without paying any attention to them, three marked by splashes of wet blood on their bodies. Curious and concerned, Allan asked Judd to investigate the source of the screams while he rushed after the warriors. Halting at the entrance to the fort, Allan drew his revolver as the Matabele men disappeared into a grove of trees.

Moments later, Judd arrived, gasping for breath. "They killed four Mashona men who worked at the general store. Executed them right in the middle of the street."

"Why?" Allan asked, bewildered.

"No idea. Old Mrs Green fainted. She was right there when it happened."

"Was she hurt?" Allan questioned.

"No, it seems they solely targeted the Mashona people. They didn't lay a finger on any Europeans, although they easily could have."

A scream from beyond the tree line diverted their attention. Straining their eyes, they could make out a man on horseback galloping toward them, with another figure following.

"Who's that?" Allan inquired.

"No clue, but they don't seem happy," Judd expressed concern. "Look, someone else is chasing them."

"Are they being pursued?" Allan ventured.

"Appears so."

Emerging from their abodes, a dozen Fort Victoria residents watched the unfolding commotion. Allan and Judd stood outside the gate, awaiting the approaching riders. As they neared, the first man reined in his horse, his arrival stirring up a cloud of dust.

"We've been attacked," the man gasped, clearly distressed.

"Who attacked you?" Allan demanded, noticing the blood splatters on the rider's chest and face.

The second rider dismounted abruptly before his horse had fully stopped. "The Matabele tribe is on a rampage," he exclaimed. "They're killing everyone!"

"What?" Judd was dumbfounded. "Why?"

"Are either of you injured?" Allan inquired of the first rider.

"No," he replied. "I'm alright. I had been walking with my Mashona guide when a group of Matabele surrounded us, and they killed him right before me. They brutally speared him."

"But they left you alone?" Allan pressed.

"Yes, but they looked at me with menace and ensured I couldn't intervene in their murder. It was horrific, I thought it was the end of me."

"I thought likewise," the second rider added, sitting heavily on the ground. He trembled in shock. "I was in my field with about fifteen workers when the warriors descended upon us. They massacred my employees while pointing their spears at me."

Suddenly, distant cries of panic reverberated through the air as terrified Mashona men and women emerged over a slight rise, dashing toward the settlement seeking protection. Not far behind them came the Matabele warriors, sprinting effortlessly and swiftly catching up to the fleeing crowd. With ruthless efficiency, they slashed and killed, the air filled with horrifying screams of death. Once satisfied that there were no survivors, the warriors confidently retreated into the bush.

Allan retrieved a silver whistle from his pocket. It was attached to a lanyard that was slung over his right shoulder. He blew three long, piercing blasts, knowing that his men would swiftly arm themselves and rush to their designated positions.

"Inside the fort!" Allan shouted loudly to settlers and soldiers alike. "Quickly."

Inside, Allan found a vantage point to peer over the wall, trying to make sense of what had just happened. Soon, two of his men joined him, one passing him a rifle.

"Thank you," Allan acknowledged, accepting the weapon while holstering his handgun.

"What's happening, Captain?" Fitzgerald inquired anxiously.

Fredrick Fitzgerald was a tall, handsome man, clean-shaven save for a thick moustache. Donning a slouch hat and a khaki shirt with rolled-up sleeves, his muscular forearms attested to his ability to handle physical altercations expertly. The Martini-Henry rifle in his hands looked like a child's toy.

"Not entirely sure," Allan replied, his gaze fixed on the distant tree line. "It appears that the Matabele are on a warpath."

Allan turned to the other man beside him, a soldier slightly shorter than Fitzgerald. Bill Napier, sporting a well-worn slouch hat in dire need of replacement, also had a full moustache. He stood alongside Allan, scanning the horizon.

"Are all the men in their positions?" Allan inquired of Napier.

"Yes, Captain," Napier confirmed, his gaze fixed in the distance.

Fitzgerald subtly nudged his rifle to the left. "Two men approaching, Captain," he whispered. "They're on foot."

"Do you think they want to negotiate?" Napier questioned.

"Seems likely," Allan nodded, barely noticeably. "Napier, please fetch Mr Lendy. I believe he should be present. Also, ask Trooper Judd to get statements from any witnesses."

"Yes, Captain," Napier replied, promptly dashing off.

Charles Lendy, who worked in the magistrate's office of Fort Victoria, was a commanding figure. With his hair neatly parted in the middle, he exuded an air of importance. Lendy diligently maintained his physical fitness, which was evident from his well-toned physique. His meticulously groomed moustache added a regal touch to his overall appearance. Dressed in a grey coat and a tie, he joined Allan and Fitzgerald at the fort gate, patiently awaiting the arrival of the two Matabele.

"Can you translate?" Lendy inquired of Allan.

Fitzgerald responded quickly, "I can, Sir. I understand isiNdebele."

The approaching warriors halted about ten yards away from the white men. The elder of the two surveyed his adversaries with a mix of pity and contempt while the younger man's eyes darted menacingly as if daring the three men to provoke them. They each held a spear and an oval shield made of dappled cowhide. Feathers were attached to armbands on their upper arms, with more around their calves and on their headgear.

Speaking in isiNdebele, the older man introduced himself, "I am Induna Manyow. I come from King Lobengula, the great ruler. This man is Induna Umgandan."

Fitzgerald translated for Lendy.

"Ask them why they're here, what their purpose is, and why they're killing the Mashona people," Lendy instructed, his gaze unwavering.

Fitzgerald translated the message and then conveyed the reply to the magistrate. "He said that the Matabele have the right to kill the Mashona and take as many cattle as they please without interference. The cattle are King Lobengula's property. He assures us they will respect the Royal Charter and refrain from harming white people. He wishes to speak to Dr Jameson, as he has a message from the King."

Lendy pondered on this for a while before responding, "Alright, inform them that Dr Jim is currently in Fort Salisbury," Lendy said, using the accepted nickname for Dr Jameson. "I will send a message to him, and he will come. Meanwhile, they must send their warriors back to KoBulawayo while these two wait until Jameson arrives. It may happen after some days."

The message was translated, and the two emissaries departed, though Umgandan shot an intimidating glare at the men before leaving.

"I don't trust that younger one," Lendy grumbled. "Captain Wilson, please have your men prepared. I don't like the look of this situation. I will send a message to Jameson immediately."

After the magistrate left, Allan and Fitzgerald were joined by Judd and Napier.

"What do you make of all this, Captain?" Napier asked.

"I'm not sure," Allan replied with a shrug. "I do know that they are not permitted to harm Europeans, and we are forbidden to harm any Matabele, however, I don't believe any agreement states that the Matabele cannot do as they wish with the Mashona."

"This could turn into a disaster," Fitzgerald remarked.

Allan let out a sigh. "I fear that if the Mashona seek our protection, we will find ourselves in a very difficult situation."

Fitzgerald shook his head. "Let's hope it doesn't come to that."

Breaking his gaze from the tree line, Allan spoke decisively, "Alright, let's get back to our positions."

***

Dr Jameson arrived on horseback almost a week later. Initially, he didn't believe the reports he had received from Fort Victoria about the Matabeles' desperate need for war. As he approached the fort and saw the devastation–burnt villages, destroyed crops, and mutilated corpses–lying across the land, his disbelief turned into grim acceptance.

Upon his arrival at Fort Victoria, Dr Jameson gathered Wilson, Lendy, and Fitzpatrick for a meeting without wasting any time. They stood beneath the flag of the BSAC that had been raised in the centre of the garrison.

"I can't believe Lobengula sanctioned this," Jameson expressed his distress at the sight of the carnage. "I know his Indunas and warriors have been pushing him to let them loose on the Mashona, but this? We came in peace and agreed to peaceful terms."

"The Rudd Concession and the subsequent Royal Charter don't give us the authority to interfere in their traditional practices," Allan interjected.

"But peace should always be the priority, Captain," Jameson replied.

"Moreover, if they kill the Mashona, they are killing our workforce, which is vital for the prosperity of this land. The Mashona are now seeking our protection, and we must provide it. Hundreds have already sought shelter here."

"I suggest you speak with the King himself, immediately, before the situation worsens," Lendy advised.

"Yes, I will," Jameson sighed. "If they harm any one of us, or if we harm them, it will amount to a declaration of war, and we must avoid that at all costs."

"If I may, Sir," Allan requested.

"Go ahead, Captain," Jameson nodded.

"If war is declared between the Matabele nation and ourselves, they will swiftly overpower Fort Victoria and Fort Salisbury. We have roughly 3,000 settlers in total, while they boast an army of approximately 80,000 warriors. Many of them are now armed with rifles, thanks to the Rudd Concession and Rhodes' generosity," Allan added with a hint of sarcasm. "We are ill-prepared, lacking sufficient rifles and heavy weaponry."

"I agree with Captain Wilson," Lendy concurred. "We cannot defend ourselves against a superior force on foot. It would be another Rorke's Drift massacre."

Continuing his train of thought, Allan continued, "If we have any chance of repelling an attack, we need a cavalry. Our men on foot are no match for them. We would be defeated before the battle even begins. Horses are everything."

Jameson pondered on this. "Then we must buy time and prepare ourselves. I will travel to KoBulawayo and personally plead with Lobengula not to kill the Mashona. Simultaneously, I will send a coded message to Rhodes, informing him of the urgent support we require. Rhodes needs to be aware how fragile the situation is."

"Very well, Sir," Allan acknowledged.

Jameson nodded. "Captain Wilson, you possess the most experience in the Zulu wars. I will arrange to promote you to the rank of Major. I will make it official before I depart south."

"Thank you, Sir," Allan accepted the offer. The promotion came as a welcome surprise.

"Step up the training of your troops for potential conflict with urgency."

"I will, Sir," Allan agreed.

Jameson, Lendy, and Allan then walked together to the gate of the fort, standing there patiently. Fitzgerald joined them as the interpreter. The Matabele noticed their arrival, and soon, Manyow and Umgandan emerged from the tree line and approached the trio. Behind them hundreds of warriors stood silently under the shade of some trees.

Lendy clucked his tongue. "Those two, they are the spokesmen, but I told them to send all the other warriors back to KoBulawayo. It looks like they didn't listen."

Jameson squinted his eyes. "Are some of them carrying rifles?"

"Not all," Allan said, "but quite a few of them. They mean business."

Unfortunately, the meeting with the two Indunas didn't go well from almost the moment it started. Umgandan arrogantly flaunted his authority as given to him by the most powerful King in Africa. Eventually, Jameson could no more tolerate such disrespect from the young warrior.

"Tell him to return to KoBulawayo with his men; they have one hour to leave this area," Jameson raised his voice threateningly. "If they fail to comply, we will pursue them. Let him know this! Tomorrow, I will depart for KoBulawayo to speak directly with King Lobengula. They have one hour," Jameson repeated.

Fitzgerald translated the message, but Umgandan simply smirked and taunted the doctor with aggressive gestures before walking away leisurely. An hour later, Jameson instructed Lendy to gather a force of thirty-eight mounted men—the entire number of their available horses—and ensure that the Matabele adhered to his demands.

As Lendy and his men mounted, Jameson came to see them off.

"If they haven't left, chase them off," Jameson grumbled.

When Lendy and his men returned, they reported that Manyow and his impi had returned to KoBulawayo, but Umgandan and his impi had refused to leave and were in the process of raiding villages and killing more Mashona. The fracas became violent, and in response, Lendy and his men were forced to open fire, resulting in the death of several Matabele warriors, including Umgandan.

Jameson penned a stern letter to King Lobengula, demanding compensation for stolen cattle and the lives lost among the Mashona. He also wrote coded messages requesting urgent protection and support from Rhodes, including heavy weapons, ammunition, horses, and reinforcements. These messages were to be carried on horseback to a very remote outpost called Tati, in northeastern Bechuanaland, and just beyond the border of Matabeleland. Tati was the northernmost point where the telegraph line from Cape Town terminated.

Jameson suddenly changed his mind, however, and tore up his letter to Lobengula, deciding to speak with him personally after all. Calling for a horse, he wasted no time in departing. As soon as Jameson was gone, Allan sought out Judd, Fitzgerald, and Napier, who were stationed at the southeastern corner of the settlement.

"I fear trouble is heading our way, gentlemen," Allan expressed his concerns.

"I expected as much," Fitzgerald acknowledged.

Judd smiled. "So, I hear you've been promoted to Major?"

"Yes," Allan grinned. "Given the circumstances, Jameson is arranging for the three of you to be promoted to the rank of Captain. I will be in charge of the Victoria Rangers, and I will need your assistance."

"You can count on us," Judd assured Allan with a curt nod.

"Thank you," Allan gratefully accepted their support. "Jameson has devised a plan. If Lobengula declares war, we will launch a two-front attack. The Victoria Rangers, us, and the Salisbury Horse will advance on KoBulawayo from the north, while the Bechuanaland Border Police will join forces with King Khama's army to attack Lobengula from the south. We can't leave until Jameson and Rhodes procure weapons, ammunition, and horses. That could take another couple of months."

Fitzgerald's brow furrowed. "Currently, we stand little chance of surviving an attack. Just with those numbers hiding behind those trees, we would have a serious problem."

Judd shook his head. "With barely forty horses, we would have no chance whatsoever."

"I know that. Jameson is proceeding urgently to talk to Lobengula to try and pacify and stall things. We desperately need time," Allan acknowledged. With only four hundred men under his command, he knew the task ahead would be gruelling.

Allan continued. "I am willing to take a risk and utilise most of our ammunition to train our men while we await replenishments. Judd, I trust you to oversee firearms training. Fitzgerald, I'm assigning you to drill exercises, and Napier, you and Lendy concentrate on fitness and physical training. Lendy is a master of physical fitness. He is also a recognised sportsman, so let's utilise his expertise."

"Understood, Captain," they replied in unison.

"I also need you to help me recruit volunteers. There will be no pay for this, but Jameson has confirmed that if we go to war and oust Lobengula, those who sign up as volunteers will be allocated free land to farm or ranch, including many free mining claims."

"That's appealing," Fitzgerald said. "It will not be difficult to recruit men on the basis of those promises."

"There's more," Allan continued. "They will each get a share in the spoils of the King's cattle and treasures."

"I was at the confrontation with Umgandan," Fitzgerald confirmed. "I don't think those Indunas expected thirty-eight mounted men to confront their number."

Allan sighed in despair. "If war does break out, remember that the lives of all the white women, children and men in this country are at stake. The Matabele won't take prisoners. We cannot afford to lose."

Uncertainty hanging in the air, the men went their respective ways to resume their critical responsibilities.

***

When Jameson entered King Lobengula's kraal, he discovered the King confined to his bed due to a severe bout of gout. Positioned just behind his King, Mjaan stood ready with his spear, prepared to act if Jameson proved to be a threat.

"Do you have your white man's medicine?" the King demanded.

Jameson nodded and administered a dose of laudanum. He waited until the King showed some relief.

"I have come to speak with you, Great King, about trouble in the settlement we call Fort Victoria," Jameson began.

"You may speak," Lobengula said.

"Your men came to Fort Victoria and slaughtered many people: men, women and children."

"Was a white man hurt?" Lobengula frowned.

"No," Jameson admitted.

"So I have kept to my side of the agreement. You have not. Your people have killed Induna Umgandan and forty of his men."

"You cannot kill the Mashona," Jameson almost pleaded.

Lobengula shook his head. "I said I would not hurt the white man, but I can do what I want with anyone else. The Mashona are a conquered people. It is our right."

"But King," Jameson said, "The Mashona have sought our protection, and we wish to provide it."

The King scowled. "You are not permitted to protect them."

"Maybe so, but we do," Jameson said with authority. "You have no use for them, you only want to kill them."

"I will kill you now. You have broken the agreement."

Jameson sighed in exasperation. "There is no agreement about how we treat the Mashona. We don't want war with you.

We came with peaceful purposes, and if you want to send raiding parties to kill and enslave the Mashona, we must protect them. Perhaps I may make a proposal, King."

"What is your proposal, White Man?" Lobengula grumbled. He had forgone all diplomacy and politeness now.

"Our big Induna wants to talk with you. I propose you send three emissaries you trust to meet our Induna, Mr Rhodes, and the High Commissioner for our Queen, Sir Henry Loch."

"And where are they?"

"Cape Town," Jameson said. He was desperate for the King to agree to these negotiations to give him time to get weapons and horses to Fort Victoria and Fort Salisbury in the event war was unavoidable.

"Why doesn't your Induna come to see King Lobengula?" the King demanded. "He has never come to KoBulawayo, and I have not met him. Is he scared of me?"

"He is a very busy man, oh King. I know he is desirous of meeting you. But if you will agree to send three emissaries to Cape Town, I will arrange for my personal friend, Mr James Dawson, whom you know and trust, to escort them and keep them safe."

King Lobengula looked at Jameson through the corners of his eyes. He did not trust him.

"Doctor Jameson," Lobengula paused and sighed. "Have you ever watched how the chameleon catches the fly? The chameleon carefully stands behind the fly and does not move for a long time. Then he moves forward, very slowly, very carefully, putting one leg in front of the other. When he is close, his tongue darts out rapidly, and the fly is gone. England is the chameleon, and I am that fly."

Jameson didn't know how to respond.

"Leave me now," Lobengula said bluntly.

Jameson obliged. He bowed respectfully to the King and went to find James Dawson.

Lobengula sat in silence for a full minute. "Mjaan!"

"Yes, my King," Mjaan replied. He immediately dropped to one knee.

"What am I to do?"

Mjaan was careful with his response. "The King seeks advice from a soldier?"

"Yes," Lobengula sighed. "My Indunas argue with me, my advisors argue with me, and now the white man is arguing with me. What do you think?"

Mjaan thought long and hard about his answer. Whether the Matabele attacked or not, the white man was causing trouble in their land. Like Lobengula, Mjaan could see that whatever the King decided to do, he was in a difficult position.

"My King," Mjaan began, "the only option I can see is to go to war with the white man. They want your land. They want to live under their laws, not yours, and they want all your gold, and all the ivory and shiny stones in the ground. The traders who visit you all the time always want from you, but they give nothing in return. They want to topple you and take your country. We must fight them and drive them all away. If we lose, it will be the end of our nation.

"If you do nothing, your own people will be angry with you. They already are unhappy. The white man has stopped us from fighting the Mashona and making our men stronger. They have stopped us from strengthening our nation with fighting men and young women. I fear your own people will rebel, and they will be the ones to topple you. There is only one outcome: to attack the white man and win at all costs."

Lobengula remained silent, and Mjaan dared not flinch. An extended period of reflection commenced, and Mjaan was uneasy; he didn't know what was going through the King's mind.

"You are right, Mjaan," Lobengula finally said. "You have spoken wisely. Do you think we can win against the white man?"

"Yes, King!" Mjaan looked at Lobengula with fire in his eyes. "We are many, and they are few. We have rifles and a lot of ammunition, just as they do. We have spears; they do not. If we fight them in the forests, they will have no chance against the might of our warriors."

Lobengula grunted. "Summon the Indunas," he demanded.

***

Mjaan returned to his hut and ducked his head as he entered. Thandiwe greeted him and noticed his drawn looks.

"Sit, my husband," she ushered him to the stool he always sat upon. "You look troubled. I will bring you some fresh beer that I brewed last week."

Mjaan forced a smile. "Thank you, Thandiwe. The day has been long."

She filled a dried calabash shell with the brew and handed it to her husband. He drank thirstily and handed back the empty container. As she went to refill it, he waved a hand, declining any more.

"What troubles you, Husband?"

"The King has decided on war with the white man," Mjaan nodded, seemingly agreeing with the King.

"Are you going to fight?" Thandiwe asked cautiously.

"No," Mjaan shook his head in disappointment. "Induna Manonda and his impi will go. He has five thousand warriors, so it will be an easy battle. The King has commanded me to go, only to be his eyes and report to him. I will not be fighting. I would very much like to, but I am the commander of the iNgubo impi, and my impi will remain here to protect the King."

"So, our son, Londisizwe, will not fight?"

"No, he is part of the iNgubo impi too. He will remain here."

Thandiwe sighed silently in relief. She wanted her son to be recognised as a heroic fighter, but her maternal instincts to keep him safe conflicted with her traditional thinking. She was also pleased her husband would not be active in the battle.

Mjaan, now an old man of sixty-seven years, was well past his physical fighting peak, but his firstborn son, Londisizwe, a strapping thirty-five-year-old, was in top physical condition. He was a big man, with a powerful chest and legs which could carry him on the run for an entire day. When Londisizwe's physical strength had proven he was a very capable warrior, Mjaan wasted no time enlisting him in his own impi, which pleased the King. Mjaan was very proud of his son, and knew that he would succeed him as the commander of the iNgubo impi.

Mjaan understood that his second in command, Ngwenya, should take over if he was killed, but Ngwenya was also getting old now, and Londisizwe was his natural successor. Mjaan had trained Londisizwe well over the years, and there was no doubt that he was a brilliant warrior.

Thandiwe carefully placed a pot of boiled meat by Mjaan's feet. "When will the men start fighting?" she asked respectfully.

"Ghaa!" Mjaan exclaimed in disgust. "Not right away. First, the King wants to talk with the leaders of the white man again. This is very frustrating. I do not understand why the King wants to talk so much. The time for talking is well past. The Indunas want to fight, now."

CHAPTER EIGHTEEN

July 1893

The Burnhams had been travelling northwards for almost three months. The country north of the Limpopo River teamed with animals and birds, and every day was a new and exciting adventure for the young family. Fred's eyes never rested. They darted everywhere, taking in the tracks left on the soil, the leaves in the trees, and the creatures that inhabited them. He noted the insects flying in the air and scurrying on the ground, the way the grasses swayed in the gentle breezes, and the various shades of colour. Nothing went unnoticed by Fred. His childhood training by the Indians back home stayed with him, and he was fascinated by both the differences and similarities of the vastly contrasting continents. He was in his element every hour of every day.

One day a similar buckboard to his, with two men driving it, overtook them. They stopped to share news, as was the custom in remote parts of the world. One man was an American named Pearl Ingram, and the other was a Canadian, Robert Bain. Fred and Blanche quickly befriended them as their heritage was comfortably similar. More than that, the new arrivals had both worked for the American government as scouts, and so Fred had a lot in common with these two men. During their conversation, comparing dates and places, Fred and Ingram discovered they were at the same fountain in California at the same hour and on the same day just before departing for Africa. The coincidence of meeting thousands of miles away in the African bush was cause for much hilarity, and a bond instantly formed between the two. Old stories were shared, mutual acquaintances discussed, and soon they felt that they had known each other for years.

Ingram and Bain were heading north to Mashonaland. A bright future in gold and other mineral discoveries had been promised by Cecil Rhodes to anyone who was brave enough to venture there. The two stayed for the night and enjoyed the Burnhams' companionship before continuing their trek northwards the following day.

Fred's buckboard and donkeys were swifter and more manoeuvrable than the Boer's ox-drawn wagons, and so it was agreed that Fred would go ahead each day and find a suitable place for the next camp. The Boers would lumber up later and outspan. By the time it took the wagons to reach the Burnhams, Fred would already have gone out hunting for food, exploring, or secretly looking for signs of gold.

One afternoon, while the Burnhams and the Boers were resting in the noon-day heat, a wagon approached them from a north-easterly direction, heading south-west in a desperate hurry. The family on board was driving hard, and the fact that the wagon was moving in the heat of the day was an ominous sign. The family stopped when they reached Fred's convoy, bearing dreadful news; the Matabele were preparing to attack the settlers throughout Matabeleland and Mashonaland. The travellers told of the incident at Fort Victoria, where warriors had freely entered the settlement and slaughtered Mashonas for no apparent reason. The travellers said that when the leader of this raiding party left, he had warned that their next visit would involve killing whites as well as the Mashona. He urged everyone to turn around and ride for their lives.

Another two wagons with families arrived in a cloud of dust and pulled by moaning oxen. The families on the wagons also brought harrowing stories of a bloodbath. The head of each family declined to outspan and rest their oxen, preferring to push on as hard as possible. They had a look of terror in their eyes. One lady pulled Blanche aside and begged her to turn around and save herself and her young son.

After the fleeing families departed, the Boers called a meeting amongst themselves to discuss the unexpected tidings. The leader of the Boer contingent, a man named Johannes Jokobus Smit, affectionately known as JJ, was a very large and powerful person with a full and unruly beard. Next to him, Fred looked like a mere boy.

"I have been involved in these African wars before. This is not my war, and I have nothing waiting for me up north yet," JJ said. "Those of you in my situation can return if you wish; there will be no embarrassment for turning around. As for myself, I wish to get as far away from the settlers south of the Limpopo as I can, so I will continue my trek north."

A second Boer sitting on an upturned box nodded gravely. "I would return, but I have a farm near Fort Salisbury. It may be that the uprising is a small matter and will be resolved soon. I think I would like to wait a little longer and get more news from travellers before I decide."

The overall consensus was to wait and see how bad the situation truly was.

"Alright," JJ agreed, "we will wait for more information."

"I have a suggestion," a man called Black spoke up. "We know that about thirty miles to the west is a telegraph line running parallel to our journey. It will junction at a station, I think it is called Tati. If some of us trek west for about thirty miles, we will intercept the telegraph line's path. Then, if we follow it, we will find the telegraph station and can get accurate news."

"That is a good idea," JJ said. "I suggest four of us look for this station. Who will go?"

Fred, being a seasoned tracker, put his hand up. Another three volunteered and immediately prepared to set off to find the telegraph line. Their names were Black, Waller and Der Huyter. Fred bade farewell to Blanche and Roderick, and the four men immediately left the laager on foot.

It took longer than expected to find the telegraph line, two wires suspended high on wooden poles. By then, it was getting dark, so the four men made camp for the night. Another half a day was needed to reach the Tati telegraph office. There they found a young man called Dennis Dillon. Fair-haired with pale blue eyes, he was twenty-six years old. His father was a Postmaster in Punjab, India, and after being educated in England, Dillon came to Africa to follow in his father's wandering footsteps and had enrolled with the BSAC.

Dillon was full of jokes and mischief, which he cultivated to keep himself sane in the isolated outpost. He would play tricks on the local people using electricity from the telegraph line, giving them mild shocks to show the 'power' of the 'white man's magic'. Seen as cruel by some but funny by others, he nevertheless thus made it known that the telegraph lines were not to be played with. This later worked very much in Dr

Jameson's favour.

"Good day to you, Gentlemen," Dillon greeted the four men as they noisily emerged from a thicket of bush.

"Good day to you, Sir," Fred extended his hand in friendship. "We are trekking from Johannesburg to Fort Victoria. Our wagons are about thirty miles to the east."

"What brings you to my humble establishment?" Dillon smiled in welcome.

"We hear the Matabele are uprising," Black said. "We have women and children in our caravan, and we need to decide whether to turn around or press on. Would you have any news on the situation?"

"I have indeed," Dillon smiled widely. He enjoyed having unexpected visitors. "Come in, and let's get you gentlemen some refreshments."

Refreshments consisted of only water or tea, but Dillon had a stash of dried and salted meat that the Boers called *biltong*. Although often on his own, with the uncertainty of events in Fort Victoria and KoBulawayo his outpost had recently received more attention than usual.

While Fred and his fellow men slaked their thirst and chewed on the delicious biltong, Dillon pulled some papers from his desk drawer. The Boers found boxes and a spare chair to sit upon, but Fred moved to the corner of the room and squatted on his haunches. His eyes studied the room intently, and he was intrigued to follow the wire down from the roof to Dillon's desk–a wire that originated in Cape Town over one thousand miles away.

Shuffling through some papers, Dillon extracted a leaf of paper and waved it in the air. "This one is from LSJ, Leander Starr Jameson," Dillon looked at Fred to confirm that he understood the initials. When there was no response from anyone, he continued. *"To CJR, Lobengula frustrated. Wants to fight. Send arms."*

Fred looked at his companions. "They're not fighting yet?"

"No," Dillon said, "but this one from four days ago says *'LSJ to CJR: Matabele entered Ft.Vic. Mashonas killed at random. Attempts to push them back resulted in 40 Matabele dead. Need weapons.'* Here's another one, *'Send men. Need support. Vulnerable. Urgent.'* And there's more, stuff like *'need horses, need ammunition'*, and so it goes on."

"Does Rhodes reply?" Black asked.

"Oh yes, of course," Dennis smiled. "I shouldn't tell you these things because it's all confidential."

"That may well be the case," Fred said calmly, "But as we said, we have women and children in our caravan, and a decision to continue or return depends on what we learn here."

Dillon continued with his almost permanent smile. "Alright, I take your point. CJR is sending people and weapons on the double. He is funding the purchase of over five hundred horses, which are being sent up as quickly as possible."

"Five hundred horses against eighty thousand Matabele?" Black mulled. "I don't like the odds."

"True," Dillon said. "I can tell you they are sending more of those new Maxim machine guns, too. That will make a difference."

Fred shook his head. "I've heard about the Maxims. They've never been tested in battle before."

"True. I can tell you something else," Dillon grinned. "I think they prefer to negotiate before they fight. Sir Henry Loch, the Cape High Commissioner, wants King Lobengula to send three of his top men to parley with him in Cape Town and settle this dispute. Lobengula has agreed. I expect these men to pass through here any day now."

Waller frowned. "So the Colonial Office doesn't want to fight, Lobengula is uncertain, and I get the feeling Rhodes wants a fight because he is sending horses and guns in a hurry."

"Defence, perhaps?" Dillon posed.

"I still don't like it," Der Huyter said.

When Dillon's ticker sprang into action, Fred and his party moved outside to sit under the shade of a tree where they could talk freely between themselves.

"It sounds as though things are getting very uncomfortable between the white settlers and the Matabele," Black grumbled. "I don't know. I think I will advise JJ we should return with haste."

"I'm not so sure," Fred mulled. "They seem to want to negotiate, so I don't see the urgency right now."

"I would agree," Waller said. "It seems they expect things to remain stable at least long enough to send reinforcements. I would suggest we proceed."

"Alright," Der Huyter sighed, "let us rest up for a while to gather our strength, and then return to the convoy to discuss this with JJ. He will make a good decision for us."

The three men napped quietly in the shade, but Fred remained alert, his eyes darting around him, taking in his surrounds. He noted that on the far side of the telegraph compound was an armed BSAC soldier, and beyond him, a small cluster of bedraggled tents. He assumed the BSAC had moved a small contingent to the compound to protect it should hostilities arise. He also noticed that the guard was not very attentive, preferring to slouch lazily under a tree.

Fred and his companions had been resting for about an hour when a lone white man approached from the north. He was tall and extremely thin. Even from that distance, his beak-like nose was prominent. Behind him walked three Matabele warriors. They were in full battle dress, and armed with spears. It was obvious to Fred that they were Lobengula's emissaries.

The tall man entered the compound with the three Matabele men and spoke gruffly to the BSAC soldier who seemed to become a little more attentive. Fred heard him tell the guard to look after the warriors, then told the three men in isiNdebele to wait. Fred didn't need to understand the language to know what the instruction was.

Fred noticed that the white man was exhausted, and when he entered Dillon's office, he stood and followed him in. Fred wanted to hear what this man had to say.

"I need water," the thin man croaked at Dillon as he sat heavily in the spare chair. "Please, water."

Dillon stood and quickly passed the man a military issue container of water. The visitor made short work of the contents.

"Thank you, I'm starving. Got anything to eat?"

The telegraph ticker sprang into action, drawing Dillon's attention. Fred passed the man a stick of biltong that he was about to eat.

"Here," Fred smiled broadly, "this will be good for starters."

"Thank you, good Sir," the visitor said as he took the proffered biltong, then offered his hand in greeting. "The name's Dawson, James Dawson."

"Fred Burnham," he returned the handshake. "Are those Lobengula's men?"

"Yes, emissaries," Dawson confirmed. "Extremely frustrating, this whole debacle."

"How so, Mr Dawson?" Fred asked with curiosity. Dawson looked as if he would not manage another day's walk.

"I'm a trader in the KoBulawayo area. Just a trader," Dawson said, then paused to drink and refill his mug of water. "Out of the blue, Jameson asks, no, tells me to escort these three men to Cape Town for a meeting with Mr Rhodes. No offer of payment or reward, no concern for my loss of business. An absolute shambles. Do you know how far Cape Town is from KoBulawayo?"

"Couldn't you have just said 'No', Mr Dawson?" Fred asked.

"Say no to Jameson?" Dawson exclaimed. "He thinks he's a headmaster, ordering everyone to do his will. If you even hesitate, he invokes the might and power of his god, Cecil John Rhodes."

"What's KoBulawayo like at the moment, Mr Dawson?" Fred kept his questioning up.

"Utterly miserable."

"Miserable?" Fred cocked an eyebrow.

"More boring than this place. A most pathetic settlement," Dawson grimaced.

Dillon returned to the conversation when his ticker went silent. "I swear Jameson and Rhodes have their own language. I wish they would just speak English."

"What do you mean?" Fred asked curiously.

"Take these latest telegraph messages," Dillon ruffled through some papers on his desk. "From Jameson to Rhodes yesterday, 'May I enact the Dunvegan Protocol?', and this one from Rhodes to Jameson today; 'Read Luke 14:31'–I don't even know if I got the numbers correct."

"They are codes," Fred smiled. "They are not meant to be understood."

"Well, they don't make my life any easier," Dillon complained.

Fred returned to his travelling companions and reported back. "That tall man who just arrived is a trader from KoBulawayo, and he is escorting the King's emissaries to Cape Town. He doesn't think there is much excitement going on in KoBulawayo. In fact, he says it is utterly boring there."

Der Huyter nodded, then stood with some effort and sighed. "Alright, people. We had best return to the wagons immediately and report our findings to our leader."

"Let's fill up with water first and bid our host farewell," Fred suggested.

When Fred entered Dillon's office, Dawson was grumbling profusely about his loss of business and the sheer inconvenience of transporting Lobengula's emissaries thousands of miles. Dillon, meanwhile, wasn't listening, but transcribing a message that had arrived only moments before.

"Excuse me, Mr Dillon," Fred interrupted. "We must be away."

"Good to meet you, gentlemen. Call past any time," he said with a laugh and shook Fred's hand in friendship.

"Mr Dawson," Fred extended his hand to the trader, "I bid you farewell and wish you safe onward travels."

"Thank you Mr Burnham. American, are you?" Dawson said with a knowing smile.

"Yes, Californian."

"Pleased to make your acquaintance. Be careful out there."

When Fred exited the office, he saw Der Huyter and Waller, talking to a BSAC Officer. Fred quickly decided to have a closer look at the Matabele arrivals. He felt he might learn something about them, which was more important than talking to the officer. His friends could fill him in later, he thought.

Approaching the emissaries, who had now found some shade and sat down, Fred wasn't sure how to engage them. Indeed, he did not know their language and was certain they knew no English. They watched him closely as he came near. When Fred arrived, he dropped to his haunches to come down to their level, pulled his tin water container from his belt, opened the cap, and offered it to the man closest to him.

The man declined by shaking his head. Fred put the bottle to his lips and took a mouthful of water, allowing some to spill from his lips. He then offered it to the man again and included a friendly smile. This time, the Matabele accepted the container, returning the smile, and took several gulps before passing it to his fellow travellers. When the container was returned to Fred, he screwed the cap back on, nodded with a friendly smile, and then left. Not a word was spoken, but Fred's sharp eyes had had a chance to study them very carefully. It was the first time he had seen a Matabele warrior.

After re-filling his water container, Fred and his three companions retraced their steps and strode off to their convoy.

"That was a useful exercise," Mr Waller commented.

"I agree," Fred said. At least, he thought, they had some useful information to make a decision. "It looks as though this is a storm in a teacup. It should all blow over. When people talk, they can settle conflicts before they escalate to war."

"I would agree with you, Mr Burnham," Black mumbled, "but I do not hold out much hope all the same."

They had been walking steadily for about fifteen minutes when they heard two shots ring out from the telegraph office.

Fred stopped in his tracks. "What do you think that was about?"

"Let's wait a moment," Black suggested.

After a further quarter of an hour, nothing more was heard. All was silent.

"Maybe just someone shooting for the pot," Fred suggested.

"Yes, perhaps," Waller muttered. "Whoever it was is not a good shot. They must learn to use only one bullet when killing for the pot. Let's continue," he said and turned on his heels.

"Excuse me," Fred said, "it's this way."

Waller looked at Fred askance, then looked at the trees and the sky. "No, it's that way."

"Gentlemen," Black interrupted. "You are both wrong. We must go in that direction."

Some urgent discussion ensued, each believing he knew the way back and each person believing he was correct. In the end, a consensus could not be reached.

"Gentlemen," Fred said, exasperated, "let us each go in the direction we believe is correct. One of us must be right. Whoever gets to the wagons first must fire two shots in the air in rapid succession every thirty minutes until we all regroup. Agreed?"

"Agreed," Der Huyter said.

"Agreed," Waller concurred.

"On second thoughts," Black said. "I think that Waller might be correct after all, and so I will go with him."

As they parted company, Fred broke into the easy loping jog that he had learned from the Sioux Indians. He was pleased he had no one along with him who would slow him down. As night set in, he began following the stars, and, close to midnight, he saw the gentle glow of the laager's fires through the trees. Blanche was still awake and welcomed him fondly.

They went to JJ's wagon and woke him, explaining what Fred had learned.

JJ sent Fred and Blanche back to their buckboard and arranged that he and the others would keep vigil and fire the two shots every half hour to guide the others back.

As Fred lay down on his mattress, he put an arm around Blanche and squeezed her. He was pleased to have her back in his arms.

"I don't know how people find it so easy to get lost," Fred frowned.

"Perhaps you just have a built-in compass," Blanche chuckled.

"Perhaps," Fred agreed. "Let's get some shut-eye."

"Good night, my darling," Blanche said dreamily.

"Blanche, Luke 14:31 is a verse in the bible, is it not?"

"Yes, why?"

"It was a code from Rhodes to Jameson."

Blanche sat up and struck a match, lit a candle and pulled out her bible from under the mattress. As she flicked through the pages, Fred lifted himself on his elbow.

"Luke 14, verse 31," Blanche whispered. "Here it is, it says, '*Or what king, going to make war against another king, sitteth not down first, and consulteth whether he be able with ten thousand to meet him that cometh against him with twenty thousand? Or else, while the other is yet a great way off, he sendeth an ambassage, and desireth conditions of peace.*'"

Fred squeezed Blanche's arm gently. "Rhodes doesn't want war; he wants peace and wants to negotiate," he whispered hoarsely. "I think that's what he is telling Jameson."

"Do you think we should keep going?" Blanche asked. The concern in her voice was noticeable.

"Yes. I don't think there will be war."

"Alright," Blanche sighed. "Roderick and I will be ready at first light."

***

Soon after Fred and his companions had left Tati, Sergeant-Major Sidney Harding woke from a deep sleep. His tent was stifling hot, and he was not in a good mood. Beads of sweat graced his forehead, and his clothing was damp and uncomfortable. In half an hour, he would report for duty to oversee the first half of the evening watch at the Tati Telegraph Office. It was an outpost of the BSAC, and Harding was less than impressed that he had been chosen for this station. Tati was a miserable place consisting of only some tents and a hut in a cleared area of hard, stony earth. All the facilities were terribly basic; even the hut of corrugated galvanised iron that housed the telegraph equipment was rudimentary.

"Nothing," Harding thought, "liked Tati; neither the animals nor the vegetation!" Trees were stunted and the grass was brown and brittle. The occasional small herd of Impala that sometimes came close to the boundary stood under leafless trees desperately seeking any available sliver of shade, huddling mournfully together.

Overseeing the watch at Tati was utterly soul-destroying. It was extremely boring, and provisions were scarce. Above all, Harding's uniform was not suited to the climate.

Stooping slightly as he exited his tent, Harding stood, yawned loudly, then straightened his tunic. He looked forward to a transfer to Fort Victoria, anywhere but here. He took a long drink of warm water from his tin canteen, picked up his rifle that had been leaning against a flimsy tree, and strode to the main gate.

Harding could see immediately that something was not right. Three Matabele warriors were sitting under the shade of a tree, with Trooper Jenkins standing beside them, looking agitated. Wasting no time, he strode to the gate to find out what had happened while he had been resting.

"Jenkins," the Sergeant-Major exclaimed, pointing at the Matabele men, "what's this all about?"

"I don't know, Sir."

"What do you mean you don't know? There are three armed Matabele warriors in the compound. Who are they? Why are they here?"

"I don't know, Sir. A Mr Dawson arrived with them and just told me to watch them."

"Where is this Dawson character?"

"In Dillon's office, Sir."

"Blimey, what's got into this place?" Harding grumbled. "I'm not having three stray Matabele loose in my camp at night. Detain them for the night. Lock them up. I'm going to speak to Dawson. And disarm them!"

"Very good, Sir," Jenkins said.

As Harding turned to go to the office, Jenkins approached the first Matabele. Tucking his rifle under one arm, he reached into his pocket and pulled out a pair of handcuffs.

The first Matabele, called Mantuse, became frightened at seeing what was about to happen. As Jenkins reached for him, as quick as a flash, Mantuse snatched Jenkins's bayonet out of its sheath, turned it and thrust it under Jenkin's ribs. Jenkins died on the spot. Another officer standing nearby tried to react but was too slow, and Mantuse charged him down, driving the bayonet through his heart. He then ran for dear life, with his colleague, Ingubo, hot on his heels.

Hearing the commotion, Sergeant-Major Harding dropped to one knee and fired two shots, instantly killing both fleeing Matabele. The third Matabele stood, traumatised and did not move. He was immediately jumped upon by BSAC men, handcuffed and arrested.

James Dawson emerged from Dillon's office to see one of his charges in handcuffs and his other two lying in pools of blood in the dust.

"What happened?" Dawson exclaimed in a daze.

"Was it you who brought these Matabele into the compound?" Harding demanded.

"Yes, I did."

"Well, what for? Who are they? Are you Dawson?"

Dawson just stared at the bodies lying at his feet. "What...."

"Mr Dawson," Harding demanded, "who are these people? Why are they here? What are you doing wandering around the bush with three armed and dangerous Matabele?"

Dawson looked blankly at Harding. He was in a state of shock. "Oh, my Lord, what have you done? This.... This is.... The implications! Oh my! This is an absolute tragedy. You have no idea what you have done!"

"Please answer me."

"Sir," Dawson composed himself, "these men are emissaries for King Lobengula. They are *en route* to speak to the Colonial High Commissioner in Cape Town. That one there," Dawson pointed to the man in handcuffs, "is Ingubogubo; he is King Lobengula's half-brother."

Harding stared at Dawson in disbelief. "Why didn't you tell us, you fool? You don't just dump strangers here and expect us to know what is going on."

"It's too late; the damage is irreparable. This can't be fixed," Dawson shook his head and sighed heavily. "Let Ingubogubo free. He will be no use to Sir Henry Loch anymore."

Dawson was right. Ingubogubo left the compound the moment he was released, returning to King Lobengula. He had news of the white man's treachery to tell the King.

This incident, the misunderstanding, had inadvertently set the wheels of war in motion.

***

Fred woke at daybreak to find Waller and Black had returned only minutes before. They had become horribly lost in the dark and found their way back by following the sound of the gunshots. Der Huyter was still missing.

Fred found JJ waving off one of his flock as their wagon turned and headed south to the Transvaal.

"You're not going back?" JJ asked Fred.

"On the contrary," Fred smiled, "I have spoken with my wife and we have decided that since we have come this far, we will keep going forward to Fort Victoria. But we have also decided to get there as quickly as possible."

JJ nodded. "I thought that might be your decision."

"My wagon can go much faster than your caravan, and I don't need as much feed as your oxen, so we will press on."

"Thank you for telling me, Meneer Burnham," JJ said, using the Afrikaans salutation for Mister. "You were good company and contributed much to our trek. I wish you and your family a safe journey onward."

"I have learned much, too. I must tell you that I don't believe there will be an uprising with the Matabele. From the things I saw at Tati and words that were spoken, I think peace will be negotiated."

"I understand, my friend," JJ nodded gravely as he ran his fingers through his beard. "I am of the same opinion."

"I wish you well then, and I hope we will cross paths again one day," Fred said with a genuine smile.

Fred shook the big man's hand and returned to his rig. Within ten minutes, the Burnham family was once again on their way. They had been travelling for almost two hours when they came across Der Huyter. He had been treed by a lion all night, and his continued trek when the sun came up left him skittish and even more incapable of finding his way back. He was therefore very grateful to find Fred.

"Follow my tracks back, and you will find your friends," Fred consoled the distraught man. "They are not far behind us."

***

Every day before dark, Fred would guide his buckboard off the track, deep into the bush, and then hide the tracks. By daybreak, the Burnhams were back on the move.

One morning, Blanche heard a wagon approaching from the rear. It was moving a little faster than theirs. Fred, who was walking ahead of the donkeys, as was his custom, pulled them to a halt, and they waited for whoever was behind them to pass. Soon, a cape cart came into view. Only one man drove the six donkeys. When he pulled alongside them, he stopped and smiled at Fred, tipping his hat at Blanche.

"I bid you all good morning," the man said. "When did you leave the American Wild West?"

Fred beamed. "It seems I left a few minutes before you. What gave it away?"

"We have identical Stetson hats. Beaver fur?"

Fred laughed. "Yes, Arizona. Yours?"

"Texan."

"Fred Burnham," Fred reached up and shook the traveller's hand. "My wife, Blanche, and my son, Roderick," he completed the introductions.

"Maurice Gifford at your service," the man grinned. "Where are you headed?"

"Fort Victoria," Fred smiled.

"Good choice, my American friend. Make haste, though; there will be trouble in the land soon."

"So I believe," Fred frowned and glanced at Blanche.

"Can you shoot?" Gifford asked with a wry smile that suggested he knew the answer.

"Yes," Fred allowed a chuckle to escape. "I worked for the American government as a scout. Got tangled up in the Apache wars."

"Ahh...." Maurice laughed. "I was a scout in Canada. We are in the same profession. You must be good. I see you still have your scalp."

Blanche didn't laugh, Gifford noticed, so quickly changed the subject. He reached back and pulled a cardboard box from the cart.

"Look what I have here," he said as he opened the box. "A brand new

Stetson beaver fur hat just like the ones you and I wear. It's a special gift for a good friend of mine in Fort Victoria. Make sure you look him up when you get there. His name is Captain Allan Wilson. He could well use someone with your skills."

"I'll do that, Mr Gifford," Fred smiled broadly.

"Well, I must be off. Time waits for no man. Mrs Burnham, Master Burnham, I bid you farewell. Mr Burnham, good to make your acquaintance, and I look forward to seeing you in Fort Victoria shortly."

"Indeed, Mr Gifford. And safe travels to you," Fred called out.

As Gifford pulled away, he turned in his seat and waved to Fred. "Captain Allan Wilson, don't forget."

Fred turned to look up at Blanche. "Well, he was a delightful person."

"Yes, wasn't he just. This country seems to have attracted a lot of Americans and Canadians."

"And Australians," Fred added. "Right, let's keep pressing on."

Not an hour had passed when Fred, who was leading on foot, abruptly stopped. He put up a hand to signal to Blanche to halt the donkeys. His eyes had been constantly scanning the ground, the trees and the grass, just as the old-timer scouts in America had taught him. Fred's attention to detail had been meticulously honed, and he never missed reading the smallest clue as to what was happening around him. He dropped to his haunches and studied the ground very carefully.

"What's wrong, darling?" Blanche asked, picking up on Fred's concern.

Fred stood, walked to his right a few paces, and carefully looked at the ground. He then signalled to Blanche.

"Come and have a look at this. Bring Roderick," he said.

Blanche put the reins down and alighted, helping Roderick to the ground. When she joined Fred, he was down on his haunches.

"What do you see?" she asked.

"Look at this footprint," Fred pointed to a barely discernible smudge in the dust.

"That's a footprint?" Blanche raised her eyebrows in disbelief.

"Yes, there's a better one. Can you see the toe prints?"

"I can," Roderick said excitedly.

"Good!" Fred exclaimed. "Now, can you see which direction he was travelling?"

"That way," Roderick continued.

"Excellent," Fred encouraged. "I can tell, by looking at this print, and the next one, that he was running, because the space between the prints are quite far apart, and almost in a straight line; not set wide. When someone walks, their footprints are closer in length, but wider apart. So, this man was in a hurry."

"Oh, surely not," Blanche said in disbelief.

"I'm serious," Fred defended his claim. "Look at that grass stalk; it's been trampled. Even that spiderweb over there has been broken. See? To me, the signs say this man was running alongside us to Fort Victoria."

"Alright," Blanche challenged him, "How do you know it was a he, not a she?"

Fred stood and faced his family. He had a huge smile on his face. "Not only can I tell it is a he, but I know who he is."

Blanche laughed out aloud. "Impossible!"

"Tell us how, Father," Roderick asked, animated by this impromptu lesson.

"When I was at the Tati compound, three Matabele emissaries arrived. They were on their way to Cape Town to negotiate for peace. Knowing they might be my enemy one day, I made a point of studying them. It was the first time I had ever seen a Matabele warrior.

"I wanted to get closer, so I made a plan to share my water with them. At first, they refused, but because they looked very agitated and suspicious about being there, I guessed they thought I might be offering them poisoned water, so I took a sip. That relaxed them, and then they were prepared to accept my water.

"While they were drinking, I studied each man very carefully. They were armed, so I studied their weapons, dress, ornaments and decorations. They all had tribal scars on their chests; they looked like burns. One man, who I think was their leader, had broken his little toe on his right foot when he was younger, and it had set badly."

Fred then crouched and picked up a small twig. "Look at this print. The person who made this footprint shows the small toe on the right foot touches the ground very lightly, almost not at all. I think this footprint belongs to that man."

Fred stood again, smiling proudly. "And that, my lovely family, is a lesson on bushcraft and scouting. It is something I love, and, as you know, it was my job before I married you, Blanche."

Blanche smiled and gave Fred a loving hug. "Very clever, darling. But I do have one more question. Why is this man running in this direction on his own, when he is supposed to be travelling to Cape Town with two others?"

"That is a good question, Blanche," Fred said thoughtfully. He cast his thoughts back to the two shots he had heard just after he had left Tati. "I can't answer that, but it doesn't sit well with me. Let's keep moving; we must make haste."

***

The remainder of the trek to Fort Victoria was uneventful. Roderick began to take more interest in the signs of the bush as they journeyed, which pleased Fred. When the smoke from Fort Victoria's cooking fires stimulated their senses of smell, the Burnhams relaxed for the first time in weeks.

Fred reported to the BSAC administration office and was allocated a place to set up camp. He then went out to find Captain Wilson, just as Mr Gifford had suggested. He was easy to find; he wore a brand new Stetson beaver fur hat. Allan was standing at the edge of the parade square watching a drill exercise. He had a swagger stick tucked neatly under his arm that cemented his seniority.

"Captain Wilson?" Fred asked, then saw his epaulettes. "Excuse me, Major Wilson?"

"Indeed," Allan replied, then smiled when he saw Fred's hat. "You must be that American my friend Maurice Gifford met on his way up here."

"Fred Burnham, yes Sir," Fred smiled. "I'm here to offer my services. I understand there is about to be a conflict."

"Thank you, Mr Burnham. I'm always looking for capable people. Gifford told me you were an American scout."

"Indeed," Fred confirmed, but felt it unnecessary to detail his vast experience.

"Good show. I would very much like to have you in my lot. We are a mounted infantry known as the Victoria Rangers."

Fred laughed. "Forgive me, Major, but where are your horses then?"

Allan chuckled. "Well observed! Yes, that is our problem. We expect the horses to arrive in two to three weeks."

"Is there anything I can help you with in the meantime?" Fred offered.

"Not really, not until we receive our horses," Allan said. "I must tell you we are a voluntary unit; there is no payment for your services, and you won't be entitled to any rank, but, if successful, Mr Rhodes will allocate land and mining claims as a reward for services rendered."

Fred nodded slowly. "I understand that, Major; thank you. Although I am happy to volunteer for possible future reward, I think the greater priority is the safety of the citizens."

"You are very perceptive, Mr Burnham. I like that," Allan smiled broadly. "Yes, you are correct, and I wish more people would see it that way. Please report to my admin office and sign up."

"I'll do that, thank you, Major," Fred saluted and turned on his heels.

***

With nothing further to do in Fort Victoria, Fred took the opportunity to visit a nearby ancient stone village that was called Dzimba-hwe. It had been discovered when the explorers visited that part of the world not too long before the Burnhams arrived. The ruins of the stone village were about thirty miles from Fort Victoria, so Fred loaded up his buckboard, and then he, Blanche and Roderick left the hustle and bustle of the settlement. They spent a week exploring the ancient ruins: the various stone walls and a most unusual conical tower. Constructed of grey granite rock and liberally covered in beautiful lichens, these structures excited everyone's imagination the moment they caught sight of them. A high wall surrounding the main part of the structures bore a striking and intricate repeating chevron pattern of rocks near the top. Explorers would walk about in silence as their imagination wondered in awe at what life had been like when the abandoned city of stone had been inhabited.

Fred panned for gold amongst the ruins, hoping he might find artefacts left behind by the original inhabitants of the stone city. To his surprise, he did find some gold beads. Blanche and Roderick were interested in Fred's prospecting activities, so he handed them the pan and went hunting. They, too, found some ancient gold beads. Excitement ran high in the Burnham family.

One evening a wagon arrived and joined their camp. It was none other than the two men they had met on the journey up from South Africa, Pearl Ingram and Robert Bain. The Burnhams couldn't be happier. The friendship Fred forged during his brief encounter with Ingram during the trek was strengthened, and many anecdotes of their time in America were shared, accompanied by much laughter. Blanche enjoyed watching Fred laugh and enjoy himself; it was a soothing balm to her because she knew how unhappy and unsettled he had been in America.

They were all sitting around a fire one evening when the conversation became more serious. The topic of the possible war with the Matabele King could not be avoided.

"The BSAC are worried about war with Lobengula," Fred broached the subject. "They are training hard at the moment."

"We could see that when we rode past," Ingram said. "Fort Victoria is a madhouse."

"We couldn't wait to leave that place," Bain added.

"I've signed up with the Victoria Rangers as a scout," Fred informed his friends. "It's a voluntary unit, so there is no pay for my service, but if they overthrow the King, the spoils are financially very appealing."

"For instance?" Bain asked.

"Six thousand acres of land for farming or ranching, and fifteen mining claims of your choice–you just have to peg and claim the sites. There is also a share of the King's massive herd of cattle. There's a good chance you could be a very wealthy man at the end of this. But," Fred continued more seriously, "that is just a part of why I'm volunteering. If the British are defeated, the King will turn on every white person in this land. Those of us who can't escape will be killed: men, women and children. And, believe me, these Matabele are bloodthirsty."

"You could escape if you saw the tide turning against you, surely?" Bain asked.

"No," Fred shook his head. "You've seen this country. It is vast and difficult to navigate. It is hot here, and we don't know where the rivers are; the land has not been mapped. Finding water is too risky. Plus, we more or less know how the Matabele work–they are similar to the Apaches. They will outrun us before we can get to the border. I would confidently say that those of us still here are well and truly trapped."

A cloak of silence settled on the friends before Ingram spoke. "Do you think the settlers have a chance of overthrowing the King?"

Fred shrugged. "Who knows? I have never seen the settlers fight. I have no idea how they work, but, as you saw, they are taking this seriously in

Fort Victoria."

"You think they need more scouts?" Ingram asked.

"I think they'll take anyone they can get," Fred nodded.

"I'll sign up when we return," Bain nodded. "I value my life, but I also want to make some money–that's why I came here."

"I've already identified some very promising claims if we win," Fred grinned.

Ingram looked sternly at Fred. "You think the Matabele are as bad as the Apaches?"

Fred shrugged. "I don't know. I have had very little to do with them. From the signs on the ground, as we trekked up, I don't think they are as cunning as the Apaches or the Sioux Indians. Their tracks are very easy to read. Some followed us on the journey, but they were not careful at concealment."

Blanche pricked up her ears. "You didn't tell me we were being followed."

Fred smiled. "There was no need to trouble you, my dear. I knew where they were all the time. I had my eye on them, and was sure we were still safe. Remember our examination of the footprints? That helped me to discern that we were still safe, as that warrior at Tati had accepted my offer of water. I have no answer as to why they were there though. Perhaps they had orders to see what was happening on this route."

"Do you think they torture their victims like the Apaches did?" Bain asked.

"I don't know," Fred shrugged. "From what I hear, they kill with spears or a stick with a ball or knob at one end. They call it a *knobkerrie*. Apparently, they use it to club people on the head; if so, it's a quick death."

"I'm going to sign up," Ingram said.

"Me too," Bain concurred. "If the lives of the foreigners, which include us, depend on winning this war, I think it is our duty to sign up."

"Seek out Major Wilson when you get to Fort Victoria. He'll sign you up. You can't miss him: a giant of a man."

Blanche suddenly laughed. "I'd say 'herculean' is a more apt description of Major Wilson, my darling, especially when you are standing next to him."

Ingram and Bain laughed at Blanche's humour.

"I'm not that short," Fred feigned a protest.

"I'd say you are," Ingram continued the joke.

Fred joined in the laughter. "Major Wilson has a very full moustache, and he's wearing one of these," Fred flicked the brim of his hat with his finger.

"He's impossible to miss," Blanche laughed again.

***

When Ingram, Bain and the Burnhams returned to Fort Victoria, the activity in the settlement had increased dramatically. The horses had arrived that morning, and so had some heavy weaponry and extra men. It was chaotic.

Captains Napier, Green, Kirton and Gifford were instructing the men at fever pitch. Even Allan threw himself in as a drill instructor. Lendy had been made a Captain, and because he had experience with cannons, he took command of the one-and-a-half-pound Hotchkiss and the seven-pounder cannon. He made it his responsibility to familiarise himself with the new Maxim machine guns. The Maxims were a fairly new technology in weaponry, invented by an American, Hiram Stevens Maxim, about a decade earlier. It was the first fully automatic machine gun ever invented. It could fire about six hundred rounds a minute, but it had never been tested on a battlefield before. Lendy took a very keen interest in these weapons and spent hours learning how to operate, service, and maintain the new water-cooled machine guns.

Allan enlisted Ingram and Bain into the Scouts division as soon as they returned from their exploration of the ancient Dzimba-hwe stone city. Then, along with Fred, they were cast out like fishing nets around the town perimeters, looking for signs of Matabele in the area.

Once all the new horses had been inspected, Allan allocated them to men based on compatible size and strength. Fred, being a short man, was allocated a small horse. Everyone was given time to get to know their mounts before they were sent to corral them for the night.

The following morning, Allan sent the men to retrieve the horse they had been paired with. Having spent most of his life on horseback, Fred found his mount straight away, but more than half the others either found the wrong horse or could not identify theirs at all.

Allan was both amused and annoyed. He pulled Fred over to his right.

"Obviously, you have equestrian skills. Stay here and help me with this mob," he grumbled.

As the mounts were reallocated to their respective owners, Fred was surprised to see how well Allan already knew his horses. After just a couple of days, Allan knew many of the horses by name, and who its rider should be. Fred immediately gained a great deal of respect for his new Commander; he felt comfortable that the Victoria Rangers were in competent hands with this Scotsman at the helm.

CHAPTER NINETEEN

September 1893

Allan inspected his troops in the parade square. He was pleased with what he saw. He felt confident that his men were ready if they had to go into battle. At the end of each day, Allan would assemble his men and give them a short speech. Without fail, he would include his thanks for their dedication and commitment to the cause.

Allan pushed his men hard, but he also understood the importance of recognition, appreciation and praise given to each and every man, but especially his captains, where at all possible. If they met in the Officers' Mess at night, he would join in and be 'one of them', but he never drank alcohol. By not partaking in alcohol, he showed leadership. By spending time with them, he fostered a spirit of teamwork. His efforts resulted in his men putting in greater effort.

One morning Allan noticed some horsemen entering the fort. He recognised Dr Jameson as one of the riders. Catching Captain Kirton's eye, he signalled that the troops be brought to order, forming up in their respective ranks. A sharp command from Kirton got the entire squad scurrying furiously. In seconds the parade square fell silent as men fell in and formed perfectly straight lines in their given ranks. Everything went quiet. Allan smiled inwardly; his squad was ready for inspection.

Dr Jameson was visibly impressed. The soldier riding to his left looked unamused, though, and frowned at the sudden change that unfolded rapidly in front of him. When they arrived at the parade square, Allan saluted Jameson and invited him to inspect his column.

Later, in the cool of a thatched gazebo, Jameson introduced the soldier

147

who accompanied him as Major Patrick Forbes. Allan knew of him, but they had never met. Although the same rank as Allan, Forbes was just thirty-two years old, five years younger than Allan. He was currently the second in command of the BSAC.

Forbes was a handsome man whose face looked much younger than his years. He had fine brown hair that he kept neatly combed in soft waves, and he sported a full moustache, as was fashionable for men at that time. His uniform was pristine and belied the fact that he had just been on a long horseback journey from Fort Salisbury. Allan took a guess that Forbes was an office-bound tactical soldier and was not keen to test his mettle on the battlefield.

Introductions over, Jameson led Allan and Forbes away from the parade square and stood under the shade of a large tree where no one could overhear them. Jameson then took on a serious tone.

"I have come here to explain my battle plan," he said.

Allan nodded gravely. He was expecting this.

"Major Forbes will command the Salisbury Horse. He has two hundred and fifty-eight men under his command," Jameson said.

Forbes entered the conversation. "My second in command is Captain Henry Borrow; a very competent soldier. I have two cannons and two Maxim machine guns."

Allan was surprised at the tone of Forbes' voice. It lacked authority; it didn't sound anything like he had expected. Caught off guard, Allan didn't reply.

Jameson broke the awkward silence. "What's your structure, Major Wilson?"

Allan snapped back to reality. "The Victoria Rangers has four hundred and fourteen men. My second in command is Captain Lendy, assistant to the Magistrate in Fort Victoria." Allan nodded at Forbes, "I assume you know him, being a member of the Magistrate fraternity? He is also in charge of artillery. I have an excellent team of scouts, in particular three Americans and one Canadian, all with extraordinary skills. I also have a fellow of mixed race called Grootboom, a magnificent tracker who can speak English, isiNdebele and chiShona fluently."

"Excellent," Jameson enthused.

"What are your armaments?" Forbes asked bluntly.

"Three Maxims, a seven-pounder Hotchkiss and a one-and-a-half-pound cannon."

Forbes frowned. "How about a signaller? We will need good communication between our two groups when in the field."

Allan nodded. "Trooper Dennis Dillon. He was stationed at the Tati telegraph station. He is a fine soldier, too."

"Logistics?" Forbes asked.

"As per Dr Jameson's instructions. Three days full rations, then what we find in the field. We have over twenty transport wagons, one prepared as a mobile field infirmary. Because we are going against the Matabele, we have no shortage of Mashona volunteers to support the column as porters, drivers, and even an armed auxiliary force."

"Arming your Mashona volunteers does concern me rather," Forbes said. "You do know the Mashona could join forces with the Matabele and turn on you at the eleventh hour?"

"That theory has been posed often enough," Allan scowled, "but I think it highly unlikely. Nevertheless, we will be on our guard."

"Very good," Jameson smiled. He had heard enough. "When the command is given to assault KoBulawayo, I want the Salisbury Horse and the Victoria Rangers to meet at Iron Mine Hill. Do you know where that is, Major Wilson?"

"I've seen it on a map, and I have someone in my force that has been there before. I will find it, Sir," Allan said.

"Good. Major Forbes will take command of the combined force once you and Major Forbes meet at Iron Mine Hill."

Allan was surprised to hear this. "Very good, Sir," he said, though he was unhappy with the arrangement.

It didn't make sense. Despite Forbes and Allan having equal rank, Allan was his senior and had over four hundred men under his command, compared to the two-hundred-and-fifty men Forbes had. Allan even had more armaments than Forbes.

What bothered Allan the most was that he had fought in three wars and had significant combat experience, whereas he was certain that Forbes had no combat experience at all. He wanted to ask about Forbes's experience in the field but then thought the better of it.

"When do you expect to issue orders to march?" Allan asked the Doctor.

"I will communicate by coded message," Jameson craftily avoided the question. "When you get a message from me that contains the word 'Dunvegan', you must commence your march to Iron Mine Hill immediately. Once there, wait for us to join you."

"What's the battle plan, Sir?" Allan pressed.

"Good question," Jameson smiled broadly. 'Once the two forces combine at Iron Mine Hill, we will march on KoBulawayo. Our route will take us from the northeast. There will be two separate columns; Colonel Goold-Adams of the Bechuana Border Police will move from Tati, from the south, and another BBP force led by Commandant Piet Raaff will come up with King Khama's forces from the southwest. If Lobengula wants to give us any trouble, he will have to fight at least three fronts. We will coordinate our marches to arrive in KoBulawayo at the same time."

"Very good, Sir," Allan congratulated Jameson.

It was Forbes' turn to add to the discussion. "Lobengula has spies all over the land, and the moment he sees any of us on the move, we suspect he will mobilise his warriors and engage us. We must use our scouts wisely to clear the path ahead of us, or at least warn the columns in good time."

"I understand," Allan nodded gravely.

It took just over a week for Allan to receive a message from Dr Jameson in Fort Salisbury. It contained only five words; *'Capt Dunvegan accepts your request'*. One hour later, the Victoria Rangers were on the move–Fred hardly had time to say goodbye to Blanche and Roderick.

***

King Lobengula sat on his royal wagon and addressed his Indunas and impis. Mjaan stood beside him, looking ominous, his face like thunder.

"You have asked me for the command to attack the whites in the north. I give you that command now," Lobengula roared.

There was a thunderous cheer! This is what his people were desperately wanting. Thousands of warriors on the outer edge of the war council heard the shout of jubilation, and they took up the joyous cry.

Lobengula waited for the noise to abate. "Our loyal spies have told me Rhodes' army has begun to move towards KoBulawayo."

Another raucous cry of exultation erupted around the meeting area. The wives in the huts surrounding the royal village immediately knew what had been decided.

"The white men have deceived us. They say they want peace, but they want war. They want our country."

There was a low rumble of disapproval that followed this statement.

"I sent emissaries to talk peace, as they themselves insisted, but they killed them instead. The time for talking is finished."

More roars of joy erupted from the gathering.

"I have chosen Induna Manonda to lead his impi to victory. Two thousand warriors will wash their spears on white men's blood. Then, when their army is defeated, our warriors will go to Fort Victoria and kill everyone there."

The howl of approval was deafening. Lobengula smiled.

"After Fort Victoria, they will go to Fort Salisbury and kill every one of the remaining whites. We will wipe our country clean of the white men."

The roar of approval erupted even louder. It was time for jubilation on a grand scale.

"But that is not all," Lobengula held a warning finger in the air. The crowd went silent in anticipation. "There are two more armies coming from the Big River in the south. I will send Induna Gumbo and two impis to defeat them."

The crowd went into raptures. They would regain their land.

Later that afternoon King Lobengula briefed his Indunas, Manonda, Mjaan and Gumbo. "Manonda, move north until your spies meet the white army, then wait for them to sleep. When the moon is high, attack swiftly. They cannot see in the dark."

Manonda bowed his head. "That will be done, my King. Our attack will be fast and decisive."

"Take Induna Mjaan. When you have beaten the whites, proceed to Fort Victoria," Lobengula demanded.

"Yes, my King," Manonda bowed his head again in reverence. "We shall run to Fort Victoria swiftly. The whites there will have no warning of our attack. I have seen their defenses in the place they call Fort Victoria. Only old men and women defend the fort."

A sinister grin crossed Lobengula's lips. "That is good. Make this a slaughter they will talk about for generations. I want the enemy to feel the Matabele's power and cunning." He then addressed his faithful bodyguard. "Induna Mjaan, you are my eyes and ears. When Induna Manonda overthrows the white army, you must return immediately and tell me about the fight. You must not remain for Manonda's run to their cities. I want to know immediately when his impi has beaten the white men's army."

"Yes, King," Mjaan bowed in reverence. "I will return with good news. I ask permission for my son, Londisizwe, to join me. I wish him to wash his spear with the white men's blood."

"Permission is granted. Now, Induna Gumbo, take your men to the Mangwe Pass. All armies from the south must pass through there. The rocks and mountains will give you protection from their bullets. You must take no survivors. Take your brother to be my eyes and ears."

"I will do that, my King," Gumbo said solemnly.

"Now go, all of you," Lobengula said. "The King has spoken."

CHAPTER TWENTY
October 1893

Allan steered his horse off to the right of the Victoria column, then halted. He watched as more than twenty wagons and his heavy armaments rumbled past, kicking up a soft cloud of dust and dried grass. Over four hundred men flanked the left and right of the wagons, protecting them from a surprise attack, all the while either watching for danger in the distance or scanning the ground for signs of the enemy.

Allan saw Captain Charles White passing. "Captain," he called.

White was in charge of the scouts. He immediately responded and rode over to his commander. "Sir?"

"We're not far from Iron Mine Hill now. Please take some scouts with you and clear the way ahead. Stay about three miles forward, and if you see signs of the enemy, send one of the scouts back to report to me."

"Yes, Sir," White acknowledged enthusiastically.

"If the enemy threatens you, engage them. We will hear your gunshots, so I will send reinforcements."

"Very good, Major," White said, wheeling his horse around.

Fred watched this exchange. He had a feeling his division would soon be called to action. He was proven correct when White selected him, Ingram, Captain Campbell, and another scout called Dollar to accompany him.

The scout group cantered forward, fanned out and began checking the ground for signs of Matabele warriors.

When the sun had just passed its zenith, the scouts found a large area where a herd of cattle had recently passed. Fred dismounted and checked the ground carefully.

"Captain White," he signalled. "There are a lot of herders following these cattle."

"How many?"

"Hard to tell, Sir. Thirty, maybe forty or more; too many for a herd of cattle. There are hoof prints both on top and under footprints. I would say these are warriors ahead and behind this herd."

"Very good. Let's follow these cattle and see what it is."

When the five scouts crested a hill, they saw a sight that surprised them. Two hundred yards ahead was a herd of cattle, three hundred strong, herded by ten men. There were about one hundred warriors ahead of the herd, and a further one hundred warriors behind them.

"Those cattle belong to the Mashona," White said. "Soon, they will be in the hills and unable to be retrieved. We must intercept them immediately and return them to their rightful owners."

"Sir," Ingram frowned, "There are over two hundred of them and only five of us. And they have rifles."

"There's no time to wait for backup," White remarked. "Besides, they can't aim to save their lives."

Dollar spoke for the first time that day. "I think they will be very surprised to find five men confronting their lot."

"I agree," White said. "Let's go. Burnham, you take the right flank; Captain Campbell take the left with Dollar. Ingram, follow me."

They charged down the hill, the Matabele stopping at the sheer audacity of what was unfolding. About one hundred yards away, a firefight erupted, forcing the BSAC men to dismount and retaliate.

White was correct; the warriors were stunned. Half ran for cover, and the other half returned fire. Once again, White was correct in his assumptions; the Matabele were poorly trained in shooting with modern weapons.

Kneeling, Fred took his time picking off his targets while listening to a hail of bullets cracking overhead. He realised one of the reasons the Matabele warriors' aim was so bad was because they fired on the run, at the same time holding their heavy shields and spears in the hand that held the rifle's stock. It was no wonder, Fred thought, that their aim was all over the place.

Suddenly, a giant of a Matabele man ran towards Fred, staring him down as he closed the distance. He was a brave man, and his determination fascinated Fred a moment longer than it should have. The Matabele stopped, threw his shield and spears to the ground, aimed at Fred, and fired.

The bullet ripped past his head, lightly grazing his temple. The sound of the knock against Fred's skull reverberated through his body. Fred lifted his rifle, but the warrior's next bullet hit the ground just ahead of him and kicked dust and stones into his face. Temporarily blinded, Fred rubbed his eyes quickly, then returned fire.

Lead was exchanged during the following seconds, but, in the end, the fortunes of war favoured Fred.

When backup arrived, the warriors were driven off. Most of the cattle were eventually recovered and returned to the rear, where they were put with the other cattle that were travelling with them. The column had formed a protective laager the moment the shooting was heard. This was a tactic that had been learned from the Boer commanders.

The return of the cattle to the Mashona had an immediate and positive effect on the Mashona who accompanied the army. Suddenly, the Mashona realised how the white man could protect them from the raiding Matabele. The hundreds of Mashona supporters that followed the Victoria Column were jubilant. This joy also eased the BSAC's constant fear that the Mashona might turn on them at any stage.

When Fred returned to the laager, Allan was immediately by his side.

"How badly are you hurt, Burnham?" he asked with concern.

"I'm fine, Major Wilson," Fred shrugged. "A graze, that's all."

"Good. Let's get you cleaned up. I think things are going to get very hectic soon."

"Captain Campbell took a bullet to the hip, Sir. Our men are bringing him up now. They should be here shortly," Fred said sadly.

"I'll advise the medical team immediately; thank you, Burnham."

Captain Campbell was the first casualty of the Victoria Column. Later that night, he became the first white man to die at the hands of the Matabele.

***

When the Victoria Rangers arrived at Iron Mine Hill, there was no sign of the Salisbury Horse. Allan sent Fred, Ingram and Bain to scout for them, then escort them to the column.

Fred found them, and the following day he led them to Iron Mine Hill, where they joined the Victoria Rangers. Jameson, who was with the Salisbury Horse, immediately called a leader's meeting.

Allan met with Forbes and Jameson under the shade of one of the wagons–Jameson's war office, which also doubled as his living quarters. There was an officer with Jameson and Forbes that Allan had not met. He was introduced as John Willoughby, Jameson's military advisor.

In his mid-thirties, Willoughby was well-spoken and very polite, but Allan could immediately tell that Willoughby was not pleased with his predicament.

Jameson took up the conversation. "Tomorrow, I want to break camp and proceed to the Shangani River, the border of Matabeleland. I would like our columns to cross into their territory the day after tomorrow if possible."

"If I may?" Allan requested permission to speak.

"Of course," Jameson nodded his agreement.

"With my experience in the Zulu wars and with what happened yesterday with the Matabele encounter, following which Captain Campbell tragically lost his life, I think we must, at all costs, avoid a direction that goes through a forested area. Specifically, the Somabula Forest."

"Please explain," Jameson asked.

"The Matabele are experts at close combat. They cannot shoot straight; they've not been trained, and I think they know that, so they rely on getting close to their enemy and utilising their spears.

"Furthermore, they have cover in a forest, and our Maxims will have a problem in that type of domain. They also have numbers–vast numbers. In a wooded area, we will be overrun easily. We need.... It is imperative that we stay in the open ground to have a chance of surviving an onslaught by these warriors."

Forbes nodded thoughtfully. "I believe the Somabula Forest stretches from KoBulawayo to Salisbury. It will be almost impossible to avoid it."

"We can follow the outer limits," Allan suggested, "and I can ask my scouts to find a clear route. But I am certain that, if we enter a forest, we will take many casualties."

"Very good," Jameson agreed. "Please put your best scouts on this task."

Willoughby turned to Jameson. "On the subject of the Maxim, you are all aware that it has never been tested in battle before. We cannot put too much hope on this new weapon."

"It will be fine," Jameson smirked. "We have trained relentlessly on them. Fear not."

Forbes moved the discussion along. "I suggest that when we laager from now on, we combine our columns and strengthen one laager, rather than have two separate ones."

Allan was hoping Forbes wouldn't suggest this. Willoughby saw the hesitation in Allan's expression.

"A suggestion, if I may?" Allan said. "What you say is sound. Ordinarily, I would agree if we were against the Boers or an enemy with smaller numbers, but experience tells me that it will not be the best idea against the Matabele."

"Your suggestion?" Forbes asked irritably.

"We keep our laagers separate and at a distance of three to four hundred yards apart. This way, the enemy has to split itself and contend with a counter-offensive from two directions. The distance apart will also allow for an overlap of our firepower and will cause the enemy to instinctively refrain from moving into the area between the two camps. Of course, if we are too close together, we risk shooting our own men if the enemy manages to get into the gap. We, therefore, cannot allow that to happen."

Willoughby nodded and looked at Jameson. "I agree with the Major. Sound advice."

"Agreed," Jameson smiled. "I can see you have vast experience in the field, Major Wilson."

"Thank you, Sir," Allan said humbly, relieved that his opinion had been accepted.

"The Mashonas and our support column?" Forbes asked. "Inside or outside the laager?"

"Outside," Allan didn't hesitate. "It will be too crowded inside if we are under attack. If we set their camp another five hundred yards from the laager, they won't be a target for the Matabele."

"Very good," Forbes nodded his agreement.

The meeting continued for another hour before they broke to plan their departure in the morning. It required a two-day trek from Iron Mine Hill to get to the Shangani River.

Allan called a meeting with his scouts and explained the importance of the route that they would need to take in order to keep the upper hand. Fred knew that, from that moment on, he would be in the saddle until they reached KoBulawayo, if they reached there at all.

***

Fred sat astride his horse and looked at Ingram, who carefully studied the ground from his saddle as they rode along slowly.

"Ingram," Fred caught his friend's attention. "That river ahead, I think that's the Shangani River."

"The distance would indicate that," Ingram agreed. "Any sign of the enemy?"

"No," Fred looked to his left. "Nothing that I can see."

"I think we would be safe to return with the news that we have found the river. The column will set up camp here tonight. Wilson will be pleased we are on schedule."

"He will," Fred grinned. "I think the Salisbury Horse could set up over there," Fred pointed to his left, "and Victoria over there," he pointed to the right. "Nice open ground between them."

"Let's suggest we put the support wagons and staff to the east. If the Matabele are going to attack, they will probably come from the west."

"Good idea," Fred nodded. "Let's return with our findings."

By late afternoon, the laagers had been formed. Men went about their preparations for war while the support contingent slaughtered a cow and boiled up a traditional maize porridge for the evening meal. Allan, Forbes and Jameson walked around the fortress and studied the Shangani River.

"Not much of a river to boast about," Allan ventured.

"Rather piddly," Jameson concurred. 'Not what I expected."

"I assume it would be significant in the wet season," Forbes mulled.

"This is the wet season," Allan smirked. "Well, that's what the experts tell me."

"As usual, they are wrong." Jameson chuckled. "Major Forbes, if Lobengula's men attacked today, or tomorrow, which direction do you think they would favour?"

Forbes looked around. "From the west, of course."

Allan cleared his throat. "Not necessarily so. KoBulawayo is in the west, of course, but I wouldn't put it past the enemy to surprise us from the east, simply because we would not be expecting that."

Forbes shuffled uncomfortably. "It really doesn't matter which way they come from; we are prepared."

"That's good to know," Jameson said in relief, looking to change the subject. He wanted to avoid a confrontation between his two commanders.

Jameson couldn't discount that Wilson had vast combat experience, had served longer, and was physically more powerful and imposing than Forbes. Wilson was also Forbes' senior by age, but Jameson chose to ignore that. He had made his decision; he wanted Forbes to be the overall commander, come hell or high water, and whether the troops believed it to be personal, or whatever they wanted to believe, he really didn't care.

Later, when Jameson and Forbes had retired to the war office wagon for the night, Allan was still walking about his laager, inspecting the guard, and ensuring shifts were functioning. His last task for the night was to check in on the scouts, and he found Fred sitting by a small fire with Ingram. Fred was writing a letter. They tried to jump to their feet when they saw him, but Allan stopped them with an outstretched hand.

"Good evening, chaps," he said with a broad smile. "Who's on patrol at the moment?"

"Bain and Gifford, Sir," Fred confirmed.

"Good show," Allan nodded.

"Ingram and I will replace them shortly."

"Perfect. Writing a letter back home, Burnham?"

"To my wife, Blanche, Sir. I left her and my son at Fort Victoria. I'm sure a rider will be heading back there soon."

"Of course," Allan agreed. "Be careful when you return from your patrol tonight, gentlemen," Allan warned. "Our men are trigger-happy at the moment."

"We're aware of that, Sir," Ingram frowned. "We were just talking about that now. Our shift will finish around five o'clock, so we will stay outside the laager until morning."

"Wise move," Allan nodded. "Be sharp, chaps. We are in Matabele country now."

"Yes, Sir," Fred agreed.

"Good night," Allan nodded and moved off.

"Well, we had better be at it then," Ingram sighed. "Bain and Gifford will be back any moment."

Fred stood. "Yes, let's go."

When Bain and Gifford entered the laager, they quickly reported to Fred and Ingram, who then silently slipped out into the darkness of the African bush. They struck out about one hundred and fifty yards, then began a stealthy circumnavigation of the entire camp. Because it was so dark they could not look for signs on the ground, so they had to rely on sound and smell.

By two o'clock, they completed the circle of the laagers and found an old tree with a naturally occurring shallow depression beside it. It was well situated, and they were suitably concealed. Both laagers could be seen, one slightly to the right and one off to the left. The support laager was behind them, hidden by some trees. In a quiet whisper, Fred suggested to Ingram that they use that hollow as their lookout for the remainder of the night. They suspected it was too dangerous to scout about and risk being fired upon by some skittish youngster from the Salisbury Horse. They settled in and waited for sunrise.

***

Indunas Manonda and Mjaan crouched behind a rock. Their adrenaline was pumping. Behind them, two thousand silent, energised warriors waited for the command to attack.

"It is time," Manonda whispered hoarsely.

"I think you should wait for your scout to return with the news that they are all asleep," Mjaan suggested in a low whisper.

"He is taking too long."

"Then let that be the reason to wait. After all, you sent him; it was your order."

Manonda wanted to grunt his frustration at Mjaan, but he knew he had to maintain silence.

A dark shadow slipped into view and silently squatted beside the Indunas.

"It is good," the scout said. "They have guards, but they are asleep."

Manonda grinned. It was so dark that there was no glint of his teeth. "Let us begin."

Manonda and Mjaan quietly moved back to the ranks of their warriors and passed the message to be ready. They all rose and silently crept forward. Mjaan moved to the tree where his son, Londisizwe, was anxiously waiting.

"My son, when you hear the first scream of death, you must run in and spear the first man you find. It is time for you to wash your spear."

Londisizwe sneered. "I will spear many."

"I will not fight; I am the King's eyes and ears. Now, you are my eyes and ears. Return quickly."

Londisizwe nodded his understanding and slipped into the dark.

Manonda was the first to step into the laager. Just as his scout had said, the guard was fast asleep and snoring. He had a rifle in his hands, which was lying across his chest. Manonda raised his spear above his head and was about to thrust it into the guard's chest, when the man turned over and muttered something in the Mashona language.

Manonda froze. He couldn't understand why a Mashona man was fighting with the whites. Carefully he brought the spear down to the man's throat. The sharp prick woke the guard instantly.

"Who are you," Manonda said in isiNdibele.

"I protect the cattle," the man said in Shona, his eyes wide in terror.

Manonda only understood the word for 'cattle', and suddenly realised they weren't in the white man's laager. In anger, he thrust the spear into the man's throat.

The guard convulsed and pulled the trigger.

***

Fred and Ingram suddenly spun around.

"What was that?" Fred whispered, trying to make sense of the gunshot.

Suddenly there was a bloodcurdling scream from the support laager, then another, then many. Fred and Ingram swivelled in their shallow hole to see where the terrified screams were coming from. They couldn't see a thing in the darkness.

Suddenly, Major Allan Wilson's powerful voice rolled across the open field from the Victoria Ranger's laager.

"Fire!"

At once, the Victoria laager erupted with brilliant flashes as men let loose with their rifles. Fred and Ingram turned to look at the laager and saw the most impressive sight. Gunfire flashes erupted from two levels, one from the top of the wagons and another from under the wheels.

"My Lord God Almighty," Fred said in awe when he witnessed the incredible show of firepower. The flashes erupting from the weapons were mesmerising.

Right behind the opening volley of fire, two Maxim machine guns exploded into life. At six hundred rounds per minute, the sight and sounds were like nothing Fred and Ingram had seen before. The Salisbury Horse sprang to life moments later, and organised pandemonium erupted. Noise, flashes and smoke suddenly turned the serene African night into a ferocious display of suffering and death. Shadows of trees and branches flickered, and, moments later, people were running in all directions.

A bullet sheered a blade of grass with a sharp click right next to Fred, and instinctively, he and Ingram ducked low into the shallow depression.

"Ingram!" Fred exclaimed. "Stay down, they can't see what they are shooting at."

"Where're they attacking from?" Ingram shouted back.

"I think they are in the support wagons."

The bullets overhead and the screams intensified, and Fred and Ingram pressed themselves harder to the ground, not that they could really get any lower.

"If the natives run to the laager for protection, they will get mowed down," Fred yelled.

"Don't sit up, Burnham. Stay down," Ingram reiterated, fearing Fred might try and stop any Mashona from fleeing.

Shadows sped past them, only to give agonising screams as bullets tore through their bodies like butter and sent them crashing into a bloody, tumbling mess.

A fleeing Mashona was shot through the heart and tumbled onto Ingram. The man was dead before he hit the ground. Ingram quickly rolled the warm, wet body away.

"Bloody hell, Burnham!" Ingram exclaimed. "They're all over the place!"

"Don't move. Wait," Fred repeated, his heart rate soaring as the disaster unfolded.

Manonda ran at full speed towards the deadly sound and sharp flashes.

He was filled with bloodlust and felt invincible. The time had come to avenge his nation and people.

Suddenly, the group of Mashona shadows he was chasing fell to the ground, screaming in nerve-shattering pain. He baulked and checked his stride. Something told him things were not right. In the darkness, a shadow ran past him in the opposite direction. He was sure it was one of his warriors, but he was not holding his spears or shield. In the flashing illuminations, he noticed the warrior was drenched in blood.

Panicking, Manonda turned on his heels and ran for safety; bullets whizzed and whined past his ears. He felt sick and ran as fast as he could. He clipped a tree with his shoulder and fell heavily to the ground, only to be bowled over by another of his impi the instant he tried to stand up. Finally, he made it to the safety of a granite rock, ducking behind it.

Mjaan was already crouched behind the rock. He was confused. He had never heard such a din from rifles. He waited for Manonda to calm down and recover his breath.

A distant voice called out, and suddenly, all at once, the shooting stopped. The deadly sound that filled the bushland was replaced by the wailing and screaming of the mortally wounded.

"What happened?" Mjaan asked. His voice was shaky.

"I don't know," Manonda said in confusion. "There are thousands of white people there. Thousands!"

"That is not so. We have both seen them on their march yesterday, and there are not many."

"Mjaan," Manonda leaned back on the rock. His breathing was still ragged. "We cannot fight them in the dark. We cannot see where the enemy is."

"It is the King's instruction to attack at night."

"It cannot be done," Manonda said bluntly, kicking his legs out before him. He was not going to stand; he couldn't, the fear sapped every ounce of his strength.

Mjaan tentatively put his head over the rock and listened to the moans of the dying. "Gather your men. We meet at the tall trees and decide how to attack them another way."

"As you command," Manonda agreed and forced himself into a crouch. He paused, trying desperately to gather himself. He signalled his lieutenants and set them to call the impi in retreat.

Mjaan got onto all fours. "I must look for my son. I must see if he lives." As stealthily as a leopard, he slipped into the darkness.

***

"Cease fire!" Allan's powerful voice boomed through the laager. The shooting came to an abrupt halt. He was standing on top of a wagon, alert and peering into the darkness. He realised their 'friendlies' were running to them for protection.

He cupped his hands and looked over to the Salisbury Horse, which was still firing randomly into the darkness. "Cease fire!" Allan repeated more forcefully.

Captain Henry Borrow couldn't hear Allan over the noise, but he saw the flashes from Victoria abruptly stop.

"Cease fire," Borrow bellowed at the top of his voice. His command was heeded.

"Maxims," Allan shouted as loud as he could, "hold your fire. Riflemen, fire on anything that moves."

It was a tough order, he knew that. The people out there were friendly, and in need of help and protection, but there was also an enemy amongst them, and in the dark, they could not tell them apart.

Somebody lit a torch, and the inside of the Victoria laager began to illuminate eerily.

"Douse it!" Allan demanded urgently. "Douse it quickly." The light in the laager would have made them blind targets. The soldier obliged immediately.

Silence reigned.

"Anyone hurt?" Allan called out. He knew Borrow would be asking the same question over at Salisbury.

A mumble of no's rumbled through the camp.

"Trooper Dillon," Allan called into the darkness.

"Sir," came the reply.

"Send a signal to Major Forbes that we are alright. Ask about his situation and warn him to expect another attack."

"Yes, Sir," Dillon called from the interior.

"Soldiers, reload and stand fast," Allan bellowed. He knew the sun would be up in a few hours, and that was when he expected the next onslaught. At least, he thought, they would have something to aim at.

"Major Wilson," Captain White called out.

"What is it?"

"Two of my scouts are still out there."

"Bugger," Allan groaned silently. "Names?"

"Burnham and Ingram, Sir."

"Bugger," he grumbled under his breath again. He looked over to the Salisbury camp and saw Dillon's Aldis Lamp flashing its message. A moment later, a reply came back from their signaller.

"Salisbury Horse–No casualties, Sir," Dillon shouted over his shoulder.

A soft rumble of relief washed over the laager.

Allan looked into the darkness and took a deep breath. Cupping his hands around his mouth, he called out the Australian 'Coo-ee', and waited for a reply. It came back a moment later, but it was the American version.

"Yee-haa," Fred's voice drifted across the open plain.

Allan smiled. They were not far off to his right.

"Are you hurt?" he called.

"No, Sir," Burnham's voice was soft but clear in the still night.

"Hold fast," Allan called back. He turned to Dillon. "Dillon, message Salisbury. Hold fire; we need to retrieve two men. I need confirmation."

"Yes, Sir," Dillon immediately started flashing his code across to Salisbury Horse.

Allan watched the flashes dancing through the night, then turned his attention to the silent bush. Groans of agony had subsided somewhat but were still distressing to hear. He grimaced. He knew they would have to listen to that all night, and it was not good for morale.

"Confirmed," Dillon called back. "You have one minute."

"Burnham, Ingram, get in here, now!" Allan bellowed. "Captain Kirton, guide them in."

Running at a crouch, Fred and Ingram ran for the laager. Kirton exited the laager between two wagon wheels and whistled in sharp bursts to guide them to safety. In seconds, they were inside, and the all-clear was sent to Borrow.

"Stand fast, men," Allan shouted across the laager. "Stay alert; they will rush us again."

***

Mjaan paced angrily around the dishevelled, humiliated impi. He saw

Londisizwe standing with a group of fellow warriors. Relieved he was unhurt, Mjaan went to him and grabbed his son's arm. He roughly led him a few paces away.

"What did you see?" Mjaan demanded.

"Ghaw!" Londisizwe shook his head in dismay. "There are too many of them."

Mjaan's ire rose. "Did you wash your spear on a white man?"

"No, Father, I could not get close to them. Nobody could. Their bullets chased us away."

"Ghaa!" Mjaan exclaimed and walked away.

He found Manonda by a tree, pretending to be brave, but he could tell he was frightened. Mjaan could not believe there were more white soldiers than they had spied on the previous day; it was impossible!

"Manonda," Mjaan confronted him, "How many have you lost?"

The Induna shook his head in shame. "Maybe one hundred are missing. Another one hundred are wounded and cannot fight. I think they will die before the sun comes up."

Mjaan looked to the eastern horizon. The sky was lightening to indigo. From what Manonda implied, the wounded were probably dead already.

"We must attack again in the daylight, so we can see them and shoot straight."

Manonda looked disheartened. He sighed heavily.

"You will attack," Mjaan said angrily, "and I will attack with you. If you do not, I will report to the King, and you know what he will do."

Manonda puffed his chest out. "We will attack, and we will win this time. Fighting in the dark is no good. If we can see the enemy, we will be victorious."

"Good, now get your men together; we move when the sun is above the trees. Place them in the Horns of the Buffalo formation, and we attack from that side," Mjaan waved to the south. "Now, go."

***

Captain Napier saw a movement in the tree line to the south. It was a fair way off beyond the open plain, but he was sure he saw a shimmer of something, perhaps the sharp edge of a spear.

When he saw the glint again, he knew he had not been mistaken. "Enemy south!" he called loudly.

The Victoria laager sprang into action, manning their posts with well-trained discipline and precision.

"Trooper Dillon," Allan shouted. "Signal Salisbury. Enemy south."

"Yes Sir!" came the quick response.

Allan climbed to the top of a southernmost wagon and stared into the distance. He was comfortable with all the open ground before them. He looked at the Salisbury laager and saw Major Forbes standing on top of another wagon shouting orders.

Anticipation heightened; weapons were at the ready. Then, as if by magic, a massive impi of Matabele emerged from the tree line. The warriors started chanting and hitting their hard rawhide shields with their spears as they slow-marched towards the two columns. The noise was intimidating, and Allan felt a cold shiver snake down his spine. The Matabeles' feathered headgear made them look taller, dangerous, and most fearsome.

"Hold your fire," Allan called, steadying his men. "Hold your fire."

The warriors advanced slowly and began fanning out. Allan could see the buffalo horn formation falling into place; he had seen it before, and it was enough to make his blood run cold. He was tempted to tell Dillon to warn Forbes of this–he didn't trust Forbes' experience in warfare. He stopped himself, though; mainly because he knew that time was not on his side. Allan simply hoped that Forbes had spotted it.

"There are thousands of them," someone shouted from the firing line.

"Hold," Allan said firmly. He raised his right arm in the air to reinforce his command. "Wait."

The chanting got louder, and the Matabele warriors began to jog faster. Then, a moment later, the chant became a war cry, and the jog turned into a full-speed sprint. Their left and right flanks began to spread out in perfect symmetry.

"Hold!" Allan demanded again.

He needed the warriors to get closer and hoped Forbes was holding fire too. He glanced towards Forbes and saw him standing like himself, right hand in the air, watching him. Allan smiled, turned to face Forbes and, with a salute, Allan handed the leadership to Forbes.

Forbes turned to face the streaming mass of warriors and picked a tuft of grass that he estimated to be about one hundred yards from his laager. He would call the command to fire when the enemy reached that point.

It came only seconds later. Forbes dropped his hand and gave the command to open fire. In sync, Allan commanded his troops to open fire too. Over one hundred and seventy bullets ripped through the Matabele assault every second. And then the cannons joined in.

The Matabele stood no chance against the whites' defences. Hundreds of brave warriors stumbled to the ground in seconds, either dead or mortally wounded.

The charge faltered, but a courageous cry from the rear rallied the warriors, and they rose to the charge a second time. They, too, were cut down instantly. A third time, they charged, but by now, the Matabele impis had been reduced to less than half in number. The warriors didn't need an order to retreat; they knew that they could not attack again. Those who were able turned and ran back to the tree line.

Allan watched the retreating army. "Cease fire!" he called. "Reload. Make ready and stand fast." He wasn't going to risk being unprepared if there was another charge.

"Captain Green, is the rear secure? Any wounded?" Allan's commands rang out over the laager.

"Perimeter secure," came Green's response.

"No wounded, Sir" someone called across the laager.

Dillon shouted from his heliograph. "All secure at Salisbury. One wounded, one dead."

Allan grimaced. "Thank you, Trooper Dillon," Allan acknowledged the various verbal reports. "Scouts, report to me."

Fred, Ingram and White left their posts at a run and joined the other scouts at the base of the wagon that Allan stood upon. He climbed down and faced the men. It was the first time he had seen the scouts in daylight since before the original engagement. He was shocked to see Ingram, covered in thick, dried blood.

"Are you alright, Ingram?"

"Not my blood, Sir. A slain Mashona fell on me during the night attack."

Allan was relieved. "Gentlemen, please scout outside the perimeter and let me know if they are retreating or regrouping for another attack. Check northwards, and I'll ask Forbes to get his scouts to check southwards. Go on horseback. Any sign of trouble, double back here fast."

The scouts responded immediately, and soon their horses' hooves were thundering across the open veldt. Quickly, though, the scouts were forced to reign in their mounts. Hundreds of wounded lay strewn in their path. The number of dead was horrifying.

Fred sat in his saddle and stared at the carnage at his feet. "Oh my Lord," he said in stunned disbelief.

He looked over at Ingram, who was also visibly shocked. Beside him, White leaned to his right and heaved violently.

"Captain White," Fred tried to draw White's attention to himself.

White retched again, then wiping his mouth across his sleeve, he looked across to Fred, a look of dread smeared across his face.

"Are you alright, Captain?" Fred asked.

White took a deep breath. "I've never seen so many dead people before–slaughter on such a scale," he stammered.

"It's alright, Captain," Fred said reassuringly. He knew he had to take White's mind off the carnage in the field. "Best we keep moving; we have a job to do."

"I must go back and tell Major Forbes what happened out here. He needs to do something." White said, then leaned forward and vomited violently again. "There's one down here who's still alive."

Fred looked back at the laager and saw Dr Jameson and some of his medical assistants moving forward. Many of the other officers were also advancing towards the battleground.

"The medical officers are coming, Captain. Let them do their job now. We must do ours."

White groaned as he sat uncertainly in his saddle. Ingram nudged his horse close to Fred.

"Fred," Ingram said softly, "he's no good to us; let him go back."

"You're right," Fred nodded in agreement. "Captain," Fred spoke up, "go back; we will complete our sweep of the area. Please report to Major Wilson, and tell him that we have gone on ahead."

White nodded unhappily, then, pulling on the reins, turned his mount and walked off. He was a broken man.

Fred looked at Ingram, a deep frown creasing his face. "How are you?"

"I'm alright. I've dealt with death before."

"This is shocking, though," Fred said as he looked at the dead bodies surrounding them.

"I must admit, I've never seen anything like this," Ingram scowled.

Fred shook his head in dismay. "This should never have happened. This was a massacre; they had no cover. Why didn't they stop their attack as soon as they saw what was happening?"

Ingram cast his eyes over the field of death. "I've never seen bravery on a scale like that. I didn't realise how deep loyalty to a King can be."

"Let's get on with it then," Fred suddenly focussed his attention on the distant tree line and spurred his horse forward.

The BSAC soldiers counted over six hundred dead Matabele in the field that day. More disturbing was the number of warriors that later fell on their spears in shame. A man they assumed to be a Matabele commander was found in a tree. He had hung himself with a leather strap.

When Fred and Ingram returned with the news that the enemy had fully retreated, they found several men struggling to deal with the massacre. One soldier was dry retching under a wagon. Allan was consoling him along with some of the other disturbed men.

"No sign of the enemy, Sir," Fred informed Allan.

"Thank you, Burnham. Please make sure you and Ingram eat something and get some liquid into you. I think we have a reprieve for the moment."

"It's hell out there, Sir," Ingram said. The sadness in his voice could not be mistaken.

"So I've heard," Allan nodded. "I'll go out there soon enough to see what happened, but, for now, I need to see to the well-being of our men."

***

Allan mounted his horse and then rode to Captain Lendy, who was attending to the Maxim.

"Captain Lendy," Allan caught his attention. "There's a meeting at the Salisbury laager. As my second-in-command, I'd like you to know what's being discussed; please accompany me. I think your knowledge of the strengths and weaknesses of our weaponry in this war will be of value."

Lendy smiled. "Of course, Major," he agreed and mounted his horse.

When they entered the laager, they found that Dr Jameson had arranged a table and chairs in the centre. Major Forbes was seated with him, together with Captain Borrow, the Salisbury Horses' second-in-command. Allan and Lendy took the two remaining seats.

Dr Jameson was smiling broadly. "All in order, Major Wilson?"

"Yes, Sir. A few close calls, but thankfully no injuries."

Forbes nodded. "Regrettably we lost a man. We also sustained one minor injury, a flesh wound, and lost one horse, along with three deaths and quite a few injuries in the support group, mostly from friendly fire."

"What were your estimates on enemy numbers, Major Wilson?" Jameson pressed.

Allan looked at Lendy. "We estimate about two thousand. You agree, Captain?"

"Yes, Sir," he replied. "Two thousand, I would say."

"We estimate that number as well," Forbes concurred.

Dr Jameson spread a map on the table. "We have never been to KoBulawayo from this direction, so I am not sure what direction to take."

"I suggest," Forbes frowned, "we follow the blood trail. It is bound to lead us directly to KoBulawayo."

"I disagree," Allan said. "We know we cannot fight them in woodland. We need open spaces, and their trail goes right into the Somabula Forest. We need to find a route that is mostly open ground."

Forbes looked indignant. "We have the upper hand. If we move fast through the forest, we will surprise them."

Lendy took the floor. "I must agree with Major Wilson, Sir. Even if we pursue them now, our wagons are slow and will be hampered by the trees. Above all, the Maxims are useless on the move. The Matabele are swift, being on foot, and will regroup fast. We must stay on open ground."

"Very good," Jameson smiled. "Major Wilson, you have a rather exceptional scout with you. Burnham, I believe. He could find us a suitable route, I am sure."

"Yes, Sir. Fred Burnham, an American. Quite a fellow."

"Good show. Please send a runner and ask Burnham to come here. I want to speak with him directly."

***

Fred rolled under a wagon and put his hat over his face. He was exhausted; it had been a long night.

"Move over," he heard Ingram say.

Fred shuffled further under the wagon and heard his friend slide into the cool shade of the undercarriage.

"Close call we had," Ingram muttered.

"Yes, it was precarious," Fred mumbled through his hat. "Let's see how much sleep we can get before we are put on lookout duty."

Fred heard footsteps approaching the wagon.

"Burnham, is that you?" Dillon asked. His voice sounded cheerful.

"Yes," Fred grunted, not removing his hat.

"Dr Jameson wants you down at Salisbury Horse."

"Me?" Fred took his hat from his face. "Whatever for?"

"No idea," Dillon smiled. "Better jump to it. You don't want to keep the Major waiting."

Fred sighed. "Ingram, please keep my place."

"Will do," Ingram mumbled sleepily.

"Can you believe it? I haven't slept for thirty-six hours, and now the Major wants to talk to me."

"Good luck," Ingram muttered as sleep overtook him.

***

Mjaan threw himself at King Lobengula's feet. He was covered in other men's blood.

"My King," Mjaan spoke into the dust. "I bring terrible news."

"Stand!" Lobengula demanded. "What news do you bring your King?"

Mjaan stood quickly but kept his head bowed. "Manonda and his impi are defeated."

"No, that cannot be!" Lobengula grimaced. "Where is Manonda? Bring him to me."

"He lives no more, my King. He was ashamed, so he took his life."

Lobengula paced heavily. He was limping. His gout was troubling him again, and he carried more weight than ever.

"The cowardly dog," Lobengula grunted. "He could not brave himself to let my eyes see him."

Mjaan looked at his King pitifully. "The white man has very powerful guns. They are of a kind I have not seen before."

Lobengula's eyes bore into Mjaan. "What kind of guns?"

"They travel on wheels, like a small wagon. They shoot many bullets very fast. We have left many of our warriors for the hyenas. Many more can no longer fight for the King."

Lobengula's eyes widened at these numbers. He had not expected that. "How many in the white army?"

"Half the number of one of our impis, my King. Yet we could not touch them."

Lobengula's ire rose, and he began to shake with fury. "Why did these people give us guns that don't work properly, yet they kept these powerful ones for themselves?" He tried hard to compose himself. "How many white soldiers did our warriors kill?"

"None, King. From what my eyes could see, we did not hurt one man."

Lobengula was exasperated. "Did you attack in darkness, as I commanded?"

"Yes, my King. We attacked in darkness, and then again with the sun. Both times, we were defeated." Mjaan wanted to say that the hail of bullets made no difference to night or day, but he knew that information would not be received well.

Mjaan continued nervously. "My eyes saw that it is better to attack when they are moving and their guns on wheels are also moving. Their protection drops when they move. Also, my eyes tell me we can't win when they are in the open. We need trees for protection. Trees stop the bullets, but our shields are like water to them."

"Your eyes tell you that?"

"Yes, my King. It is what I see. Also, our spies say they have been watching one man who has magic that can make him see in the dark."

Lobengula fumed. "How can he see in the dark?"

"We do not know. He rides a brown horse silently in the dark, and leads others and tells them where to go. When he walks without his horse, he is as silent as the leopard. Our spies struggle to see him when he walks alone. That man wears a strange hat with dents in it. I think his magic is in his hat."

"Ghaw!" Lobengula exclaimed. "How can that be?"

"*The one who sees in the dark* wears his hat both at night and in the day. The magic surely must be in his hat."

Lobengula grunted in disgust. "This is the man that must be killed first. Call a war council for this afternoon. The King wishes to make plans for the army. Leave me now."

Mjaan bowed and left the royal enclosure.

***

Fred walked to the Salisbury Horse laager. He could have taken his horse, but he wanted it to rest and graze. Besides, it was only a short walk. Entering the wagon enclosure, he noted there was no sign of the hustle and bustle seen at the Victoria Rangers. All seemed more relaxed, *'But then,'* he thought, *'maybe that was because there was only half the number of people in this camp.'*

The war council at the centre of the laager was obvious. His commander, Major Wilson, was seated at the only table, talking to Dr Jameson, Major Forbes and Captain Borrow. Captain Lendy also had a seat at the table.

"Sirs," Fred said boldly as he announced his arrival. He gave a salute to the officers.

"Ahh..." Jameson smiled, cutting Lendy's contribution to the discussion off. "Thank you for coming over so promptly, Burnham."

"At your service, Sir," Fred affirmed. He was dog-tired, but duty was duty.

"Got through the skirmish alright?" Jameson asked. "I hear you got caught outside when it started."

"Yes, Sir," Fred grinned. "I must say it was quite spectacular watching the two laagers jump into action in the dark. Very impressive, Sir."

"Well, I'm pleased you weren't hurt."

"Oh, it was close. Ingram and I nearly added to your tally," Fred chuckled.

"Must have been nerve-racking, Burnham," Forbes said.

"Not too bad, Major," Fred frowned. "I've been under fire often in my time."

Forbes nodded his understanding. "First time many of my men have been under active fire. Myself included. I must say it was tense for us."

Lendy looked at Allan surreptitiously and raised an eyebrow at that comment.

Fred chuckled. "Tense would be a good term, yes."

Jameson cleared his throat. "Burnham, we have a problem that I would like your help with."

"Certainly, Sir," Fred replied, immediately serious.

"We are expecting the Matabele to attack us again. We know the number that attacked us this morning is just a small handful of Lobengula's army. The next onslaught will be significant. We need to get to KoBulawayo without delay to catch them unprepared.

"We have two problems to consider. Firstly, we don't know exactly where KoBulawayo is from here. Secondly, we cannot be caught in the forests. If the enemy has trees for cover, they will easily advance very close to our laagers. To make matters worse, the dense trees will shield them from our bullets. We must, at all costs, travel through open land wherever possible. I want to task you, Mr Burnham, to find a suitable route to KoBulawayo, specifically to scout for an open way to Lobengula's Royal Village."

"I can do that, Sir," Fred agreed, keeping his reservations to himself.

"I need not remind you that the lives of all in Fort Victoria and Fort Salisbury depend on the favourable outcome of this conflict. The fate of the BSAC's endeavours also rests on winning this war. It is critical–I cannot express this enough–it is critical that you find us a clear route to Lobengula's capital–and with haste."

The pressure thus put upon Fred was not lost to those around the table.

"A question, Sir," Fred asked. "Why me?"

"I believe you have extraordinary skills as a scout. Major Wilson speaks very highly of you."

"Thank you, Sir," Fred acknowledged humbly. "May I take someone with me? It would work better if we were a team."

"Of course, I was about to insist that be the case," Jameson smiled.

"Please may I take Captain Gifford, from the Salisbury Horse? He has experience with scouting and tracking Indians in America. I know him, and I know I can rely on his abilities and knowledge to complement my own. Above all, he has travelled to KoBulawayo in the past."

Forbes frowned and leaned forward. "Sadly, I can't allow him to go with you. He is the only effective scout we have with the Salisbury Horse, and I need him here."

Fred was disappointed. He was then about to ask if he could take Ingram, whom he knew was also a great American scout, but he was interrupted by Jameson.

"Major Forbes is right. Gifford must remain here. I suggest that you take Trooper Vaversol. He is a very accomplished scout. He also knows these parts well and can speak isiNdebele fluently. He will be very useful to you."

"Very good, Sir," Fred said hesitantly. He wasn't confident about taking someone he didn't know. On a mission such as this, it was important that they could work together and understand each other. The value of the fact that Vaversol was fluent in isiNdebele, however, could not be dismissed.

Jameson then became gravely serious. "This mission is extremely critical, Burnham," he reiterated. "If either of you is injured during this mission, and you cannot continue, the other must leave the incapacitated person to fight it out on his own and complete the mission alone. Do you understand?"

"Yes, Sir," Fred nodded, a frown creasing his brow. To fight it out on their own effectively meant there would be no return for that man.

"Find Thabazinduna, the Mountain of the Chiefs," Jameson continued. "KoBulawayo is at the base of Thabazinduna. It's a flat-topped mountain with steep cliffs. If you find the mountain, you have found King Lobengula's capital."

"I will do that, Sir," Burnham nodded.

"Thank you, Burnham. You may be excused. I'll send Vaversol to you shortly. Make haste."

Allan stood. "If the meeting is over, Sir, might I accompany Burnham back? I have some instructions for him."

With that, the meeting ended. Allan, Fred and Lendy walked back together.

"You up to this?" Allan asked Fred once they entered the open ground.

"Yes, Major," Fred nodded.

"You haven't slept in a while."

Fred smiled, "I'll sleep when we rest the horses and let them graze."

"Be careful," Lendy warned. "Your success is vital to the country's future and, more importantly, our loved ones."

"I'm aware of that," Fred grumbled; he didn't need reminding.

"Major," Lendy lowered his voice, even though no one was close by, "did I hear right? Did Major Forbes admit he had never been in a battle before?"

"That's what I heard," Allan agreed. "He said this was the first time he had been in an active engagement."

"I heard that too," Fred added. "That's certainly how I understood his comment."

"So why is Forbes the joint commander of this lot? You should be the joint commander, Major," Lendy scratched his head.

"Maybe I'm just not part of Jameson's gentlemen's club," Allan laughed.

"No, seriously," Lendy pressed. "You're both the same rank, but that's where it stops. You have far more experience than Forbes, command a unit twice his size, and are his senior in age."

"I know, but there's not much I can do about it, Gentlemen," Allan said. "My concern is for the Victoria Rangers and all who serve in it. I want to win this war, and I don't want to lose anyone to it."

"Doesn't it bother you that everything you suggest, Forbes counters or disagrees with?" Lendy asked.

"Yes," Fred quipped, "and not just you, Major Wilson. Dr Jameson gave me a mission critical to the war, this country and all who live in it, yet when I asked for Maurice Gifford, Major Forbes denied my request, and his refusal was upheld without question."

"Exactly," Lendy agreed.

"It's not that Gifford is my friend," Fred continued, "it's because I regard him as the most capable person for this mission. You would think a mission of this so-called importance requires the best. But no, Major Forbes wants him in camp, and Jameson just agrees with him."

Allan frowned. "Yes, it is a problem, and I understand your feelings entirely, Burnham. There must be some connection between Jameson and Forbes, and I don't know what it is."

Lendy grunted. "A lot of blokes in the Salisbury Horse are talking, and so are our blokes."

They had reached the perimeter of the Victoria laager. Allan quickly got the last word in.

"There is not much we can do about it, Captain," Allan closed the subject. "Burnham, make ready. If there is anything I can assist you with, just ask."

"Yes, Sir," Fred saluted and slipped into the laager.

Fred wanted to let Ingram know what he was doing, but Ingram was so deep in sleep that he left him alone. At a time like this, it was vital that sleep was taken whenever it was available. Instead, he informed Captain White of his mission and asked him to update Ingram when he awoke.

***

Lobengula had spent a troubled night wondering how he would overcome the invaders. Mjaan's account of the battle at the Shangani River was very insightful. He called for a war council, and all the Indunas, along with their impis, gathered outside the Royal residence waiting for their King to emerge.

"Induna Manonda's impi was weak, and they were humiliated by the white man," Lobengula proclaimed loudly as he faced his army.

Jeers and ridicule aimed at the defeated impi was the enthusiastic response.

Lobengula smiled. "Who among you is better than Manonda's impi?"

A roar from the assembled warriors erupted. This pleased the King.

"Here are the King's orders," Lobengula called in a loud, deep voice. "The enemy must only be attacked when they are on the move. Never attack them when they are stopped and surrounded by their wagons. The enemy must be attacked in the day, never at night.

"iMbizo impi, you will lead the attack. But first, you must climb to the top of Thabazinduna. You will see the dust that they make and will know where they are. Go to them at night and wait for them to move when the sun arrives. Take the iNgubo impi with you. Take iSibiza impi, and take iHlati impi. You will all fight when the iMbizo impi strikes."

The roar from the warriors was resounding. This was going to be the battle they were all waiting for.

Once they had settled, Lobengula continued. "aMavene impi, iQobo impi and iNsukamini impi, you must be there for the second wave. Do not hesitate. We will have ten thousand warriors on the battlefield against their half a impi. Two thousand must carry rifles. Eight thousand must attack with spears. They must be overrun and defeated quickly.

"Induna Gambo, take four thousand men and march quickly to Tati in the south. Our spies tell me two columns of white men are coming from that side. Do not let them through the Mangwe Pass. Kill them all. Now go to your victory! The King has spoken."

With cries of jubilation and determination, the impis formed up, waiting for the order from their particular Induna to march. Mjaan was excited. He was desperate to go into battle, just as he had in the old days.

"Mjaan," Lobengula called the leader of the Royal Guard to come close.

Mjaan obliged and got down on one knee, waiting for his order.

"You will remain here when they go to fight," the King commanded.

Mjaan was heartbroken. "My King, I will lead my impi into battle. I will fight for you."

"No," Lobengula said gruffly. "Send Ngwenya to lead your impi. I want you here, I have a duty for you."

Mjaan lowered his gaze. "Yes, my King. I am here. I will do as you command."

"Come close," Lobengula lowered his voice. "I fear if the white man is victorious."

Mjaan jerked his head up. "They will never be victorious, King."

"I know, but if they are, what am I to do?"

Mjaan looked at his leader in disbelief.

"Mjaan, your job is to keep me alive. Not so?"

"Yes, my King."

"Then we make arrangements if things go wrong. Arrange that my wagons and cattle follow me northwards. Arrange for all the women, children and old men in the capital to move with me also. If the white men conquer our army, then I want to be well ahead of them when they arrive in KoBulawayo."

Mjaan was shocked to be hearing this from his King. Never in his wildest dreams did he expect his royal commander to be planning an escape. He was dumbstruck.

"Do you hear me?" Lobengula asked sternly.

Mjaan snapped out of his stupor. "Yes, my King, I hear you," he said forlornly.

"I want to start moving before the sun is there," Lobengula said, pointing to a position in the sky that indicated about two hours hence. "Stay here with some men. If we are defeated, you must order them to set fire to the whole village. Everything must burn. All the gunpowder, grain, ivory and my treasures; all must burn. I will not leave any of it for the white man. When the village is destroyed, follow my tracks and join me as fast as you can.

"If we are victorious, a swift messenger must follow us and tell me. I will return immediately. But if we are defeated, I must be well away from the white settlers. I will find a new land to the north and rebuild our nation where the white men will leave us alone forever."

"I understand," Mjaan said. He was devastated, but the plan was sound.

"Bring only my cattle and all the gold sovereigns the white man gave me. The gold seems to have much value to them. It seems it is the only thing they like to bargain with. To me, the gold coins have less value than the buttons they wear on their shirts. Now go, make these arrangements."

***

In a small pouch, Fred packed some maize meal cakes and biltong sticks for nourishment, some cotton thread to be used to activate an early warning system, a small mirror for signalling and some short fuses for a flash of light in the case of emergency. He had been taught well by the old men of the Wild West, and he knew he had to be prepared for any eventuality.

Fred mounted his horse and left the fortifications of the Victoria laager, heading back to the Salisbury laager. He saw a lone man on a horse walking towards him.

Trooper Vaversol was a large man, well-built and sporting a full beard and moustache. His eyes were dark, and constantly on the move, taking in his surroundings. He spoke with a thick Afrikaans accent. After a brief greeting, the two men turned west on their hunt for a clear way to KoBulawayo. Behind them, the order to break camp was heard, and oxen, wagons and men began to move.

"Have you ever been to KoBulawayo?" Fred asked his companion.

"Once, a long time ago," Vaversol replied. "And you?"

"No. I believe the mountain is formidable, so it should be easy to find."

"I've only seen KoBulawayo from the west, man. Not from the east," Vaversol frowned, "so I have not seen Thabazinduna. They tell me these Matabele throw people off the cliffs if they disagree with the King. Maybe we will find a lot of bones at the base of the cliffs."

"I hope not," Fred scowled.

"At least we will know we have arrived at the correct mountain."

Fred and Vaversol had been riding at a steady walk throughout the day and came to a halt just before sunset. They had found several traps that had been set for them by the Matabele and avoided a number of obvious ambushes. Fred was certain that they were being watched, and Vaversol agreed with him.

Coming to a halt, Fred dismounted and checked the ground. "These traps are inferior to the Apache traps. I think we can count our blessings."

"Ja, that one over there," Vaversol pointed to his right, "is so obvious it's laughable, man."

"That's because they want us to see that and go the opposite direction, where an ambush waits," Fred said quietly. "Let's go this way instead. I saw some deserted huts over there. They would never expect us to go there."

"Good thinking, man," Vaversol agreed. "Perhaps we can find a stash of corn for our horses as well."

The huts were indeed abandoned, and some stores of corn were discovered. As night was falling, they led the horses into a depression where their silhouettes would not be seen against the starry sky, then took turns to sleep. At midnight, they began their hunt for Thabazinduna again.

It was slow progress in the dark, with every bush a potential trap. The men depended not only upon their five senses, but on those of their horses too. They watched their ears, which way they turned their heads, and for any stiffening of a shoulder or neck muscle. Fred was in his element; this was what he had been trained to do. Through all this, he kept an eye on where he was, just in case he had to backtrack. As Holmes had often instructed in the Arizona Desert, a scout will only get lost once. To get lost is a death sentence.

When the sun came up there was no sign of the fabled mountain, just small hills in the distance. Fred and Vaversol were becoming increasingly disappointed and irritable. As they walked along the banks of a stream they chanced upon two old women carrying water in large clay jars on their heads. They took fright and dropped the jars, running for their village. Vaversol immediately wheeled his horse in front of them and cut them off, telling them to stop.

In fluent IsiNdebele, he greeted them in their polite customary way and showed much respect for their seniority. This calmed them down and allowed him to explain that he was a friend of the land and that he had met many of their chiefs. He used the various chiefs' names often and soon got the old women to engage in conversation with him. Fred waited on his horse nearby, watching for Matabele warriors. He noted a group with spears, along with some carrying outdated muskets, obviously forming an attack plan.

"Matabele approaching," Fred urged Vaversol to hurry up. "Three minutes."

"So, I am lost now," Vaversol said without looking at Fred. "Is the

Shangani River that way?"

"No," one of the women replied. "It is more that way," she pointed slightly over Vaversol's shoulder.

"Oh, so then the Bembezi River must be there?" he scratched his head in mock confusion.

"Yes, that is so," the woman smiled pleasantly.

"So, where is Thabazinduna?"

"Ghaw," the woman mocked Vaversol's lack of knowledge. "That is Thabazinduna, just over there." She pointed to a small hill not five miles away.

"That is Thabazinduna?" Vaversol repeated, in genuine surprise.

"Yes, that is Thabazinduna." The other woman nodded in confirmation.

Vaversol looked at Fred, then turned back to the women.

"So that small one must be Matshumhlope?"

The women laughed.

"Yes," said the old lady. "I can see you have been here before."

"Vaversol," Fred warned.

Vaversol bowed his head politely. "I thank you, grandmothers of your village, for helping me. Please pass my greetings to your chief. We will go now, and I am sorry that we frightened you."

Once the women were out of sight, Vaversol spoke to Fred. "Thabazinduna is nothing but a small hill!"

"That's surprising," Fred grumbled. "Not what we had been told at all."

"Let us return to Jameson quickly and tell him we have found the route."

"No," Fred objected. "I think we must climb that hill near Thabazinduna and look at KoBulawayo with our own two eyes. If that is not Thabazinduna, we will lead the columns to their deaths."

"Ja, alright, good thinking, man. Let's go."

They wheeled their horses around and galloped away from the threatening warriors, moving out of their range and heading for the distant hill identified as Thabazinduna. Cresting a low hill, Fred and Vaversol saw the remarkable sight of King Lobengula's Royal Village, and his capital, KoBulawayo. They were elated. It was a huge kraal, with thatched huts in neat rows encircling a massive round hut in the centre. This hut was obviously the King's residence. Dotted around the outside of the circle of huts were large storerooms that contained the King's treasures of ivory, weapons, gunpowder, and gold.

They had found the route to the King, and now they had to return to Jameson and the columns. Time was of the essence.

"Let us ride hard," Vaversol said. We must tell the Doctor urgently."

Fred shook his head slowly in thought. "I disagree, my friend. If we ride hard, our horses will be completely knocked up. They are already exhausted. The enemy will be in our path, too. They want to stop us, and they know we are here and why we are here."

"What is your suggestion?"

"We go carefully and avoid the warriors looking for us. We must walk our horses wherever we can. You and I must also get some much-needed sleep–we will make mistakes if we don't."

Vaversol knew Fred was right. "I agree, my friend. Let us go."

When the two scouts reached a huge open grassy expanse, they walked their horses as close to the middle as they could. Then, on a long rope, they let the horses graze while Vaversol lay down and slept. One hour later Fred woke him and immediately took his turn to sleep. An hour later, Vaversol woke Fred with a stick of biltong and some water.

"It's time to go," he warned Fred. The warriors have seen us, and they are surrounding our position."

Fred sat up and looked at the surrounding line of trees. "Most of the warriors seem to be on the eastern side."

"That's the direction of the columns. It is the direction they expect us to go."

Fred frowned. "Let's ride towards them. Just before they charge, we must turn north and go through that gap there," he indicated surreptitiously with a nod.

Vaversol agreed, and they mounted, walking slowly towards the bulk of the threatening warriors. In a coordinated flash decision, Vaversol and Fred turned north and bolted for the gap. The ploy worked flawlessly, and in moments they had left the agitated warriors behind.

Darkness came early–clouds had begun to form on the horizon. Carefully, quietly, they picked their way through the forest. Suddenly, they felt moisture settle on their faces. A thick mist settled through the trees and blotted out even the starlight.

At about midnight, Vaversol pulled up to Fred. "Meneer," he

whispered. "I think we are going in the wrong direction. We should be travelling more to the east."

"This is the correct direction," Fred said confidently. "I know where I am going."

"I must disagree this time," Vaversol insisted. "We need to be moving in a northerly direction."

"That is where I am going," Fred argued. "I am using my memory of how we came. This is the right track."

"I have a compass," Vaversol pressed. "Let us see which way the compass points."

"Alright," Fred reluctantly acquiesced.

The two men crouched down on the ground and laid the little compass on the dirt. Covering the compass with their hats, Fred lit a small fuse. The brief light was blinding after the near-total blackout. It showed the men were travelling in a northeasterly direction.

"I am right," Vaversol whispered.

"I can't believe this compass," Fred shook his head. "I know I am right."

"Well, my friend, I wish to go that way, according to the compass."

Fred gave the situation some thought. "Fair enough. You go that way, and I will go mine. Hopefully, one of us is correct, and we can catch up with Jameson."

Vaversol and Fred stood. They shook hands and parted company. Fred had gone only one hundred yards when he heard a soft call off to his left. He called back, and soon Vaversol re-joined him.

"Meneer, I have lost confidence in my compass, and it is not easy to see the needle in the dark. I will come with you and put my faith in you."

Fred smiled in the darkness. "Very good, my friend. Let us proceed."

Not long later, Fred's horse twitched. It hung his head low and stopped. Fred dismounted and stood by his mount's head, wondering what it was doing. It seemed to be smelling the ground. Fred got down on his hands and knees and sniffed the earth, then stood, smiling.

"Vaversol, smell the ground. I can smell a horse has been here. This is the place we first stopped to let the horses feed."

Vaversol frowned. "I am sorry I doubted you, my friend."

"No apologies are necessary," Fred said kindly, "but we must push on urgently. Meneer Vaversol, can you hear those warriors to the right of us?

Their heading will cross our path just now."

Not far off, in the dark and the mist, a column of Matabele warriors were walking in a similar direction to them, but their paths were closing all the time. They were too close for comfort now, and Fred was worried a clink from the metalware on the horse's bridle, or the sound of a soft neighing might alert them to their presence. They were so close now that they could hear some warriors talking amongst themselves.

Vaversol nodded. "I can hear them, and I can understand what they are saying."

"You can?" Fred was impressed.

"They fear the white man because they fight at night and in the day. They are also heading towards the column. They know where it is. They have said that the column is travelling in the wrong direction, and plan to overtake it and wait in a strategic place to ambush them."

"Then we must make haste and warn Jameson," Fred said, nervously. "There is no time to lose. We will have to push the horses to their limit."

Fred and Vaversol pressed forward, pushing their horses as quickly and quietly as they could, avoiding intersecting with the Matabele warriors' path. The sun was cresting the horizon when Fred and Vaversol emerged from the forest, and they soon found the track made by the columns. They chased the columns down and, with their horses on the brink of collapse, reached Major Forbes just before noon.

"Major," Fred called out urgently. "We have found a way to KoBulawayo, but you cannot proceed in the direction you are heading. Lobengula's army is not far ahead, waiting in the trees."

Forbes' moustache bristled. "How do you know they are ahead? You have only just arrived from the rear."

"We heard their movements and their conversations during the night. They are going to overtake you and intersect the column up ahead."

Forbes looked at Fred disbelievingly. "No, we are on the right track. We will proceed."

Fred was taken aback by this response. "Sir, you are walking into a trap if you hold this direction. The safer way to KoBulawayo is that way," Fred pointed to the open route, free of forest.

Vaversol, his horse slower as it carried greater weight, had just caught up with Fred and joined the conversation. "Major, the enemy is just ahead."

Forbes frowned. "You have just come from a different direction. How could you possibly know?"

Suddenly, Allan, Borrow and Lendy joined the small group.

"Did you men find a route?" Allan asked.

"Yes, Sir," Fred nodded, pointing to where they had emerged from the forest to make his point.

Fred shot a glance at Forbes, who remained silent. He was curious as to why Forbes was not jumping to action.

"We need to turn around," Fred said in desperation. "There are thousands of Matabele up ahead, waiting to ambush us."

"That is true, man," Vaversol said. "They almost intersected with us last night. I could hear their conversations. They know where you are and in which direction the column is moving."

"What are you suggesting?" Allan asked Fred.

"Change course immediately," Fred said, exasperated. "There is a large open expanse not far off. We need to get there and laager as quickly as possible."

"I don't think that will be necessary," Forbes said calmly. "We are ready for them, and we know how to fight them. Besides, we have no proof the enemy is where these scouts suggest. We will keep moving forward."

Fred looked at Allan and Borrow. There was confusion in his eyes. Fred could not believe Forbes' stubbornness.

Allan looked Forbes squarely in the eye. "And the fact that our scouts say the safe route to KoBulawayo is in a different direction?"

Forbes looked blankly at the horizon in thought, then at Allan. "If the enemy is observing us, and they see us do an about-turn, they will regard that as a retreat, and it will show weakness."

"Oh heavens," Allan exclaimed. "You are so 'by-the-book', aren't you? I will remind you that a retreat is ordered when under enemy action, and one is being overwhelmed. This is not a retreat. It is a calculated manoeuvre."

Fred, uncharacteristically, interrupted. "Sir, Dr Jameson sent us on a critical mission; to find an open route to Lobengula's capital, and I am telling you that we have found it–that way. We are also telling you the enemy is waiting in ambush ahead of you, and that there is a perfect spot to defend ourselves in our suggested direction."

"Order the about-turn, Forbes," Allan threatened, "or I will see Jameson about this."

Forbes looked flustered. He was about to say something when Fred looked ahead and suddenly pointed forward. Two horsemen were galloping back to the columns.

"Look!" he said. "Those are your forward scouts, are they not? They are galloping. They must have seen the enemy."

"All right," Forbes capitulated. "Turn the column around."

"Burnham, Vaversol, take the lead," Allan ordered before Forbes could say anymore, then spun his mount around to organise the Victoria Rangers.

***

Ngwenya called the other Indunas to him. Even though he was only the Ingubo second-in-command, the fact that Mjaan was his superior gave him extra status in the impis.

"How far are the white soldiers?" he asked impatiently.

"They should be here any time now," the iMbizo Induna said. He was just as anxious to order his warriors into battle as Ngwenya was.

The Induna of the iHlati impi joined them, a little out of breath. "My spies have returned. They report the whites have turned around. They are going back to the Bembezi River."

"Ghaw!" Ngwenya exclaimed. "Why do they do that?"

"It is that white man who rides alone in the dark," the iMbizo Induna said. "He is the one who tells them which way to go."

"We call him 'The One Who Sees in The Dark'. He has white man's magic in that strange hat that can make him see in the dark."

"It is true," another Induna agreed. "He wears that hat at night."

"These people are like the snake in the grass," the iSiziba Induna complained. "The snake puts its head up, looks around, puts its head down, then comes up somewhere unexpected, ready to strike. These white men must be treated like snakes."

The iMbizo Induna spoke with authority. "I think we must go back to the Bembezi and wait for them there. We can get there before they do."

"I agree," Ngwenya concurred.

"Wait," the iSiziba Induna put his hand in the air. "I worry about the light, and if they are moving. Remember what the command is. We fight only in the day, and we fight only when they are moving. Also, we must fight in the trees, not in the open."

IHlati nodded. "I agree. I propose we move quickly to the Bembezi now and hide behind the cliffs of the riverbanks. When they draw near, we watch to see what they do. If it is daylight, and they are moving, we attack. If they stop and make their fort, then we rest and wait for the morning."

The Indunas considered this for a moment, and then unanimously agreed. The impis were rallied, and the army was quickly on the move. Spies kept the commanders updated on the enemy's position, and very quickly–and secretly–the foot soldiers overtook the rumbling wagons. Ten thousand warriors were silently ensconced in the low cliffs of the Bembezi River.

The ambush was re-set, and the warriors were shaking with excitement. The sun had passed its zenith; the timing was perfect. Ahead of them was about a hundred yards of thick forest before it opened into a vast open plain. They could see the dust of the white men's column approaching. They would wait for the wagons to reach the forest, then attack. The time for killing was upon them.

***

Fred and Vaversol rode side by side, ahead of the column. The land opened up to a flat grassy plain in front of them, a line of trees–part of the Somabula Forest was just to the west. Beyond that the Bembezi River, and, two days' march after that, King Lobengula's capital.

"How are you doing for sleep?" Fred asked. "We have been going a long time, you and me."

"Ja, I'm tired, but I will sleep soon."

"A rest will be good. We will laager here," Fred casually waved a hand at the open land ahead.

"Meneer Burnham," Vaversol said, "I want to thank you for standing by your conviction when my compass failed. You saved our lives, and that of the entire column, no doubt."

"Perhaps your compass didn't fail. I have been thinking about that, and it is possible we laid the compass too close to the barrel of a rifle, or perhaps there was a stone of iron under the soil we rested it on. I'll tell you a secret, though, my friend," Fred grinned, "I was not worried about being lost until you came back. When you re-joined me, I realised I had a responsibility for your life, too, and that made me very nervous."

Vaversol slapped Fred on the shoulder with a monstrous hand. "Well, we achieved our mission, and that's what matters. Neh?"

"Yes," Fred said, but he was frowning. "I still cannot understand why, after being sent on such a critical mission, Forbes wanted to ignore our findings."

"Agg..." Vaversol shrugged. "He is young. Luckily you have Major Wilson to quietly put things right."

"Still," Fred grumbled, "it should not be like that. Changing the subject, would you mind leading the Salisbury Horse into the plain? I'm going to lead the Victoria Rangers up that rise to the right."

"Ja, no problem Meneer," Vaversol said, and veered off to the left.

Fred dropped back, then signalled Captain Lendy to make for the top of the grassy rise. Lendy confirmed the instruction, and Fred saw the Victoria Rangers break neatly away from the Salisbury Horse. He looked over his shoulder and took in his surroundings. He smiled to himself; if they came under attack while in laager, this was the best position they could be in. '*The perfect position,*' he thought.

The two laagers were set up in double-quick time, and lookouts were posted one mile out from the perimeter in every direction. Allan looked over his laager and was pleased with his position. It was just as Fred had explained. He had a clear view all around, from an elevated position. It suited his artillery well, and even Captain Lendy seemed pleased. When Fred entered the laager Allan called to him.

"Burnham, you say KoBulawayo is just two day's march from here?"

"Yes, Sir. It's plain sailing from here; I know the route, and it is open all the way."

"Excellent. Thank you. Now, find somewhere to put your head down."

"Thank you, Sir," Fred smiled and immediately rolled under a wagon. Almost as soon as his hat covered his face, he was fast asleep.

***

Ten thousand bloodthirsty warriors crouched or sat in absolute silence. They feared the punishment for making a noise. The cliffs running along the east bank of the Bembezi were a good few hundred yards long in that area, and well over six feet high. They were perfectly concealed, and the enemy wagons were heading right into their ambush.

A spy sidled up to Ngwenya and the iMbizo Induna, who crouched beside each other. "They have stopped and are making their kraals now," he said.

"Ghaw!" Ngwenya exclaimed in annoyance.

The iMbizo Induna signalled for all Indunas to join them. Once together, he explained the situation.

"They will not move until morning. We will have to wait," he said.

"We can wait," the iHlati Induna said. "If the killing happens today or tomorrow, it doesn't matter."

"Good. Tell your warriors to be absolutely quiet, and be prepared for the morning. We will wait here and not move. This is the perfect position to be in. They will not see us until they are upon us."

All Indunas agreed and swiftly moved to their impis to explain the approved strategy.

***

Troopers Thompson and White rode their horses at a gentle pace westwards, towards the thick tree line. When they reached the trees of the Somabula Forest, the Salisbury laager was a good mile behind them.

"I'll be pleased when this campaign is over," Thompson grumbled. "Already they have put us on half rations. You'd think they could plan better."

"I don't know so much about Forbes," White said. "He can't seem to make up his mind about anything. He says one thing, then Jameson comes out of his hidey-hole and says something else, and Forbes just hands out a *'Yes Sir, whatever you say, Sir'* business."

"Wilson is another animal altogether, don't you think?" Thompson said. "When he shouts his orders to his troops, even we can hear him from the Salisbury laager. I'll bet that irritates Forbes immensely."

"Once this lark is over, I'm collecting my six thousand acres of land and heading down to Cape Town for a few weeks. The girls are very pretty there. You want to come with me?" White winked.

"Oh, yes, consider me a part of your follies," Thompson laughed.

They had reached the tree line, dismounted and tied their horses to a tree. Immediately the horses began to graze.

"See any Matabele?" White chuckled.

Thompson laughed. "They've run to KoBulawayo, like little girls."

The two troopers walked a little way into the trees, enjoying the shade and cool, gentle atmosphere of the forest. Trooper White found a fallen log and sat upon it. He felt for a cigarette in his top pocket, but it was just a reflex; he had run out of cigarettes five days prior.

Thompson walked a little deeper into the forest, planning to relieve himself. Just ahead of him was a gulley, eroded by rain. Thinking that might be a nice place to drop his trousers, he sauntered to the edge.

Suddenly, he was looking down at dozens of Matabele warriors, sitting in the shade that the gully provided, waiting, conserving energy for the attack that was planned for the morrow. They looked up at Thompson. A stunned silence hung over the landscape for an awkward moment as realisation dawned on all present.

Thompson turned on his heels, screaming, and ran for his life. As for the Matabele, with their cover blown, their immediate instinct was to attack. Despite the orders to wait for the white man to be on the move, and in forested areas, the time to kill had come, and nothing would stop them now.

White swivelled on the log he was sitting on and saw a confusing sight. Thompson was running furiously towards him, and behind him hundreds of Matabele, carrying spears and rifles, came pouring out of the ground like a nest of angry wasps.

Thompson, in sheer panic, ran for a tree and frantically began to climb it. He didn't get far before several hands grasped his ankles and hauled him forcefully to the ground. Several assegais ensured he was dead within seconds of hitting the earth.

White witnessed his colleague's violent death and suddenly considered his own life. He leapt from the log and bolted for his horse. He had about a twenty-yard head start, and, when he reached his horse, he jumped for its back. Unfortunately, his adrenaline was pumping so violently he almost cleared the horse entirely, clipping the saddle with his knees and falling to the ground on the other side.

Rolling to his feet, he kept running. He drew his revolver, and, throwing his arm backwards, fired a shot. One mile ahead he saw safety. Thirty yards behind were hundreds of spears and bloodthirsty warriors. He threw his revolver away, put his head down and ran.

***

* * *

"Captain Judd," Allan walked over to the tall officer. "Please keep a few fellows on watch on the east and south perimeter. I'm going to concentrate our defences on the west."

"Yes, Major," Judd agreed.

"Any sign of a problem, let me know immediately and I'll...."

A distant, muffled shot rang out. It was more like a soft pop. Everyone suddenly stopped what they were doing and strained to listen.

"What was that?" Allan said, already bounding up to the top of one of the wagons.

Allan stood precariously on the edge of the wagon and scanned the open ground immediately below. The Salisbury laager was established, and it looked like everyone was on high alert. A muffled roar rose up from the distant tree line. Then, almost comically, a lone man came running out of the trees, and almost immediately behind him, thousands of Matabele emerged in full flight, spears at the ready.

Allan immediately realised what was happening. "Matabele attack," he shouted down to his men. "Captain Lendy, bring the artillery to bear. Captain Napier, prepare maxims, Captain Green, ready rifles. On my command."

Trooper White was about three-quarters of the way to the Salisbury laager, and it looked like he was increasing the gap between himself and certain death. The men in the Salisbury laager began shouting encouragement at White. Cheers went up as soldiers stood to get a better view. The cheering was contagious, and the Victoria laager joined in.

Trooper White was beginning to tire, and the lead Matabele warriors were gaining on him. The cheering from both laagers increased immeasurably, and suddenly Allan became concerned his men wouldn't hear his order to fire.

"Lendy!" Allan shouted to his second-in-command. "Aim the cannons one hundred and fifty yards out from Salisbury. When that man is about one hundred yards from the Salisbury laager, open fire."

"Sir!" Lendy acknowledged and swung the seven-pounder around. Allan saw the Hotchkiss also adjust aim.

The cheering from the settlers and the war cry from the Matabele blended. The scene was surreal. White was losing ground, and the warriors were now very close. When he crossed an imaginary line that

Lendy deemed to be one hundred yards, Trooper White's legs began to buckle. The lead warriors were closing fast.

When the seven-pounder boomed into action, the Salisbury laager opened up with all they had. With bullets screeching past White, he staggered the last gruelling stretch of his run, and collapsed at the edge of the laager. He was quickly dragged inside by three waiting men.

The Matabele, however, baulked at the onslaught of lead. The seven-pounder round exploded amongst them, and each burst of the maxims cut down the front row of their charge. Warriors fell upon warriors, and many died where they lay. The intensity of the firing stayed constant. The warriors with rifles fired back, but with their lack of training, their rounds usually went high.

At the Victoria laager, Allan was directing fire like a conductor at an orchestra. At regular intervals, he checked the situation around the laager, but all was quiet. It was clear the attack was coming from the river only, but he was disinclined to take any chances.

A second wave of attackers surged through the trees, but they were cut down quickly, and then a third wave came through. Within forty minutes, the Matabele military force was destroyed, and the attack was called off. Those who could, limped back to KoBulawayo, ashamed and defeated.

Allan didn't waste any time. "Reload," he bellowed. He didn't know if there was another wave coming and would be prepared regardless. "Casualty report!"

His captains came to him one by one, Judd, Kirton, Napier, Fitzgerald, and Greenfield; there were no casualties, but a stray Matabele bullet had killed one horse.

"Major Wilson," Dillon called from his heliograph. "Salisbury says they have one killed, ten injured. Three horses lost."

"Thank you, Trooper Dillon. Please report back no casualties from here. One horse killed."

A check of the battlefield revealed that over two thousand five hundred Matabele warriors had been killed. No one could guess how many others were wounded. The battle had been very one-sided.

After a long night, Allan and Captain Lendy rode down to meet with Jameson, Forbes and Borrow at first light.

Jameson did most of the talking. He was desirous of getting to Bulawayo as fast as possible and rapidly laid out strategies, some of which were obviously impossible to achieve.

"A mounted cavalry could get there today," Allan suggested, "it's only about forty miles away, but that would be dangerous. Besides, our horses are in no condition to take into battle after the march we have just undertaken."

"And with the wagons?" Jameson asked.

"According to Burnham, two full days, Sir."

Jameson sighed deeply. "I really need to get there as soon as possible."

Allan noticed his anxiety. "Why is that important, Sir?"

Jameson paused to choose his words carefully. "As you know, two other columns are coming up from the south to support us. We plan to meet at KoBulawayo simultaneously—well, that was the plan. Colonel Goold-Adams will be leading the Bechuanaland Border Police, the BBP, and Commandant Piet Raaff will support him with a group known as Raaff's Rangers.

"What worries me is that Goold-Adams was instructed to participate in this exercise by the British High Commissioner, Sir Henry Loch. If Goold-Adams gets to KoBulawayo first, Loch may claim Matabeleland for the Crown. He hates the fact that a private company, owned by Rhodes, could own a country. I think he may even despise Rhodes himself. If we get there first, we will claim Matabeleland for the BSAC and Mr Rhodes. So, as you can see, Major Wilson, it is a race against time."

"Do you not think Goold-Adams and Raaff will encounter resistance like we did?" Lendy asked. "Surely, he would be slowed down considerably. With the speed we defeated our attackers, I would think we will get to KoBulawayo well ahead of them."

"Indeed, it would seem so," Jameson frowned, "but I don't want to risk losing Matabeleland to the Crown. We must make haste."

After some final instructions, Allan and Lendy rode back to their column.

"Sounds to me, Sir, that this attack on Lobengula was planned a long time ago," Lendy said.

"It certainly seems that way, Captain," Allan said. "There are complicated politics at play here."

Suddenly, to Allan's left, a deep thunderous boom rumbled overhead.

"What was that?" Lendy asks in surprise.

"I have no idea," Allan pulled his horse to a halt and looked to the sky.

Birds had taken flight in surprise.

"That was a massive explosion," Lendy ventured.

"Yes, and coming from the direction of KoBulawayo. Let's get back to the laager quickly."

Once in the safety of the laager, everyone there seemed excited. Questions were being thrown helter-skelter.

"Sir," someone shouted, pointing to the sky. "Look."

A huge billowing cloud of black and grey smoke appeared above a distant line of hills and was gently rolling towards the heavens. It was definitely coming from the direction of KoBulawayo.

"Burnham!" Allan called.

Fred responded immediately and ran to meet him. "Sir!"

"Are you rested?"

"Yes, Sir."

"And your horse?"

"Fully recovered, Sir."

"Good. Please get to KoBulawayo as soon as possible and find out what the hell is going on there. Take Posselt with you. He is a strong rider. Be careful, there are a lot of Matabele stragglers out there."

"Will do, Sir. May I take Ingram with me as well?"

"Of course, three scouts are better than two. Please hurry; I need to know what's happening. I'll get Vaversol to lead the columns to the capital."

Within minutes Fred, Ingram and Posselt left for KoBulawayo. They used every trick in the scouting book to avoid any Matabele stragglers. The sun was just setting when the three scouts arrived at the outskirts of the royal kraal.

The entire place was on fire. Some buildings were still actively burning, others smouldering. They saw two men standing on the roof of a building that was as yet untouched by fire. The two had seen the scouts and were climbing off the roof. Ingram and Posselt dismounted and got into a kneeling position, aiming their rifles at the approaching men.

Fred had a pair of field glasses and studied the men carefully. "Wait," he exclaimed. "They are white men."

The two men were traders called Usher and Fairbairn. They had been prisoners of Lobengula and quickly related what had happened in KoBulawayo the days before the declaration of war.

"So, where is King Lobengula?" Fred asked.

"Gone," Fairbairn said.

"Took off after you clashed at the Shangani River," Usher added.

Fairbairn continued. "We heard you lot were attacked twice, first at night, then in daylight, and the Matabele suffered big losses both times."

Fred scratched his head. "So Lobengula had already left before we met at Bembezi? It seems he knew he was defeated even before we clashed at Bembezi?"

"Seems so, doesn't it," Fairbairn shrugged.

Usher shuddered involuntarily. "His Indunas wanted to kill us before he left, but Lobengula said no, he didn't want to hurt an innocent white man."

"Really?" Ingram was astounded.

"Yes, that's how we survived."

"Well," Ingram cocked an eyebrow at Fred. "Sounds like Lobengula is a pretty decent man after all."

"We'll need to tell this to Jameson. He is making his way here now," Fred said. "Meanwhile, we need to get back to the column and tell them what's happened. Will you be alright here?"

"Yes," Usher said. "This place is deserted. There's not a soul here apart from us, but there are some whites still in the trading settlement. Go ahead, we'll wait for you."

The next day Fred, Ingram and Posselt reconnected with the columns. Fred made sure he saw Allan before Jameson.

"Lobengula blew his village up. There's nothing left," Fred said. "That's what the black cloud was; his gunpowder store is no more."

"Heavens," Allan exclaimed. "And the King?"

"Absconded. He left after his army's defeat at Shangani."

"Shangani?" Allan said in surprise. "Come, we must tell Jameson immediately."

Jameson was delighted with the news. His main concern now was if Goold-Adams reached KoBulawayo first.

By lunchtime the following day, Jameson was strutting around the ruins of King Lobengula's once vibrant capital. Some of his treasures were recovered from the ashes, but apart from that, everything had been destroyed.

Jameson was over-excited. "We must rebuild this city without delay.

The white trader's camp outside the village must be relocated here, immediately," Jameson directed. "We must find Lobengula and make a treaty for peace. We need an administration to control this land. Rhodes must know KoBulawayo has fallen, and we have it. Major Forbes, bring your notebook."

Meanwhile, Allan gathered his Rangers and secured the village, sending out scouts to look for possible enemy hideouts, and to look for tracks that would indicate where Lobengula was headed. He set up parties to organise water and food supplies, to consult with the remaining traders in the white camp, and others to construct rudimentary shelters because he was sure the rains were on the way. The Victoria Rangers wasted no time in performing their duties; they knew their rewards would come in good time.

"Major Wilson," Jameson called; he was talking fast. "I don't know where Goold-Adams is. There is a rumour that his column was totally annihilated by an Induna called Gambo. I need to get a message urgently to Mr Rhodes. Oh, he will want to hear this news. Where is Burnham? Please get him for me. And we need to raise the Company flag. Find me a BSAC flag. We must raise it immediately."

Jameson was almost out of control. Allan gave him a wide berth and went to find Fred.

"Burnham," Allan called him over. "Jameson is going to want you to take a message to Tati. Are you and your horse up for that?"

"Yes, Sir. I've been to Tati before, but only from the south."

"One more thing; Goold-Adams is missing and believed to have been vanquished by one of Lobengula's impis. Raaff's Rangers are also missing. The way to Tati might be treacherous."

"I'm alright with that, Major Wilson. It shouldn't be a problem."

"Alright, please go see Jameson and offer your services. Be wary; he is in a very excitable way at the moment."

"Yes, Sir," Fred saluted and smiled his understanding.

When Fred saw Jameson, he immediately realised what Allan had meant. Jameson put a folded note in Fred's hand.

"Please get this message to Tati and have them send it to Rhodes with the utmost priority. Rhodes needs to know KoBulawayo is ours, and the King has fled. He must know we were the first here, and the company flag flies above KoBulawayo. This is vitally important."

"Yes, Sir," Fred obliged the doctor.

"And if you come across any of Goold-Adams column, or Raaff's Rangers, tell them to get here on the double. We need their support urgently."

"I will leave this instant, Sir."

"Good man. Thank you, Burnham. Here, this is for you," Jameson handed Fred a tin of cocoa powder. "For your troubles. Make haste, please."

"Thank you, Dr Jameson," Fred smiled. He had not tasted chocolate in a very long time.

Fred returned to Allan. "You were right," Fred chuckled. "Excitable is a fitting description."

"He'll get over it. Got your marching orders?"

"Yes, Sir. Urgent messages for Mr Rhodes. I must make a speedy dash for Tati. It seems the Mangwe Pass could be tricky. May I take someone with me?"

"Of course," Allan smiled. "Let me guess, Ingram?"

Allan had seen Fred and Pearl Ingram sharing a laugh on many occasions on the march to KoBulawayo. They would mock each other jokingly in what he perceived to be American humour. They always seemed to know what the other needed, and somehow anticipated each other's moves. They worked like a well-oiled machine and were very good friends to boot.

Fred laughed. "You know me well, Major. Ingram and I have done many things together. He is an excellent scout, and we each understand how the other works."

"I know," Allan chuckled. "Take another scout with you–someone who knows the land and can talk the lingo. It's always better to go in threes."

"Any suggestions, Sir?"

"There's a Mashona man who has been with me since Victoria. Very reliable. He goes by the name of Dabson. Top bloke. I'll send him to you. Ride safely and return as soon as possible."

"Thank you, Sir," Fred smiled and threw his commander a salute.

Dabson turned out to be an excellent tracker, and to Fred and Ingram's delight, he was a first-class cook too. As a joke, Fred asked Dabson if he knew how to make a chocolate cake using ground maize meal instead of flour. His effort was exceptional and drew hearty accolades.

***

Fred, Ingram and Dabson found Goold-Adams of the Bechuanaland Border Police on the far side of the Mangwe Pass, about sixty miles southwest of KoBulawayo. Induna Gambo had indeed engaged Goold-Adams but had been defeated. Gambo and his impi had dispersed, heading north to join the King. Amongst the granite rocks of the pass, Fred found smouldering fires and signs of walking wounded.

The BBP's chief scout, an intrepid explorer called Fredrick Courtney Selous, took a shine to Fred and Ingram and exchanged many scouting stories and tips. Selous had been injured in the skirmish with Gambo and his warriors, but not badly enough to prevent him from leading Goold-Adam's column to KoBulawayo.

The second BBP column, led by Commandant Piet Raaff, had not been heard from, and Goold-Adams was concerned it had become lost, or, worse, been annihilated by the Matabele. He was particularly concerned that the Raaff Rangers had not reached KoBulawayo because they were a well-trained unit, mostly made of rough-and-ready Boer commandos. These men had earned the nickname Raaff's Riff-Raff.

After completing their business with the BBP, Fred and Ingram made their way toward Tati. The following day, a man appeared, riding towards them with secret messages for Goold-Adams and Dr Jameson. Like Selous, he was another larger-than-life individual named Johan Colenbrander.

Colenbrander had seen a great deal of action in various Zulu wars and carried some impressive scars from spears to show it. An attribute he had that envied many was that he could speak many of the common African languages fluently. His messages for Jameson and Goold-Adams were so urgent he could not waste another minute. He bade them farewell and disappeared into the bush.

Fred and Ingram would soon cross paths with Colenbrander again, but in a most troubling way.

CHAPTER TWENTY-ONE

November 1893

After a hard journey, Mjaan arrived at Lobengula's fleeing wagons. He had Ngwenya with him, and his son, Londisizwe, who had both been involved in the battle at Bembezi. Ngwenya had sustained a flesh wound on his shoulder from a passing bullet but was otherwise fit for duty. Mjaan was very relieved that Londisizwe had escaped unharmed although he was very shaken. Londisizwe had seen many of his impi violently cut down. Mjaan was dreading telling the news to Lobengula, but it had to be done.

"I see you, my King," Mjaan said forlornly and dropped to a knee when he reached the royal wagon.

Lobengula looked drawn. "Tell me what happened."

Mjaan shuddered involuntarily. "We lost most of the impis, my King. We are defeated."

"Then we must make haste for the Great River in the north and rebuild our nation. I know the white man will send more soldiers after me."

"I have sent some old men to stay near KoBulawayo and act like farmers. I have told them they must let the white man capture and question them. If they ask where the King has gone, they must say he has gone to Inyati, which is to the east of where you are moving. We have already laid some false trails to confuse them."

Lobengula grunted in satisfaction. "You have done well. That is a good strategy."

Just then, Londisizwe approached the wagon and knelt slightly away from Mjaan. Lobengula called him over.

"My King," Londisizwe spoke to the ground in respect. "A Mashona man has arrived with a message for you."

Lobengula looked shocked. "How did a Mashona dog find me?"

"He was asking our people to bring him to you as he has a message from Dr Jameson."

Lobengula weighed this revelation carefully in his mind. "Bring the cowardly dog to me," Lobengula grumbled.

The messenger was a young man in his twenties. He was petrified to come before the King. Mjaan ensured he got onto his knees forthwith. Taking a folded piece of paper from him, Mjaan passed it to the King.

An old man who had been taught the basics of reading and writing in English by the missionary Moffatt was sent for.

"What does the message say?" Lobengula demanded of the old man.

"My King, it is a message from Doctor Jameson. It says: To King Lobengula. The war is over. It is finished. You must return to KoBulawayo immediately and surrender. You will be treated properly and shown respect if you return now."

"Is that so?" Lobengula grinned. "I have a message for Jameson."

Mjaan looked respectfully at Lobengula. "My King, before you send a message to Jameson, may I speak with you?"

Lobengula nodded. "Take this Mashona dog away from me until I have my answer."

Londisizwe and Ngwenya unceremoniously dragged the messenger away from Lobengula's presence.

"My King," Mjaan lowered his voice. "When this messenger takes your reply back to Jameson, he will tell him where you are."

Lobengula frowned in consternation; Mjaan was right. "What do you suggest?"

"I suggest we kill the messenger immediately. Then one of my men will deliver your reply to KoBulawayo and hand your letter to the first white man they see. Let that white man deliver the letter to Dr Jameson, not the Mashona messenger."

Lobengula smiled. "You are very clever, Mjaan. Arrange for this right away."

***

Allan was studying a map outside his tent when a trooper from the

Salisbury Horse ran up to him. He saluted Allan and handed him a note. The wet season had set in and drenched every man and horse with torrential downpours. Allan didn't particularly enjoy the wet weather.

"From Dr Jameson, Major," the trooper said, quite out of breath.

Allan opened the note and read it immediately. He had been summoned to the good doctor's tent. It seemed that some urgency was required.

"Thank you, Trooper," Allan smiled. "Please take my horse over to Captain Judd. Let him know I have been called to Dr Jameson."

"Will do, Sir," the trooper saluted again and took the reins.

Allan strode over to Dr Jameson's tent. When he ducked through the entrance, he faced a group of people around a table, two of whom he had never met, although he had an inkling of who they may be.

"Major Wilson," Jameson beamed. "Come in. May I introduce you to Colonel Goold-Adams of the Bechuanaland Border Police and Commandant Raaff of Raaff's Rangers? Gentlemen, this is Major Allan Wilson."

Brief introductions were made, and Allan took the seat that had been provided for him. Opposite was Major Forbes and John Willoughby, Jameson's military advisor. Allan nodded his acknowledgement, then quickly studied the two newcomers.

Goold-Adams was a distinguished-looking gentleman with fine white hair, combed neatly with a perfectly straight parting on the left side of his head. Despite the white hair, he sported a heavy black moustache. It made his features striking, but also made it difficult for Allan to judge his age. Allan settled on the estimate that Goold-Adams was in his mid-fifties. Regardless of age, the Colonel was the most senior military man in the room. His military uniform was immaculate, and he displayed an air of confidence.

Commandant Raaff was quite the opposite. His scruffy, untidy beard and moustache matched his uniform. He was in need of a barber, and his hair, which he parted down the middle, was flattened down with hair cream. His eyes were sad, and Allan felt Raaff could tell more than a few depressing stories. He was younger than Goold-Adams, probably in his mid-forties, making him perhaps five or six years older than Allan himself. Raaff didn't seem pleased to be in the meeting.

Jameson continued. "I will recap for Major Wilson's benefit. Lobengula has fled, but I need him to surrender to end these hostilities and allow us to get on with developing this land. I have instructions from Mr Rhodes that Lobengula needs to return to KoBulawayo and disband his army. I have sent a message to him requesting that he surrender, and assuring him that we will treat him correctly and honourably. I received a response this morning."

"I didn't realise that," Goold-Adams said. "And?"

"Well, it's a bit confusing," Jameson said. "He said he would stop fleeing, but he wants to know what arrangements we have made for his accommodation, and specifically asks where his emissaries are."

Forbes entered the conversation. "He knows damn well where his emissaries are. Two were shot dead at Tati, and the survivor made off to tell him so."

"Who killed his emissaries?" Goold-Adams asked.

Jameson answered. "A very unfortunate accident, I'm afraid. I was stalling for time and arranged with Lobengula for three of his emissaries to meet with Rhodes and Sir Henry Loch in Cape Town. I sent them down with a well-known trader in the camp called James Dawson as their guide."

"James Dawson?" Allan interrupted. "A Scot?"

"Yes," Jameson smiled, somewhat bemused. "You know him?"

"If it's the same man, yes. We attended the same school when we were youngsters. Tall, thin man?"

"Indeed. Anyhow," Jameson returned to the subject, "when Jimmy Dawson got to Tati, he was exhausted and probably petrified from walking through the bush with three savage Matabele. He handed them to the care of one of the BSAC troopers at Tati without proper instruction and went in search of water, which he had been without for an extended time. There was some confusion, and a breakdown of understanding as a result of Jimmy's absence, and a fight broke out. Two emissaries were killed, and the other escaped. They killed two BSAC troopers in the melee."

Goold-Adams sighed. "Of course Lobengula knows then. The emissary who escaped would have wasted no time in telling him."

"Especially as the man is his half-brother," Forbes added.

Allan raised an eyebrow at that comment.

"In Lobengula's reply, he also wanted stationery," Jameson frowned. "He sounds confused."

"I would say he is stalling for time," Allan added.

"That's exactly what I think," Jameson agreed. "So, this is what I will do: I will form a patrol to pursue Lobengula, preferably to bring him back alive, or to kill him if it comes to that. The Matabele army must be neutralised, and this can only be achieved with the King's capture or death.

"Lobengula is heading north, to Inyati; we know that. I want Major Forbes to form a patrol of competent men. The Company cannot afford to pay them, so Mr Rhodes instructed that they must be volunteers, and we will reward them as usual. I want the patrol selected from the Salisbury Horse, Victoria Rangers, the BBP and your Rangers, Commandant Raaff.

"Major Forbes, you are to command the Salisbury Horse, Major Wilson, the Victoria Rangers, and Commandant Raaff will have command of both the BBP and the Raaff's Rangers, but," he paused, "I place Major Forbes in overall command of the column."

Then Jameson said something that confused everyone present.

"Major Forbes, although you command the joint forces, you must consult Commandant Raaff on everything you do."

Allan furrowed his brow and sat back in his chair, a look of confusion on his face. Even Willoughby looked perplexed. Colonel Goold-Adams, the most highly ranked member of the column, was not in the column, and Major Forbes, the most junior of them all, was in overall charge. To make matters even more unusual, Raaff, an Imperial Officer who was more senior to both Allan and Forbes in age, rank and experience, was reduced to the role of advisor to a commander who was not only a lower rank, but younger and less experienced in active battle than all of them. Allan couldn't help but wonder what was going on behind the scenes to cause such a strange chain of command.

Allan looked at Raaff, expecting to see some reaction, but he was poker-faced. Willoughby just shook his head in resignation, causing Allan to believe Jameson was not listening to his advisor.

"Gentlemen," Jameson concluded, "please gather your volunteers and prepare to leave at first light."

Just as everyone exited the tent, Allan turned to Jameson as an afterthought.

"Excuse me, Sir, do you know if Mr Dawson is in camp?"

Jameson smiled. "Yes, I believe he is. He has a tent about a mile out of town, where all the traders have set up."

"Marvellous. I'll make a point of visiting him later today. I haven't seen him for many years."

"Good show," Jameson beamed. "Do me a favour, will you? While you are there, please ask Jimmy, on my behalf, to get the word out to all the traders and prospectors at the camp to relocate their tents and wagons. I want them all here, on the site of Lobengula's royal village."

"I'll do that for you, certainly," Allan agreed.

"Unfortunately, the current traders camp is in a slight depression, and with the rains upon us, they will soon become bogged in. Some traders have more permanent wood and thatch huts, especially the Jews and the Greeks. They will have to abandon them, I'm afraid. Tell Dawson that if they resist, he must suggest the threat of a Matabele attack. That will get them moving."

Allan frowned. "Are you expecting an attack?"

"No," Jameson almost laughed. "The Matabele are well and truly defeated. But, we must capture or kill the King. That is paramount. Mr Rhodes has demanded it, and we won't let him down, will we?"

***

Allan gathered his captains and allocated tasks to them all. He knew that by sunrise the Victoria Rangers would be organised and ready. Jameson had instructed each man to be issued with one hundred rounds of ammunition—this task Allan gave to Captains Fitzgerald and Napier. Captain Lendy reported directly to Forbes because he would be in charge of one of the Maxims, and he needed a different quota.

They would be taking provisions for four days only. Jameson believed they would reach the fleeing King in two days, and it would take less than one day to capture or kill him. Knowing the rains had arrived, Allan instructed his men to make sure they took suitable clothing and protection. Once all was in motion, Allan walked down to the trader's camp to seek out James Dawson.

The trader's camp was disorganised, with tents, wagons and the odd hut randomly placed between trees and bushes. Mud splashes from the rains had stained the base of every tent, and overall the camp looked quite a mess.

Allan roamed about for a bit, taking in all there was to see. Mostly, people seemed very relaxed, and an air of lethargy hung heavily over the camp. He came across a fairly large, square building made from mud and pole walls and rusted corrugated iron sheets for a roof. Two smartly dressed young men sat on makeshift stools outside. A large sign that said 'Langbourne Bros.' hung above the door. The two men looked miserable.

"Good afternoon, Gentlemen," Allan greeted them jovially, hoping to elicit a smile.

They both jumped to their feet, returning his cheerful greeting with the smile Allan had hoped for.

"Good afternoon, Sir," the younger brother replied, "How may we help you?"

"I'm looking for a trader named James Dawson. Have you heard of him?"

"Indeed. That's his tent over there," the other said, pointing to a bedraggled awning not far off.

"Nice setup you have here," Allan looked at the wooden structure. The corrugated iron roofing was uncommon.

Big raindrops started to thud on the roof. "Best you make your way to Mr Dawson's tent before the rain starts," the older brother said, casting a glance at the sky. "I'd offer you some shelter in here, but I think it's drier outdoors."

Allan laughed. "I'm delivering a message to Mr Dawson that he must arrange for everyone to move to the location of the Royal Village. Dr Jameson has instructed that this camp be abandoned and moved there. It might do you good to have a chat with Dr Jameson soon as he will allocate a new plot to you. Also, you're going to get bogged in soon."

"Thank you for the advice, Sir, we will most definitely do that. My name is David Langbourne, and this is my brother, Morris. Pleased to meet you, Sir."

"Wilson, Allan Wilson," Allan shook hands with the brothers. "Thank you for the directions. I'll be away for a few days. I'll look you up when I return; looks like you may have an interesting outfit here."

Allan walked briskly to James Dawson's tent as the rain increased in intensity. The tent flap was open, and he found Dawson reading a book.

"Well, if it isn't Wilson himself," James looked up with a forced smile.

"Fancy meeting you here," Allan laughed. "How are you, Dawson?"

They shook hands amicably and exchanged some pleasantries. Allan delivered Jameson's message.

"I heard you are engaged to be married to May Thompson," James wasted no time broaching a subject close to his heart.

"I'm not sure if the engagement is still on. I've been in Africa for sixteen years now, and correspondence is poor at best. She may well have moved on, and I would respect that."

James smiled softly. "Are you going back to Scotland?"

"Yes. I'll visit May and take it from there. I had resigned myself to returning to Fochabers and, in fact, was about to tender my resignation when this hullabaloo with Lobengula started, but first, I want to see what Jameson will reward me and our men with. It seems there will be some interesting concessions in land and mining claims."

"I see," James nodded his understanding.

Allan frowned. "I have one more mission to complete. We leave tomorrow, but I should be back before the week is out."

"Right-oh," Dawson smiled weakly. "Best of luck. By the way, why did you steal the belt the headmaster used as a tawse?"

"Oh," Allan laughed, "that wasn't just me; I got a few of my friends to help me break into his office one night. We started a rumour after we stole it, saying it was taken in protest of the girls being beaten."

"Did it work?" James asked.

"Yes, the beatings stopped, but I heard a few years later a new headmaster reintroduced it. What did you do with the thing?"

Dawson laughed and slapped his belly. "I'm wearing it."

Allan looked at the belt around James' waist. "Good Lord," Allan smiled. "At least it found a useful purpose."

Dawson reached over and shook Allan's hand. "Go well, Major Wilson."

"Allan, call me Allan."

"They call me Jimmy. Pop in when you get back from your mission."

CHAPTER TWENTY-TWO

14th November 1893

Londisizwe ran to Mjaan and crouched by his feet. "Father, the warrior we sent to KoBulawayo with the message for the white soldiers has returned."

"What news does he bring?" Mjaan scowled.

"He gave the King's letter to a white man who successfully gave it to the Doctor. We know this because the white men are moving to Inyati, just as you planned."

Mjaan grinned. He was pleased with this news. "Good. Now when our spies are interrogated by these white men, their soldiers will move faster after the King, and further away. Send the messenger to me, I wish to ask him questions."

"Yes, Father," Londisizwe smiled broadly and quickly obeyed. He was proud of his father.

The messenger arrived and dropped to his knees in front of Mjaan, who told the man to stand.

"The white men did not suspect you to be a Matabele?"

"No, Induna," the man shook his head confirming this. "I did not see their Induna, and he did not see me. A lesser soldier took the message to their Induna. These men are not clever."

"Good. My ears tell me they are going to Inyati."

"Yes, Induna. They move to Inyati, as you say."

"Did you see how many?"

"Yes, Induna. Less than half those we met at Bembezi."

"How many wagons?"

The messenger held up his hands and splayed his fingers, showing ten wagons. "About that many."

"What about the 'sigwagwa'?" Mjaan asked, using their new nickname for the Maxim machine guns.

The messenger held up one hand, showing four fingers.

"What about the big guns?" he pressed, meaning the Hotchkiss.

One finger was held aloft.

Mjaan smirked. He was pleased to hear they had a vastly reduced force. "That is good. You have done well. Stay close to Londisizwe, I may have more instructions for you."

"Thank you, Induna," the messenger bowed and retreated backwards in respect.

Mjaan caught up to the slow-moving wagons that escorted King Lobengula and waited for the column to halt. Going through the bush was tough, and several times they had to change direction to avoid thickets or rocky outcrops. The intermittent rain muddied the ground, also hampering progress.

Mjaan tapped on the wooden side and waited for the invitation to enter. When he heard Lobengula grunt permission he jumped lightly onto the wagon. Lobengula was resting and looked very uncomfortable. A sheen of sweat glistened on his forehead.

"My King," Mjaan wasted no time in passing on the good news, "the white men are moving to Inyati. They are going the wrong way, and their force is reduced."

Lobengula grimaced as he shifted onto his elbow. "So, I was right; they are coming after me. They do not wish to negotiate."

Mjaan hadn't thought of it this way. The King was correct. "Would you like me to send my men to attack and kill them? They are few, and we still have many warriors."

"No," Lobengula frowned. "We will be beaten again. The weapons they have, which they did not give us, will defeat our men quickly. We must keep moving as fast as we can."

Mjaan nodded, accepting his orders, and left the wagon smartly.

***

The town of KoBulawayo was a hive of activity when Fred and Ingram dismounted. Their journey back was uneventful, and each night when they retired they commented on how easy the day had been. No Matabele to harass them, and no fresh spoor to be concerned about.

A BSAC soldier stood guard outside Dr Jameson's tent. Fred approached him and advised that he had messages to deliver to the good doctor. Both Fred and Ingram were ushered into the tent without delay. Jameson was pleased to see the men and asked them to wait while he quickly cast his eye over the mail.

"All seems to be in order," Jameson smiled broadly. "Thank you for your services, Gentlemen."

"Our pleasure," Fred smiled back. "We should probably report to Major Wilson now."

"Ahh...." Jameson cleared his throat. "He is not in camp. The Victoria Rangers have gone in pursuit of the King. It is imperative he be brought back to surrender."

"Do you wish us to follow them?" Ingram offered.

"Well, actually," Jameson hesitated, "of course I would like you to assist them, but I cannot ask that of you after all you have done."

Fred could tell by Jameson's tone that he was hoping they *would* offer their services again. He glanced at Ingram seeking confirmation. He registered a slight nod.

"We would be happy to continue our service under you," Fred said.

"It is on a volunteer basis, I'm afraid," Jameson frowned, "however, there will be compensation from the Company once the mission is successful, as usual."

Fred and Ingram had heard in Tati that the shares in the British South Africa Company had doubled since the news of the taking of KoBulawayo had reached London.

"We understand," Fred smiled. "As before, we would gladly accept a share of the spoils of the war as payment. Even Company shares would suit us. Not so, Ingram?"

"Indeed," Ingram confirmed.

"Good show!" Jameson's eagerness surprised the scouts. "But first, I cannot allow you to go without a medical examination to see if you are fit and well enough. Meet me at the infirmary in half an hour."

Fred laughed. "You'll find Ingram and I are made of biltong. When may we leave?"

"If you pass the medical," Jameson said, "you may leave tomorrow morning. The column left yesterday and should reach Inyati tomorrow. Inyati is about forty miles north. You should reach there in a day."

The medical examination went exceedingly well, leaving Jameson scratching his head as to how robust the two Americans were. They left the following morning, just before sunrise, and re-joined their column just as the sun was setting.

***

Commandant Raaff walked over to Forbes, who was in a heated discussion with Allan and Colenbrander. Colenbrander had been asked to join the patrol as their interpreter. Cowering at their feet was a captured Matabele youth. His hands and feet were bound by leather straps.

"What is the problem?" Raaff asked.

"Commandant," Forbes acknowledged the man but was not pleased he had joined the discussion. "This youth was captured and questioned about the flight of the King. He said he saw him pass this way yesterday."

"Do you believe this boy?" Raaff asked.

"Yes," Forbes replied, "what he says makes absolute sense."

Allan interjected. "I don't believe him."

"Nor do I," Colenbrander added.

Raaff looked at the hapless youth at his feet. "Meneer Colenbrander, as a man who understands their language fluently, why don't you believe him?"

Colenbrander shrugged. "Because I have lived with these people all my life."

"And Major Forbes, what makes you believe him?"

"Because, Commandant," Forbes face flushed, "Dr Jameson said Lobengula was heading this way. All herders we have found here have confirmed it, and even this man confirms what is known. What do you think, Commandant?" Forbes threw the question at him in frustration.

Raaff looked at the captive again and paused in thought. "I say he is lying."

Forbes grunted. "Well, I do not, and we will press on."

"As you say, Major," Raaff said despondently.

"May I make a suggestion?" Allan asked. When nobody objected, he continued. "Those two American scouts joined us last night. They can find a needle in a haystack. I suggest we send them forward to look for the

King's spoor. His wagon tracks will be very difficult for most people to spot; they are obscured by an impi of warriors, herds of cattle and a civilian population on foot following him. But it will be easy for those Americans to find; they have an incredible ability to read the signs of the land. If they locate the wagon tracks we press on, but if not, we return to KoBulawayo and report that we have failed to locate Lobengula."

"We cannot fail this assignment," Forbes said through gritted teeth.

"Gentlemen," Raaff spoke softly, but with authority. "If we fail, it is not of our doing. Firstly, we were not provisioned properly. We were allocated four days of supplies for a task that should have taken three days. Already we have used our entire allocation, and we are yet to find the tracks of the King's exodus. Our men are discontented. There is much complaining. We have too few wagons to laager for effective protection. If the Matabele mount an attack, we are doomed. What I also find unacceptable is that Dr Jameson, himself a medical practitioner, has sent us out here without any medical supplies. I find this nothing short of incompetent."

Forbes' brow furrowed, his face turned a deeper scarlet, and he struggled to control his breathing.

"Alright," he finally acquiesced, "send the Americans out. Let's see what they say."

Fred and Ingram spent the day scouting for tracks but found nothing. That evening, they reported their findings to Forbes, who was now in an uncomfortable dilemma. He decided to retire to Shiloh, which was about halfway back to KoBulawayo, just a little more to the west. There, he knew, he would find a mission outpost that had some food and shelter, although not enough to sustain his column.

Three riders were sent back to KoBulawayo, requesting that Jameson send provisions to Shiloh on the double and meet them there. The effect of turning around sowed further discontent amongst the ranks, including the officers.

When the column reached Shiloh the following day it was raining hard. The men were hungry, tired and openly disgruntled. There was no food at Shiloh, which didn't help matters, and the re-supply from KoBulawayo was to take yet another day to arrive. With the ground getting a good soaking, and the mud making travel more difficult, the Maxims were becoming a liability rather than an asset.

While the soldiers grumbled under whatever shelter they could find from the rain, Fred, Ingram and Bain went out again and returned later that afternoon.

"Sir," Fred approached Forbes, "we have found the King's tracks."

"What?" Forbes frowned. "Are you sure?"

"Yes, Sir. He is heading north with thousands of warriors and even more cattle. We estimate he has five wagons with him, and he may only be a day or two ahead of us."

This was bittersweet news for Forbes. He was finally pursuing the King, but his gullibility in listening to the natives had been proven, and his authority sorely tested.

CHAPTER TWENTY-THREE

2nd December 1893

The King's column was settling for the night. The women folk had started the campfires and begun cooking the meals for all the men and children. A light rain had fallen throughout the day, and everyone was soaked.

Mjaan was crouching under one of the King's wagons. His wife had made a thin soup over an open fire and passed him some in a clay pot.

"Thank you, Thandiwe," Mjaan smiled at his loving wife.

"You have walked far today, Husband. You must rest tonight."

"We have all walked far. The days will be difficult soon, but we must keep moving."

"Tell me again how powerful our son is. Tell me how he fought the white man."

"Ahh...." Mjaan sighed, then blew some steam off the top of the clay pot. "He is a fine warrior. He is very brave and very strong. My heart was pleased when I saw him in battle."

Thandiwe smiled lovingly. "I always knew he would make a fine warrior."

Ngwenya suddenly appeared and ducked under the wagon. "Induna, I have news from our spies."

"What is it?" Mjaan's mood changed abruptly.

"The white men changed direction and are now in Shiloh."

"Shiloh?" Mjaan reiterated in surprise. "Why did they go to Shiloh?"

"I don't know, Induna. But, their scout, *the one who sees in the dark*, he has picked up our trail."

"Ghaa!" Mjaan exclaimed. This was not good news at all. "We don't have enough distance yet. The King's wagon moves very slowly."

"My spies say they think they have run out of food and are waiting for more."

Mjaan pondered for a moment. "Alright, I will speak to the King. Send the spies back. I need more information."

Ngwenya smiled. "I have already sent more spies; those with fresh legs. They will be there before the sun comes up."

"Good," Mjaan nodded. "Thank you, Ngwenya."

***

Provisions had arrived at Shiloh, and just in the nick of time. The members of the column were at breaking point; tempers were strained, and insults aimed at Forbes were commonplace. Allan refrained from involving himself with the ill feelings, choosing instead to stay with his troops and keep the team spirit intact. Raaff's Rangers and Forbes' Salisbury Horse were openly angry.

Forbes called Allan and Raaff for a meeting at his tent. He needed to discuss options, but, although it would outwardly be a discussion, Forbes had already made up his mind on the action he planned to take.

"The column is too large and cumbersome, and we are being hampered by bad weather," Forbes stated. "It needs to be trimmed down."

"What do you have in mind, Sir?" Allan asked curiously.

"I have enough rations for three hundred men for twelve days, so I want to reduce the column to three hundred. The rest must go back to KoBulawayo. Call your men to parade in half an hour and I will ask for volunteers. Of those who volunteer, please select only the strongest and best men for the job."

"Forgive me, Sir," Raaff said quietly, "I have just over ninety members of the BBP under me. They are an Imperial Force, so they are not volunteers."

Forbes controlled his exasperation. "Very well, they are exempt, but your 'Riff-Raff' are not. We will lighten the column and take four wagons, four maxims and the Hotchkiss."

"I am still concerned that you do not have a hospital wagon," Raaff continued in his calculatedly soft tone. "I believe that is a mistake."

Allan noticed Forbes' face start to redden.

"My hands are tied, Commandant. Besides, we will only be away for a few days, and the King's forces are depleted and defeated. Now, please, if you will, call your men to parade."

Allan and Raaff left Forbes' tent and called their soldiers to attention on a level piece of muddy land. Forbes strutted out of his tent and explained the situation; only three hundred men would be selected, and volunteers were to step forward. All three, Forbes, Allan and Raaff, were shocked by what happened next.

Of Forbes' regiment, the Salisbury Horse, only seventeen men stepped forward; of Raaff's ninety-strong contingent, only four men took a pace forward. Surprisingly, every single one of Allan's Victoria Rangers stepped forward and volunteered without hesitation.

Allan's pride in his men skyrocketed. Forbes' face turned scarlet. Raaff shook his head in embarrassment and walked away.

The following morning the company split, almost half heading south to KoBulawayo, and two hundred and ninety men heading north, hot on the heels of Lobengula. Captain Borrow commanded twenty-two men of the Salisbury Horse, as before. Raaff took the Rangers consisting of twenty men, and Captain Coventry commanded seventy-eight men of the BBP.

Allan's Victoria Horse consisted of one hundred and seventy men all up. On his team were Fred, Ingram, Bain and Colenbrander. Allan looked over his men as they started their march; he was a very proud man. Unknown to him, his men were just as proud to have him as their leader.

Despite the reduction of the size of the Patrol, the going was so difficult that, after only seventeen miles, Forbes reduced the column's size by almost half again. With just over one hundred and fifty men and only two maxims, the Patrol struck out in pursuit of Lobengula.

**

Ngwenya ran to Mjaan. It was a hard run, but he was not out of breath.

"Induna, the white men began moving on our trail this morning."

Mjaan looked at the treetops in contemplation.

"There is other news," Ngwenya continued, "half of them are returning to KoBulawayo, together with some of the sigwagwa guns."

"That must be because they can't move the big guns fast in the rain." Mjaan hypothesised.

"But now that they are less, they can move much faster."

Mjaan frowned. "Yes, but I also think they have no idea how big our army is. It makes no sense why they would reduce their force and weapons."

"Yes, it doesn't make sense," Ngwenya agreed.

"Alright. Thank you, Ngwenya. I will speak to the King."

Mjaan trotted to the lead wagon and knocked on the wooden side. Lobengula acknowledged the request, and Mjaan leapt into the vehicle. The King seemed to be in pain but attempted to hide it.

"My King, the white man has found our trail and has begun to move forward."

"I expected this," Lobengula frowned. "They want me dead; they do not want to negotiate. All they want is gold."

Mjaan wanted to suggest he surrender, but he also knew it was too late, and they both knew the white man could not be trusted. He crouched in silence, careful not to topple over in the swaying wagon. Lobengula opened a metal trunk by his side and withdrew two cloth pouches. They were held closed by drawstrings. He tossed them to Mjaan, who caught them easily. They made a soft clinking sound as they landed in his hands.

"These are gold sovereigns, the kind the white man likes. Send a messenger to the leader of the white army with these sovereigns and say that they must stop their advance immediately. This gold is my guarantee that I will surrender and return to KoBulawayo and stop fighting. If they accept the gold and continue to advance, then I will regard that as a sign that they want to kill me, and I will fight to the death."

Mjaan nodded forlornly. "I understand, my King."

"Now repeat that to me."

"The white army must stop advancing immediately. This gold is my guarantee that I will surrender and return to KoBulawayo. If they accept the gold and continue to advance, then I will regard this as a sign that they want to kill me, and I will fight to the death."

Lobengula nodded. "Say it again."

Mjaan repeated the message.

"Good. Now send a messenger. Send an old man so that they do not think the messenger is a warrior and shoot him."

"It will be done," Mjaan said, then left the wagon.

***

Trooper William Daniel and Trooper James Wilson, both British subjects, were stragglers. Miserable in their demeanour, they always found their way to the column's rear, where they were not supervised properly and therefore contributed little to the cause. They were lazy, and, because of their common desire to do as little as possible, became good friends.

Always quick to complain, ridicule or offer sarcastic comments, they weren't particularly liked by the other soldiers. As a result, they were often left alone at the back of the column. They had only joined the volunteer column to be able to claim the spoils of war, not to participate if they could possibly help it. They were relegated to 'batmen', servants to officers, to carry and care for their kit during a campaign.

The column had been following the King's trail for two days, and Daniel and Wilson were lagging about a mile behind the column, as was common for them. Up ahead, they saw an old Matabele man standing with his arms outstretched above his head.

"What's he doing?" Daniel asked.

"I haven't a clue," Wilson said. "Ask him."

Daniel could speak a little isiNdebele. He waved the man to come forward. The old man hobbled closer and stopped a couple of yards in front of the two horses.

"What do you want, old man?" Daniel gesticulated rudely at him.

"I have a message for your leader from my King. Please take me to him."

"No," Daniel said condescendingly, then pointed ahead. "You can find him yourself. He is that way."

"Thank you, Boss," the man said and turned to leave.

"What'd he want, eh?" Wilson asked his friend.

"He has a message for Forbes from Lobengula."

"Oi!" Wilson shouted at the Matabele and gestured for him to come back. "Ask him what the message is," he said to Daniel.

"Old man, what is the message?"

"I have a message for your leader from my King."

"Alright, alright, I know that, but what is the bleedin' message?"

"My King says: Stop your advance immediately and I will surrender. Take this gold as my guarantee that I will return to KoBulawayo. If you take the gold and do not stop your advance, I will understand you want to kill me, and so I will not stop fighting."

Daniel looked at Wilson and cocked an eyebrow.

"What?" Wilson said.

Daniel didn't answer Wilson, instead, he turned back to the old man. "I can pass this message to my leader. I will go faster on my horse."

The old man nodded his acceptance of this offer.

"Where is the gold?" Daniel asked.

The old man reached into an antelope skin bag he had slung over his shoulder and withdrew two pouches.

"Give it to me," Daniel demanded.

The old man reached up and handed it to Daniel. He weighed the pouches in his hand and almost whistled in disbelief at how heavy they were, however, he checked himself.

"You can go now," Daniel said. "I will deliver the message now. Off you go."

Once the messenger had vanished into the bush, Daniel tossed one of the pouches to Wilson. They loosened the drawstrings and looked into the leather containers.

"Blimey!" Wilson exclaimed. "What do you think this is worth?"

"A bloody fortune, that's what it's worth," Daniel shook his head in disbelief.

"What's it for?"

"Lobengula wants to surrender. The gold is to pay for Forbes to stop hunting him. If Forbes takes the gold and continues, Lobengula will attack."

Wilson gave this some thought. "So, if Forbes attacks, there is a very good chance he will get killed by the Matabele."

"Exactly," Daniel sneered.

Wilson grinned and looked at Daniel. "You know, nobody knows about this gold except us."

"My thoughts exactly," Daniel smirked.

The damp grass and trees smothered their raucous laughter.

***

Mjaan jumped into the Royal wagon. He thought Lobengula looked worse.

"My King, the gold was delivered to the white man, but they continue to advance."

Lobengula grunted. "It is what I thought. They only want to kill me."

The two men held their silence as thoughts swirled through their minds. Finally, Lobengula spoke.

"Mjaan, I want you to think of a way to get me and my people across the Great River before the white man catches us. Can you do that?"

"Yes, my King. I can do that."

"Where are we now?"

"We are about to cross the Shangani River. We are about halfway to the Great River."

"If I recall," Lobengula grunted as he shifted position, "the bush is difficult to pass after the Shangani River."

"It is difficult, my King. The white man will catch us soon if we don't move faster."

"What do you suggest, Mjaan?"

"We must move you from the wagon and let our warriors carry you on a different path. I want to wait at the Shangani River and fight the white man there. I have a plan to defeat them if we wait at the Shangani River."

"What is your plan?" Lobengula asked.

"The rains are upon us. I want the white men to cross the Shangani, then when the water flows hard, which will be very soon, they will be trapped and will not be able to go backwards. They will be in the forest and can't use the sigwagwa guns properly. We can take our time to kill them. They will run out of bullets quickly, and nobody can bring them more. If anyone tries, I will have men in place to stop them. They will run out of food, and, again, nobody can bring them more."

Lobengula nodded gravely. "Alright. That is a wise strategy. It must be done. Arrange to move me to the Great River, and set your trap. Do not fail mc, Mjaan."

"I will not fail you, my King," Mjaan bowed his head in respect, determined to succeed.

Jumping out of the wagon, he signalled Ngwenya to his side.

"Find Londisizwe and tell him to bring our people over the Shangani River quickly. I want everyone across the river by tomorrow."

Ngwenya nodded that he understood.

"Now, Ngwenya," Mjaan became very serious, "I want you to take three hundred of our best warriors back the way we came. Put mud on your bodies, and grass in your hair. You must look dirty and tired. Walk like you are hurting. When you find the white man's army, tell them you are returning to KoBulawayo to surrender to Jameson. Tell them you are tired and sick, and unhappy with the King, and you do not want to fight any more."

Ngwenya looked at his commander in astonishment.

"Then," Mjaan continued, "after you pass the army, turn to the west and then north again, and come to the place where we will cross the Shangani River. *The one who sees in the dark* will not see your tracks this time. Do not cross the river, but hide. When the white man's army arrives, wait until you see them follow our tracks over the river. I do not want them to see that you backtracked to the river. When they are all across the river, move to the banks and block them. They must not return. If a white man tries to cross back over, kill him. If anyone brings food and bullets to them from KoBulawayo, kill them also. Do not let them cross the Shangani River."

"That will be done," Ngwenya nodded vigorously.

"Now go. May the ancestors watch over you well."

***

Forbes called the column to a halt. Ahead, hundreds of Matabele warriors began emerging from the bushes. They did not seem to have a leader, and looked like a disorganised, pathetic group of defeated men.

"Colenbrander," Forbes called to his interpreter.

Colenbrander sidled up to Forbes, and was immediately joined by Allan and Raaff.

"What do you make of that?" Forbes asked.

"No idea," Colenbrander said. "They're coming our way."

"Let them come," Forbes said quietly. "They don't look aggressive."

"I don't trust them," Raaff said under his breath.

A huge number of Matabele walked past at a gentle pace. They certainly looked defeated. They were filthy and emaciated and had clearly been living rough for some time.

Colenbrander shouted at one of the men to stop. "Where are you going?" he asked.

"Back to KoBulawayo," the man said in surprise; he didn't expect a white man to speak isiNdebele so fluently.

"Where have you been?"

"We were with King Lobengula. He is sick and defeated, and we no longer wish to serve with him. We are returning to Doctor Jameson."

"Where is King Lobengula?"

"That way," the warrior pointed in the direction they had come from.

"How far is the King?" Colenbrander pressed.

"Near. He is soon to cross the Shangani River."

All the while the questions were being asked and answered, Matabele continued to walk past the column. Colenbrander related what had been said to Forbes.

Forbes nodded. "Alright, let them pass."

"I don't trust them," Raaff objected.

"What do you expect me to do, Commandant?" Forbes snapped back. "Most of them have already passed us. They are clearly defeated."

"Disarm them at least," Raaff scowled.

The all-too-familiar scarlet hue began to rise in Forbes' face. "No, it will delay us. There are hundreds of them, and the King is just up ahead."

"I think Commandant Raaff is right," Colenbrander said. "They should be disarmed."

"No, we press on," Forbes ordered. "KoBulawayo can tend to that."

"I don't trust them," Allan said as he watched them pass. Deciding there was no point in arguing with Forbes at this point, he spurred his horse forward to re-join his unit.

CHAPTER TWENTY-FOUR

3rd December 1893

The shallow waters of the Shangani River lapped gently over Mjaan's feet. He stood in the middle of the soothing flow of water and gazed at the opposite bank. It was only about thirty yards across, but he knew one more heavy thunderstorm, bringing with it plenty of rain, would swell the river to more than ten times its width. It would also deepen the river considerably and make it impossible to cross.

Mjaan smiled to himself; they had arrived in time, and his people could cross without hindrance. He wished, though, that the sangoma was near at hand to perform a rain ceremony. Once across the river, a flash flood would solve all his problems. Nevertheless, he knew he could not depend on a flash flood just at the time he wanted it, so his other contingencies were still important.

Turning back, he splashed through the water, careful not to slip on the smooth, rounded pebbles that formed the riverbed. He signalled the first of the King's wagons across, then stood aside as it rumbled past him.

Once safely across the river, with the remnants of the KoBulawayo population and Matabele warriors following behind the Royal Convoy, Mjaan arranged for the transfer of the King onto a makeshift seat attached to long poles, to be carried swiftly by a team of strong warriors. With the King safely on his way, Mjaan turned to set his military strategy in place; his aim was to stop the settlers' advance once and for all.

***

"This is the Shangani River on the right, Sir," Colenbrander informed his commander.

"Not a significant river," Forbes grumbled.

"We should have no problems crossing it, providing the rain doesn't intensify," Captain Borrow mused as he looked at the stream.

"Very good," Forbes nodded, then looked at the sky. "We make camp here for the night."

"I'll call the halt," Borrow said and rode off to issue instructions.

Forbes saw Fred returning from his scouting excursion and waited for him.

"Sir," Fred exclaimed excitedly, "the King has crossed the river just upstream, about a mile further on."

"Very good," Forbes smiled his pleasure. "How far ahead is he?"

"I would say he crossed about mid-day."

"Excellent, we are gaining on him. I suspect we will have him tomorrow."

"Sir, I have a concern."

"Go ahead, Burnham."

"Just beyond where the King crossed the river is a dense forest a little to the south, on this side of the river. I fear there are warriors in that forest. I saw some movement in the trees. I cannot be sure they are warriors, but it would be a perfect trap if that is the case. You will be cut off if you cross the river."

"Have you seen tracks indicating a breakaway from the King's column heading for that forest?" Forbes asked.

"No, Sir. I looked but saw none, but to be certain, I ask permission to scout that forest."

"No, that will not be necessary. It's more likely to be villagers than warriors. Stand down for the night. Tomorrow will be a significant day."

Fred saluted, dismounted, and walked his horse to the river for a drink.

"Major Wilson," Forbes called for Allan.

Allan pulled away from a group of his men and walked his horse over to him. "How may I help, Major?"

"Burnham has informed me that the King crossed the river just a mile or so upstream. There are about two hours of daylight left. I want you to take a patrol of twelve men and go to where the King crossed, then ford the river and see if you can find him."

"Very good, Major," Allan nodded.

"I want you back before sunset. Understood?"

"Understood," Allan nodded curtly and turned his horse around.

The men of the Victoria Rangers watched Allan approach.

"Everything alright?" Captain Fitzgerald asked.

"It seems the King is just over the river. We need to reconnoitre. I require twelve volunteers for a patrol, please."

Allan rode over to where Raaff stood, organising his men to set up camp for the night.

"Commandant, Major Forbes is sending me to reconnoitre the river crossing a little further upstream. It seems the King crossed there earlier this afternoon. He is near."

Raaff looked up at the skies. "It's a bit late for a reconnoitre patrol, don't you think?"

"He told me to be back before dark," Allan confirmed.

"A bit of a pointless exercise, if you don't mind me saying so," Raaff scowled. "Has not your scout already reconnoitred the route?"

"Yes," Allan agreed, "but he has not crossed the river."

"Be careful, Major," Raaff warned. "Something makes me feel uneasy. With all my years in this land, I feel something is not right."

"Thank you for the warning, Commandant. I will be cautious."

Allan returned to Fitzgerald. There were twenty men grouped around him, all astride their mounts.

"I only want twelve men," Allan laughed.

"Come on, Sir," Captain Greenfield said with a laugh, "we want to join you. Please let us have some excitement, and a break from Forbes."

"It's only two hours," Captain Judd added.

"Don't turn us away," Trooper Dillon pleaded.

"Forbes won't care if you take twelve or twenty," another shouted.

"He won't even notice," yet another said.

Allan looked at the men who were gathered around him. "There are eight officers in you lot. We will be too top-heavy."

"Come on, Sir," a chorus of objections rose from the men. "Let's go find the King; we want to go home."

Allan laughed again. It was hard to turn them away. "Alright, let's go. Two hours, men."

As they rode off, Captain Kirton called over to a man lighting a fire. "Keep my dinner warm," he laughed. "I'll be back before dark."

The group of men rode past Forbes, and Allan threw him a salute. Forbes returned the salutation and noted the group numbered more than twelve men, but decided to ignore it. Once they disappeared from sight, Forbes looked out to the forested area that Fred had expressed concern about. It looked very benign. Behind him, he saw Fred crouch down to wash his face in the river.

"Burnham!" he called.

Fred got to his feet and strode over to Forbes. "Yes, Sir?"

"I've just sent Wilson and some of his men to cross the river to follow the spoor. They will be back before dark. Follow them quickly and help them track."

Fred's heart sank. He had been in the saddle all day, and he was exhausted, as was his horse.

"My horse is knocked up, Sir."

Forbes thought for a moment. "Take mine. Follow them quickly. Go, before you lose them."

Forbes jumped off his horse and passed Fred the reins. Fred quickly adjusted the stirrups, mounted, and spurred the horse forward. He could tell that the horse still had good energy reserves. After he had gone a mile he realised he had left his jacket on a branch by the river where he had been washing. A drizzle of rain touched his face, and he shivered. Fred wanted to kick himself for having left that jacket behind. He consoled himself, however, with the knowledge that he would be back before dark, which wouldn't be long in coming.

Fred caught up with Allan's patrol as they were crossing the Shangani River. The horses splashed through the shallow water with ease. The bank on the other side had collapsed where Lobengula's wagons, people and cattle had passed, making it easy for the horses to negotiate. Allan noticed Fred join them.

"Burnham, what are you doing here?" Allan asked, concerned.

"Major Forbes sent me, Sir."

"Why?"

"He told me to get here and help you scout for the King. He gave me his horse, too."

"I can see that." Allan's concern persisted. "Right-oh. You and Bain take the lead and show us the King's route."

As Fred levelled with Allan, he stopped, "Sir, I was at the river a few hours back, and I'm convinced the level has gone up since then."

"I'm not surprised with all this rain. Thanks, Burnham. I'll keep that in mind."

Fred moved to the front of the column and joined Bain. They were about fifty yards ahead of the patrol, carefully studying the ground as they went.

"With this cloud cover it will get dark soon," Bain commented. "It will make tracking difficult."

"Yes," Fred agreed, looking at the clouds. He, too, was concerned. "The river has started rising rapidly. I don't like it."

They moved forward silently for a while, veering to the right as they followed the disturbed earth.

"Burnham," Bain broke the silence, "what made you come to Africa?"

Fred looked at his partner. "Africa is a new frontier, and I wanted something different and exciting. Maybe to find my fortune as well."

"Then why are you in this war?" Bain persisted.

"I left my wife and son in Fort Victoria. We became trapped there when the war broke out. Jameson said everyone would be slaughtered if we lost this war."

"So you joined the fight?"

"Yes," Fred agreed. "I want to protect my family first and foremost. I also wanted to find my fortune and seek adventure. What about you?"

"I wanted to find my fortune too. I have no family, but like you, I value my life and believe what Jameson said. I was hoping Jameson would divvy out the spoils of war when we reached KoBulawayo so that I could make my plans. I didn't expect to have to go on another mission."

Fred nodded as he scanned the ground. "So why did you come out on this patrol?"

"My loyalty to Allan Wilson, I suppose. When he asked for volunteers, I couldn't help myself. In any case, the rewards for capturing the King will be better."

Fred smiled. "This way," he gestured slightly to the right.

The light was fading as they entered a vast open grassy plain surrounded by dense forest. Suddenly, the men noticed several cooking fires in the bushes on either side of them. As they watched, more and more cooking fires lit up. A hint of woodsmoke became noticeable.

"Bain," Fred cautioned his companion, "I think we have walked into the middle of the Matabele. I suspect that this is the King's camp."

"We are surrounded. Let's get back to the patrol and warn them," Bain suggested.

Fred and Bain quickly retraced their route and joined the patrol.

"The Matabele have made camp just up ahead, Sir," Fred informed Allan.

"Thanks, Burnham," Allan acknowledged the warning as he signalled his men to bunch up around him.

"There are thousands of them, Sir," Bain added.

Allan frowned in consternation. "Right-oh, let's advance cautiously and have a closer look. Stay close, gentlemen."

As the patrol reached the spot where Fred and Bain had halted, they nervously looked at the bright points of cooking fires all around them.

"This is a massive camp," Fitzgerald said.

"And they're all around us," Greenfield added, concern in his voice.

"I'm sure the King must be here," Napier asserted.

"Keep pressing forward," Allan encouraged. "If they have seen us and we retreat, we will look weak. They are expecting a massive army, not just a twenty-man patrol. It is obvious we are here to negotiate, not fight."

The column walked determinedly ahead. Matabele women and children noticed them and stopped what they were doing, staring at the small group of white men and horses.

"Captain Napier," Allan called out, "please ride up to those people and tell them we are messengers from Dr Jameson and want to speak to King Lobengula. Explain that we do not want to hurt him; we only want to deliver a message."

***

Londisizwe watched the small group of white men ride toward a scherm, an untidy tangle of sticks and twigs for temporary protection, that a small family had set up for the night. A lone white man broke away and approached the family. He could hear him talk in broken isiNdebele, but it was easy to understand. The white man wanted to know where the King was.

Wasting no time, Londisizwe ran to the closest family to him under the cover of the foliage and grabbed a young boy by the arm.

"Go to that man. Do not be afraid, he will not hurt you. Tell him you will show him where the King is. Then run slowly to the King. You understand? You must lead them there slowly."

"Yes, Uncle," the young boy said nervously.

"Just before you reach the King, run into the bush and hide. I will send another boy to run fast to warn my father, Induna Mjaan, that the white man is coming. Do you understand?"

"Yes, Uncle," he repeated.

"Go!" Londisizwe ordered.

The young boy turned and walked into the clearing, mustering up all his courage.

Londisizwe silently made his way to the next scherm and found some warriors who were watching events unfold, their confusion and consternation obvious.

"Stand up!" Londisizwe admonished them. "Do not be afraid. Run to all the scherms and tell every warrior you find to follow those men as they move towards the King. Follow them and close in behind them. Go now!"

Turning to a slender boy of about ten years old, Londisizwe gripped him by the shoulder. "Do you know where Induna Mjaan is?"

"Yes, Uncle, I know where he is. He sleeps near the King's wagon."

"Run there very fast and tell him the white man is coming. He must be alert. Do you understand me?"

"Yes, Uncle," the young boy nodded vigorously.

"Then go now, fast. Very fast."

Before Londisizwe could blink, the boy vanished into the forest.

***

Napier followed his commander's order and went forward. Approaching a small scherm with a barely visible fire, a young boy emerged from the bushes and spoke to Napier. He said the King was very near, and that he would lead everyone to him. Napier told him to wait while he spoke to his leader.

Napier returned to Allan and passed the message to him. On hearing what he had to say, the excitement in the group rose rapidly. *'Finally!'*, they thought collectively. The pursuit of the King would be coming to an end, and then they could go home, away from the bush, the hunger, the wet and the cold.

"Tell the boy to please lead us," Allan ordered Napier.

Napier returned to the young man and asked him to lead the way. He immediately jogged off ahead. Fred, seeing the youngster suddenly run off, instinctively turned his horse and trotted beside him. Fred noticed the boy wasn't running fast, so assumed the King was close by.

Just as the remainder of the patrol began to follow Fred, someone called out to Allan from the rear.

"Major, Sergeant Judge and Corporal Ebbage's horses have gone lame. They are further back and struggling to keep up."

"Alright," Allan acknowledged. "Tell them to go back to Forbes as best they can and re-join him. Right, the rest of us follow Burnham. Quick!"

They soon came to a stretch of open land, surrounded by dense forest. The boy slowed, so Fred peered into the dense bush ahead, expecting to see something significant, however when he glanced back at his guide, the boy had vanished. Fred pulled his horse to a halt.

"The boy has disappeared," Fred called to Allan, who was not too far behind him.

Allan halted and pulled his officers together. "What are your thoughts, men?" he asked. "Either we push on to find the King and arrest him, or we go back to Forbes and bring the column forward in the morning with the Maxims?"

"I say we go get him now," Fitzgerald said. "By the time we return tomorrow, the King would have bolted into the bush. We won't catch him after today."

"I agree," Judd concurred. "It's now or never."

"It's almost dark," Allan warned.

"No matter," Greenfield said. "This is our only chance. Let's finish the job here and now."

"Alright," Allan frowned. "Those were my thoughts too. Let's do the deed. Burnham, lead the way."

They cantered through the scherms, frightening the Matabele as they pounded ahead, but very quickly came to a small clearing that had been fortified with poles. Behind the poles, silhouetted by some campfires, were two wagons. The King's white horse was tethered to one of the wagons. The patrol was elated. This was the end of the road; they had found the King.

Allan looked at Lobengula's encampment with suspicion. Suddenly he realised that capturing the King wasn't going to be that easy after all. The rain was intensifying, and smaller fires were being extinguished.

"Napier," Allan called his interpreter, "call to the King and tell him we are messengers from Dr Jameson, and we have come to escort him back to sign a peace treaty. Explain that we will not hurt him, but he needs to return with us. Be respectful."

Napier pushed his horse forward, right up to the pole fortifications. He drew a deep breath and shouted as loud as he could.

"King Lobengula, powerful ruler of the great Matabele nation, we have been sent by the great white Induna, Dr Jameson. His message for the great King is to return to KoBulawayo and sign a peace treaty. We are here to escort you safely to him."

All that could be heard were the large raindrops that began hitting the leaves of the trees around them. Napier turned to look at Allan for further instructions. Allan tossed his head in the direction of the enclosure, indicating for Napier to repeat what he said.

As Napier began, a deluge of rain lashed the men. Lightning streaked across the sky, and thunder rolled overhead. Allan looked around and, in a flash of lightning, saw that many Matabele warriors had surrounded the patrol. Suddenly, the situation had become dire.

Once Napier had delivered his message for the second time, and a deep roll of thunder had subsided, only the lashing rain could be heard. Water was dripping off the brims of the mens' hats. The sudden downpour had completely blotted out the remaining light from the sunset, and the darkness was unsettling.

There was another brilliant flash of lightning, and Allan immediately noticed that the warriors were now standing very close to them; they had crept up to just yards away, and their spears and rifles were raised, readied for attack.

"Retreat!" Allan shouted at the top of his voice as the next clap of thunder reverberated around them.

***

Forbes paced anxiously. It was dark now, and Wilson's patrol had not returned. As always, Forbes thought, Wilson had gone against his instructions, this time, disobeying a direct order, and Forbes was angry. He saw Raaff standing at the edge of the camp, looking in the direction Allan had gone. Taking a deep breath, Forbes strutted over to Raaff.

"I told Wilson to be back before dark," Forbes complained. "I didn't think he would lower himself to disobey me."

"Maybe he is lost," Raaff suggested without taking his eyes off the bush.

"He's got several competent scouts with him. I doubt he is lost. He has also taken most of his officers with him. Why would he do that, I wonder?"

"I don't know, Meneer," Raaff said softly, still staring into the blackness.

"I told him to take twelve men, so he took twenty. That is insubordination. I think he wants to capture the King for himself so that the Victoria Rangers get all the credit."

Raaff broke his gaze and looked Forbes in the eye. "You think so? Does it really matter who captures the King?"

"Of course it matters. Why else would Wilson disobey my command?"

"Meneer," Raaff changed tack, "did not Scout Burnham tell you he saw movement in that forest over there?" he asked, pointing vaguely in the direction Allan's patrol had gone.

"Yes, but I didn't think much of it. It could have been villagers; anything really."

"Look. You see that?" Raaff said softly and pointed to the forest.

Forbes looked into the darkness, and a sickening feeling drained into his stomach. Far ahead, he could see hundreds upon hundreds of cooking fires.

Forbes hesitated, then spoke cautiously. "Do you think those are Matabele warriors?"

"Those are not herders, Meneer. I would say there is a full impi in that forest, maybe two impis, and they are waiting for you. I would say there are easily two thousand people around those fires."

Forbes froze with dread. He was in a very difficult predicament.

"What are you going to do, Meneer?" Raaff asked coldly.

Forbes began to panic. His mind was racing, but he could not think clearly to strategise.

"What do you suggest, Commandant?" Forbes finally realised that he had to ask for help.

"Knowing these people, as I do, I would say your options are limited. Firstly, you must hope that Major Wilson comes back here before morning because you cannot get there to help him. The river is in flood now, and people will drown if they try to cross it in the dark. What is more, you will never carry the maxims across that torrent of water. The Matabele impi is lying in wait for you to attempt the river crossing. If you do manage to cross the river, you will not be able to turn back. You will be trapped on the far side of the river, and you have no idea what awaits you there. We will all die. It is a trap."

"They set a trap?" Forbes asked in disbelief, fearing the answer.

"Yes, a very good trap. Perhaps you should have taken more notice of what Scout Burnham told you," Raaff said in disgust.

"How do we outsmart them?" Forbes asked with an uncertain quaver.

Raaff laughed. "You will not outsmart them. They have won. Firstly, just hope that Wilson manages to return soon. Secondly, resign yourself to the fact that the King has escaped for now. You will not catch him. You have neither enough ammunition nor food. I'll say it again: if you attempt to cross that river, you and your column are doomed. We will all die."

"So, you are suggesting we retreat?"

"Meneer Forbes, I hate the word retreat, because I have been in that situation before. You must avoid it at all costs because your people will be cut down, believe me. But, in this case, I say you only have one option: to retire before sunrise."

"We can't retire now," Forbes scrabbled for courage. "We are so close."

"My friend," Raaff dropped all formalities and turned to face Forbes, "in the morning, if you send some scouts out there, they will confirm that there is an impi waiting for you to cross the river. Scout Burnham has already told you so, but you chose not to believe your own scout. Once you cross the Shangani they will cut you off and cut you down as soon as you try to come back over the water. I can tell you something else. On the other side there are even more impis waiting for you, and while they fight you with your back to the river, the King will be rapidly absconding. You must resign yourself to the fact that the King has escaped. Your job now is to save your column," Raaff glared at Forbes in the firelight.

Forbes met Raaff's stare for a moment, then turned on his heels and stormed back to his tent. He was *not* going to accept defeat.

***

Allan's patrol scattered immediately. They tried to find their way back from whence they came. The sheets of driving rain blotted out any visibility, and they could only find their way by following the bent grasses and muddied tracks made earlier, seen by the infrequent brilliant flashes of lightning. Allan hoped everyone heard his command to retreat over the sound of thunder. He had hesitated after he called the command to retreat to make sure everyone had heard him. Not seeing anyone in the driving rain, he spurred his horse on and fled the scene.

Galloping after his men, he found that they had regrouped under a thin growth of trees; the rain was lashing them unmercifully. Realising that they needed better protection, Allan shouted orders and got his men to follow him to a thicket of bushes and trees close to the river where they had originally crossed.

They all stood, drenched, along with their horses, listening to the roar of the rain. There was some protection under the trees, but not nearly enough. Water dropped furiously from the brims of their hats and off the leaves of the trees. Finally, the squall passed, and the gentle pitter-patter of lighter raindrops filled the air.

When Allan was comfortable that all was under control and no attack was imminent, he called to his men–just loudly enough for them to hear.

"Gather round, chaps. Roll call; names please."

As the names were spoken, Allan counted them off on his fingers.

"We are missing some people," Allan announced, concern evident in his voice. "Check for your mates; who's missing?"

"Captain Hofmeyer is not here," a voice came from the dark.

"Colquhoun? You here?" someone called.

There was silence.

"I haven't seen Bradburn," another voice punctuated the dark.

"Damn!" Allan exclaimed. "They were the rear guard. They probably didn't hear my order to retreat over the sound of that thunderclap."

A very uncomfortable feeling settled on the huddle of men. Allan was particularly concerned for the missing soldiers. He knew if the Matabele had not killed them during the shambolic retreat, they would be killed at sunrise if they were discovered.

"I must find them," Allan mumbled.

He quickly called his officers to gather around him. He needed to hear their opinions, in case he was missing something. Sitting in their saddles in a circle, their horse's heads almost touching in the centre, Allan asked the officers if they felt they should return to the column, or ask Forbes to bring the column over the Shangani River and join them with the Maxim guns. He also asked if anyone could suggest a better plan.

It was decided to wait on this side of the river and tell Forbes to bring the entire column over as soon as possible. It was imperative to bring the Maxims. If Forbes could get across the river before sunrise, they might have the King before he could escape.

It pleased Allan when they came to this decision because, although he didn't say it at the time, he was not going to return without looking for his missing men. Against all the odds, it was just possible that they might be alive and hiding in the bush somewhere.

"Captain Napier," Allan said, "will you get that message to Forbes for me?" He had noticed that Napier was not well, and had deteriorated through the day. Every now and again he had witnessed Napier shiver involuntarily. If they had to fight the next day Allan didn't think Napier would be up to strength.

"I can do that, Sir," Napier agreed.

"Good show. Take Bain with you; he knows the way. And take someone else in case you have a problem."

"Two should be enough," Greenfield suggested. "We should not reduce our force here."

Allan disagreed, "It's important that three messengers go. This is a critical message. If something were to happen, there would be a better chance of the message getting through if three messengers carried the same message. Besides, I'm not concerned about reducing our force because Forbes should join us before morning."

"I'll take Robertson," Napier said.

"Good. Gather the men and bring them to me first. I want you all to have the same message for Forbes in case one or two of you don't reach him."

Napier quickly brought Bain and Robertson to Allan. The message was conveyed clearly and concisely.

"Now make haste, Gentlemen, and please stress how important it is for Forbes to bring the Maxims. It is crucial, and it is urgent. Don't take no for an answer. You are my senior officer, Captain Napier. Forbes should heed your words."

Napier, Bain and Robertson left immediately and were instantly swallowed up in the darkness.

"Burnham!" Allan called for his scout in the blackness.

"Here, Sir," Fred said, walking his horse over to Allan.

"I must find those lost men, Burnham. Please help me backtrack and search for them."

Fred was soaking, and, being only in his shirtsleeves, he was freezing cold. He knew it would be an almost impossible task. "Major Wilson, Sir, the ground has been trampled by cattle, horses, men with boots and barefoot warriors. The area is drenched, and it is pitch black out there. I fear that finding their tracks will be well-nigh impossible."

"It is a tough request, Burnham, I realise that. I cannot leave my men out there if they are alive. Let's at least give it a try. I'll come with you."

Fred nodded; he would do his best. The two men turned their horses away from the group and walked into the darkness. After a while, Allan stopped.

"I think this is where we might have lost them," Allan whispered.

In the trees surrounding them were sleeping Matabele; the occasional glow of embers from cooking fires indicated just how close they were to the enemy. The two dismounted, and Allan took Fred's reins while Fred dropped to his hands and knees, and, calling on all that the Sioux had taught him when he was younger, he felt the ground with his fingertips, hoping to find the curved shape of a horseshoe.

Fred was very cold, and, being lightly dressed with a drizzle of rain running down his neck and back, his fingers began to chill to the point that he was losing sensation. He was floundering, and he knew it. Lack of sleep, poor diet and excessive physical exertion over the last three or four days was taking its toll.

He cursed himself as he touched the soil lightly, not knowing what he was looking for anymore. In a time of need, he was failing, and under the eye of his commander to boot. He was ashamed.

"Burnham!" Allan whispered sharply. "Stand up."

Fred got to his feet and rubbed his hands together, trying to get some warmth into his fingertips.

"Here," Allan took off his cape. "Put this on. You are freezing."

Fred took the cape and put it on. His mind was numb.

"Burnham," Allan continued. "I know you Americans are good at what you do. I've seen your work before, and you are better than all the others combined." He took Fred by the shoulders and, with his huge hands, rubbed his shoulders to loosen him up. "Show me what you Americans can do."

Allan's actions spurred Fred to a new level of energy and determination. Never before had a commander offered him his personal cape and encouraged him like Allan had, and, for Fred, the impact was immediate. He nodded his acceptance of the encouragement and got back down on his hands and knees.

Soon, his fingers picked up a curved horseshoe shape in the soil. He checked the direction and then estimated where the next impression should be.

"Sir, please put your foot here and mark this print for me."

Allan did as he was asked and then he saw Fred crawl forward a little and touch the ground again.

"Something there?" Allan asked anxiously.

"No," he whispered. "But if the horse was galloping, the next print should be about here," he said and reached forward a little further.

Fred froze. "I have it, Sir. This horse is heading that way at a gallop."

"That's a different direction to that in which we retreated," Allan controlled his excitement in a whisper. "Well done, Burnham. Let's keep going."

Bit by bit they advanced, Fred checking for spoor until they were, once again, uncomfortably close to the King's enclosure. In the starlight that finally broke through a gap in the clouds, Fred could see a line of trees on a slight rise.

"If these prints belong to their horses, our men will be in those trees over there," Fred whispered to Allan. "It's a long way off."

"I think we should call for them," Allan said.

"What!" Fred exclaimed in a hoarse whisper. "The Matabele are all around us. We'll be dead in seconds."

"Regardless, I must make the attempt," Allan determined. "Mount up and get ready to ride like the wind, Burnham."

Fred thought Allan was losing his mind, but complied and mounted his horse. Allan cupped his hands around his mouth, and, at the top of his voice, shouted out the Australian outback call.

"Coo-eee!"

Fred immediately stiffened. The call caught him right off guard. Immediately, there was a commotion in the Matabele scherms. Men grumbled, women screamed, and children began to cry. As the hullabaloo died down, Allan and Fred listened intently for a reply.

"Nothing," Fred ventured.

"I think the natives are petrified of that noise. They've never heard it before," Allan smiled to himself. He cupped his hands and called again as loudly as he could. "Coo-eee...."

Again, another round of unhappy voices came from the bushes around them.

Fred smiled this time. "Yee-Haa...." He yelled. "That's cowboy for coo-eee."

As the uncomfortable murmuring died down around them, they heard a very faint reply.

"Coo-eee...."

"They're alive," Allan smiled. "Come, let's move."

Three more calls received a reply, each time the answer getting closer until the men reunited. They eagerly shook hands, Hofmeyer telling his fellow soldiers that he had heard that Wilson was a man to die for, and now he understood why.

With greatly lifted spirits, the five men returned to the thicket where the others anxiously awaited them.

***

A sentry's shout caused everyone in the Forbes laager to become instantly alert.

"What is it?" Forbes asked the lookout. He was slightly out of breath from the dash from his tent.

"Two riders coming in," he pointed to some shadows slowly moving towards them.

The two riders were Corporal Ebbage and Sergeant Judge.

"Why just the two of you?" asked Forbes when they arrived. "Where are the others?"

"Our horses became lame, Sir," Judge replied. "Major Wilson sent us back to you. We were no good to anyone."

"How far are they?" Forbes pressed.

"Only about five or six miles ahead, across the river."

"Did Wilson send a message for me?"

"No, Sir. He sent a man back to us to tell us to return to you."

"Do you know what his plans are?"

"I think he wants to sleep out there tonight," Ebbage said vaguely. "Maybe he'll go after the King in the morning?"

"I told him to return before…. Never mind," Forbes was exasperated. "How many Matabele are there? Did you see any?"

"No, but the man who told us to return mentioned they asked a Matabele boy how many guards the King had, and he said it was just a few."

Raaff had joined the conversation. "I wouldn't trust what a Matabele boy would say."

Forbes ignored the comment. "Did Major Wilson say anything about reinforcements?"

"No," came the succinct reply from Corporal Ebbage.

"But," Sergeant Judge added, "I did hear him say the track was good enough for the Maxims."

Forbes stood with his hands on his hips for a moment. Their answers did not help him much. "Alright, stand down. Get something to eat," he said and walked briskly back to his tent.

Just before midnight, the sentry called out again, alerting everyone in the camp. This time it was Napier, Bain and Robertson who came walking into the laager leading their horses. They were freezing cold and hungry. Some of their colleagues brought them blankets and food. When Forbes arrived, he noted their exhaustion.

"Just the three of you?" Forbes looked surprised. "Where are the rest?"

"They are staying on the other side of the river, Sir," Napier said through a shiver. "Major Wilson has a critical message for you, Sir."

"What is it?"

"The King is not far. We must apprehend him at sunrise or we will lose him. Major Wilson requests that you mobilise the column and get to him before sunrise."

"Impossible," Forbes exclaimed. "We cannot move in the dark."

Napier pulled himself to his full height and puffed out his chest. "Sir, the enemy number is immense on the other side. The column and the Maxims are urgently needed. Major Wilson said the Maxims are critical to capturing the King."

Forbes shook his head. "How big is the King's army? Did you see them with your own eyes?"

"Yes, Sir. There are thousands of warriors. Those Maxims are vital. Without them, I would say Major Wilson and his patrol are doomed."

Forbes looked into the darkness where he had earlier seen the cooking fires. Suddenly he wondered if he was, in fact, being surrounded by the Matabele. He noticed Raaff was standing quietly beside him.

"What do you think, Commandant?"

"I think there is only one option left to you, Major," Raaff said coldly. "You need to get a message to Major Wilson to return immediately. He must re-join the column and we must abandon our pursuit."

"Impossible," Forbes immediately dismissed the advice. "We have come so far and now, just when the King is within our grasp, you say we should return? What would Jameson have to say about that?"

"The chase is lost," Raaff advised calmly. "If you proceed, you will be cut off after you cross the river. The Matabele are watching you. The moment you cross the river they will advance to the bank and prevent you from returning. Your men have informed you there is a large army on the other side of the Shangani. You have seen the enemy in those trees on this side," he pointed into the darkness. "If you wait for sunrise, they will cut you off before you can cross the river. It is open land, and you have no cover, therefore your only defence will be the Maxims, and you have scant ammunition. You will be cut down very quickly."

Raaff scratched his head in sheer exasperation, then continued. "If *you*," Raaff accentuated that word, "cannot cross the river, neither can Major Wilson, and he will be cut down. You have only one option, Major Forbes, and that is to retire. You are trapped. To save the lives of your men, you must retire, now."

Forbes turned back to Napier. "Wilson wants the entire column and Maxims to come now?"

"Yes, Sir. That is the message he gave the three of us. He felt this message was so important he gave the same message to all three of us in case one or two of us did not reach you. On another matter, Sir," Napier continued, "the river has risen quite a bit since earlier this evening, and it is flowing a lot faster. If you don't get the maxims across soon, you won't be able to, and Major Wilson's patrol will be unreachable."

Forbes did not like hearing this news. He gave the situation serious consideration as he was now in a very precarious position. Many eyes in the camp were looking his way. He needed time to think.

"Stand down, I will give this consideration," he said and turned to walk back to his tent.

"One other thing, Sir," Napier said. "Lieutenant Hofmeyer, Corporal Colquhoun and Sergeant Bradburn are missing. We had to retreat in a squall, and we were separated."

Forbes heart sank. This was terrible news, and it affected him deeply.

"Is Wilson going to search for them?" Forbes asked anxiously.

"I don't know, Sir. It's as black as ink out there, and the bush is riddled with Matabele warriors and civilians."

Raaff cleared his throat. "I would say, knowing Major Wilson as I do, that is another reason why Wilson won't come back here. He won't leave knowing three of his men are missing in hostile territory."

Raaff was absolutely correct. Forbes restrained an exasperated sigh. He turned and stormed off to his tent.

***

While Allan's men rested, huddled uncomfortably in the wet grass, some only in their shirtsleeves, Allan paced anxiously, peering hard into the darkness. He guessed the time to be close to midnight. Apart from the chirrups of nocturnal insects and the occasional croak from a frog, Allan heard nothing. He walked over to Fred and woke him.

"Burnham, I would be most grateful if you would go back along the track towards the river and listen out for Forbes and the Maxims. If you hear them, report back to me immediately."

Fred stood. The lack of sleep was testing his resolve, but he would do anything for this commander. "I'll do that, Sir."

"Thanks, Burnham. I know your eyes are trained for the dark, and your hearing is better than most men. I need you for this job."

"Of course, Sir," Fred agreed and slipped into the darkness.

It was just short of an hour before Fred returned. He didn't have good news. What he had to report was troubling.

"I can't hear the column, Sir," Fred said sadly, "however, I could hear hundreds of Matabele closing in. I fear they are cutting us off."

"You could hear them?" Allan asked in surprise.

"Yes, they are not far from our position. I could hear feet squelching in the mud, plants hissing from people moving through the undergrowth, that sort of thing. There are many people moving from the west and east.

Also, the river is flooding; I could hear it from where I was."

Allan went silent for a moment. "I had a feeling they would do that. Thanks, Burnham, get some rest."

***

Forbes emerged from his tent almost three hours later and sent a messenger to find Captain Borrow. He arrived a minute later.

"You wanted me, Sir?" Borrow saluted.

"Yes, I'd like you to select twenty-two men and form a patrol to cross the river and assist Major Wilson in capturing the King."

"Yes, Sir," Borrow immediately agreed.

"Wilson has twelve men over there, fifteen if the three lost men find him. If we add you and twenty-two men, he will have a force of thirty-nine. That should be a formidable enough number to capture Lobengula."

"Very good, Sir. Will we require the one hundred round allocation each, Sir?"

"Yes, draw them from the store. One hundred rounds of ammunition each will do."

"How many Maxims?"

"None," Forbes said bluntly.

"No Maxims?" Borrow said in surprise.

"No. Are you alright doing this?" Forbes asked.

Borrow looked at Forbes in confusion. "Of course I'm alright with it, Sir, but I would feel better with a Maxim in support."

"I'm not letting the Maxims go. Hold on a minute while I confer with Raaff."

Forbes found Raaff standing by the edge of the laager, spoke briefly with him, and then returned to Borrow.

"Right, please have your men mounted and ready to leave in fifteen minutes. Take the American, Ingram, as your scout. Leave Captain Napier with me; he is ill."

"Very good, Sir," Borrow saluted and left.

From the edge of the laager Raaff watched Forbes instruct Borrow. Captain Lendy and another officer, Captain Francis, who had been lying on the ground by Raaff's feet, stood up. They had heard the conversation Forbes had had with Raaff.

"You can't let Forbes split our force, Commandant," Lendy objected.

242

"We are virtually surrounded, and Forbes is reducing our number."

"Captain," Raaff said forlornly, "it makes no difference what I say to Forbes; he has made up his mind."

"He is sending Borrow over without Maxims?" Lendy questioned. "Wilson and his men will die, and now Captain Borrow and his twenty-two men will die along with them."

"I am not the overall commander of this column," Raaff said. "I cannot change Major Forbes' mind. You know what he is like."

Francis shook his head in dismay. "Forbes is sending twenty-three fine young men to their deaths. Surely, he must know he is sending them to die."

"If there is an inquiry after this," Lendy said, "and if I live through it, I can assure you I will have something to say about Forbes."

***

Mjaan stood on the bank of the Shangani River, watching the far side very closely. A lone warrior was working his way towards him. The water was up to his thighs, and he was working hard to ford the swiftly flowing river.

Only once the man reached the shore did Mjaan realise it was Ngwenya.

"Induna," Ngwenya was breathing heavily from the exertion, "there is a group of them coming. They have just left their camp."

"How many?"

Ngwenya indicated with his hands about twenty men.

"Do they carry the sigwagwas on wheels?"

"No, Induna. They have no sigwagwas."

"That is good," Mjaan scowled in deep concentration. "Go back and tell the impis to let them pass, then to wait. If the big group with the sigwagwas start to move in the dark, wait for them to cross the river, then attack when they are in the water. Do not let the sigwagwas cross to my side.

"But, if the sigwagwas start to move when the sun arrives, then attack them before they cross the river. Stay in the trees and let them waste their bullets. Keep them on your side of the river. When their bullets are finished, then attack and kill them all."

"It will be done, Induna," Ngwenya smiled.

"Go quickly, before the small group arrives. Let them pass and then close behind them. You must kill all the men on your side tomorrow."

"Yes, Induna," Ngwenya smiled, then turned on his heels and made his way back across the Shangani River.

***

Allan found his way to Fred and touched him on the shoulder. He reacted immediately.

"Burnham, sorry to ask you this, but please go out on the track again and tell me what you hear."

"Yes, Sir," Fred spoke through bleary eyes. He stood and stretched before riding off towards the river.

At first, he heard nothing but the pitter-patter of raindrops, and the happy calling of insects. The rustle of the warriors had stopped, so he assumed they had gone to ground while they waited for sunrise.

Then he heard a different noise. He thought it was the soft tread of horse hooves, but he wasn't quite certain. Fred strained his ears and suddenly realised it was definitely horses moving up from the direction of the river. Elated, he got back to Allan as quickly as possible.

"Sir, the column is arriving. I could hear the horses moving through the wet earth."

"Good show, Burnham. About time. I wonder what took Forbes so long."

Allan quickly woke the rest of his patrol in readiness for the column's arrival. They were all drained. The cold of the night had sapped their energy, and, having left the column the evening before without their supper, they were hungry and weak. Knowing the arrival of the column was imminent, their spirits rose.

Ingram was in the lead; Borrow and his men were directly behind him. Borrow walked up to Allan and dismounted.

"Major Wilson, we have come to support you in capturing the King."

Allan looked into the darkness from where the support column had come. "Where are the rest?"

"This is all you have," Borrow said. "Major Forbes sent twenty-three of us to support you. Unfortunately, two of my men became lost as we crossed the river. I think they would have returned to Forbes. We are only twenty-one now."

"How many Maxims did you bring?" Allan asked, disbelief creeping into his voice.

"None."

"None? Why not?" Allan struggled to control his anger.

An uncomfortable shuffling could be heard from Allan's men as they moved closer to hear the conversation.

"Major Forbes said you would not need them," Borrow said nervously, casting a look about himself as he felt the others' presence close in.

"I told Captain Napier to specifically tell Forbes we urgently needed the entire column and the maxims. Did Napier not get to Forbes?"

"Yes, Napier came," Borrow said, "and he told Forbes you needed the Maxims; forcefully."

"So...." Allan looked at his men's expectant faces. "Why didn't Forbes send them?"

"He said you didn't need them. Apparently, the King doesn't have a lot of warriors protecting him."

"Who told you that?"

"Judge and Ebbage, when they came in with lame horses. They said you had spoken to a young boy who said the King only had a few people around him."

"Why would I request maxims and the entire column to come here urgently if the King had just a small number of people guarding him?"

Borrow frowned. "Forbes never suggested to me that your predicament was dire."

Allan took his hat off and ran his fingers through his hair. He was exasperated, exhausted and angry. His first instinct was to get back to Forbes as soon as possible if only to punch him in the face.

"Did you see any sign of Matabele after you crossed the river?" Allan asked.

"No, but...." Borrow signalled to Ingram. "Please come here, Mr Ingram. Mr Ingram believes he heard many in the bushes, but we didn't see any, nor were we confronted."

"I heard them, Sir," Ingram agreed. "They were all around us, but I couldn't see them. To be honest, I felt that their movements were such as to clear a path for us."

Allan sighed. "They were letting you through."

"You need to know, Sir," Ingram added, "that the Shangani River is in flood. I doubt you could get the column over now. We were lucky to cut across it."

Allan shook his head. "Captain Borrow, kindly ask your officers to mount up and meet me just over there with my officers. I want to have a meeting with you all."

The officers mounted and moved just outside the group of men. With the horses standing in a circle like the spokes of a wheel, noses touching noses, Allan addressed the officers of the Patrol.

"Gentlemen, Major Forbes has abandoned us. He has specifically ignored the information I sent him and my requests. He has not sent any Maxims, just an additional twenty-one men to capture the King. Captain Borrow, how much ammunition have you got?"

"One hundred rounds each, Major."

"There are thousands of warriors out there," Greenfield said. "Lobengula's entire surviving army has surrounded us."

"Not entirely," Borrow said. "We believe about three thousand warriors are on the other side of the Shangani. They have positioned themselves on the column's left flank."

Allan let out a low whistle. "We have been led into a very elaborate trap, Gentlemen. Forbes is not coming. He has been cut off from us, and we have been cut off from re-joining him."

"It looks like this is the end, Gentlemen," Judd said.

"What do you think is the best move, Captain Kirton?" Allan asked.

"There's no best move, Major," Kirton shook his head in dismay.

"We are in a hell of a fix," Fitzgerald said. "I see no way out."

"Thirty-seven of us, and each with one hundred rounds," Judd spoke softly, "against ten thousand or more of them? We could never cut our way out. We have come to the end."

"I'd like to meet the Matabele Induna who planned this," Allan smiled bitterly. "He is very smart; make no error."

"Much smarter than Forbes, it seems," Greenfield chanced.

Allan rubbed his chin in thought and felt his stubble. "I must say I am very disappointed in Forbes. He knew the situation very well. He knew he had the enemy on his left flank and we had a serious problem here, yet he sent Captain Borrow and twenty men to us without Maxims. We are now a force of thirty-seven, which is too small for an attacking force and too big for a reconnaissance force. In so doing, he has reduced his force by thirty-seven, which also makes no sense."

"With due respect, Captain Borrow," Fitzgerald said bitterly, "I feel Forbes deliberately sent you on a suicide mission. We are not going to get out of this."

"Gentlemen," Allan spoke authoritatively, "I see only two options. We either cut our way back to Forbes and attempt to defeat the Matabele at our back and cross the river if we can get to it, or we go forward and capture the King. My feeling is, why sell our lives cheaply to the warriors behind us? Rather, let us go for the King. If we do not capture him, we may at least kill some of his Indunas and higher officers. If we capture him, then we can force him to stand his impis down and surrender. Lobengula is our only ticket out of this."

"I agree," Fitzgerald said.

"Agreed," Judd echoed.

"I concur, Major," Greenfield grimaced.

"I'm in agreement with you, Major Wilson," Borrow nodded.

Allan frowned with deep concern. "Alright, Gentlemen, gather your men; the sun is almost upon us."

CHAPTER TWENTY-FIVE

4th December 1893

It was daybreak, and Forbes had not slept well. He had been awake since three o'clock that morning and had decided, against Raaff's warnings, to move across the river. Almost everyone in the column was sleep-deprived, cold to the bone, wet, hungry and, above all, exhausted. The situation was not good.

The troops could sense that a merciless and savage army surrounded them on three sides; only the Shangani River on their right gave them some protection. Men were tense. One Maxim at the front left, and the other at the rear left, the column began to move on Forbes' command.

The ground was muddy in places, sometimes bogging down the Maxim carriage wheels. It became evident very quickly that this was going to be a tedious advance.

To the right, a new sound grew louder with every footfall–the roaring of the Shangani River in full flood.

***

Fred took the lead, moving about fifty yards ahead of the patrol, and retraced the patrol's tracks back to the King's wagon. With the dawn of a new day, it appeared as if they hadn't been that far from the wagon after all, and they arrived at the open ground near Lobengula's enclosure quicker than expected. Fred halted, waiting for Allan and the patrol to catch up.

"Just over there, Sir,"

"Thanks, Burnham," Allan locked his eyes on the wagon inside the enclosure, looking for movement. "Can you see anything?"

Fred strained his eyes, but all was eerily quiet. "It looks empty to me, Sir. I can't see anyone."

"I hope he hasn't left already," Allan said under his breath. "Wait here." Allan moved forward about twenty yards and, in a loud voice, called out to the King's wagon.

"King Lobengula, we have come from Dr Jameson with a message for you. Come back with us, and we will treat you with the respect due to a King. The war is finished."

A heavy stillness settled on the land. It was a strained silence and everyone hoped, even prayed, that the King would emerge and end their suffering.

Allan swivelled in his saddle. "Burnham, please go forward and look inside the wagon."

Fred gently spurred his horse forward and walked calmly to the wagon. He saw that a canvas flap had been lifted and left open. Craning his neck, he peered into the opening; it was empty.

"No-one here, Sir," Fred called back. "The King is not here."

Allan's heart sank. His thoughts confirmed they were in a deadly situation. All hope of gaining a bargaining edge was lost.

***

Mjaan watched the Patrol advance towards them as they entered the open ground. He counted over thirty men and saw no Maxims. He grinned. The river was in full flood, and he knew his trap had been sprung.

"Londisizwe," he whispered to his son, "take two warriors with rifles and spears and position yourself over there, by the wagon. When the shooting starts, you must shoot the *one who sees in the dark*, the man with the hat that has white man's magic; he is a big problem for me. Make sure you kill him."

"Yes, Father," Londisizwe complied instantly and scurried soundlessly into the tall grass.

Mjaan stole off to his left and crouched by a large Matabele man who commanded a group of three hundred warriors.

"Wait for me to give the command," he whispered to his lieutenant. "Let them come close."

He watched as the patrol halted. A big man, whom he assumed was their leader, moved forward and shouted something to the wagon. He did not understand the white man's language, but he had a good idea of what was implied.

Suddenly, Mjaan's grin broadened when he saw *the one who sees in the dark* ordered by his commander to inspect the wagon. This was better than he had hoped for; the scout was now very close to Londisizwe. Mjaan watched the scout call back to his leader, and he interpreted that they had realised King Lobengula was no longer there.

Mjaan decided the time for killing had arrived. He stood to his full height, filled his lungs with air, and then bellowed as loud as he could.

"Ghee!"

***

Londisizwe had his sights trained perfectly on Fred's torso. His finger was twitching on the trigger. He desperately needed to hear the shooting start so he could kill the white scout.

Suddenly, his father's command to attack roared over the plain and rifle fire immediately erupted from the far tree line. Londisizwe pulled his trigger.

Fred, who was waiting for another instruction from Allan, heard the war cry and then the crack of hundreds of rifles from the far left. He was startled and spun to see where it was coming from, drawing his rifle across his saddle. But he was riding Forbes' horse, and because Forbes had very minimal experience in active combat, his horse was not accustomed to sudden rifle fire. It was spooked, and bolted to the right. The sudden jerk caught Fred off balance, and he slipped sideways in his saddle, just as he felt a bullet brush past his face.

Trying desperately to get back into the saddle, Fred realised that his horse was now galloping for some thick bush from which three large Matabele warriors had emerged. They were heading straight for him. The leader was a big man with a broad chest. The starkly defined muscles in his arms and shoulders bulged with power and determination. Fred knew he was in serious trouble; the man was only yards from him and closing fast.

Londisizwe fired again, but his bullet went high, missing Fred's head by inches. He tried to load another round while in full flight, but the breech seemed to jam. Londisizwe glanced down at the weapon and forced the mechanism, but quickly realised he would be upon *the one who sees in the dark* before he could reload. He looked up and saw his victim struggling to regain his balance on the horse's saddle. A sinister grin crossed his face; a spear was a better end for this white wizard, he thought, and dropped the rifle, tightening his grip on his spear.

Fred was seated so badly in his saddle that he was watching the event unfold from under his horse's neck. He pulled desperately at his pommel and righted himself, swung his rifle around with one hand and, instinctively, pulled the trigger. It was the snap-shot he had practised in the Arizona desert, and he hoped he still had the skill because he would not have a second chance–the warrior was almost upon him and was now brandishing a deadly-looking spear.

Fred's bullet hit Londisizwe squarely in the chest, and the brave warrior dropped like a stone at the horse's hooves. Mjaan saw this from his vantage point, and his wrath rose, burning violently. He wanted that white man more than any of the others. He would send a message that the one with the magic hat must be brought to him alive.

Forcing himself to tear his attention back to the battle, he looked at the white man's patrol. They had dismounted and were lying in the grass.

"Kill them!" Mjaan's voice crackled as he issued his command. "Kill the horses first!"

***

Captain Lendy turned to Commandant Raaff the instant they heard the shooting on the other side of the river. It was not far, not more than a mile or two away.

"That's Wilson," Lendy said.

"I know," Raaff concurred. "Caution. I think we will come under attack imminently."

Raaff was quickly proven correct. From the forest on the left came the aggressive sound of spears hitting rawhide shields. The hollow thudding merged into a dull rumble as thousands of warriors warned the enemy of their impending death. It was disturbing, through to the soul.

"Maxims–take your positions!" Forbes called his men to attention. Suddenly rifle fire erupted from the left, and hundreds of Matabele warriors emerged with rifles, spears and assegais.

"Take cover!" Forbes shouted at the top of his voice.

The problem was there was hardly any cover at all. They were caught in the open, on the move, and their enemy was under cover of the forest.

***

Allan spun around to see where the firing was coming from. Like Forbes, he and his men were well and truly caught out in the open. One of the horses suddenly fell to the ground.

'Dismount!" Allan yelled. He needed a moment to think.

His men dropped to the ground and began to return fire, but Allan knew they only had one hundred rounds each–not enough for a sustained battle. He remembered passing a large anthill, at least ten feet high, and decided that they should retreat to that. They desperately needed to get out of their current situation.

"Hold your fire!" he commanded. "Mount up and retreat to the anthill; three men hold the rear!"

As everyone re-mounted, Allan took stock of the situation. Bullets were still whizzing by, but thankfully all were going high. He noticed two horses were down, and one of his men, Trooper Britton, was struggling to stem a flow of blood that was gushing from his face.

"Double up," Allan shouted to the men without horses. One of them was Fitzgerald. Ingram surged past him and reached down, hoisting him onto the back of his horse.

"Dillon!" Allan yelled. "Cut the saddlebags from the dead horses."

"Give me your reins," Kirton shouted as he snatched at Dillon's horse.

Dillon tossed his reins to Kirton, then ran, unsheathing his knife. He slashed the straps of the ammunition bags in quick order and, with the bags hoisted over his shoulders, ran back to Kirton and his horse. Kirton manhandled Dillon into his saddle, then they bolted for the anthill. The retreat was in progress, with hundreds of warriors chasing them. The Matabele were filled with blood lust, spurred on by the knowledge that they were finally going to kill the white men.

As Allan and his men fled for the anthill, they heard Forbes' column come under fire. They now knew for a certainty that there would be no rescue.

Allan ordered his men behind the anthill, where the horses were at least somewhat protected, then rapidly climbed to the top to instruct his patrol. They took their positions and waited for the warriors to come into range.

At one hundred yards Allan gave the command to open fire. The shooting was so concentrated and accurate that dozens of warriors fell, instantly dispersing the onslaught and forcing the Matabele back into the cover of the trees.

"Cease fire!" Allan yelled. "Preserve your ammunition; make sure that every bullet finds its mark."

Fred lay on the red dirt of the anthill, rifle pointing ominously at shadows that moved between trees and bushes. They were fleeting, and the patrol could sense that there was much reorganising happening.

There was a very short lull, and then, barely a minute later, the warriors, whom they had passed only minutes earlier, had come level with them. Now, suddenly, the back of the anthill was exposed.

Fred heard a dull thud, and a Salisbury Horse trooper who was lying beside him grunted, then groaned in pain. A bullet had hit him in the back, just under the shoulder blade, and exited near his collarbone. Fred quickly looked over his shoulder and watched a horse collapse onto the grass.

"Behind us!" Fred managed to shout.

Shooting broke out immediately; four more horses fell, and two of Allan's men were seriously hurt. They had to move fast. Their situation was untenable.

"Retreat!" Allan ordered.

The men with uninjured horses galloped up to the injured and waited for them to be passed up. Those without horses encircled the group, forming a protective shield. Meanwhile, three men bravely stood their ground on the anthill until the retreat to where they had spent the previous night was fully underway. They then re-joined the patrol. Fred had just leapt onto his horse when a bullet clipped his rifle, and it clattered to the ground. Kirton scooped it up and tossed it up to Fred.

"You dropped something," Kirton shared some comic relief before dashing for his mount.

With the attack easing, Allan moved his men into a dense thicket of vegetation close to where they had bivouacked the previous night, taking advantage of the cover it afforded. Allan understood why the firing had subsided; the Matabele knew the white men had nowhere to go. They could take their time now, and risking the lives of warriors had become unnecessary. Meanwhile, across the river, the men heard the familiar sound of the Maxims come to life.

***

Allan had sent Fred and Captain Judd to lead the patrol back to the thickest part of the forest. He had taken the rear with Captain Borrow. For about a mile they walked carefully, left alone by the Matabele. Allan studied the injured men doubled up on horses, slumped over in pain, holding onto their comrades. He was horrified at what had happened, at what he saw.

"Captain Borrow," Allan sidled up to his new second-in-command, "I want to try and send someone out to inform Forbes of our desperate situation and to request that he come across as soon as he is done with his action."

Borrow frowned in concern. "Sir, I don't think we can hold off long enough for Forbes to join us."

"I know. I fear that too; but there is another reason I want to try to get someone out."

"Go on," Borrow frowned.

"We are in a desperate predicament. If there is an enquiry, I want someone to be there as a witness to Forbes' actions."

Borrow nodded. "I agree. I think he handled this very poorly. He misinformed me about the situation here while he was well aware of it. He has knowingly sent me and twenty good men to our deaths."

Allan sighed. "I thought that too, but I didn't want to say so. By attempting a break-out, our force will be reduced. I want your opinion first."

"Send someone, Major. I support your decision."

"I want to send three men. One alone will never make it, but three have a better chance."

"I agree," Borrow nodded while he scanned the edge of the forest. "Whom do you have in mind?"

"If anyone can make it, Scout Burnham can. I have seen how he works in the bush," Allan said.

"Agreed. Who else?"

"You, Captain Borrow. I want you to go. If you make it, and there is an inquiry, someone from the Salisbury Horse should give evidence."

Borrow shook his head. "With respect, Major Wilson, I won't leave my men. I will die with them. May I suggest Trooper Gooding? He is a fine soldier and rides hard, and his horse is in the best condition."

"Very good, Captain," Allan nodded his acceptance of Borrow's suggestion.

"Who else, Sir?" Borrow asked.

"The other American, Scout Ingram. His horse is still up to it. Besides, I know Burnham will ask if he can take him. They work very well together. It may increase their chances of escape."

"Very good. Let it be so."

They spurred their horses to the front of the line and joined Fred and Judd.

"Burnham," Allan began. "Can you break out of here and return to Forbes?"

"I don't think so, Sir," Fred said as he cast his eyes to the surrounding forest. "No, I really don't think it would be possible."

"I want to get a message to Forbes, and I want someone to bear witness to what has happened here. You have the strongest horse, and I believe you have the skills, and, therefore, the best chance."

Fred looked around uncomfortably. "If I break out, I will certainly die, and I will die alone. I would prefer to die with these men, Major."

"I understand, Burnham," Allan allowed a smile of appreciation. "You won't be alone. I am sending two others with you."

Fred squirmed in his saddle, then shrugged. "I'm going to die here today, so I guess it doesn't matter where I fire my last bullet. I will try for you, Sir."

"Good man, thank you, Burnham."

"Sir, may I take Ingram with me? We have done much together. It would be fitting that we die together. I would like that."

"Yes, Captain Borrow and I have already discussed this, and we have selected Trooper Gooding to go with you and Ingram. He is a strong rider. I believe he is an Australian, and those Australians are tough."

Fred stood in his saddle and surveyed the area. He selected a route that he thought would give the three of them the best chance of survival. He turned to Allan and Borrow, leaned forward, and shook their hands.

"It was an honour to serve under you, Gentlemen. May God bless you both," Fred said unhappily.

With that, Ingram and Gooding were summoned and Allan quickly advised them of their mission. He also briefed them on what was to be reported if they made it over the river.

In a flash the trio wheeled their horses and galloped at full speed for the western edge of the open grassland. The moment they crashed into the woodland, they realised that they had run upon the tip of one of the Matabele 'horns of the buffalo' regimental formations.

***

Forbes was returning fire at a tree line, but could not see his enemy. It suddenly occurred to him that his column was wasting ammunition. There were only two thousand five hundred rounds for each maxim, and at six hundred rounds per minute, each burst was expensive.

"Conserve your ammunition!" Forbes called out, but his voice was drowned out by the noise of the firing.

A horse fell in front of him, then another, and then a third, and Forbes realised that the Matabele were aiming at the beasts. He knew that without the horses they might not survive the Matabele onslaught in the vast, open African wilderness. At a crouched run, he found Captain Finch and ordered him to run to the river and see if they could hide the horses under the cliffs alongside the riverbank.

Finch hurried to the river, but what he saw shocked him. The river was a raging torrent of water, and he knew they could never cross over. The opposite bank had been about twenty yards away the previous day; today it was over seventy yards away.

White foam, rolling waves, logs and whole bushes tore along in the swollen waters. It was possible to hide the horses under the cliffs, but if the enemy flanked them from upstream or downstream, or worse, both, there would be no way out. Furthermore, he realised that if Matabele armed with rifles formed up on the opposite side of the river they would be completely exposed, and the Matabele would be close enough to fire at them.

Finding Forbes with Raaff, Finch gave his commander the bad news. He had interrupted a heated discussion between the two of them, which resumed as soon as Finch delivered his verdict on the Shangani River.

"You cannot cross the river," Raaff declared in anger, "nor can you advance. You have no cover. You must order a retreat immediately."

"It will show weakness if we retreat. We will not!" Forbes insisted.

"Then we will die here. Do it!" Raaff demanded.

Captain Lendy, who was supervising a Maxim nearby, overheard the argument. Crouching behind the machine gun, he turned to Forbes.

"We cannot sustain this!" he yelled.

Forbes' face reddened. Men above and below his authority were testing him, and this would not do.

***

Fred wheeled his horse to the right and bowled over some startled young warriors. They screamed in fright as they fell and dropped their weapons. Fred hoped that he had opened a small path for Ingram and Gooding to follow. Clearing the fallen warriors he turned left, then right again. They were in thick bush with young trees whose trunks were only as thick as his wrists. It was troublesome for the horses, but manageable. He pushed his mount hard and broke through.

Looking back, Ingram and Gooding were right behind him, but the warriors were lost to his view behind the dense foliage. Only once he decided that he had managed to gain reasonable ground did he slow down. His horse needed a breather. His companions joined him, breathless and anxious from the near-death experience.

"They're coming," Ingram said as they heard branches and bushes crack against a rush of humans.

"This way," Fred pointed to his right. "At a walk; calm the horses."

The trio pressed on through the forest, zigzagging at every opportunity. Suddenly, Fred pointed left; he could smell the sweat from overexerted bodies.

"They are there," he strained a whisper at his companions. "Change direction."

They moved off in the opposite direction until they came upon an open grassland.

"Ingram," Fred pointed to his right, "walk your horse across this open land. When you reach the forest, walk your horse in a big circle in a clockwise direction then backtrack to this position and conceal yourself. Gooding, go to the left and do the same, but walk your horse anti-clockwise. Meet back here and join Ingram. I will go back slightly and walk in a figure of eight. I'll meet you fellows back here in five minutes."

Ingram objected. "They will figure it out."

"The American Indians would figure it out, yes, but not the Matabele. I have seen how they track."

The men split up and did as Fred had instructed. They confused their tracks, then moved back to the edge of the forest where they re-assembled and concealed themselves. Not long after, over three hundred excited young warriors arrived, saw the tracks and plunged into the bush.

Fred, Ingram and Gooding quickly rode the other way, straight for the river. It didn't take long to reach the north bank of the Shangani, where they stopped in their tracks, dumbfounded.

"We can't cross this," Gooding groaned. "Yesterday it was in flood, but passable. Not anymore."

The water boiled, angry and brown in front of them. A massive fully-grown tree, green leaves still attached, tumbled quietly past them. A bush the size of a small horse was sucked into an eddy and disappeared. Off to the right they could hear Forbes' battle underway, with the Maxims singing their tunes in short bursts.

"We're dead if we try to cross that," Ingram concurred.

Suddenly, a swarm of warriors emerged from the grass behind them, and spears took flight. Without a second thought, the three men spurred their horses and yelled encouragement at the top of their voices. Taken by surprise, the horses leapt into the water and began swimming hard for the other side.

Holding firmly to the pommel of the saddle, each man kicked his feet out of the stirrups and stretched out over his horses' rumps, trying to lessen the drag. It was heavy, exhausting work. They had not yet crossed the halfway point before Fred began to think that his end would come by drowning and not a bullet. An old dry log bumped into him and threatened to pull him and his horse under. A quick manoeuvre with a freed hand allowed the log to pass unhindered. This was by no means the last log to threaten the three. Fred's horse finally found purchase on the muddy bottom of the river and hauled itself out of the water. Fred, on the point of exhaustion, walked his mount to the edge of the river and was confronted by a sharply eroded cliff. Behind him, Ingram and Gooding emerged, unhurt, but also near total exhaustion. Frustrated warriors on the far bank, their remaining spears unable to fly across the tempestuous torrent, turned to rejoin the battle unfolding on their side of the river.

"We must get to Forbes," Fred said between gasps for air.

"Our horses are knocked up," Gooding said, looking at the three horses whose heads hung low, breathing heavily.

Fred listened carefully. "I'd say Forbes is about a mile away. We have drifted quite far downstream."

"I doubt our horses could manage to walk even that short distance," Ingram said despairingly.

"I doubt we could even walk them up over the edge of the bank," Gooding noted.

Fred shrugged; he knew that. "We must try. The column will need our help."

"There's a cutaway in the bank over there," Ingram pointed to his right.

"Perfect!" Fred immediately took the bridle of his horse and walked to the cut.

Climbing out of the floodplain was harder than Fred had expected. The sand kept slipping out from under his feet. Coupled with his exhaustion, hunger and lack of sleep, this latest exertion caused him to feel the strain greatly. It occurred to him that the last time he had had anything to eat was at three in the morning of the previous day, when Forbes first sent him out to scout the way ahead. Thankfully, he thought, hunger was not his biggest problem–he had trained for this in the Arizona desert– but he was now feeling shaky, and that bothered him.

Bedraggled and worn to the bone, the three men took stock of themselves once they emerged from the riverbank. The sound of Forbes' fierce battle was louder from this vantage point. Off to the right, just beyond the northern shore, they could hear the gunfire from Allan Wilson's battle. The three men looked at each other but said nothing. A hollow feeling sat in their stomachs–they knew all too well what the outcome would be, and that only a miracle could save their comrades-in-arms now.

Fred reached for his horse's bridle and nodded at his companions to start moving. They moved, dejected, side by side, a dark heaviness pressing down on them. Water squelched in their boots and dripped from their hats, and Fred was cognisant of the fact that the waterlogged saddles and leather on the horses added to their discomfort too.

**

The men of the Allan Wilson Patrol gathered in a small clearing in the forest. They knew the end was near. Allan had the injured placed on the ground and positioned his men in strategic points around them.

"Make every bullet count, Gentlemen," Allan said, grimly. "Aim for the edge of the tree trunks. If anyone puts their heads around a tree, nick the edge of the trunk."

Everyone acknowledged their commander and resigned themselves to a fight to the death. Many of the men prayed silently. Adrenalin replaced their hunger, cold and fear. They were ready.

"Here they come," Greenfield warned.

Within seconds the patrol was surrounded by hundreds of Matabele. A young warrior ran towards them and hurled a spear. It came whistling through the air, and, with a dull thud, pierced a horse through its ribcage. It whinnied pitifully and dropped to the ground. Bullets and more spears followed immediately. Allan called on his men to return fire, and Matabele warriors began dropping all around them.

The battle went on for what seemed to be hours. Allan didn't take cover; he stood in the centre of the ring of men and horses directing fire. He had taken a bullet in his left arm and a tourniquet had been tightened around the wound. When an attack strengthened from one area, he directed fire in that direction. Allan halted fire when the warriors seemed to be retreating, but, to his dismay, he could see more warriors arriving to take their place. During the momentary lull Allan quickly took stock of the situation. He realised that none of the horses would survive the coming onslaught. Of his thirty-three men, four were dead either by spear or bullet, and half of the remainder were injured. Of those injured, only five could still put up any sort of a fight.

"Gather the horses in a tight circle. Quickly," Allan ordered.

Those who could, pulled the mounts in close to them. They knew what the next order would be.

Judd suddenly called out. "Fresh attack coming!"

Allan was dreading the next order, but it had to be done. "Shoot your horses, men. Make it quick."

There was a quick round of firing, and the remaining horses dropped where they stood, forming the men's only protection. They ducked behind the bodies of the faithful mounts that had served them so well and took up defensive positions. Judd was right, the fresh attack began in earnest.

***

* * *

Fred, Ingram and Gooding walked their horses towards Forbes' battle, their horses' heads drooping low. They rounded a thicket, and there stood three young Matabele warriors. They locked eyes with the youths, and an awkward silence hung between them.

"Greet them, and keep walking, chaps," Fred ordered impulsively and threw a casual salute towards the warriors.

Ingram and Gooding were dumbfounded but went along with Fred's suggestion. They raised their right arms and saluted casually, nodding a greeting and forcing a smile at the same time.

The three warriors nodded back, frowning in confusion.

"Keep walking," Fred almost sang out.

They trudged along, expecting at any moment to feel a bullet in their backs. Only after they had walked about one hundred yards did the young warriors come to their senses and start firing at the trio. Fred and his companions had covered more than enough ground by this time, and he immediately commanded that they remount and ask their faithful horses to give them just another two hundred yards.

The horses obliged and cantered off towards Forbes' raging battle. When the three arrived at the rear guard, they were allowed to enter the makeshift laager. Dismounting, the men ran to take a position to help with the defence. Fred saw Forbes lying behind a tuft of dry grass, firing into the forest. Fred ran straight to him and crashed into the ground by his side.

"Sir," Fred said calmly. "I report that the three of us are the only survivors of Major Wilson's party."

Forbes looked at Fred critically. "Don't say anything about this to anyone until we have finished with this action." Then, without a word, he continued firing at phantoms in the forest.

Without Forbes giving him any orders, Fred took the initiative and looked about, trying to work out where he would be best placed to help defend. He noticed something strange–Raaff seemed to have taken over command. He saw Lendy struggling with a Maxim, so he quickly ran to him in a crouch.

"Can I help, Sir?" Fred asked as he dropped to the ground on his belly.

"Cover that clump of bushes for me whilst I help these men reload," Lendy pointed slightly to his right.

Fred aimed his rifle at the thicket Lendy had indicated; there was nothing happening from that direction. "Is it my imagination," Fred asked, "or is Raaff commanding this battle?"

Lendy swung the Maxim around, satisfied it was reloaded. "Forbes is technically still in command, but we are taking orders only from Raaff from now on."

Fred raised an eyebrow and cast a fleeting sideways glance at Lendy, who returned it with an equally brisk glance. Without further discussion, the two men got back to the business of defending their position.

***

Ammunition was running low. Without prompting, those who lay wounded at Allan's feet were loading rifles and passing them to those who could sustain fire. Smoke filled the air, and, between the noise of firing from within the ring of death, beyond the trees came the sound of warriors beating their shields with their spears; a story of despair and sorrow for some, and victory and joy for others, was being indelibly written.

As if by invisible command, all the warriors suddenly ceased firing. Allan quickly called the order to follow suit. A sinister lull filled the clearing as the smoke drifted off in the light breeze.

"Captain Borrow," Allan called to his second-in-command.

"Here, Sir."

"Situation?"

Borrow quickly assessed their position. "Not good, Sir." He didn't call out the number of dead–there was no need.

Allan turned to look at the men at his feet. It was a sorry sight. The wounded were loading the rifles of those who had died, ready for those still able to fire the weapons.

"Sir," Dillon called. "They are retreating."

Allan couldn't believe it. He looked back at the trees and saw dark shadows slinking away. For a moment, he wondered how they could have survived through this. Bodies of dead Matabele lay piled on top of each other at the tree line. He estimated there were a few hundred dead. The shooting accuracy of his men was proven to be outstanding. To Allan's disappointment, however, his fleeting hopes of a possible resolution were shattered when he witnessed a fresh impi swiftly taking the positions of the men who had withdrawn.

Suddenly Allan noticed a lone, elderly warrior walk to the edge of the trees. He stepped over the first body, then looked at the hundreds of young warriors who lay dead in the white man's field of fire. The old man looked directly at Allan, and their eyes locked.

There was a look of disdain in the old warrior's eyes, along with a look of sadness. Allan recognised this man as the brilliant Induna of these brave warriors. He squared himself to the man and pulled himself to his full height. Then, as only soldiers know how, Allan nodded in appreciation for and recognition of a superior adversary.

Everything in the forest went deathly quiet as the two men spoke without speaking. The wordless discussion was watched by both sides. Allan broke the visual contact and turned to his men.

"We are offered the chance to break out," he said.

"I'm not leaving my men," Captain Greenfield said.

"Neither am I," Captain Borrow affirmed softly.

Trooper Dillon looked up at Allan and smiled. "I'm staying with you, Major Wilson."

A soft chorus of 'hear hear' and words of agreement rose from the soldiers.

Allan nodded his acceptance, then looked at Mjaan. He gave a barely discernible shake of the head. Mjaan indicated his understanding with a look of sadness.

"It's time, Gentlemen," Allan turned to face his men. "It has been an honour to fight with you all."

"It's been an honour serving under you, Major Wilson," Borrow said.

Lieutenant Hofmeyer struggled to his feet. A wound in his shoulder from a spear was bleeding profusely. "I was always told you would die for your men, and you proved that to me. It is my honour to die with you, Sir."

***

From the tree line, Mjaan watched some white men struggle to stand. Some had to be helped. They stood beside their commander, and to Mjaan's utter astonishment, they took off their hats and began to sing.

"Ghaw!" Mjaan said under his breath. "They are about to die and they now sing. Are they not fearful of death? What kind of bravery is this?"

Dumbfounded, the Matabele stood quietly watching the spectacle. When the settlers had finished singing, they gave three cheers, then all shook hands. Replacing their hats on their heads, the men crouched down and took their positions. The leader looked at Mjaan one last time.

Mjaan shook his head solemnly, filled his lungs, and bellowed the command to attack. Instantly, the air was filled with the roar of gunfire, smoke, and the screams of death. The battle was short-lived; the settlers had finally run out of ammunition.

When the pall of smoke lightened, a lone man stood. He was bleeding badly, and he held a revolver in each hand, with which he continued firing. In reply, those warriors who had rifles shot back. Their aim was true this time, and a bullet to the white man's hip dropped him to his knees. Still, the man kept firing until his revolvers made quiet clicking noises. The time had finally arrived, and, with a cry of victory, the Matabele warriors rushed their enemy.

As Mjaan's men danced and shouted in jubilation, he stepped forward and angrily ordered them to silence. He purposefully walked around the ring of death, looking at his defeated enemy. He then walked around the outer circle, inspecting his fallen warriors. Mjaan estimated his losses at over five hundred.

He made his way to the inner circle and counted the white men—just thirty-four. Thirty-four men in total. Looking at their faces, Mjaan was shocked; they were young men—too young to be fighting a man's war. Their bravery shook him.

Mjaan cast a menacing eye over all his men. They stood in trepidation of what their Induna would say to them. He looked angry.

"You will not molest these dead people!" Mjaan shouted. "You will not mutilate their bodies. You will not take anything from them."

Looking around to ensure everyone had his attention, he continued. "They were men of men, whose fathers were men before them. They fought and died together. They could have saved themselves but chose to remain and die with their brothers. Do not forget this!"

Mjaan glared angrily at the warriors gathered around him. "You did not think the white men were as brave as the Matabele, but now you must see that they are men indeed, to whom you are but timid girls. These men did not scream or groan in death. Therefore, as they died in silence, so we shall respect them in silence."

He looked at his warriors menacingly. He dropped his gaze, and, as he walked away, the warriors quietly stepped aside to let him pass. There was no joy for Mjaan in this victory.

***

Commandant Raaff called the retreat as soon as there was a lull in the attack. With a strategically placed rear guard, the calculated withdrawal began. Raaff ensured that it happened as quickly as possible. Once they reached the place where they had camped during the night, a defensive position was set up.

The almost continuous firing that they had heard from the northern side of the river petered out. Fears for Allan Wilson's Patrol haunted the men. It didn't take long for the realisation to spread through the troops that Major Wilson's patrol had perished. An ominous feeling of certain defeat settled on the column. Eventually, even Forbes had to admit that the chances of the Wilson Patrol re-joining him were slim-to-none. Forbes became withdrawn, which made it easier for Raaff to take over full command.

Sporadic firing from the Matabele on Raaff's side of the river kept up throughout the day. The biggest fear was that their column might be flanked along the riverbanks, both upstream and downstream.

Raaff quickly briefed some of the men of his plans, and told them to repeat his message to those unable to hear him. Raaff felt that the men needed to know what was going to take place so that they fully understood the situation and would work with him as a team.

"We are surrounded on three sides," Raaff announced. "We have the Shangani River in flood on our left, which is our saving grace. We have injured men, some seriously, and we have no provisions left. The pursuit of the King has ceased. We will follow the Shangani River. When we get closer to Inyati we will break from the river and turn towards Inyati itself. I will send riders back to KoBulawayo to tell Jameson to send support, food and medicine to meet us there. It will be a difficult retreat, but it is our only chance of survival. Most of our horses have been killed, so the retreat will be on foot. What you take, you will carry yourself, so choose wisely. Our friends who went to the other side of the river were cut off and surrounded. I think you will agree that we are not likely to see them again. As we move, we will come under further attack, and our ammunition is low. Preserve your bullets and make every shot count. Reveille is at three o'clock in the morning; we move out fifteen minutes later. Be prepared."

Fred and Ingram lay on the ground, trying to sleep before they were called for duty. Although they were allocated two hours' sleep, they were woken by Raaff after only half an hour.

"Scout Ingram, I would like you to deliver an urgent message to Dr Jameson in KoBulawayo. Will you do this for me?"

"Yes, Sir. Of course," Ingram said groggily as he gingerly sat up.

"You heard my message to the men?"

"Yes, Commandant. You will follow the Shangani as far as possible, then break for Inyati. Jameson must urgently send food, weapons and medicine to meet us."

"Very good. Thank you. I will ask Lynch to accompany you in case one of you can't make it. He has a strong horse and is a good rider. Burnham, I want you with me to scout ahead and find a suitable route for us to take with our injured and the Maxims."

"Yes, Sir," Fred acquiesced.

"Thank you. As soon as it gets dark, Ingram, you must set off with Lynch," Raaff said, then reached over and grasped Ingram's shoulder in appreciation. "The success of your mission will be the difference between life and death for us all," he said gruffly.

"I'm aware of that, Commandant," Ingram said.

As night set in, Forbes ordered flares to be set off in the hopes that any survivors on the north bank would see where the column was situated so that they could make their way to them under the cover of darkness. By eight o'clock that effort was abandoned because another massive storm lashed the camp. During the peak of the storm, Ingram and Lynch set off. Their plan, as commanded, was to follow the Shangani River until they were clear of the Matabele, then cut south and head directly for KoBulawayo.

At three o'clock in the morning, Raaff ordered the men to reveille and to prepare for retreat. Just as Raaff had instructed, fifteen minutes later the column was on the move. The retreat was difficult, especially as the men were exhausted and on the verge of starvation.

At about ten o'clock that morning, as Fred returned from a scouting expedition, Forbes pulled Fred aside.

"Burnham," Forbes said, "I want you to cross the river and backtrack to where you left Wilson and see if there are any survivors."

Fred looked at Forbes in disbelief. "Sir, Wilson and his men have perished. There is no possibility of any survivors. Besides, the river is impassable."

"Yes, there is a possibility of survivors. You don't know if they have all perished. None of us do. Besides, you have already successfully crossed the river in flood."

Fred decided that Forbes had become momentarily overcome with guilt. 'Sir, with respect, I was there. There is no hope for any survivors. They each had one hundred rounds–nothing more once those rounds were finished. And we heard their gunfire cease."

"I don't care, Burnham. There may be a chance that someone survived."

"If you send me there, I will certainly die. You know that, don't you?" Fred wanted to remind Forbes that this is exactly what he had done to Captain Borrow but held his tongue.

"I want you to backtrack and check this for me, Burnham!" Forbes stated aggressively.

"Alright," Fred replied angrily, then turned to get his horse.

Ten minutes later Fred returned with his mount. His eyes were burning with anger.

"Major Forbes," Fred said loudly enough for everyone to hear him. "I will do as you say and cross the river to look for survivors, but you must make it an order, not a request."

Forbes pulled himself up to his full height but said nothing.

Fred waited for the order, then continued. "I have never refused an order, Sir. Make that an order!"

Forbes stared at Fred for a moment, then spun on his heels and walked away, leaving Fred fuming with anger.

Fred didn't cross the river, but later that afternoon, he went out again and scouted for the next section of the route. To his absolute delight he found the hoof print of Ingram's horse, named Brandy, and Lynch's horse, named Soda. They had made it through, and the column would be saved. Fred's joy didn't last, though. On top of Brandy's hoof print was the tell-tale footprint of a Matabele youth. Ingram and Lynch were being followed.

Fred went back to the column and sought out Raaff. On telling him what he had found, Raaff called Colenbrander, who was well-versed in the ways of the African bush, and they returned to Ingram and Lynch's trail.

"What do you think, Meneer Colenbrander?" Raaff asked.

Colenbrander prodded the edge of the footprint. "It's a young man, running light."

Fred, who had been scouting about thirty yards ahead, called the men over to look at what else he had found. Another thirty-odd runners had joined the lone runner.

"What worries me," Raaff studied the footprints, "is that Ingram and Lynch would be walking their horses to conserve their strength, and so these men are running faster than they are walking."

Fred concurred. "If Ingram is unaware that they are being chased, the Matabele might catch up to him."

Colenbrander scratched his head thoughtfully. "Knowing the Matabele as I do, especially the young ones, they don't have the disposition that your American Indians do. If they don't see Ingram and Lynch after one or two days of chasing, they will give up and return to the main Matabele army."

"That's some consolation," Raaff said softly, "but we cannot be certain of that happening."

Colenbrander frowned in consternation. "If we let this discovery be known to the column, it may lead to a further drop in morale. Our men are already abysmally dispirited."

"I agree," Raaff said. "Tell no one, not even Forbes. We must just pray that Ingram and Lynch get through to KoBulawayo."

***

As the sun touched the horizon at the end of their first day in the saddle, Ingram and Lynch stopped to drink and partake of some of their meagre food reserves. Ingram looked over his shoulder and studied the land they had just ridden through. The bush was still quite thick, and difficult to traverse.

"Lynch, I'd like to backtrack a little to see if we were followed."

"Of course, but I doubt the Matabele saw us leave in that storm."

"I agree, but, from my experience with the American Indians, it would be prudent to check our tail."

"Are those American Indians that good?" Lynch asked, amused.

"You bet. They are cunning, and far more astute in tracking and bushcraft than any people I have ever known."

"Very well, if you feel it is important," Lynch agreed.

Instead of following back along their tracks, Ingram and Lynch circled back, hoping to intersect their tracks a few miles farther back and see if there were warriors after them. There proved to be no need to find their tracks, though, because soon they saw, through the trees, a group of Matabele following the trail they had left.

Lynch nodded his appreciation to Ingram.

Ingram smiled broadly. "Let's lead the Matabele away from us, shall we?"

CHAPTER TWENTY-SIX

10th December 1893

Commandant Raaff often scouted ahead with Fred. It bothered Fred because Raaff was the most experienced soldier in the column, and being away from the main body, sneaking through the bush in and around the enemy, was a very dangerous exercise. He expressed this concern to Raaff, but Raaff was not worried. He believed that these reconnaissance excursions gave him a good feel for the situation, which would enable him to make plans or change tactics quickly if necessary.

The two would leave the camp between two o'clock and three o'clock, in the early hours of the morning, and quietly walk in amongst the enemy's positions, gauging their numbers and locations. Then they would walk a safe distance away, conceal themselves and take some time to sleep before returning to the column and setting the course for the day.

On one of these nightly scouting excursions, at two o'clock in the morning, Fred was out scouting on his own. He discovered that the enemy had grouped in large numbers. Tethering his horse safely to a tree, Fred crept closer to the enemy positions. The Matabele were all soundly asleep, without having posted guards, which made his excursion into their camps easy. He realised, though, that in the morning they would see his prints and know he had been amongst them. This didn't worry him. On the contrary, it made him smile, but he also knew he wouldn't be able to be this bold again because they would be more alert and post guards for the next time.

Fred had discovered that the Matabele had positioned themselves to launch a major attack on three fronts. There was only one way for the column to proceed–they had to traverse a deep gully that crossed the route of their retreat. The Matabele had worked this out and set a cunning trap that would be difficult, if not impossible, to avoid.

Cutting his scouting expedition short, Fred returned to the column to tell Raaff, Forbes and Colenbrander of his findings. Drawing a rough map in the sand, he explained how dire their predicament was.

"Gentlemen," Raaff said thoughtfully, "it is true. We are surrounded, and our only option is to push through."

"We could wait for the relief force," Forbes suggested. "They should be with us soon."

Raaff sighed. "We cannot depend on them. We found tracks that indicated Ingram and Lynch were being pursued by the Matabele."

"Why didn't you tell me that?" Forbes demanded.

"To lessen dejection in the troops," Raaff said bluntly. He, as well as several others, knew Forbes couldn't keep a secret to himself. Too many times he had confided in troopers, or those close to him.

"What are our chances of pushing through and keeping the Matabele at bay?" Colenbrander asked.

"There are too many of them," Fred shook his head. 'I have scouted through their camps. It would be folly to even try."

"There is no other way then," Forbes said, defeatedly.

"There is," Raaff said softly, "but it is extremely risky."

The other three men, crouching on the ground, looked at Raaff in anticipation.

"We must cross the gully as soon as possible, in the early hours of the morning when the warriors are at their deepest sleep. But, we cannot make a sound. One sound will alert them, and they will attack when we are at our most vulnerable."

Fred shook his head. "The Maxims won't get up the other side. Are you suggesting we leave them behind?"

"We are not leaving the Maxims," Forbes said firmly. "Even if we do manage to cross the gully, we would be dead within hours without them."

Raaff nodded. "Ja, Meneer, I actually agree with you this time. We will take them, but we must leave the carriages behind, and carry the Maxims out of the gully wrapped in blankets and on horseback. Then I want to use the carriages as a decoy. If we cut logs and fashion them to look like the barrels of the Maxims, the Matabele will think we have remained in camp, and will come here to fight us. If we make it look good that we plan to remain in camp, they will have to advance very carefully. This will take them a while, and will buy us some extra escape time."

Fred shook his head in consternation. "Then you must hope they don't see our tracks as we move past them."

"It is a chance we must take," Raaff said.

Colenbrander nodded. "It is a good plan, Commandant, but I fear we will make a noise when we move. It will be almost impossible to move silently."

Fred agreed. "We have bridles and stirrups that jingle, and horses' hooves are not silent. Furthermore, we have seriously injured men who have no pain relief. If they are to be carried out, they will be heard."

"I know," Raaff agreed. "My plan will not be easy. All metalware, everywhere, must be wrapped in cloth. All horses' hooves must be wrapped in leather or blankets. The men must be told they can take one thing with them other than their rifles, only one. If they want a cape, they may take a cape. If they want a blanket, they may take a blanket, but not both. This will be a very tough order for men already suffering. All men who have dogs must put them down."

Fred's heart sank. There were seven dogs in the camp, animals which had faithfully followed their master's into battle and were loyal companions to them. He knew how devastated the men would be to have to end their dogs' lives. Fred was right; it was the hardest thing those men had to do. Even as trained soldiers, who could hold their own in a raging battle, disposing of their dogs brought those seasoned men to tears. It was heartbreaking to see.

The sleeping men were woken, and Raaff's plan was immediately set in motion. The fires were stoked high so that they would burn and smoke well into the morning and weaker horses were left tethered to trees to look as though the camp was occupied. The Maxims were wrapped and tied between pairs of horses that were fit enough to carry the load. The remaining blankets covered mounds of abandoned equipment to look like sleeping men. The maxim carriages were strategically placed, and deliberately poorly camouflaged. Their fake barrels protruded menacingly. Where possible, the soldiers made effigies to look as though the camp was occupied and guarded.

Then, moving off in the dead of night, the men led the horses into the gully, very slowly, one careful step at a time. The leather or fabric foot coverings silenced their steps. Somehow, even the horses seemed to sense that they had to be quiet, which fascinated Fred, especially as he thought he knew equine temperaments better than anyone in the column.

The wounded were carried over their comrades' shoulders, and not once did they make a sound, even though they were in great pain. Fred led the column out of the ravine. It took just over two hours to traverse the Matabele's killing zone. Finally, when they were clear of the gully, they moved through the inky darkness and put as much distance between themselves and their enemy before sunrise.

When the sun came up, Raaff's plan to present a camp to the Matabele where the men were taking a day off, paid dividends. At first, the Matabele thought it was a trap, and kept their distance, waiting to see what the white man had in store for them. Eventually, a brave spy crept up to the camp and peered in, only to find it deserted.

The soldiers realised that it was because of Raaff's experience and knowledge of the Matabele that they had lived to see another day. By now, most men had worn their shoes to the point that they were almost useless. They were forced to cut leather saddlebags or canvas coverings to create makeshift soles. Some men were on the point of giving up, longing for an assegai to end their misery because their feet were so painful. Clothing was in tatters from the thorns and branches, and men had lost so much weight that they looked like walking skeletons. Many had been on the march since early October, others since mid-November, on short rations and with no support. They were exhausted.

Moving forward, they arrived at a shallow river. The Matabele were now hot on their trail, and catching up with them. Raaff wanted to cross over as quickly as possible. In the distance, they heard the warriors call out excitedly as their spoor was picked up. Elated, the Matabele warriors came running to engage the fleeing column.

The crossing was not difficult, but in their rush to get across, the ammunition for the Maxims was left on the far bank. Forbes called for volunteers to retrieve the boxes, but by then everyone had all but given up and collapsed on the sandy bank, dejected. It was a sorry sight. In the days since the retreat was called, the column had been attacked on four occasions and escaped at least that many times again. Time and again men were on the verge of giving up. They sat down in despair, feet bleeding, suffering from immense exhaustion, pain or hunger, but their comrades forced them on. This seemed to be just that one disaster too many.

Eventually an emaciated man called Tancred waded back across the stream and lifted the boxes. Fred thought his thin legs would snap under the weight. As he staggered back some men found the strength to go into the water and help him across. Ammunition in hand, the column gained incentive, and quickly made their way to some open ground not far off. When the Matabele saw the column waiting in a defensive position, with the sigwagwas set up, armed and aimed straight at them, they gave up the chase.

The following day, Fred was scouting ahead of the column, and in the distance, he saw two riders walking their horses in his direction. As they got closer, Fred recognised one of the men—Frederick Courtney Selous, the hunter and scout under Colonel Goold-Adams' column whom he had met near Tati. After twenty-five days on the march, with only five days' rations to start with, the column had been found.

***

Dr Jameson came up with the relief column and immediately got to work tending to the injured and sick. Fred and Bain were last on his list, as they seemed to be the only two who were relatively healthy.

Jameson marvelled, "How is it that you and Bain somehow survived better than the others?"

Fred grinned. "We know some of the ways of the Indians in America. When our food ran out, we had to eat our starving horses. The meat of a starving animal loses all nutrition, but, thanks to the Indians, we know that the brain is always the last organ to lose that nutrition, so we ate the brains. The Englishmen are so stuck in their culture that they wouldn't dream of touching the brains of an animal. This meant that there was more for us."

"Well, I never," Jameson smiled. "Of all of this group, you two are the only ones who I believe can walk the last forty miles to KoBulawayo."

"Are Ingram and Lynch alright, Sir?"

"They are," Jameson confirmed. "They are safe in KoBulawayo. They were very fatigued, though, and their horses were on their last legs. I have admitted them to the infirmary there until I am satisfied with their recovery."

"I'm pleased to hear that," Fred smiled. "I was concerned about them."

Jameson laughed heartily. "I'll tell you a funny tale, Mr Burnham. Mr Rhodes came up to KoBulawayo after the King fled. A short while ago he rode out towards Inyati with his friend, Sir Charles Metcalfe. Rhodes was unarmed; he has a severe dislike of weapons. He saw two riders walking in, looking exhausted, and Rhodes said, 'Metcalfe, I believe those are scouts from Forbes' and Wilson's patrol; they are utterly exhausted,' and Sir Charles said 'No, I would suspect that they are policemen out on patrol.' When they met, Mr Rhodes asked who they were, and they said they were Ingram and Lynch, and Ingram said he had a message for Mr Rhodes. Rhodes said he could give him the message, but Ingram told him to go to hell. If he wanted to know what the message was, he would have to go to KoBulawayo and ask Rhodes himself. Rhodes then explained who he was, but Ingram said Rhodes wouldn't be such a damn fool as to be riding outside KoBulawayo unarmed. With that, Rhodes and Metcalf escorted Ingram and Lynch back into town where I immediately introduced Mr Rhodes. Poor old Ingram, he was so embarrassed, but Mr Rhodes commended him for being so determined to keep his message confidential."

Fred laughed at that. "Well, good for Ingram."

"When we get back to KoBulawayo, I want to have a discussion with you about this entire incident."

"I'm at your service, Dr Jameson."

"Good show, Mr Burnham. We will leave tomorrow and begin a very slow march to KoBulawayo."

***

Safely at Inyati, Fred left Jameson's wagon and saw Raaff and Lendy sitting in the shade of a messy thatch shelter. They were in conversation, so he walked over to greet them.

"How was Jameson?" Lendy said sarcastically.

"Alright," Fred replied. "He gave me a clean bill of health. He said he wanted to talk to me when we got back to KoBulawayo."

"I'll be putting in a scathing report about Forbes," Lendy said. "He has no idea what's coming."

Fred could imagine the venom that would be evident in that report. After all, in peacetime, Lendy was Fort Victoria's magistrate assistant.

Fred held his tongue; he wasn't quite sure how to react to this.

Raaff leaned back against a pole and sighed. "My report will also be scathing about Forbes. I have much to say about him. My attack will also be levelled at Jameson. Your Dr Jameson is directly to blame for the loss of Major Wilson and his Patrol, as well as *all* our men who died fighting the Matabele."

"Oh, I agree," Lendy said angrily. "What man would send men on a three-week patrol with five days' worth of provisions? What man would send one hundred and sixty men with one hundred rounds of ammunition each to face an enemy of over ten thousand? If that wasn't enough, he then, on a whim, put an inexperienced man in command."

"What do you think, Meneer Burnham?" Raaff asked.

Fred shuffled uncomfortably. "Gentlemen, I have to agree with you, but I'm an American who has got tangled up in a British war. I don't know that I have an opinion on the matter."

"Of course you do," Lendy frowned.

"Well, think about it; I am a volunteer, I'm not paid by the BSAC, and I was engaged as a scout, not a soldier. Unlike all of you, I have no rank. I'm just 'Scout Burnham'."

Lendy's frown deepened.

"So," Raaff asked, "why did you volunteer?"

"For the reward. Jameson, the Administrator of Mashonaland, promised six thousand acres of workable land to farm or ranch, and twenty mining claims. They even offered us a portion of Lobengula's cattle. I came for the adventure and to farm and mine. Not to fight, and certainly not to overthrow a ruling King and take over a country."

"But you did fight," Lendy pressed.

"I have a wife and son in Fort Victoria. They told me.... you told me," Fred pointed at Lendy as he corrected himself, "if we lost the battle the Matabele would kill everyone in Fort Victoria and Fort Salisbury. I fought to protect my family."

"And this brings me to why Jameson is to blame, more than anyone else," Lendy continued. "The King was defeated; we didn't need to pursue him and capture him. All of this could have been negotiated."

"I have to agree there," Fred scowled. "It was badly handled. So many needless deaths on both sides. I'll say one thing, though: I have come to admire the Matabele. I have never experienced such courage and determination. They came at us, in defence of their King and their land, time and time again–despite the inequality in weaponry. They are brave and loyal warriors."

"There will be a Court of Inquiry," Raaff said. "Captain Lendy will ensure it happens. Will you testify, Meneer Burnham?"

"Of course," Fred said. "I will answer any question they ask me, with honesty."

"Meneer Burnham," Raaff allowed a rare smile to appear on his lips. "I want to thank you for what you did for us out there. We are alive only because of you."

"No, Sir," Fred was quick to deflect the praise. "It was your command that saved us."

Lendy cleared his throat. "The men are talking, and they all agree you led us to safety, Burnham. Without you, we would have died. They also have the highest respect for Commandant Raaff. You are right," Lendy frowned, "we are fully aware that Commandant Raaff played a significant part in saving us."

"We all played our part," Fred frowned, "even the wounded and the animals."

"That is true, Meneer," Raaff nodded sadly. "That is true."

***

When the column finally marched into KoBulawayo, those who had remained behind greeted them in the centre square with cheers and applause. Rhodes was there to greet the men and shook hands with everyone who passed by him; however, he turned his back on Forbes and refused to shake his hand. When Raaff entered the square, a raucous round of applause was given, with a hip-hip-hooray salute. Forbes, who was in quiet conversation with Jameson, did not miss this.

Later that evening a feast was held for the columns, and some of the emaciated men gave impromptu speeches. Forbes, who didn't attend, was roundly criticised by all who spoke. Raaff and Lendy included Dr Jameson in their verbal attacks, which somewhat surprised the attendees. Raaff's speech was particularly brutal as he let his anger flow freely, and Lendy was utterly scathing about Forbes. Fred stayed well out of the politics, insults and fist-thumping.

The Court of Inquiry was convened only days later. Raaff was unable to attend because of a sudden severe case of food poisoning that he suspected he got at the welcome feast. He tried to submit a written report from his hospital bed. He was so sick, however, that his submission was confusing and of no help. Dr Jameson was unable to help Raaff, medically, and a few days later the Commandant passed away. His cause of death was said to be peritonitis, from indulging on rich food too soon after his acute deprivations.

Captain Lendy testified at the inquiry and submitted a blistering account of the Shangani Patrol's demise. He held back no punches when it came to Forbes' command.

Boasting a high level of fitness, Lendy was the proud owner of a pair of dumbbells and trained every morning and evening. He attended an impromptu sporting competition after his testimony and, while putting the shot, became wracked with abdominal pain and was rushed to the infirmary. Dr Jameson attended to him and declared he had ruptured his intestine. Two days later he was dead.

Forbes, as expected, came out of the inquiry very badly. Despite all the accusations levelled at him, however, no charges were laid against him. He departed for England as soon as he could.

Once Fred and Ingram had testified at the inquiry, they left for Fort Victoria. Fred was yearning to see Blanche again, and he knew she was waiting anxiously to see him. When they arrived on the outskirts of the Fort, Blanche and some of her lady friends were waiting on the road. They had received a message that Fred and some of the men were on their way, so the womenfolk had set up a welcoming party with picnic blankets, food and refreshments.

After the emotional reunions were over and stories had been exchanged, Fred sat on a picnic blanket slightly away from the others, Blanche by his side.

Blanche squeezed Fred's hand lovingly. "There is talk around town that you were the main reason so many lived through the battles."

"That's not true, Blanche. I was just a small part of the entire operation."

Blanche smiled sweetly. "Well, that's not what everyone is saying. Some are saying it was the efforts of the American scouts that enabled the settlers to win the war. I was worried about you. When I heard that poor Allan Wilson and his men were killed, I worried that you were a part of his group."

Fred shook his head in sorrow. "That was so tragic. I *was* a part of his group, Blanche, but he sent me, Ingram and a man called Gooding to escape with a message for the commander. We nearly didn't make it."

"What happened that day?"

"It's a long story, Blanche. I'll say one thing though, I have a lot of respect for the Matabele Induna who commanded their force. Once he realised that the Matabele army was no match for the Maxims, he set an elaborate trap against an enemy that was far superior weapon-wise to his. Had we all crossed that river, the entire column would have been doomed–and then they would have turned around and retaken KoBulawayo and everyone in it. I think they suspected that we were short of manpower, arms and ammunition, and we were!"

Fred looked up at the leaves of the tree they were sitting under and sighed heavily. "The history of this country changed on the banks of the Shangani River that day. Major Wilson along with his thirty-three men died a brutal death on one side of the river, and we couldn't get to him. His remains and the remains of his men are still out there somewhere. It is very sad."

"That's terrible, Fred," Blanche shuddered. She knew only too well how close she had been to becoming a widow.

Fred shook his head forlornly. "And on the other side of the river we were driven back mercilessly; we were resoundingly defeated, and yet, against all expectations, the Matabele have stopped fighting."

"Why?" Blanche asked curiously.

"I don't know, Blanche. I don't think anyone knows. It's a mystery."

Fred and Blanche sat in silence, close together, as memories swirled in their minds. Emotions were high, and the companionable silence was a welcome balm to anguished thoughts.

"Shall we go to Roderick now?" Fred broke the silence with a smile; he was keen to see his son.

"In a moment. I want to sit with you a little longer. Roderick and Major Wilson's son are having lessons with Mrs Thatcher right now."

"Poor child," Fred said sadly. "How old is he now?"

"Herbert is years old," Blanche frowned. "I wonder what his future holds now. I would think the BSAC will have some responsibility for him."

Fred nodded. "There is an extremely wealthy man in Cape Town called Barny Bernato. He is a friend of Mr Rhodes. They say his wife and Major Wilson's late wife were sisters, so Herbert has an aunt. Rumour has it they will be adopting him."

Blanche sighed softly. "I'm pleased to hear that. He has been on my mind. So tragic for that young boy at such a young age."

After a pause, Fred changed the subject. "We have been allocated a lovely plot in the new settlement of Bulawayo. It's a corner stand, and just a short walk from the town centre. I've also been awarded dozens of licences to claim gold mines, and six thousand acres of land to farm," Fred winked.

Blanche laughed. "You hate farming. Look at what citrus did to you!"

"I know," Fred said sheepishly. "I cannot think of anything worse. I'll be turning that offer down, in favour of shares in the Company."

"What's Dr Jameson like?" Blanche became serious again.

"He's a gentleman," Fred smiled, "a really nice man. His personality is alluring and captivating. Jameson is a brilliant doctor, I have seen him work, and as an administrator, I think Rhodes is very lucky to have Jameson controlling his affairs. He is efficient, and effective and gets things done quickly. I think he would make for an excellent politician. Militarily, I'm not so sure. He is excitable and doesn't seem to heed his advisors. Let's just pray he never engages in a military campaign again."

"Well, I do pray there is peace over this land from now on," Blanche said softly.

"Tomorrow I want to pack up our things and take you and Roderick to KoBulawayo to begin building our new home. We have so much work to do."

Blanche squeezed Fred's hand. "Stay here a few days and rest, darling. You must be totally exhausted."

Fred laughed. "Me? Never. Tomorrow is already too far away."

Blanche chuckled softly. "You haven't changed one iota, Fred Burnham."

CHAPTER TWENTY-SEVEN

February 1894

It had been two and a half months since the Inquiry when Dr Jameson poked his head into the dim shed that James Dawson had constructed.

"Jimmy," Jameson smiled happily. "Glad I have found you."

"Good morning, Doctor. Come in," Dawson invited, warily.

"Nice place you have here," Jameson looked about the shed.

"This is just temporary. I will be travelling south at the end of the year."

"Jimmy, I have a big personal favour to ask of you."

Dawson did not like Jameson's requests for help. They invariably cost him time, money and hardship. "How can I help, Sir?"

"I am losing sleep over the thought that the remains of Major Wilson and his men have been left abandoned in the bush. I would appreciate it if you were to find where they died and bury their remains. You are a respected trader with the Matabele, and you speak their language. That is why I am asking you."

Dawson was inclined to decline any request from Jameson immediately, but this one was hard to refuse. Wilson and his men had become heroes overnight, and he felt he owed this to their legacy.

"Would you be funding this venture?" Dawson asked. "I have no money right now; I lost everything in the uprising."

"Of course. The Company will make all arrangements for you."

"Very well," Dawson agreed. "I will leave tomorrow."

***

James Dawson, together with a friend named Riley, left Bulawayo early the next day. With the help of Matabele villagers, whom they met along the way, they eventually found the point at the Shangani River where the Wilson Patrol had crossed over.

The river was no longer in flood, but it was still flowing at about two feet deep in the centre. A young Matabele saw them cross over and greeted them. Having explained their mission to him, the young man led Dawson and Riley to the site where the fateful battle had taken place.

It was a pitiful sight, and Dawson was moved to tears, his emotions difficult to keep in check. There, in a small grouping, were the skeletal remains of both humans and horses.

The young boy noticed Dawson's tears of sorrow. "Sir, I have been waiting for you."

Dawson looked at him in surprise. "Why do you wait for me?"

"Our leader said I must stay here until you come. He wishes to speak with you."

"Your leader wants to speak with me?" Dawson responded in surprise. "Alright, let us speak," he agreed.

"I will return with him tomorrow. He lives far."

"I will wait," Dawson confirmed.

As soon as the young man had left, Dawson and Riley scoured the area and looked for paper, notebooks or anything else that Allan's men may have recorded something on before they perished. They only found some scraps that had been destroyed by the rain, white ants and the intense sunlight. The remnants were utterly useless.

They identified the skeletons of thirty-four men, but only thirty-three skulls; one was missing. There were no uniforms or possessions that could be used to identify the soldiers' remains, and no weapons remained. Dawson also noticed that the tree trunks all around the circle were nicked with bullet marks. Wordlessly, Dawson and Riley studied the fateful site and could discern how fierce the battle had been.

They extracted two shovels from their wagon and began digging a large grave beside a tall Msasa tree. As the sounds of their spades worked at the hard earth, groups of young boys and girls gradually appeared from nearby villages and patiently watched them dig. They only finished excavating when the sun was about to set. Exhausted from their exertions, they set up camp and retired for the night.

The following morning an elderly man was brought to Dawson and

Riley. They exchanged traditional greetings; a high level of respect shown by all parties.

"My name is James Dawson. Doctor Jameson has sent me from Bulawayo to find the bones of the white men who died here."

The man nodded his understanding. "I am the leader of the Matabele warriors, and my name is Mjaan. I have been expecting someone to come."

"I seek your permission to bury the bones of these people in the ground with the white man's customs."

Mjaan nodded gravely. "You have that permission."

"We thank you," Dawson said and bowed slightly to enforce his sincerity. "Does King Lobengula still live?"

"The King is no more. I was with him when the Great Bull Elephant died," Mjaan said sadly.

"We are sorry to hear that," Dawson said. It was a genuine sentiment. "Do you know how he died?"

Mjaan looked into the forest briefly, formulating his answer. "He was very sick, but before the sickness could take him, he died of a broken heart. He was very sad at what the white men did to him and his people."

Dawson was not able to answer this comment, although he had expected something like it to be said.

Mjaan continued. "I buried him in a cave with all his royal belongings, as is our custom for a King's burial. I plunged my spear into his belly, and the calf of the elephant belched. My burial job was now complete, and I sealed the cave."

Dawson nodded his understanding. He knew it was the Matabele tradition to open the bodies of the dead to free their spirit. "We found the bones of thirty-four men; one skull is missing," Dawson said.

"That is correct," Mjaan said. "We took one head to show our King that we had indeed defeated the white men."

"Many Matabele have returned to Bulawayo," Dawson said tentatively. "They have handed in their weapons and gone back to their villages. Is it true that the Matabele have stopped fighting with the white man?"

Mjaan nodded. "Yes, it is so."

"Why?" Dawson could not stop himself from asking. He knew that the Matabele could mount another attack and drive the white population away if they continued fighting. The whites were on the brink of defeat.

Mjaan looked around the circle of the dead. "There are no men braver than these boys," he said solemnly. "They didn't need the sigwagwas to fight. When the battle was over, I looked at all the dead, and I thought, how can so few young boys kill so many of our warriors before we could kill them? We then feared our victory; we thought, what will happen when the bearded ones, their fathers, come and say 'Where are our boys? Who killed them?'. I decided it is best we fight no more in order to save our nation. I am the one who ordered our people to stop fighting."

Dawson looked at Riley and cocked an eyebrow.

Mjaan continued. "It was also clear the settlers would stop at nothing to kill our King. Even the gold he sent to guarantee his return would not stop them."

Dawson was shocked. "The King sent gold to guarantee his return?"

Mjaan nodded. "That is so. The King gave me two pouches of gold sovereigns to give to your commander. I sent a man to deliver it with the King's words. This he did. But your commander did not stop, which was the sign that they wanted to kill the King, and not to capture him to negotiate peace."

Dawson sighed in dismay. "The gold was not received."

Mjaan shook his head emphatically. "No, they did receive it. My courier missed the front of your column, it was moving too fast, but he caught up with the men at the back. It was given to two men at the rear. They promised to give the gold to your commander."

"Induna Mjaan," Dawson said, "I will report this to Dr Jameson. He will want to know this. I have one more request to ask of you."

Mjaan studied Dawson for a moment, then nodded.

"It is clear to me that many people died here on that day. All were brave warriors; your people and our people. They all fought like good soldiers. There is no one man who is less brave than his comrade. I would like to make a mark on that tree," Dawson pointed to the Msasa that towered over the empty grave. "It will be the mark of the Great Spirit of the white man, a cross, but it will be on a tree rooted in your land, the land of the Matabele."

Mjaan looked at the tree and frowned. He said nothing.

Dawson continued. "In that mark, I would like to inscribe some words to recognise *all* the brave men that died here on that day."

Mjaan nodded gravely. "Then let it be so."

* * *

When Dawson and Riley placed all of the human bones that they could find in the grave, they were about to begin shovelling soil when Dawson held up a hand.

"Forgive me, Riley, but there is something I would like to do," he said as he passed his companion his spade.

Dawson undid his belt and pulled it free from the loops of his trousers. Gently folding the belt in half, he studied the black leather for a moment, then, carefully, he tossed it into the grave.

"For you, Wilson. May you rest in peace."

Riley looked confused. "Are you alright, Dawson?"

"Yes," Dawson smiled. "That tawse always belonged to him."

"That's a belt, not a tawse," Riley said.

"It was used as a tawse by our headmaster," Dawson grinned sheepishly.

"You knew him? Wilson?"

"A long time ago. Not a great academic, but a great sportsman."

"You think Wilson should have been the leader of the column?"

"I do," Dawson sighed, deep in thought. "Without a doubt."

Riley nodded. "You know, Dawson, Induna Mjaan stopped a war because of the bravery of Major Wilson and his thirty-three men."

"Yes, that certainly seems to be the case," Dawson smiled and retrieved his spade from Riley. "Right-oh, shall we continue?"

Once they had filled in the grave, Dawson withdrew his sheath knife and etched a fairly large cross on the Msasa tree. The dark grey bark gave way to a pale inner trunk. It was quite striking. He stood back and admired his handiwork.

"What inscription are you going to carve in the cross?" Riley was curious.

"I want the inscription to represent the brave men of both sides. We lost thirty-four men, but they lost over five hundred."

"And so?" Riley asked cautiously.

Dawson frowned, deep in thought. *"To Brave Men,"* he declared.

THE END

Maj. Allan Wilson

Dr Jameson

Fred Burnham

Capt. Charles Lendy

Induna Mjaan

Capt. Henry Borrow

King Lobengula

Blanche Blick-Burnham

Cmdt. Piet Raaff

James Dawson

Maj. Patrick Forbes

Some Officers of the Victoria Rangers 1893

Standing (Left to Right) : Lieut. Stoddart, Capt. Judd, Major Allan Wilson, Capt. Napier, Capt.Fitzgerald, Lieut. Hamilton, Lieut. Williams. *Seated* : Lieut. Sampson, Adj. Kennelly

Funeral for the men of the Shangani Patrol.
Fort Victoria,1894.

Photograph copy obtained by Mr Neville Wilson from the National Archives of Zimbabwe.
Mr Wilson advises that the young boy on the right is his father, Herbert Wilson.

Left: The Mopani Tree on the north side of the Shangani River where Dawson engraved the cross and the words *'To Brave Men'*. Photo Credit: www.zimfieldguide.com
Right: The engraving 130 years later. Photo Credit: Sue Finaughty

AUTHOR'S NOTE:

With an event of this significance, there are obviously some controversial theories that researchers have put forward, but as this book is a novel and not a technical book to reference, I have not referred to them nor offered an opinion.

Although not mentioned in the book, James Dawson returned to Scotland and married May Thompson, fulfilling his lifelong dream. The city of Fochabers declared Allan Wilson a hero and erected a drinking fountain monument in his honour. The inscription reads:

"Erected by the natives of Fochabers, and others,
to commemorate the heroic stand made against the forces
of the King of Matabeleland by Major Allan Wilson of this town,
who with a small band of gallant comrades fell bravely fighting
against overwhelming odds near the
Shangani River in South Africa on 4th December 1893."

A high school in Salisbury, Rhodesia (now Harare, Zimbabwe), was named after Major Allan Wilson. A significant monument was also erected in the Matopos Hills, near Bulawayo, commemorating the Shangani Patrol, where the remains of Major Wilson and his men are interred. The inscription reads:

TO BRAVE MEN
To the enduring memory of
Allan Wilson and his men
whose names are hereon inscribed and who fell in fight
against the Matabele on the Shangani River
on December 4 1893.
There was no survivor.

Just days before this book was published, I was contacted by Neville Wilson from Western Australia, who said he was the grandson of Allan Wilson. His father, Herbert Wilson, was a nine-year-old boy at the time of Major Wilson's death. What Neville told me was extremely interesting, and he supplied a photograph that showed a young boy at the funeral ceremony of Major Wilson and his men in Fort Victoria in 1894. In all my research, I found no reference to Major Wilson having a son. Without time to study this further, I will leave this exciting development open to historians of the Shangani Patrol, who I know will find this most interesting.

Very little is recorded about the final years of Mjaan, save that he did live a full and long life. Some of his warriors gave interviews to Foster Windram, a reporter for the Bulawayo Chronicle, in 1937. The detail and accuracy of their accounts of the battle were surprisingly good, despite the length of time that had elapsed.

The tree upon which Dawson engraved the cross and the words 'To Brave Men' was felled, and the stump with this inscription was relocated to the safety of a museum, where it remains to this day. My thanks to my friend, Sue Finaughty, for the photo featured in this book depicting the engraving 130 years later.

Dawson's report about the incident of King Lobengula's gold offering incensed Dr Jameson, who identified Troopers Daniel and Wilson as the culprits. They were arrested, tried and sentenced to seven years of hard labour, but a court in Salisbury overturned the ruling two years later and they were set free. Neither they nor the gold were ever seen again.

Dr Jameson handed all the documents from the Bulawayo Court of Inquiry to Sir Henry Loch. A highly critical submission by Jameson's military advisor, Sir John Willoughby, later went missing and is yet to be found. Dr Jameson was an exceptional administrator for Mr Rhodes and went on to establish the very successful country of Rhodesia. He was later elected as Prime Minister of the Cape Colony, where he served from 1904 to 1908.

Fred had a most remarkable career and befriended many notable people including US President Franklin D. Roosevelt, Rudyard Kipling and Lord Robert Baden-Powell, who modelled the Boy Scouts Association on Fred's teachings. Fred is the only non-British subject to receive the Distinguished Service Order from King Edward VII. Pearl Ingram married Blanche's sister, thus becoming Fred's brother-in-law. They remained lifelong friends. A mountain peak in the USA was named in Fred's honour. Fred died in California at the age of 86, and Blanche at the age of 77.

I take this opportunity to extend my heartfelt gratitude to the great-grandchildren of Fred and Blanche Burnham, namely Russell A. Burnham and Roderick D. Atkinson in the USA. Their invaluable support and contribution have played a pivotal role in the completion of this book. I am deeply humbled by their generosity in offering me the necessary insights and materials, as well as their willingness to provide any copyright permissions relating to Fred and Blanche. Their kindness and assistance have been truly outstanding.

Equally so, I am eternally grateful to Tim Tanser, whom I regard as one of the leading authorities on the Shangani Patrol, for kindly agreeing to cast his critical eye over my manuscript and point out some significant errors I made. Without your input and genuine encouragement, Tim, I probably would not have published this book.

My deepest thanks are given to Martin Robinson and Cindy Kramer for the considerable time they gave to editing, fact-checking, and turning this book into something readable. It was a herculean task, and I am extremely grateful to them and for them. Also, to my wonderful cousin, Nancy Rich, for helping me research several genealogy mysteries.

As always, I thank my step-daughter, Rachel De Bruyn, for her dedication and enthusiasm in designing the cover of this book—so many hours to get it just right and always happy to oblige.

My thanks to my proofreading team, Mary Power, David and Karen Cutlack, Sue Arkell, Ros Brown, Eamonn Giblin, Anne Dix and my lovely wife, Sharon, for sharpening their pencils and doing the painfully necessary polishing.

Excerpts from an interview with Foster Windram
Reporter: The Bulawayo Chronicle, 1937

Ginyalitsha : November 1937
"When the white people saw the Matabele would not listen, all of them took their hats off their heads and sang and then shouted: "Hip hip hooray" and then they said no more and fought to the end. I am not certain, but from what I know now I think they sang God Save the Queen."

Nabeni Khumalo: November 1937
"I was present at this fight. The white people dismounted and stood back to back in groups. When all the horses were shot they took shelter behind them. There was one of the white men who never took shelter. He stood there all the time with a little stick in his hand. There were forty men; the man with the stick was the man who was killed last.

The Allan Wilson Patrol Roll of Honour
(Age in brackets if known)

Major Allan Wilson (38)
Captain Henry Borrow (29)
Captain Frederick Fitzgerald
Captain Harry Moxon Greenfield (33)
Captain William Joseph Judd
Captain Argent Blundell Kirton (37)
Lieutenant Arend Hermanus Hofmeyr
Lieutenant George Hughes
Troop Sargeant-Major Sidney Charles Harding (33)
Sergeant Clifford Bradburn (26)
Sergeant Harold Alexander Brown
Sergeant William Henry Birkley
Corporal Frederick Crossley Colquhoun (18)
Corporal Harry Graham Kinloch (31)
Trooper William Abbott
Trooper William Bath (38)
Trooper William Henry Britton (24)
Trooper Edward Brock
Trooper L Dewis
Trooper Dennis Michael Cronly Dillon (26)
Trooper Harold John Hellet
Trooper George Sawers Mackenzie (24)
Trooper Matthew Meiklejohn
Trooper Harold Dalton Watson Moore Money (22)
Trooper Percy Crampton Nunn (39)
Trooper Alexander Hay Robertson
Trooper John ("Jack") Robertson (27)
Trooper William Alexander Thomson (23)
Trooper Henry St. John Tuck (26)
Trooper Frank Leon Vogel (24)
Trooper Philip Wouter De Vos
Trooper Henry George Watson
Trooper Thomas Colclough Watson
Trooper Edward Earle Welby

AND

Over five hundred brave Matabele warriors.

RESEARCH MATERIAL

Books and material consulted in the research :
(Listed by date of publication.)

Rhodesia Past and Present - SJ Du Toit (1897)
Three Years in Savage Africa - Lionel Decle (1898)
On the South African Frontier - William Harvey Brown (1899)
Southern Rhodesia - Fergus W Ferguson (1909) (Rare Book)
Old Rhodesian Days - Hugh Marshal Hole (1928)
The White Whirlwind - TV Bulpin (1961)
Encyclopaedia Rhodesia - The College Press (1973)
Rhodesia Before 1920 - National Gallery of Rhodesia &
National Historical Association of Rhodesia (c.1975)

On the Shangani Patrol:
Downfall of Lobengula - Wills and Collingridge (1894)
With Wilson in Matabeleland - Charles Donovan (1894)
Sunshine and Storm - F C Selous (1896)
Burnham Scout - Albert Curtis Brown (1901)
Scouting on Two Continents - F R Burnham (1927)
Rhodesian Genesis - Neville Jones (1953)
The White Men Sang - Alexander Fullerton (1958)
A Time to Die - Robert Cary (1968)
Pursuit of the King - John O'Reilly (1970)
A Splendid Savage - Steve Kemper (2016)
Matabele - Chris Ash (2016)
Taking Chances - Major Frederick R Burnham (2021)

Photo and Research Credits:
Sue Finaughty
www.zimfieldguide.com
Wikimedia Commons
Wikipedia
And the descendants of the Burnham Family:
Russell A. Burnham and Roderick D. Atkinson

'To Brave Men'
A Landau Books Publication
www.landaubooks.com

ABOUT THE AUTHOR

Alan Landau, born in Salisbury, Rhodesia (now Harare, Zimbabwe), led a diverse and interesting life before turning his hand to writing novels.

From serving in the British South Africa Police (formally the BSAC) and the Zimbabwe Republic Police, to transitioning into the commercial sector and eventually migrating to Australia, Alan's experiences have undoubtedly shaped his unique perspective.

After retiring in 2012, he delved into the realm of Historical Fiction writing, with a particular focus on his family's migration to Africa in 1893, as portrayed in the successful 'Langbourne Series'.

Even during the difficulties of the Covid-19 lockdowns, Alan continued to push himself creatively, exploring new genres such as a Romantic Thriller with '*Of Sand and Stars*'. He further challenged himself to write that in the style of a female author, using the pseudonym, Brenda Kate.

His dedication to storytelling, especially in the retelling of historical events, like '*To Brave Men*', sets him apart as an author who believes in the power of narrative to preserve and convey the past. Alan's style of historical fiction as a means of preserving and passing down important events and stories is both unique and captivating.

Other Books By
Alan P. Landau

The Langbourne Series

A Landau Books Publication
www.landaubooks.com

"Of Sand and Stars"
by
Brenda Kate

In the vast Australian outback, FBI agent Mandy Richardson and an enigmatic Australian astronomer kindle a forbidden romance while unravelling a sinister plot. Their combined knowledge uncovers a scheme for mass destruction, forcing them to navigate dangers and reconcile loyalties. Racing against time and torn between duty and desire, they must conquer ruthless adversaries and protect humanity. Prepare for a thrilling journey where love defies rules and survival hangs in the balance.

Another Landau Books Publication
www.landaubooks.com

www.ingramcontent.com/pod-product-compliance
Lightning Source LLC
Chambersburg PA
CBHW030603120726
47904CB00006B/1747